Dreaming Under
an
Electric Moon

by
Kris Powers

Illustrations by Clovis Batebola

www.dreamingunderanelectricmoon.com

Chapter One

"Rose!" Tommy Howser screamed before he fell from his bedroom balcony onto the concrete walk two stories below.

His mother, Daphne, was having late afternoon refreshments with a host of her colleagues when Tommy's body slapped the pavement. Light brown hair rested on concrete and brown eyes would remain forever closed.

The sunlight passing through the protective dome over the underwater town cast refracted patterns across his broken body. A gap in the cloud cover far above released a ray of sparkling sunshine on little Tommy before returning to a muted, foggy grey.

A full second of deathly quiet drenched the estate before Daphne's screams broke the silence. She flew from her seat, upsetting a wrought iron table with a glass top in the process. Hair, the same color as her son's, broke free from a purple hat matching her dress, and sunglasses fell from her bulging blue eyes. The round, glass top shattered across the concrete, accompanied by everyone's glasses of iced tea. Daphne's well-dressed friends stared at each other, paralyzed in their seats. Streaks of eyeliner and mascara traveled down their cheeks once Tommy's khaki shorts and tee shirt leaked a small puddle of crimson.

Daphne crouched at her son's side. Her shaking hands kept moving to hold him, only to stop inches from his small body. Her laced hand covered her mouth as it screamed, seemingly all on its own.

Her friends' collective intakes of breath drew Daphne's attention to the balcony where his nanny, Rose, stood. The bereaved mother's face was broken with grief, but Daphne's eyes hardened as Rose's face filled them. She shrieked a heart-withering scream at the sharp-featured woman staring down at her, eyes wide.

A moment later, two security guards in dark suits yanked her from the balcony, wrenching Rose's arms behind her back as they cuffed her. A second and third guard attended to the casually-dressed Reginald Howser slumped on a leather couch against the back wall in Tommy's large bedroom.

"He looks like he had a heart attack," one of the pair in black suits said to the duo holding the nanny.

The security guards handled Rose even rougher now, hauling her out of the room without her feet ever touching the floor. While the black-clad men rushed Rose across the walk, she kept glancing over her shoulder at the sight of Daphne, crouched and crying over her son's body. Rose's mouth moved, but the sound of blaring sirens erased the words on her lips.

***

Two police officers opened a steel door and shoved Rose into a small, black interrogation room. The only decor was a single, broad steel table accompanied by two chairs and a large mirror embedded in one wall. The two cops forced Rose into a seat across from a burly man in black. One of his colleagues stood in each corner of the small interrogation cell.

Without saying a word, the man across from Rose took a stack of large photos and threw them across the desk. Rose smirked at the sight of Tommy's small, thirteen-year-old body splayed across the concrete in every photo.

"Fresh from the crime scene," the man said, directing his own grimace at Rose.

"My," she said, swallowing hard, "you guys do work fast. God, it smells like rat piss in here!"

"Compliments of the *vU* and the rats," the husky man said. He sat in his seat and moved it to within a few inches of the table. "'Course, you've got your own technological advantages, don't you? Care to share?"

Rose placed her right hand in her lap, covered it with her left, and scowled at the man opposite her.

"Men?" he asked, looking around him. Before Rose could leap from her chair, all four men in black suits surrounded her. Two held her in place while the other pair separated her hands and held Rose's right arm up in the air. The unnamed man with a narrow, black tie got up from his chair, a vPhone on his wrist. "It's required for evidence and we are well within our rights to do it."

"Not in the Western States of America," Rose bit out.

"Good legislation they passed, I'll admit, but this is the SS of A," the man said with a smile. "Now show us the little guys and we can continue." Rose struggled against their grip, but the man's scowl filled her world. "We can do this the easy way or we can have a surgeon dig out those things, and don't think we'll bother to knock you out first!" he exclaimed as hot breath rushed across her face.

"I'm so glad to see how much you guys enjoy your work."

"You murdered a thirteen-year-old boy!" he yelled. Droplets of spittle rested on her flinching face.

"I didn't touch the kid! Okay, okay!" Rose exclaimed, feeling her eyeliner run as tears forced their way down her cheeks. She held up her right hand and squeezed her eyes closed. Three transparent tubules the length of a pinky finger popped out from between her knuckles.

The sweaty man began flashing photos from different angles. Once Rose saw the flash from the man's vPhone several times, she retracted them into her hand.

"I want a few more pictures," the burly man said, nudging her with a fist.

"You've got enough evidence. Now, where's my fucking phone call?" Rose yelled. She shrunk into her chair as the towering men returned to their corners.

"Those little things are how she gets into people's heads?" one of the other four asked from behind sunglasses, lacquered ginger hair and a puffy face.

"It's how they get at the vChip in your head," another cop replied, "and your mind."

"They speak!" Rose exclaimed in mock shock. "You all look like you belong at a nineteen-fifties funeral. Bunch of Greatest Retros! Worst fad in twenty years."

"A joker and a mindhacker," the middle-aged hulk remarked from across the table. "You got into Reg's head, didn't you? They said the father had a heart attack at the sight of his son going over the balcony, but I'd bet you lobotomized him after you got what you needed from his mind. The boy walked in on you committing the crime and over that balcony Tommy went just to shut him up!"

"That sounds pretty stupid of me," Rose said, a thin smile on her lips, though her hands trembled. "I'd get caught."

"You panicked."

"Just so he could scream my name and fall to his death because I pushed him?" Rose asked, rolling her eyes. "Buy a brain, 'detectives', and figure it out: I was framed."

A broad smile of yellowed teeth appeared on the man's broad, red face. "Framed, right, boys?" he asked, looking around the other faces in the room, their expressions mirroring his. "Yeah! You wanna tell me who would frame some worthless, filthy mindhacker like you?"

"Where's my fucking phone call?" Rose demanded, crossing her arms.

"Phone call?" the man repeated. He regarded his comrades with a smug smile under the room's harsh, buzzing fluorescent lighting. "What phone call?"

"I am a citizen of the Western States of America and I want my phone call."

"Ah," said the man, pale light shining off his feathery, white hair. "Citizens get phone calls, terrorists don't."

"Fucking Southern States! This would never happen in the WSA," Rose said under her breath.

The large, sweaty man's smile widened before he leaned against the desk, the edge of his thin, black tie resting on it. "The Western States. Bunch a tree-hugging faggots, if you ask me. I'm not surprised you're from there."

"And we have an extradition treaty with you."

"I never signed it," the man said, crossing his arms and staring at her with a salacious smile. His phone rang out an incessant beep into the ambient, dead silence between them. The unnamed man glanced at it for a moment, almost shoving it back into his pocket, before his eyes flashed at the name on the phone. "Hang on."

"Yeah, whatever," Rose mumbled.

The detective got up from the table and waddled from the room while Rose's eyes moved between the four sets of eyes boring a new hole into her head. The man returned a minute later and sat down, causing the metal chair to creak as he dropped into it.

"Something wrong?" Rose inquired, a sickly-sweet smile spreading across her face.

"Nothing," he replied, straightening in his chair. "I'm just sad to say that you'll probably get the death penalty for this."

"You're actually sad?"

"Oh yeah," he said, gesturing for her to lean into the table. It was a gesture she didn't obey. "You see: I don't believe in the death penalty."

"How unlike the rest of this country."

"Call me a rebel, but I believe that people should rot in jail and suffer day after day in the worst possible ways than get the easy way out," he said.

"Evolved thinking," Rose remarked. "I wouldn't call you a rebel, though."

"Yeah, what would you call me?"

"A mother fu—" Rose began before she was interrupted by the sound of the door behind her opening and closing with a loud, metal clang. Shortly afterwards, two people in business dress walked into view.

"Well, I'll leave you to your interrogators," the man said, getting up from his seat. As all five police officers left the room, he stopped and looked at the male half of the duo. "Please, *don't* take it easy on her."

The pair waited until the other group in their fifties-style suits had left the room before the male agent rolled his eyes. "We're not interrogators."

"But you're the one in charge," Rose said, looking up at him.

"Why do you say that?" he asked, raising an eyebrow.

"Because the last guy talked to you, first."

"Actually," the woman said, taking the only other seat in the room, "I'm the one in charge." She straightened her grey blazer and plum blouse just as a tapping came from the mirror, but the lead agent kept her eyes on Rose's face.

"WBI?" Rose asked, looking up at them with doe eyes.

"FBI," the woman corrected. "I'm Zahra Washington and this is Mason Deane."

Rose waved away the introductions and blew a raspberry. "The FBI? As in the Former Bureau of Investigation? You guys don't have any power! No wonder those SS officers are watching from the other side of that glass. You're, what, a tenth of what you used to be?"

"Our staff may have decreased in size but the Treaty of Disbandment allows our organization to act as though the USA still exists under certain circumstances. That gives us a lot of power in this case, which is lucky for you, as you are now our responsibility," Zahra said.

"How awful for you."

"Yeah, I know. We don't get many child killers and we like to keep it that way," Mason said, wincing as he glanced at the fluorescent lights on the concrete ceiling.

"Mason—" Zahra began before Rose interrupted him.

"Who said that I murdered the kid?"

"His name was Tommy Howser and it seems like the entire SSA has," Mason replied, moving a lock of light brown hair away from his blue eyes.

"Oh yes, the SSA," the mindhacker sneered. "The same people who routinely lynched or shot people without a trial for being black. They are a bunch of backward, inbred, country turnips."

"That was over a hundred years ago," Zahra interjected, just as a loud tapping came from the mirror.

Rose leaned forward and smiled. "And some things never change. Now they just execute them after letting them rot in jail for a few decades."

"They also execute child-killers," Mason said.

"You've got it so wrong," Rose said, with a laugh, "not that it matters. The real people you answer to are on the other side of that glass."

"I can assure you that we are in charge here," Zahra said.

"Tell that to them," Rose remarked, pointing a finger at the two-way mirror.

"All I have to do, is to remind those gentlemen that the treaty the WSA has with the SSA is current and that they cannot interfere in a prisoner transfer. As this is a matter between two different federations of states, the FBI is called in to conduct the prisoner transfer and investigate. We have complete authority here," Zahra said, just as an angry banging shook the mirror.

"I don't think they agree," Rose said, nodding her head towards the glass.

"Then I would remind them," Zahra said, raising her voice as the banging intensified, "that the President of the SSA, himself, has approved our presence here and that he also sent a platoon of marines to make sure his orders are carried out to the letter. I believe they're heavily armed."

"Very heavily," Mason remarked with a nod and a boyish smile.

The banging stopped.

"Better?" Zahra asked.

"That's a start," Rose said, relaxing in her heavy, metal chair. "But I don't want to say anything with those redneck bigots listening in. Clear that room, and you have a deal."

The door opened before Zahra could answer and the heavy-set man's pimpled head popped into the room. "We need to talk."

Zahra smiled and got up from the chair with Mason. "Wait here," she said, turning for the door.

"Go talk to your masters!" Rose exclaimed just before the door closed behind her.

A dozen men lined a hallway with a haze of humidity hanging in the air, and the same large, white-haired man stood in front of her. "We are not leaving that room and you are not taking that child-killing freak with you. I think it's time you were gone."

Zahra raised a watch that looked like it had escaped from the 1950s to her lips, pressed a button on its side, and spoke a single word. "Uncooperative."

"So?" the man asked, looking her up and down.

"You'll see in about sixty seconds. I wasn't kidding about the platoon of marines or about how heavily armed they are."

"You're bluffing," the man said, curling a lip. "I'm not stupid. There's no marines coming, so why don't you start moving before we make you move?"

"Care to accompany us to the elevator?" Zahra asked, lowering her wrist.

"I'd be delighted," he replied with a stiff smile. As they walked down the corridor, the rest of the policemen formed a line behind them.

"Just asking: Are we going to disappear into that elevator and never be seen again?"

"Naw," the man said. "We're not like that."

"I bet. What was your name, again?" Zahra asked as they neared the elevator doors.

"Mister Beckwith."

"No first name?"

"Not for the likes of you. That won't be a problem soon, though," Beckwith replied, just before the elevator opened to the sight of half-a-dozen marines armed with rifles. Beckwith gulped and put a hand on the pistol in his holster.

"I wouldn't do that," Zahra said, looking at Beckwith's hand. "The rest of the squad is coming down the other elevators, and you'll have these troops in front of you and another twenty behind. Do you really want to do this?"

Zahra stared down the man whose white dress shirt had several growing sweat stains across it.

"Hey, we didn't mean anything," Beckwith said, slowly taking the gun out of its holster by the tip of the handle with a trembling hand. He carefully placed it on the concrete floor and raised his hands. Behind him, the rest of his cohort did the same.

Zahra shrugged and glanced at her partner. "Hey, neither did we! We did do a little digging into your background before we arrived, though. Did you know that this police station has had more than a dozen prisoners go missing?"

Beckwith slouched as more marines dressed in grey camouflage came up behind his group of cops, who were already putting their hands on their heads. "No kiddin'."

"It's true. Now that's something that normally wouldn't fall under the FBI's jurisdiction anymore, but it's also true that two FBI agents went missing in this area just a few years ago, and two missing agents in this area does fall under our jurisdiction. At the time, your people claimed they never arrived. That couldn't be your fault, could it? This God-fearing town doesn't make people disappear, do they?"

The man shook his head and stared at the floor. "No, not our kind of people."

"Now, I don't like taking really long elevator rides and neither does my partner, at least, I don't think he does," Zahra said, pausing to look at Mason, who smiled and quickly shook his head. "You realize that this incident is something that I'm going to have to report, which means I'm going to have to detain you and your friends for questioning. While there, I think it's time we got down to what happened to our missing agents.

"Now, Rose in there was right: we don't have the kind of staff we used to. Our nearest office is in Birmingham. I hope you enjoy the ride."

"But," Beckwith said, looking at the angry faces around him, "that's two hours away!"

"Oh, I know."

"You should bring a book," Mason said, a wide grin firmly fixed on his face.

Beckwith returned to staring at the floor while the officers broke his cadre into smaller groups and escorted them from the building.

"Thanks, Major," Zahra said to the senior officer, who nodded and began to follow Beckwith into the elevator. Her eyes settled on a few drops of blood on the back of his hand as he turned Beckwith around. "Did one of them cut you, Major Peterson?"

"Oh," the major said, looking at the back of his hand. "I'll get the medic to look at it, but I'm sure it's nothing."

"Thanks, again. By the way, Beckwith?" The slumping man looked up at her as he was escorted into the elevator. "I would have appreciated your first name. Without it, it's going to take about three times as long just to process you. All we have to go on is Mister Beckwith!"

The man began to roar in response, but the elevator door muted most of his protestations as it closed on his red, puffy face.

***

"All taken care of," Zahra said, returning to her seat. "The police are on their way to Birmingham and the station's being run by the SSA military for the next little while. There are two marines guarding this room as we speak."

"Okay," Rose said, crossing both arms across her chest. "You got it done. I'll tell you what I know. I just can't believe the FBI sent you."

"Why's that?"

"You're Black!" Rose exclaimed.

"And you're Japanese. Your kind isn't liked around here much more than mine is."

"Which is why I'm glad to be sitting with you rather than them. Do you know how many people disappeared around here in the last ten years alone?" she asked.

Zahra held up her slender-fingered hand in response. "We heard. Now why would you kill a little boy?"

"I was framed," Rose said, shifting in her chair.

"Why would someone frame you?" Zahra asked, tightening her eyebrows.

Rose leaned towards the partners. "Because I just stepped in something that's way more than I was contracted to handle."

"So, you were contracted to get something from Howser," Mason said.

"Yeah," Rose said, looking away for a moment at a patch of floor next to her chair, before locking eyes with them. "But I swear that my contract wasn't to murder rich dads or their little princes."

"He was spoiled?" Zahra inquired.

"No more than any other kid, I guess. He was my way in, you know? Get close to the kid, then his father. People like you and me do what we need to get the contract done," Rose replied, looking up at Mason.

"People like you and me?" he repeated, his forehead wrinkling.

"Come on," Rose said, tapping her temple with an index finger. "You're a mindhacker, too. I can feel it. There's some kind of buzz or something when we get around each other. Does the FBI know what causes it?"

Mason smiled and then kneeled on the concrete floor behind the table. "It's because our implants cause some kind of feedback when we're in close proximity to each other. Look, I've got to say that it does look like you were contracted to lobotomize him."

"My contract was for information, that's all," Rose said, uncrossing her arms and putting her hands flat on the table. "I didn't do it, but I can point you in the direction of who did."

Zahra crossed her hands on the steel table. "Okay, tell us what happened."

"Reg's company's got new code coming out that will help mindhackers be even more effective than they were before."

"And you were paid a lot to get that information," Mason said with a knowing smile.

"A fortune, but there was something different about this one."

"Like what?" Zahra asked.

"You know that every mind is different, right?"

"Wouldn't they be?" Zahra asked, shrugging her shoulders.

Rose smiled before replying. "Hacking into a person's mind is like hacking into their internal world, their *innermind*, where they live in their dreams. Everyone's different, so the world they live in is like a fingerprint: unique."

"I saw someone's innermind that looked like a world out of a fantasy. It was incredible," Mason interjected.

Rose nodded. "Some of them are like that. Some are kinda bland, and some are pretty scary."

"What was Reg's innermind like?" Zahra asked.

Rose chuckled at the question. "Ordered. It was like some kind of old-world office; You know like they had in the 1920s with all of that wood paneling and Tiffany lamps? There was even one of those old-style radios with the round tops playing ragtime music, but the only desk in the room had this computer from the nineties sitting on it. It was like Art Deco with tech. Weird, right?"

"So, what happened then?"

"I had to get at his controls to get the info I needed," Rose replied.

"Controls?" Zahra repeated.

"She means the controls to a person's mind. They can be just about anything," Mason said, loosening the vibrant blue tie around his neck.

"Like the wheel of a ship," Rose said, nodding at him.

"Or, it could be the cockpit of a plane, or a fuse box," Mason said, returning the nod, "or even a desktop computer from the nineties."

"Right, but there was someone else at the controls instead of Reg," Rose stated.

"That's impossible!" Mason exclaimed, scowling at her.

"Why?" his partner asked, looking between their faces.

"A mindhacker goes into someone's head, gets information, and gets out. They can't just leave a copy of themselves behind. It would be like you visiting someone's home and leaving a clone of yourself behind; You can't do it."

"I thought so, too," Rose remarked.

"Who was it?" Zahra asked, leaning towards her.

"The guy who killed Tommy and put Reg in a coma," Rose replied.

"So, you were nowhere near Tommy when he fell over the balcony?" Mason asked.

"I was on the other side of the room just coming out of Reg's innermind when Tommy screamed my name and fell over the balcony," Rose said, her voice breaking as she talked.

"A mindhacker who leaves copies of himself behind in someone's head? You know how that sounds, right? It's more likely that you're making all of this up to get out of going to an SSA prison," Mason said.

"Which is why I was framed! Think of it, FBI: Why would I get the information I needed, wake up, have Tommy come in on us and then stop him from talking by throwing him over the balcony when I knew his mother was having lunch with her BFFs below?"

"Yeah," Zahra said, putting an elbow on the desk and placing a fist under her chin. "Why would you do something that cruel to all those rich people who never understood you?"

"I couldn't care less about what her or her friends thought about me," Rose said, rolling her eyes. "They were too boring to hate. Now ask yourself something else, Agent Washington: if I already had that information why wouldn't I just leave?"

"Oh, all that security would stop you if Tommy cried out for his daddy."

"So, I make it a million times worse by killing him. Come on," Rose said, directing a tight frown at her. She shook her head and dropped both of her arms to her sides. "Look, all I wanted was the information. If everything had gone according to plan, Reg wouldn't even have known what happened and I would have left a note the next day saying I had a family emergency and then just never come back."

"But Tommy did walk in on you," Zahra said.

"Tommy was already there," Rose said, rolling her eyes. "He goes online for three hours every day. His father's rules. You can check the time on the *vU*: Tommy was online until seconds before he went over that balcony."

"So, this control guy in Reg's head was the one who did it?" Zahra asked, raising an eyebrow.

Rose sighed and nodded. "Ask your partner: if someone can do that, then they're really dangerous and they need to be stopped."

"I need a name," Zahra said, standing up.

"You got it, but only after I've been transported back to my country and have a whole detachment of agents around me. Oh, and I want immunity! I also want into that, what do you call it, where they give you a new life?"

"The Witness Protection Program?" Zahra supplied.

"Yeah!"

"That's a lot to ask just for the name of a person you found in someone's head," Zahra remarked.

"Sure is," Mason said, also getting to his feet and wiping away the dirt from the knees of his simple suit.

"You know that person shouldn't have been there!" Rose exclaimed, slamming her hands against the table. "He couldn't be, but he was! I know what that means and so do you."

"If you're lying to us…" Zahra said, leaving the sentence hanging in the air.

"I'm not."

"Mind if we talk outside for a minute?" Zahra inquired.

"Knock yourself out," Rose replied after a shrug. "Although, I bet that once the locals find out what you did here, they're probably going to want to do something about it."

"Excuse us," Mason said with an easy grin before crossing to the door and leaving with Zahra. It was only once it was closed behind them that she spoke again.

"This sounds absolutely insane to me. Mindhackers that stick around in someone's head and a boy who's somehow lured to his death by a phantom Rose pulled out of her hat?" she asked, crossing her arms.

"I know it sounds farfetched," Mason admitted, "and the explanation that she's behind all of this is the simplest one."

"But, it doesn't fit," Zahra said with a shake of her head. "Something about all this doesn't feel right. What about her story that this guy's somehow virtually possessing people?"

"It's supposed to be impossible to do that in the Virtual Universe, but if they could get in someone's head, take it over and leave a copy of themselves behind," Mason said, with a deep sigh, "then they could be behind any face."

"That's assuming that she's telling the truth."

"I think she is," Mason said.

"Why do you say that?"

"For one thing, her story's too preposterous to be made up. She would've been better off telling us Elvis Presley was still alive and he's our guy!" Mason exclaimed, raising his eyebrows.

"And, did you notice how she spoke about Tommy?" Zahra asked. "She used the present tense a lot. He's still alive to her because she's not ready to accept he's dead yet. Even her voice breaking when she talked about Tommy's death seemed real."

"You believe her?" Mason asked.

Zahra nodded. "I wish I didn't."

Mason sighed and looked at the scratched, metal door of the interrogation cell. "Yeah, I do, too. I'll check the times on the vU when she said Tommy was online, but I've got a sneaking suspicion that it'll only corroborate her story."

"Contact the WSA. We're going to need to get a lot of balls rolling on this and Rose wasn't wrong: the locals are going to show up sooner or later and there is no way I want to be here when that happens."

***

Zahra gazed out of a crystal clear window onto the ruins of the outlying suburbs of Memphis. She frowned when the train slowed as it passed street after street of radioactive, burned-out homes and businesses.

"Are we there yet?" Rose asked, placing her bag in the overhead storage of their compartment. A mischievous red smile spread across her face.

"We left less than a minute ago."

Rose sighed and collapsed into a grey upholstered chair in a small cabin holding four such seats. Coincidentally, the seat complimented Rose's black slacks and blazer over a simple blouse of dark grey. Mason sat opposite Zahra with his seat reclined and eyes closed while his partner kept an eye on their charge.

"At least you got me out of that underwater colony. I kept having nightmares about drowning. The water made pretty patterns on the ground, though."

"Maybe you shouldn't go after targets that live in underwater colonies."

Rose rested a chin on her hand and shifted her gaze to the cabin's only exit. Zahra glanced at her and then returned her attention to the holographic display on her phone. "If you need to go to the bathroom, we have to accompany you," she said, bringing up the holographic news on her vPhone.

"What if I want to go to the bar?"

Zahra sighed and glanced at her. "Then you're buying and I'm having club soda."

"You guys are seriously no fun."

Zahra smiled and continued to look at the latest holographic news on her vPhone. "Good."

"Why don't you just go online in your head?" Rose asked, looking at Zahra's obsolete method of accessing the vU.

"Too distracting," she replied.

"Not for him, apparently," Rose said, pointing at Mason, who was reclined with his eyes closed.

"How do you know he's not asleep?" Zahra asked.

"I can tell the difference," Rose replied, looking at Mason. "People who are asleep, they're more relaxed, you know: not there? But, people who are online whether it's a chat room or a game, they look more like they're just resting their eyes."

"I see."

"Ugh!" Rose exclaimed before straightening in her chair. "How long is this gonna take?"

"Five hours, total."

"I need a drink!" Rose said, tapping her armrest with a red-lacquered nail.

"Five hundred miles an hour isn't fast enough for you?"

"I don't know why we couldn't take a plane."

Zahra rolled her eyes. "Because you kept saying that you're scared of flying."

"I was trying to get you to get me high for a while!" Rose complained.

"It didn't work," Zahra said, flipping through 3D images on her vPhone.

"Can't you at least let me on the vU?"

"No."

"Come on!" Rose exclaimed. "I'll behave!"

Zahra looked up from her phone with a flash of her eyes. "You sound like someone who should go to one of those NA meetings."

"Netholics Anonymous?" Rose said. "Please, it's because there's nothing to do here!"

"I've already told you: if you go online, even for a minute, someone could trace your location. You did say you were in danger, right?"

Rose pursed her lips and looked out of the window as the ruins of Memphis rolled past it. "I am. Whatever he was doing in there, his face was the last thing I ever wanted to see."

Zahra looked up at her words. "You didn't like *him* and you already *knew* him?"

Rose's jaw dropped open, but she closed it a moment later and nodded. "It's more like, I already knew him by reputation, but it was definitely him."

"Who?" Zahra asked, softly.

"I'll tell you when we're safely in San Francisco. Now, give me your vPhone."

"For what?"

"So I can play a game or something!" Rose exclaimed, squirming in her seat.

"It's almost supper time. It'd be better to get it served in our cabin."

"Can't we go to the dining car?" Rose asked, putting both hands together in a pleading gesture.

"I don't think that's a good idea."

"I will sit in the deepest, darkest corner," Rose said.

"What if they have flashlights?" Zahra asked, a thin smile on her lips. At the sight of Rose's sullen face, she straightened in her seat. "As I said from the beginning: you sit where I tell you to sit and if anything happens, you do exactly what I tell you to do. Right now, I'm telling you to stay put and enjoy your dinner."

"Okay, okay!" Rose said, crossing her arms, before looking at the reclined Mason seated next to Zahra. "What about him?"

"We'll text him when it's time to eat."

"I bet he's in a game right now. Probably fantasy. He seems the type."

"Okay, it's done. I'll call the waiter in with a couple of menus. Cabin: pull up the dining table."

"I think I will have the lobster!" Rose exclaimed. A thick, sturdy white surface popped up from the floor and snapped into place a moment later. Zahra called the dinner car and waited for their menus to arrive.

Chapter Two

Mason stood up from a black leather couch on an open deck in the vLibrary and took a deep breath of air faintly smelling of the sea. A wall stood behind him completely covered in tall bookcases standing against a bright, green sky. In front of Mason was an impossible vista of open silver skyscrapers, with every level full of packed bookshelves.

People sat on decks like his and read or walked among the infinite rows of wisdom, looking for something new to consume. Some flew up hundreds of feet from parks like winged angels to land on an exposed floor of a skyscraper. There, they would peruse tall shelves of books mere feet from a precipitous drop. Small groups sat around tables on randomly roaming platforms, discussing books, politics, or the latest episode of their favorite show. Beyond the skyscrapers and interest groups, the library city stretched to a horizon dominated by a small, emerald sun.

"That's enough news for today," Mason said. He dropped a newspaper with the headline: *Tenth Anniversary of Edward Blunt's Death* onto the couch behind him. Now that it no longer had a reader, the paper vanished on a draft of wind.

"I want to go to Sword & Sorcery," Mason said. He blinked and the view of impossible scrapers was replaced with old stone buildings and thatched roofs from centuries past. His clothes changed from a deep blue Italian suit to those of a medieval adventurer, complete with leather garments and a quiver and bow hanging from his back. The FBI agent's face was now that of a rugged male adventurer with a shaggy mop of hair and a boyish smile always tugging at the edges of his lips.

Mason looked down a cobblestone street with a row of low cottages not far from the banks of a vast river. The buildings on the side of the street in front of him went from the low-built cottages nearby to two and three-story buildings just a short way away. Mason's grin widened at the sight of the many shops and bars where quests abounded by the dozen in the small village of Lothering.

The hamlet rested next to an incredibly wide sapphire river shimmering in the light of two yellow moons. On the opposite bank, one could just make out a remote cottage with a single lamp hanging from one of its windows.

Mason headed for a two-story inn near an intersection. A wooden sign in the shape of a shield hung from an iron pole above a set of double doors leading into a roomy bar filled with conversation. *The Bard's Quest* was etched across the top of the sign's surface. Below those golden letters was the image of a young male bard with a lute and a bow slung over his shoulder.

Mason began an easy walk towards the inn and pub. He stopped at the sight of an older man in grey robes sitting on the bank of the river, contentedly puffing away on a long pipe. He looked at the image on the inn's sign and then back to the man a short ways away.

"Why not?" Mason asked himself aloud before walking towards the robed figure who had taken a seat on the side of a fallen tree trunk. He walked across the lawn, inhaling the scent of grass mixed with flowers near the perfect river until Mason was standing just a few feet away from the man who had one foot on a rock and the other on the ground. The old man gazing across the river jumped once he realized someone was standing next to him. Mason smiled at the reaction, which set the man into a fit of laughter.

"I'm sorry," he said, after slapping the log with a hand in surprise, "I was deep in thought."

"Here?" Mason asked. "What's so special about here?"

"All of you new gamers: you don't realize what it was like before virtual reality. Back then, we just saw and heard."

"Wait," Mason said, eyes widening, "you're not an NPC?"

"Whatever gave you that idea?" the bearded man asked, mouth hanging open.

"Well, it's just that I see you here all the time," Mason replied. "Every time I've played this game you're always out here looking across the river. I thought that you were a Non-Player Character who was locked in place because you were—"

"A quest giver?" the old man replied, smiling.

"Yeah."

"No, I just like the view. What's your favorite game, anyway?" he asked, shifting his weight towards Mason.

"This one."

He took a long draw off his pipe and puckered his lips. The words: "Good man!" traveled out on a trail of smoke.

"How old are you, anyway?" Mason asked.

"Even older than my avatar! I'm OverForty506, by the way," he said, offering a hand to shake.

"Hey Over," Mason said, accepting the handshake with an amused smile. "You are old school. I'm AntiFed386. So how far over forty are you?"

"More than just a few years. You?"

"I'm not as young as mine, but not by that much," Mason replied, looking at the rough hands of his avatar, a dark-haired beefcake of no more than twenty-one. "Most people don't talk about that kind of stuff here, you know."

"I'm not most people. In here, just like in real life, you have touch, taste, sight, sound – all of it! Haven't you ever just stopped and looked at this incredible world?"

"It's not the only one," Mason interjected, focusing on the distant cottage across the river glittering in the light of the moons. "There's thousands."

"Tens of thousands," OverForty506 corrected. "The vLibrary is a close second to this world for me, but that's why you should realize just how special each one is. Take a bit of time to appreciate everything that went into the creation of something like this." He bent over, picked a blade of grass from the lawn and showed it to him. "I can touch this, smell it, even taste it if I want to. You couldn't do that thirty years ago. This is all so *real*."

"I never really stopped to consider it."

"You should some time. What's your real name, if you don't mind me asking?"

"Mason," he replied.

"I go by De."

"That short for Deforest?" Mason asked.

"Something like that," he said with a smile and a nod.

"Thanks for getting me to stop and smell the roses, De," Mason said.

"And, you are very welcome. I'm glad you stopped to ask what I was doing. Most don't and the ones who do think I'm a, you know, NPC."

Mason turned to walk away, but curiosity turned him back around. "By the way: what is it that you're always looking at?"

"What?" OverForty asked, having already returned to gazing across the river. "Oh, I was looking at that cottage across the way."

"What for?" Mason asked.

De smiled and leaned towards him. "Do you know how old this game is?"

"No. Does that have something to do with what I asked?" Mason asked, crossing his arms.

"Yes, if you can be patient with me for a minute," OverForty replied, giving him a sour face.

"I know it's been around for a long time now."

"It's the first completely virtual game built by Edward Blunt, himself. It's had a lot of upgrades, but you can still tell that it's old. You know how?" De asked, directing a raised eyebrow at him.

Mason looked at the river and thought for a moment. "Boundaries?"

"Yes! Boundaries!" De exclaimed, clapping his hands once. "If you approach the edge of the world in most games now, you find yourself feeling like you're moving through thick mud."

"And then the game turns you around," Mason interjected.

"Yes, but the boundaries of this vWorld are all impediments that are impossible to pass. Those mountains over there," he said, pointing at the distant but impressively high peaks huddled like giants across the southern horizon. "Those mountains can't be climbed or passed, and this river here is too deep and too rough to swim or boat across."

"And there's the desert in the east," Mason said.

"Exactly! You can wander in that desert for days, but all you'll do is kill your avatar and then you have to start all over again!" OverForty exclaimed, clapping his hands again. "That's how you know a game is old, not the feeling of walking through a wall of mud, no it's those barriers! I was playing this game probably before you were even born, do you know that? It isn't the same as it was though; things are perfect now. There used to be small bits of discoloration and pixilation you could see when you examined a flower up close."

"So, what does this have to do with what you were looking at?" Mason asked, raising his brow.

"Oh! I've been playing this game for a long time, and even then, I couldn't help but pause here and think about that cottage across the river."

Mason followed his gaze to the cottage's broad, stone facade, bathed in bright moonlight. At its center was a wide, red door with two equally spaced windows on either side of it. Even though it was far away, he discerned a large, green round window in the door glowing with light coming from somewhere inside. "What about it?"

"In this world, it's really there. It has an interior, supposedly furnished, should someone find a way to look through those windows. Who knows what the programmers put in there, but you can't ever reach it, can you?"

"Well, no," Mason replied, glancing at the broad, impassable river separating them.

"I just can't help and think about what I would find if I could just explore that cottage, but we can't, can we?"

Mason smiled and shook his head. "It's been nice talking to you."

"Yes, yes. They all leave once I tell them what I'm looking at," De said, returning to his inner thoughts.

Mason left De for *The Bard's Quest* tavern where he could ask around about work in the area.

He soon stood beneath the sign of *The Bard's Quest*, took another breath of the fresh evening air and turned the door handle. Mason opened it briskly to the sight of a small, cozy pub lit by candles and warmed by conversation. A roaring fire burned on a hearth of stone on the opposite wall. In front of it stood a female bard singing songs of ancient times. Mason was about to sit down next to a bejeweled woman in purple vying for his attention when a jarring reminder came from reality in the form of a loud ping.

Mason sighed and tapped the digital vPhone flashing on his wrist. The action brought up a small screen with the text 'About to have dinner' printed across its surface.

"Great. Save game," Mason said aloud, hearing a ping of confirmation a moment later. "Quit."

***

"Ooo," Rose said, perusing the dinner menu. The setting sun gave the woods outside a strange red glow and bathed the room in twilight. "What's the limit on meals for the FBI?"

Zahra looked at her and then back at her menu. "Just don't have a twelve-course meal."

"So, no more than eleven," Rose said. "Note taken."

Zahra set her menu on the table and looked at Rose, still eye-deep in hers. "What happened after you saw him?"

"What?" Rose asked, looking up from her menu for the first time.

"I know you won't tell me his name but you said back at the police station that, when you entered Reg's mind, you found this other person there. What did you say?"

"I didn't say anything. He did," Rose replied. "When that guy saw me, he got this strange smile on his face, a cruel smile, and told me how my chrysanthemums are doing."

"Say again?"

"Oh, I forgot to mention how I got Reg into a conversation was through his love of botany. I knew about it before and thought it might get me somewhere so I studied up. Whole imaginary garden up here to talk about," Rose said, tapping her temple.

"Which is how you got him alone," Zahra said, nodding. "Then what happened?"

"I had told Reg something off-hand like my chrysanthemums were doing well this year and when I was in his head that man quoted back to me exactly what I had said to Reg, word for word," Rose said, putting her menu down.

"How did he know that?"

Rose looked out of the window as though someone might be watching from the darkening woods and then back at Zahra before lowering her voice. "Because he was the person I was really talking to, not Reg. Not anymore."

Zahra leaned into the conversation. "This guy, whoever he was: You're saying that he was in complete control over Reg Howser?"

Rose brought her face closer to Zahra's. "I'm saying that he is Reg now, or was."

"What did you do once you realized that?"

"I freaked!" Rose exclaimed in a hushed whisper. "What do you think I did?"

"What did he do?"

Rose frowned and settled back into her chair. "He told me that I was just the thing he was looking for and then kicked me out of Reg's head."

"He kicked you out?"

"Like that," Rose said, with a snap of her fingers. "That's one more reason you should be worried."

Zahra straightened in her chair and regarded the darkly dressed Rose. "Just the thing he needed? What did he mean?"

"He meant that I was the perfect scapegoat to pin a murder on."

"So, you really think he had something to do with Tommy's death?" Zahra asked.

"Why else would he need me? No, he did something to that kid. He's gonna pay for that," Rose said, tapping the top of the table with her index finger.

"I'm glad to hear it, but how did he make a thirteen-year-old kid jump off a balcony? I thought mindhackers can't hypnotize someone to death."

Rose buried her eyes in her menu again. "I don't know, but that kid wasn't stupid. He wouldn't just jump off a balcony because someone told him to."

"But, wouldn't that mean he's stronger than other mindhackers?"

Rose looked up from her menu. "Who said he's a mindhacker?"

"I meant," Zahra began before her wristwatch rang out the familiar chorus from the song 'Bang Bang'. She pressed a button on her vPhone. "Hello?"

A woman appeared from nowhere in the empty seat across from Zahra. She looked completely solid in her formal grey suit until the holographic image of the silver-haired woman flickered. From time to time, some part of Zahra's body would block out part of the image as though someone had erased a foot or hand-shaped piece from the hologram.

"I've got a fucking army in my police station and I hear you're the one who put them there!"

"And this is?" Zahra asked with a practiced smile.

"Brandi Blanc, mayor of that same city that you just staged an insurrection in!"

"Oh, no!" Rose said, unable to keep herself from giggling. "The mayor is mad as a cow!"

The mayor's image scowled at Rose and then directed a sharp stare at Zahra. "Can we talk somewhere a little more private?"

"I can switch my phone to private," Zahra said. "Hang on."

"No. We talk alone. Now."

"I—" Zahra looked up to see that Mason had just returned from his travels on the vU. She waved at him, muted her phone, and then pointed at the mayor's flickering image. "Can you take care of our charge here for a few minutes? I've got an angry mayor on the line."

"Go ahead," Mason replied. He sat up in his seat while his partner squeezed past him. Zahra hurried off into the empty corridor and Mason picked up a menu. "So, what's good here?"

"I don't know. I've been waiting to find out. Where's the waiter, anyway?"

Mason looked around the room, still shaking off the haze in his mind from being online. "Was he already here?"

"He brought the menus. Kinda stiff, if you ask me."

"Oh?" Mason asked, looking at the Better-Than-Steak menu.

"He looked more like a boxer. Even had a bandage on the back of his hand. Maybe that's what he does on the weekends," Rose said, putting her menu down. "I *will* have the lobster!"

The door opened and closed as the waiter returned. "Have we decided?" a voice asked from their left. Mason glanced up from his menu at a familiar face.

"Major Peterson?" Mason asked, recognizing the same soldier who had secured the police station just an hour ago. The major stood in front of them, wearing a waiter's outfit complete with a black bowtie.

Mason immediately went for the pistol at his side, but he reacted with surprising speed.

Before Mason could retrieve his sidearm, the waiter and officer had already placed his right hand just an inch from the FBI agent's left. His other hand held Mason's immobile on top of his gun with incredible strength. Three tiny tubules exited between the knuckles of his right hand, piercing the skin on Mason's left. The agent slumped in his chair moments later. Before the agent had closed his eyes, the major was already taking a gun from his pocket and pointing it at Rose.

"Well, shit," Rose said. The waiter/soldier smiled in response, but Rose caught him off-guard by diving for the door. His speed was still superior to hers, however, and of the two explosive bullets he shot from his gun, one blew a hole in the table, and the other turned her stomach into a mess.

She collapsed across two seats from the pain just as Zahra returned to the cabin. The FBI agent already had her gun drawn and leveled at the major, who lunged at her in response, but even his speed couldn't match Zahra's training and hair-trigger finger. The man's chest had a hole blown in it the size of an orange a split second later. Zahra was at Rose's side before the major hit the floor. The mindhacker's hand rested over the broad, deep wound in her stomach – one that was bleeding profusely.

"I'll get help," Zahra said, getting back up, but Rose shook her head at the words.

"Don't bother."

Zahra sunk to her knees and regarded the dying woman in sympathy. "Is there anything I can do?"

"I meant what I said," Rose began before moaning at the pain radiating from her stomach. "I want Moloch to pay for killing Tommy."

"Moloch?"

"That's who you're looking for," Rose said as her sight began to darken and crimson began to spill from her lips.

"But, who is he?"

"That's what he's goes by online. He's king of the mindhackers. Earns top dollar," Rose replied, her lip movements slowing to a stop.

"Rose?" Zahra asked tentatively after a moment, but too late. Rose's lifeless eyes stared off into empty space. Zahra activated the vPhone on her wrist, getting a hold of the conductor within seconds. "Stop the train now."

Chapter Three

Mason opened his eyes to the sort of surroundings seen only in his dreams. He blinked again to ensure he wasn't imagining things, but his internal world, his *innermind*, was still there in front of him. At least twenty different estates encompassing entire worlds began at a small, emerald lake and expanded out from it like pieces of a pie.

This imaginary World Showcase boasted a tall, forested hill in one zone and a frozen wasteland in another. One held a colossal, crumbling castle on a wooded butte, while another possessed a grim prison.

A circle of food trucks sat near Mason with menus boasting pizzas, cakes and ice cream bars, among other favorites of his. At the center of the trucks was a picnic table with Zahra sitting on one side, but her attention wasn't on the food trucks around her, but on himself. He smiled in response to Zahra's enigmatic one and turned to regard the grand view in front of him.

"Somebody knocked me out. That's the only explanation," he said aloud to no one in particular.

"Bingo!"

Mason spun around on one heel at the unfamiliar voice. He faced a dark land, just a hundred feet wide at its entrance, but it stretched on towards the horizon, becoming broader with every mile. In those dark recesses were raging red eyes, hands with talons, and brutally evil faces only visible during the occasional flash of lightning. From that dark land, a person appeared as though he had stepped from the surface of a mirror.

"You're not supposed to be here," Mason said, scowling at the unknown man. "I've never seen you before in my life which must mean you're a mindhacker."

"A logical conclusion," the man said, taking another step towards him. Now that he was in the light of the full moon overhead, Mason could just make out the stranger's facial features. He was tall, had black eyes, pale white skin, and a thin smile somehow alien in its makeup. His dark eyes were complimented by inky-black hair set off by prominent cheekbones. The man would have been handsome if not for his cold, cruel smile.

"Care to introduce yourself?" Mason asked, crossing his arms over a vibrant blue jacket.

"Everyone calls me Moloch," he said, putting his hands in the pockets of his tailored, black suit.

"Is that everyone online, everyone in the world, or just you?" Mason asked, chuckling at his name.

"Oh, the name's appropriate, I assure you."

"From what I remember, Moloch is a demon," Mason said.

"Did you get that from over there?" Moloch asked, pointing at part of the showcase where hundreds of tall shelves, filled with books, stood.

"It does represent my knowledge," Mason replied, following his gaze. "You're welcome to take a look, if you like."

"There's nothing in there that I don't know already. How about looking into a few things over there?" Moloch asked, pointing at a wedge of the showcase composed of a broad brick building with a single red set of double doors. The only feature on the building was a large neon sign spelling out 'The Wide World of Porn'. "I bet you have an extensive library of smut in your head. Are you one of those creepy guys who spends all of their time in a strange smelling bedroom in their parent's basement?"

"An arrogant, assuming mindhacker," Mason replied. "Who would've thought?"

"I never said I'm a mindhacker, but I will take this body. I've probably already taken your partner's by now if my host did what he was supposed to."

"You're in my mind, but you're not a mindhacker. So, what are you?" Mason asked.

"It's not important. What is important is that I know about that boy in your class, James, wasn't it? They were bullying him. They beat him right in front of you and you did nothing to stop them. You just stood there and shook like some scared little girl! Why? Was it because you were afraid of being their next target? That's it, isn't it?" he asked, smiling down on him.

Mason shifted his weight from one foot to another. "So, I'm not important but you're still going to try to make me feel guilty for something that happened when I was a kid? I learned something from that, you know: I promised myself that day that I'd stick up for others, no matter what it might do to me."

"Doesn't matter. You're not going to exist pretty soon, but don't worry, I'll take good care of this body," Moloch said, looking around at the many strange and wild estates around him.

"So, you're evicting me from my own head? Where do I go, if I'm allowed to ask?"

Moloch's tie turned to a deep, glowing red as he turned around to get a good look at the world around him. "It usually takes about thirty or forty minutes to take over a body, but I've got to admit that this is one hell of a fuckin' mess. This job will probably take closer to an hour, unlike that simple partner of yours. Luckily, the train will take five hours to get to California, so I've got plenty of time."

"I would think my partner would put up a bigger fight than that. My guess is it would take at least... forever," Mason said, shaking his hand, "plus or minus a few minutes."

"A sense of humor," Moloch remarked, returning his grim gaze to Mason. "I like that. It's too bad you've got to go. There's a lot of interesting things in here. What's that? A prison? Were you in lock-up? Maybe, became some hairy guy's bitch?"

"A prison isn't always literal, you know," Mason said, looking at the tall prison across the showcase.

"Oh, you blame yourself for something. Is that it? Does it have anything to do with the shrine in that church over there? The plaque below it says: 'In loving memory of John Tate'. Was he someone close to you, like a brother or a boyfriend?"

"Full of questions, aren't we?" Mason said, picking at a hole in his jeans.

"A hole in a pair of jeans in your mind and a palace over there, but it looks like it hasn't been lived in for a long time. You once had dreams of wealth, but abandoned them to join the FBI, didn't you?"

"Maybe."

"And then there's your partner sitting next to all of your favorite foods. Is she there as a friend, or is she, like the foods, one of your favorite things?" Moloch asked before holding up an index finger and wagging it at him. "Tut, tut, tut, Mason. Don't you know not to shit where you eat? Ever heard that curious little expression? I think it comes from the early twenty-first century."

"Why all the questions?"

"Because this will all be gone soon and I want to preserve some of it for posterity," Moloch said, a casually cruel smile returning to his lips. "Besides, I am just a little curious, especially about that guy you had sex with when you were twelve. Being gay's a sin you know."

"Fuck you! Is that a direct enough answer and what makes you think that I'm going to disappear forever?" Mason asked, his eyebrows meeting.

Moloch sneered at the question. "Funny, stupid Mason. They all disappear once I'm done. That Major Elliot Peterson who infected you with my nanobots: his mind was like an army base, but then I saw what was in the basement: That's where I found the real Eli. Both of his parents abandoned him. Did you know that? Sad story, but that's why he joined the marines. It offered him the order he never had as a child."

"I remember now!" Mason exclaimed. "Your host had to get really close to me and inject me with nanobots. That means you're not controlling minds remotely! You're taking over people's heads directly and are what, building an army of you?"

Moloch shrugged his shoulders and kept examining the showcase around him. "Maybe."

Mason watched him looking around the lake and sighed. "What are you looking for?"

"The control panel. Everybody has one. It's kind of the command center for your brain. You're an amateur in these sort of matters, so I doubt you'd understand."

"I've always called it the controls, like everyone else, but control panel isn't bad if you're into old-school computers," Mason said, holding up a gold-plated mobile phone. "Looking for this?"

Moloch's eyes darted to his, making Mason shiver. "How do you know about control panels? And, you've made sure that yours is on you at all times. No common man would know how to do that. These worlds, they're not all yours, are they? They're parts of other people you exploited which has to mean," he said, searching Mason's eyes for the answer, "you're a mindhacker!"

"You seemed to know everything else about me. I thought you'd already know that," Mason said, before taking a second look at a curiously glowing stone cathedral. "Wait, you're just seeing what's here without knowing anything about it, so you haven't actually hacked my mind yet, have you?"

Moloch's eyes went from black to red. He jumped on Mason with the rage of an animal, biting and tearing at him with teeth and nails. In moments, Moloch had transformed into a demonic minotaur and was doing his best to rend the agent limb from limb.

Mason yelled in protest as he felt sharp, piercing talons digging into his flesh and teeth gnashing at his neck. As the beast began to consume him, Mason's stomach dropped at the thought that he may indeed be about to disappear in a much more frightening way than he ever thought possible.

"Yes. Good," Moloch Minotaur said, leaning back and looking up at the bright moon above him. Blood covered his mouth and bits of flesh hung from his teeth. "There is much fear in this meat."

Mason summoned all the strength he had left to fight off the beast, only to feel the horrific sensation of his left arm being wrenched from his body. Mason's screams became frantic as he felt his midsection begin to cave in under tremendous force. All he could see above him in the moonlight, which seemed to be getting darker by the second, was two long bullhorns reaching up into the darkness to frame the moon. The sight gave him an idea of where the demon's head was located, and with the last ounce of his strength, Mason placed his right hand within inches of the horned beast and clenched it into a fist. Three tubules popped out of the spaces between his knuckles and entered the demon's left temple.

The FBI agent knew that his injectors didn't really exist in his mind, but he also knew they represented his nanobots and code. It was a last-ditch effort that was rewarded when the demonic minotaur on top of him roared in pain. Moloch turned into a silhouette of white light and vanished.

Mason woke up a second later, grabbing for his lost limbs only to discover they were still attached. A pair of hands were on his a second later, resulting in him instinctually fighting back, but a familiar voice stopped vacant struggle.

"Mason, Mason, it's me, Zahra!" a panicked voice exclaimed from above him. Mason looked around himself, realizing that he was on the floor of their cabin. He pushed himself up on his elbows and looked around.

"What happened?" Zahra asked while he focused on his surroundings. Her hand rested on his chest, which she withdrew after some hesitation.

"I could ask you the same," Mason said, gazing at a large spot of blood on the floor.

"Rose is dead," Zahra replied.

"What happened?"

"It's a long story. I was so worried about you. You've been unconscious for almost five minutes!" Zahra exclaimed. "An ambulance is already on its way!"

"I met our killer."

"Where?" Zahra asked.

"In here," Mason replied, tapping his temple.

"How did that happen?"

"Zahra, he's not getting into people's head remotely. It's much worse than that: He's taking over people's bodies with his nanobots and turning them into copies of him."

"How is that possible?" Zahra asked, creases forming across her brow.

"I'll tell you once we get out of this cabin. I don't want to see it again for the rest of my life."

***

By the time both agents had finished their stories, their rented car had reached the outskirts of Birmingham, the location of the only FBI headquarters in the state. A thick, ethereal mist had appeared just after sunset and was guaranteed to become an impenetrable fog by nightfall. Even the vehicle's bright, overlapping cones of light couldn't pierce the thick soup as the agents approached the city limits. Zahra lounged in the front seat facing Mason, who sat in one of the bucket seats at the back of the vehicle.

"It was my fault," Zahra said, looking out of the window.

"You know it wasn't," Mason said, putting a bandage over two puncture wounds on the back of his hand. "You were called out and handed our witness over to me just as protocol demands. That mayor wasn't exactly being reasonable. You couldn't have known that a marine disguised as a waiter was going to inject me with some kind of freaky, new nanobots!"

"And now this is spreading across the world?"

"Like a virus," Mason said, nodding. "He can take over anyone's mind and body."

"Have you seen anything like that before?" Zahra asked, taking her gaze away from the wall of fog outside the window.

"No, it was strange," Mason replied, looking at the ceiling of the car while thoughts of the past played across its dim fabric. "That major injected me through the skin on the back of my hand. Our nanobots have to be injected in the temples to access the vChip."

"I always wondered: Why is that?"

"Mindhacking nanobots only last for seconds before they start to break down and are absorbed into the bloodstream. So, they have to go in close to the chip, because they'll be gone by the time they reach it if they're injected somewhere else in the body."

"But, these new ones don't break down that fast?" Zahra asked.

"They can't. Do you have the major's body?"

"I'm having an autopsy done as soon as he arrives at the morgue, which should be in about fifteen minutes. From what you've said, we should be able to extract some of his blood and find out what we're dealing with," Zahra replied, glancing at the vPhone on her wrist for updates.

"Don't count on it. Those nanobots might expire when the host dies," Mason said.

"How do you know that?"

Mason shrugged and glanced out of the fog-filled window. "It's what I would do. I have to admit that whatever, whoever, that was, he wasn't something that I've ever dealt with before. It was like he was demonic. He even calls himself Moloch."

Zahra turned the vPhone on her wrist off and tapped the armrest of her seat. "Isn't that just a projection? Do you know who he really is or what he is?"

"No."

Zahra sighed and cocked her head to the side.

"I didn't have time to get him to put a name tag on!" Mason exclaimed, resting his chin on his hand. "He said that I would disappear once he was done and I have a feeling that I almost did. Whatever he is, he isn't a run-of-the-mill mindhacker."

"So, what is he?"

"Something new," Mason said. He looked out the window and pondered the hazy orange streetlights just starting to penetrate the wall of fog around the car. "I'll tell you this: whatever happened to Tommy and Reg, he was the one behind it."

"Are these drones of his, like the major, are they mindhackers?" Zahra asked.

"I've already thought about the major. There's nothing in his file about being a mindhacker and there was no buzz in my head when he got close. He still had injectors, though, and he was unnaturally strong, and really fast—"

Zahra looked up at his remark. "Yeah, what was that? He was like something out of a superhero movie."

"I know! Mindhackers don't have those abilities. Even with that, how did he hope to stop both of us? One of us would have taken him down before he got to Rose. That phone call was really convenient," Mason opined.

"Mmm, too convenient," Zahra said, turning the vPhone on her wrist back on.

"You think the mayor was in on it?"

"You said Rose noticed the major had a bandage on the back of his hand, right?"

"Yes," Mason replied slowly.

"I did too and I remember when I was talking with the mayor that she also had one on the back of her hand. What if they're all covering something up?"

Mason touched the bandage on his hand and nearly jumped out of his seat. "Injection sites! You can't get to a person's neck or head easily without drawing attention. You can get to a person's hand easier than any other exposed part of the body!"

"And you've got a bandage on the back of yours after being attacked," Zahra said, smiling, but the smile disappeared immediately afterward. "I am so sorry for what you went through."

"Hey, I survived it. That's all that matters."

"But, he was so certain that you'd disappear like all the others. Hey, I'm glad you didn't, but why were you any different?" Zahra asked.

"It had something to do with me being a mindhacker. When he figured out that I was one, he went nuts. It was like he attacked me so I didn't have time to defend myself."

"Or maybe he needs to prepare himself somehow before he does it," Zahra interjected.

"Yeah. Maybe mindhackers have some kind of defense against him that others don't."

"Well, then maybe that's something we can use to our advantage," Zahra said, selecting a phone number to call. "In the meantime, let's see if the bureau can bring the mayor in for questioning. Hang on, I'm putting this on private," Zahra said before her eyes darted to the projected image of a receptionist, sitting on the empty car seat in front of her. Her mouth moved, but there was no sound Mason could hear, "Yes, we're going to need to bring the mayor in for questioning and we're going to need a few more agents to cover our six." Mason watched as her eyebrows met and her eyes widened. "What? How? Yeah, you might as well."

"I'm getting the sinking feeling that something just went wrong," Mason said once the image of the receptionist faded from view.

"The mayor was found dead in her office a few minutes ago. Massive heart attack."

"Seriously? How old was she?" Mason asked, noticing a glowing sign indicating they had just arrived in the community where the FBI headquarters was located.

"Forty-nine. The SSA's health system isn't what it used to be, but a heart attack at her age is still abnormal."

"Moloch's covering his tracks," Mason said. "The major is dead and now the one other person we could question is dead, too."

Zahra's brown lips became a thin line as she thought on the subject. "It looks like we're back to square one."

"Maybe not," Mason said. "Rose said that she was kicked out of Reg's body because she found Moloch inside of his head, right?"

"Yes," Zahra said, nodding. "Howser's still alive, but he's a vegetable."

"Doesn't matter. If he's alive then Moloch might still be in there."

"Car?" Zahra directed at the dashboard of the vehicle.

"Yes, Zahra?" a soothing voice replied.

"We've got a new destination."

Later that evening they arrived at the hospital where the vegetative Reginald Howser was being cared for. A doctor in a white coat barely concealing his beer belly greeted them at the back door. Bushy brown eyebrows sat above tiny, round spectacles and a tall mustache crowned a small, frowning mouth. "I'm Doctor Prendergast. I got your message. The patient's state hasn't changed. He's completely unresponsive, which is in line with these type of cases," he said, showing them into the building. He rushed them down a corridor, all the while taking quick glances around him as he went down empty, echoing halls dimly lit for the night shift. "I just don't understand why you need to see him. He won't respond to questions."

Zahra rolled her eyes at Mason before regarding the doctor, whose lumbering bulk shifted from side to side as he quick-marched through the hospital. "I'm aware he can't respond to questions, Doctor, but I can't discuss the specifics of what we need with you. We can assure you, however, that he won't be harmed."

Mason heard three people tap dancing, only to look down and realize how quickly one shoe was following the other. "Are you in a hurry for some reason?"

The doctor continued on his trajectory even as he replied. "If you must know I'm scheduled for a meeting in five minutes, wait, four minutes, with about twenty of the executives that run this hospital."

"Sorry to delay you, Doctor. You can leave the second you show us the room," Mason said.

Doctor Prendergast narrowed his eyes at them but nodded once at the suggestion. "Good enough."

He rounded a corner and stopped at a hospital room marked 42. The doctor then motioned with his hand to the doorway and rushed away at a quick pace.

"Well, he did do his job."

"Yeah, can't argue with that," Zahra said as the duo entered the hospital room. It was small and dimly lit, but it was hard to miss Reginald Howser lying in a hospital bed with numerous tubes going in and out of his body. The occasional silhouette of a person marred the set of frosted windows on one side of the room, while the opposite set looked out on a bank of fog glowing orange from the sodium streetlights in the nearby parking lot. There was a chair on either side of the bed and a bathroom, dark and vacant, sat just off the main room on the far wall.

"This'll do," Mason said, pulling up a chair.

"No," Zahra said, pointing to the chair on the other side of Reginald Howser's hospital bed. "Use that one. It's further from the door."

"Yes, Ma'am!" he exclaimed. Mason crossed to the other side of the room, pulled the other chair up to the bed, and sat down.

"Mason, won't he kick you out just as easily as he kicked Rose out?" Zahra asked as she checked how full her pistol's clip was. In it was a line of bullets with glowing tips which exploded on impact.

"Rose has only been a hacker for about a year. She's inexperienced and Moloch was able to catch her off-guard. Besides, I've got a few tricks up my sleeve."

"From the time you were a mindhacker?" Zahra asked.

"And working for the FBI. Don't think I'm not being careful, though. I barely got away from my last encounter with Moloch alive."

"Anything you need?"

Mason shook his head. "No, just keep an eye on me."

"Always do," Zahra said, keeping her pistol ready.

Mason leaned towards the unconscious Reginald and put his hand, now clenched in a fist, next to his head. Three glassy tubules exited from between his knuckles and pierced the skin at Reg's temple. As Mason closed his eyes and entered another reality, Zahra dimmed the lights in the room to minimum and slowly backed into the darkness of the bathroom, leaving the door open just a crack.

***

Mason opened his eyes to the sight of a large office in the Art Deco style. This office, however, was far from Rose's description of an orderly one: It looked like a powerful quake had shaken the place to its very core. The round room's high-placed windows had shattered, giving one a view of starless night, and much of the lighting above them was burned out or flickering, creating shadowy ghosts with every flash.

The rest of the office, once decorated in bright colors and brass, was now tarnished, and the paint was peeling where there was actual plaster on the walls. One had collapsed, with row upon row of old file cabinets bursting from the wall in disarray. The battered cabinets looked like they were in the middle of vomiting up file folders from their open drawers.

A gramophone, with a dusty, red horn, stood in one corner of the room. It played a ragtime tune, but one distorted to the point that it sounded eerie and alien. At the center of the room was the simple desk Rose had described, now in a state of advanced decay, with a yellowed desktop computer from the nineties sitting on it.

Moloch sat in front of its flickering screen but he was a different man from the one Mason had barely fended off in the recesses of his mind. This Moloch had hazy eyes, white hair, and a hunch as he perched at the ancient computer like a vulture. Moloch looked up from the monitor's cracked surface only to grin yellow teeth at the person standing several feet away.

"Another tourist. There's not much left to see," the old Moloch said in a gravelly voice. He snapped his fingers and made a double-take at Mason once he didn't vanish. "Still here? You have defenses that other one didn't."

Mason narrowed his eyes. "You shouldn't be surprised and you're hiding what you're really thinking. What you really want to ask is: 'Why is another mindhacker here?'"

The old Moloch calmly got out of his seat, momentarily straightening his tattered, dusty, grey suit before he replied. "Tell me: What's going on out there?"

"We're closing in on you."

Moloch's eyes searched his for a moment before a broad, yellowed smile crossed his face. "You don't even know what I'm up to, do you? I can see the ignorance all over your face. You're here for information."

Mason smiled wryly at the statement. "I don't suppose that you'd be willing to just tell me what I need to know?"

"You're really going to ask that?"

"I thought I'd give it a try," Mason replied with a sigh. "So, what do we do now?"

"I transfer myself into your brain," Moloch said, his grin turning into that of a serial killer.

Mason shook his head and snorted. "You've already tried that."

The comment brought another frown to Moloch's lips. "You look like you're telling the truth. You *have* met me before. No, wait it wasn't the real me, was it? You ran into one of my hosts!"

"Hosts!" Mason exclaimed with a guffaw. "Is that what you're calling them?"

"What else would they be called?"

"How, about drones or slaves?" Mason asked. "You don't seem like the kind of person to use euphemisms, unless you're implying that you're a parasite, in which case, yeah, I'll go for that."

"You're reasonably intelligent. That will make your brain easier to rewire. Tell me, how many of my hosts have you encountered? Am I everywhere now?"

Mason sighed. "We're back to asking lots of questions again, aren't we?"

"It doesn't matter if you answer now," Moloch said, chuckling. "Once I'm in your mind, I will sift through everything I need before I delete it."

"Did you do that to Tommy Howser who was all of thirteen years old when he went face-first into a concrete slab?" A frown briefly passed across Moloch's face, causing Mason's eyebrows to shoot up. "So, you did take over his head! The person who screamed at Rose like she was pushing him over the balcony wasn't really Tommy, it was you! You planned it to distract from what you did to Reg and then you blamed it all on Rose!"

"You talk too much," Moloch snarled.

"Now *I* talk too much?" Mason asked before Moloch raised his hands. Pulses of bright light flew from his fingertips. In response, a semi-transparent bubble appeared around Mason, absorbing the attack.

"You've got some training. Good. The last one wasn't challenging at all," Moloch said.

"Do you ever shut up?" Mason asked.

"Fine." Moloch divided into two Molochs, who then divided into four. Before Mason knew what was happening, there were dozens of them, and they ran at full tilt directly for him.

The sight of a small army of Molochs was bad enough, but when it turned into a mass of demonic Minotaur Molochs, sweat began to bead on the agent's brow. Mason shook the fear from his head and imagined a small, black ball into his hand, which he smashed across the floor. The many Molochs paused their mad march at the sight of a great cloud of smoke filling the room.

"Nice try," Moloch said before the swish of fan blades came from above. The room was clear again in seconds, with Mason still standing in the same place as before, but now holding a pistol. He began firing at the many Molochs, but they shrugged off the bullets and continued their advance while the original Moloch led the way.

Mason raised his hand to create a blinding light, but the Moloch mob jumped on him, tearing into his body with myriad sets of sharp teeth. As they reduced Mason's body to a pile of bloody pulp, the other Molochs collapsed into the first. The monstrous minotaur paused his feasting on the mutilated corpse, sniffing the human remains stuck in his talons. Moloch raised his bloody face to the ceiling as though God himself had just spoken to him.

"There's no fear in this meat," he said, tossing it on the floor with a grimace. "This isn't real." Moloch's eyes darted around the room and spotted Mason standing at the computer, his hands working furiously at the controls. He lunged for the agent but was only able to swipe his talons through Mason's fading image.

As he retreated from Reg's vegetative mind, Mason heard Moloch's parting words: *It won't do you any good.*

***

Zahra heard the echo of someone's shoes tapping across the floor before she saw anyone. The tapping ended with a long shadow stretching across the room from the doorway. The specter proceeded to the bed and stood over it. Zahra saw the gleam of a needle in the fluorescent light coming from the corridor. Realizing Mason was on the other side of the bed, the shadow-man walked around it.

She kept her pistol ready, crept out of the bathroom, and then turned the light switch beside the bathroom door to maximum. Zahra hesitated at the sight of Dr. Prendergast hovering over Mason, his hand poised to deliver the contents of the syringe into Mason's arm.

"Freeze!" Zahra hollered at the man, who didn't jump, but stopped what he was doing and turned his head towards the exclamation. Zahra kept her finger on the trigger but found herself trembling once the man's formerly anxious face changed. His eyes became black, and his mouth stretched into an impossibly wide grin.

Her training was the only thing that saved Mason once the doctor tried to push a syringe into his arm with tremendous speed. Zahra squeezed the trigger and hit the doctor squarely in the chest, killing him instantly. She lowered her sidearm and leaned against the wall, breathing heavily. She looked up at the sound of movement to see Mason regaining consciousness in his chair.

"I missed something again, didn't I?" he asked once he took in the full needle next to Dr. Prendergast's bloody body on the tiled floor.

Zahra's eyes bulged out of their sockets as she replied, "You could say that."

"Did you fire?"

Zahra did a double-take. "What does it look like?"

"I was just making sure because I thought weapons fire sets off the alarm."

Zahra was about to answer when red lights began flashing in the hallway and were followed by a loud klaxon sending tidal waves of sound across the hospital.

"Forgot about that."

Before the words were out of her mouth, another alarm went off, this time from Reg's heart monitor, as he went into arrest a second time.

"This is one day I wish I called in sick," Zahra remarked, shaking her head.

Chapter Four

Zahra and Mason sat in the hallway amidst a buzz of activity. Several police officers leaned against one wall while a team from the morgue exited Reg's room with a filled body bag between them. A second body bag containing the expired doctor soon followed the first. Several nurses and doctors hovered around the two FBI agents.

"As I said, he came at me with the intent to kill," Zahra replied to one nurse's accusation, but the staff's heckling drowned out her voice.

The nurse and her colleagues looked down on the seated agents. "He was going to kill you with a hypodermic?"

"I believe that needle contains poison," Zahra said, pointing at the small syringe still lying on the hospital room floor.

"You were sure enough to shoot and kill a medical doctor?" a man in a white coat demanded from her left.

"Could you two give us some room?" Mason asked.

"Or what," one of the nurses demanded, "you'll shoot us, too?"

"That's not what I meant."

"And just what do you think you meant?" the same nurse demanded, now turning a rosy shade of red.

"They mean that you're harassing two FBI agents," a man in a black suit said as he approached with his partner. "I'm Ben Coates, head of the FBI's regional department. Now, if I need to call in more agents to control this situation, I will. Hopefully, though, I can count on the local police to escort these people away."

The men in blue leaning against the wall looked up at Coates before reluctantly straightening up. They approached the dozen staff members gathered around Zahra and Mason.

"Come on, we'll take care of this. Go back to your duties," the officers said, gently guiding the angry nurses away from the two agents.

"Thank you," Zahra said, getting up as Ben and his assistant approached.

"Don't thank me yet, Zahra," Ben said, poking his head through the doorway of the hospital room.

"That doctor tried to kill Mason," she said, pointing at the syringe lying on the floor. "You just need to test the contents of that needle and you'll see that we're telling the truth."

"Hey," Ben said, raising his hands in a placating gesture, "I believe you, but you're starting to build up a body count and I'm obligated to investigate. You know that. If you could come back to H.Q. with us, we'll conduct a few interviews, gather evidence, and then get you on your way. I shouldn't have to tell you, though, this doesn't look good for us, or for you."

"I know," Zahra said, taking a deep breath.

"Mason," Ben said, directing his dark brown eyes at him, "did you get any information from whatever that thing was in his head?"

Mason looked at Zahra and sighed. "No, it was too late. His brain was fried. All that was left of the guy by the time I got in there was a body in the rubble."

"I see," Ben said, nodding to Zahra. "I think it's best we get you back to H.Q. and debrief there. Don't worry, I've got more agents on their way to clean up here."

"Okay," Zahra said, starting towards the door.

"After you," Ben said to Mason once he noticed the agent was lingering behind them.

Mason joined Zahra in front of their superiors when he and his partner felt their arms being pulled behind their backs, followed by the feeling of metal closing around their wrists.

"What the—?" Mason demanded as he became aware that both he and his partner were being relieved of their sidearms.

"I'm sorry I have to do this," Ben said, continuing to guide them to the elevators, "but I've got a lot of mad people in the SSA I have to answer to right now. One thing they insisted on was that you be led away in handcuffs. Don't worry, once we're past the press, I'll take them off."

Zahra resisted at first but then relaxed her posture once he finished. "The press?"

"There's a crowd of them just outside the door. Rumors are already flying about the mad mindhacker and his Black handler."

"Seriously?" Zahra said before eyeing the silver elevator as it opened. "I'd rather face an FBI board than the press around here."

"Funny," Mason remarked as they entered the elevator, "I'd rather face the press."

"You would!" Zahra exclaimed, taking her place between the two agents.

Mason stood next to her and Ben pressed the button for the hospital's garage.

"Sir?" Zahra asked Ben, still turning from the elevator's control panel. "I really am sorry about all of this."

"I know you are, Zahra, but," Ben said, taking his pistol from his holster and directing it at Mason, "I'm not so sure about him. Whatever was in Reg's head might've taken him over, too. What does Moloch call them? Hosts?"

Mason's eyes narrowed at the sight of Ben's gun barrel. "Where did you find out that his name is Moloch and how did you know he called his victims 'hosts'? We only found that out in the last few hours and we haven't reported in, yet. By the way, nice bandage on the back of your hand. Same to your partner."

"Hmm," Ben said, holding up his bandaged hand and nodding, "so you did meet me in there. I was worried about that. You found something you weren't supposed to, didn't you?"

Zahra looked from Mason to Ben, her mouth hanging open. "Moloch?"

Ben's smile became impossibly wide on his mahogany face, and his brown eyes turned black. He pressed a button on the elevator's panel, and its progress down the shaft suddenly stopped.

Zahra frowned at the devilish change in the man's features. "What happened to Ben and his assistant?"

Ben snorted. "The host doesn't survive my takeover, but Mason already knows that and now he knows too much for me take his mind. Don't worry, Zahra, we can still salvage you, but it might take me more time and more convincing. It won't be pain-free, I'm afraid," Moloch-Ben said, reaching out for her face. "I bet your mind is like some beautiful, serene fantasy."

Zahra jerked her head away from Ben, which was all the distraction Mason needed to tear apart the handcuffs on his wrists. By the time the possessed FBI agents realized he was free, Mason had already thrown Ben's assistant into the wall, knocking him unconscious.

Ben turned the gun towards Mason, but he kicked it from the host's grip with lightning-fast speed. Moloch-Ben rubbed his hand for a moment. "You got a hold of more code than you should have, mindhacker. You learn fast."

A dark, veiny hand shot out at Mason with incredible speed, but he moved his head out of the way with time to spare. What followed was a storm of punches and kicks between the two, who were literally bouncing off the shaking walls of the small space. Zahra couldn't help but stare at them before she heard Mason's voice come from the blur of action.

"Get that agent's gun!"

Zahra turned her head away from the storm making its way around the elevator and did her best to retrieve the agent's gun with cuffs on. Just as she was balancing it in her hands, a fist came to just inches from her face, only to be pushed away.

She did her best to aim the gun but realized that all she could see was a blur of two bodies furiously fighting each other. Zahra pointed the pistol above their heads and shouted: "Hangman!"

"Wait… wait a second!" Mason exclaimed. Zahra watched in awe as Ben's head emerged from the blur with Mason's hand firmly around his throat. "Now!!"

Zahra fired the gun. Even with the disadvantage of the handcuffs, she managed to hit Ben in the head. She looked away as much of her former friend and superior's cranium disappeared. Mason let him go and the body tumbled to the floor.

"I'm glad you taught me those code words."

"Thanks, now what the fuck was that?" Zahra demanded.

Mason pressed the button for the garage and leaned against the elevator wall. "You have no idea how much energy that takes. I think I could eat an entire Las Vegas buffet by myself."

Zahra stared at his reply, shook her head, and repeated her previous question. "What the fuck was that? You moved like those drones, or whatever they are, of Moloch's and then there's Ben: He was one of those guys?"

Mason tried to catch his breath and reply simultaneously while Zahra removed her handcuffs and retrieved their weapons. "They both were. I realized that as soon as he mentioned Moloch's name and I saw the bandages on their hands."

"I thought you said you didn't find anything in there," Zahra said.

"With what I just found out, I knew I couldn't trust them."

"What?" Zahra asked. "What do you know?"

"I can't tell you until we're somewhere safe."

"Like where?" Zahra asked as the downward movement of the elevator stopped.

"Somewhere there's nobody else at all."

"What, like Wyoming?" Zahra asked, raising an eyebrow.

"No, like a car."

Mason trained his gun on the door as it opened, discovering that the garage was, thankfully, empty. He led the way to their car, keeping alert of everything around them.

"Did you send the information on the rental to the office, yet?" Mason asked, just as the forest green, oval vehicle came into sight.

"I was going to do it at the end of the week along with all the other paperwork."

"Good," Mason said, collapsing into the back chair while Zahra got into the seat beside him. "That means not even the FBI can trace us right now."

"Why wouldn't we want that?"

"Because, as we just saw, Moloch's already infiltrated it. No one there can be trusted, especially if he's managed to get as high up on the chain as Ben," Mason replied.

Zahra looked at him and sighed. She placed a hand on his shoulder. "Are you okay? You look a little tired."

Mason slapped his belly and smiled. "Hungry is more like it."

"Where to?"

"Head for the EUS. We have to get out of this country. It won't be long before people start to come looking for us. We shouldn't use this car for too long, either."

"What about the press?"

"I don't think there is any. Moloch just wanted an excuse to get those handcuffs on us."

"Car, go to Richmond," Zahra said. The car accelerated for the exit after a brief acknowledgment. "Now, what is all of this about?"

"I can't tell you yet," Mason said, leaning back in his seat and closing his eyes.

"What, you're going to take a nap now?"

"No, I'm preparing myself," Mason replied.

"For what?"

"To enter someone's mind," Mason answered.

"Whose?"

"Yours!" Mason replied.

Zahra sat up stock-straight and glared at him. "Now I know that you don't think I'm going to let anyone do no mind-job on me!"

"It's the only place where we can do this without Moloch knowing about it!"

"How do I know I can trust you?" Zahra demanded.

"Because I can't trust anyone else!" Mason exclaimed, opening his eyes. He relaxed and sighed before meeting her stare. "Because we've been working together for a year now and you've known me to be nothing but on the level with you. Don't worry, I won't look around."

"You better not," Zahra said, staring him down. After a moment, she shook her head, braids bouncing and sighed. "Okay. Fine. But this better be good."

"Just relax and make yourself comfortable," Mason suggested.

"What about those cuts and bruises? I should take a look at them," Zahra said, turning towards a small compartment on one side of the vehicle.

"We can do that after. Just sit back and relax!"

Zahra reclined in her seat and regarded him with a pleading expression. "You promise not to look around?"

Mason laughed and leaned forward in his seat towards her. "I promise. Have you ever had someone do this before?"

"You know the answer is no!" Zahra exclaimed.

"I'm just making sure. This is going to feel a little strange."

"How so?" Zahra asked, closing her eyes.

"It's like blinking and finding yourself in a completely different world. Some people feel dizzy, some get nauseated, some people piss their pants."

"What?" Zahra said, snapping up straight.

"Just kidding. Bit of an ice-breaker."

"It didn't work," Zahra said, leaning back into her seat again and closing her eyes. "Okay, just do it before I change my mind."

Mason placed his hand near her head. Injectors leapt from between his knuckles and punctured the skin at her temple. The inside of their rental car changed to that of a grand showcase like that of Mason's innermind; only this one had tourists milling about. Balloons bobbed in the blue sky and the smell of buttery popcorn was on the air. The sun was high, having just passed its zenith. At the center of it all was a tall Gothic church surrounded by a large park filled with grass and trees swaying in a gentle breeze.

"I always saw it in my head," Zahra said, staring at the smiling tourists around her. "Just not like this."

"A showcase, not that different from mine," Mason said, appreciatively nodding.

"It's always been like that for me," Zahra said.

"Hey, great minds think alike!"

"I… guess so."

"Okay, you're going to need your controls to bring us somewhere else. Wow!" Mason exclaimed, staring at something on their right. "You've got a dark side, too! Mine looks pretty close to that one."

Zahra's head snapped around to take in a place on the edge of the pavilion a hundred feet wide, and the further away it stretched, the broader it got. This part of the showcase was dark, with pairs of red eyes staring out from flashing fog. The vague lines of a shadowy building lay deeper within a misty, dark forest. Zahra's jaw dropped at the sight of his stare into her dark side.

"You said you weren't going to look around!" Zahra said, stepping in front of him and his view.

"I know, it's just that building in there looks like an old bungalow, kind of like the one I grew up in," Mason said, shielding his eyes, but not before another sight caught them. "You've got a cathedral in your head, too? Mine's got a shrine in it. Does yours?"

Zahra averted her eyes from the gothic church at the center of the park. "What? No. Wait, you've got a shrine in your church, too? What for?"

"Ah, nothing," Mason replied, mirroring her posture and turning away from the church. "I'll tell you some other time. What's that?"

"Mason!" Zahra exclaimed, turning around to see the new target of his interest.

"It's me!"

Mason stared at a copy of himself while Zahra felt her stomach shrivel. His doppelganger stood next to a tree with a few balloons bobbing above him. Mason stared at himself for a moment before frowning. "Zahra, why am I wearing khakis and a cardigan? I look like I'm going out on a date."

Zahra turned Mason away from the fantasy version of himself and pointed at a group of food stands gathered around a small collection of white outdoor dinette sets. "Hey, those are my favorite foods! Why don't you go take a look?"

Mason blinked at her, wearing a cynical smile that turned into a genuine one once he glimpsed the menus a moment later. "Burritos! You've got one stand just for burritos! Twelve kinds. No wonder I always see you snacking on one."

"Yeah, now where would my controls be so I can get us out of here?" Zahra asked.

"That's easy: It will be on something or someone important to you. Pizza! Oh, vegetarian. I'll take a look, anyway."

Zahra glanced over her shoulder at Mason's double. "Ah, yeah. You should try it. You might like it." She patted him on the shoulder as he walked to a food stand where a mustached man smiled from behind a painted counter covered in New Yorker style pizzas.

Once Zahra saw Mason fully immersed in delectable delights, she walked up to Mason's smiling, but silent copy and held out her hand. He responded by pulling an older model Smartphone from his jacket pocket and handed it to her. She gripped the phone, his hand lingering on hers for a moment before pulling away.

"Thanks," she said to the other Mason, who nodded and smiled. Zahra nodded back, her eyes catching his before she returned to the real Mason, gorging himself on a veggie pizza. "I got it."

"You know," Mason said, turning around, his mouth stuffed with pizza, "I never thought I'd like vegetarian pizza, but it tastes so good here!"

"Maybe you should try it in real life, sometime. Now, I got—"

"Chocolate Mousse Cake?" Mason said, pronouncing it *mouse* instead of *moose*. At the center of the counter at the adjacent stand was a large, multilayered chocolate confection topped with a ring of strawberries. Behind the counter and the cake stood an older lady with wild, curly hair and a smile adorned with hastily-applied red lipstick. Mason read from a small sign next to the cake: "Grandma's Mouse Cake? Look's good!"

Zahra looked at the woman behind the counter with a wistful smile. "*Mousse* cake and, yeah, it always was."

"You got the control panel?" Mason asked, accepting a slice of cake from the elderly woman.

Zahra's soft gaze dwelled on her grandmother's smiling face for a moment. "Yeah, right here," she said, handing over the Smartphone.

"Great!" he said, putting the cake down after swallowing down a few more bites. He took the phone, swiping through stills of a myriad of memories. "We'll just pick a random, yet harmless memory."

Mason tapped one of the many little squares on the screen. The view of the showcase and all its tourists changed to that of a metropolis at night. This wasn't the brightly lit downtown of a city, however, but an area lined with single-story bungalows and Mom & Pop shops.

Mason took in his surroundings of a lane bathed by streetlights under a starry sky. He looked beyond it, glimpsing a much wider road populated by three and four-story buildings lit by sodium streetlights where traffic buzzed back and forth. He looked down the street to see old-fashioned poles complete with power lines.

"Interesting," Mason remarked. "Where is this?"

"It's where I grew up," Zahra replied. "My early years here weren't the best, but by the time I was in my teens I used to have a lot of fun on nights like this one with my friends."

"I see. Good memories. Well, they ended up being good memories."

"Yeah, now what's going on?" Zahra asked.

Mason sighed and looked at the sidewalk. "Not a comfortable place to have a conversation," he said, looked at the pavement and blinked. A broad couch appeared with blue upholstery and a couple of green throw pillows.

"Better than standing here," Zahra said, taking a seat on the couch in the middle of the street. "Although we're not really standing here, are we? Speaking of which: Do we really have the time to redecorate my childhood neighborhood?"

"It's like being in virtual reality. Hours in here are like minutes out there. We've got plenty of time to smell the roses," Mason said, before snorting, "and eat Grandma's Mouse Cake."

"Gran's *Mousse* Cake. So, who is Moloch?"

"I don't know," Mason replied.

"Now, see," Zahra said, sitting up and shaking a finger at him, "that's the first thing I'd want to know if I was digging around in someone's head."

"Look, when you're doing a mind-job, it can take some time to find the information you need, but a good mindhacker can find it in seconds, if they know people well enough and know where to look."

"Shouldn't his name be right at the top of the pile?"

"You'd be surprised," Mason said, thinking back to the old-fashioned nineties computer in Reg's vegetative mind. "Someone like Moloch doesn't want their real name to be known, so they bury that information. I had a fraction of a second to access his mind, so I took what looked important and left. And, there's something else."

"Uh-huh?" Zahra asked. "Hey, I feel like a coffee, can I just," she began before a full, hot mug appeared in her hand.

"Yes, you can just think one up."

"Mmm," Zahra said, savoring the steaming coffee, "it even has two cream and two sugars, just how I like it."

"You're actually pretty good at this, you know, for a beginner."

"Thanks, now what did you want to tell me?" Zahra asked, savoring her cup of coffee in a deep mug.

"Moloch has managed to find hard-code to change some of the basic settings on his implant. It's the reason why I was able to do what I did in the elevator."

"I noticed. What's hard-code, again?"

"Soft-code is everything out there that involves vWorlds, vGames, and most other programming. It's something that can be changed relatively easily, but hard-code—"

"Is like the engine of a car: without it, the car won't work," Zahra interjected. "Now I remember."

"That's it. There's hard-code in every mindhacker's implant to keep it working," Mason said.

"Sounds like something you don't want to mess with," Zahra said, taking another sip of her coffee.

"Normally you wouldn't, but this code was surprisingly easy to install and we wouldn't have gotten out of that elevator without it. That code altered my implant and it gave me enhanced speed and strength."

"Isn't that a little dangerous?" Zahra asked.

"I knew you were going to say that and I know what a temptation it could be. If I had a choice not to use it, I wouldn't, but we were about to get shot. You have to admit that it does help to even the odds against Moloch's drones."

"Yeah, about that: why would his hosts have those abilities, too?" she inquired.

Mason pulled a can of beer out of thin air, opened it, and took a sip. "Why wouldn't they? When it comes to his hosts Moloch's got a hold of their controls now. He can increase their heart rate, get their adrenaline pumping, or even force their brains to do more than they should be capable of. It would have to come at a huge cost for the hosts' bodies, though. I don't think Moloch cares about what he's doing to them, but at least by using the code we stand a fighting chance."

"Okay, okay, just use it for good and not evil, you know?"

"Got it," he replied, with a smile and nod.

"How did he get this code?" Zahra asked, taking another sip of her coffee.

"Okay, I did find that one out," Mason replied. "Moloch stumbled onto some info a few years ago that mindhackers could be upgraded with major enhancements to the point they wouldn't be mindhackers anymore; they'd be bodyhackers. What you saw is just the tip of the iceberg. Now, guess who developed this new code?"

"Oh God," Zahra said, putting a hand on her forehead. "Please, don't tell me it was the FBI."

"The one and only," Mason confirmed. "Moloch couldn't get what he needed from the FBI because they realized it was a bad idea years ago and they were supposed to have destroyed all the data."

"That should've been the end of the story," Zahra said, looking into her mug. "And that is the end of the coffee."

"Just think up more," Mason said. At the suggestion, the mug was again full, and he continued. "The FBI destroyed the data, yeah, but they had the research done by a dozen different private companies, and none of them followed the same data disposal policies that the FBI did."

"Are you telling me that all of these guys forgot to empty their trash bins?" Zahra asked, smiling down at her bottomless cup of coffee.

"It's more like they didn't purge the backup, of a backup, of a backup, but basically, yeah. Moloch's got most of the pieces of the puzzle, now. A few months ago, he assembled the hard-code he needed to become a new kind of mindhacker—"

"A bodyhacker," Zahra interjected.

"Yeah, but he's not finished."

"Why?" she asked. A cruller on a plate appeared next to her. Zahra picked it up with a relishing grin. "Finally, a zero calorie cruller. Well, outside of those vRestaurants anyway, but I don't go to those."

"Zahra?" Mason asked, watching her take a bite of it. "Eyes on the ball?"

"Oh," Zahra said, looking up from the baked good, "believe me, I'm listening to every word."

"Moloch has the power to create entire armies of him, but it's worse that than. Eventually, most of the population would be made up of billions of Molochs."

"Is that really possible?" Zahra asked, setting down both her drink and snack on a Queen Anne end table that appeared once it was needed.

"It would take a while, but yeah."

"Is that what happened to Tommy and Reg Howser?" she asked, giving him her full attention.

"That was a screw-up on his part. Moloch heard about new research that would reduce the conversion time of his hosts to under an hour. Before, it took twice that long and that was really slowing him down. So, he found a way to isolate Tommy while he was on lunch at school. After that, he just had to wait until Tommy could get Reg alone for an hour, which he did."

"Can you imagine trusting your child only to have them do something like that to you? It must've been heartbreaking for Reg," Zahra said.

"I know better than most. Moloch kept the memory of Reg's sadness at the sight of Tommy betraying him, just for fun. Anyway, Rose showed and that gave him an idea: He sent Tommy over the edge of the balcony, gave Reg a massive stroke and then the police blamed it all on her. If the plan had worked, we would've been none the wiser."

"But I thought it did work," Zahra said, picking up her cruller again.

"Almost. Reg wasn't supposed to survive that stroke. Moloch needed to get rid of that copy of himself as soon as possible, but there was too much activity around him for those first few hours. It's likely that he took over Dr. Prendergast for the sole purpose of slipping something into Reg's I.V."

"He waited to make his move until after we arrived?" Zahra inquired.

"This all happened in less than twenty-four hours. We got there before the doctor had a chance to act, so Moloch sent Prendergast in to take care of all of us."

"Jesus," Zahra said, "Well, I guess we found Tommy's murderer, although I don't know how I'd ever explain all of this to his mother. Technically, the case would be closed, except—"

"Except that we now have some psycho out there who's got delusions of world domination," Mason interjected, slumping into his seat.

"Shouldn't we get the FBI involved?"

"You mean the same FBI who just tried to kill us?" Mason asked, taking one of his few sips from his can of beer.

"No, Mason! There are other regional heads. There's even the main office in D.C."

"And we can't trust any of them. Moloch could already have agents in all of those offices and we can't afford to have him know where we are."

"Then we need to get to the bottom of that code if we're going to stop him. I say we follow his tracks and find those same pieces of the puzzle," Zahra said, finishing the rest of her baked goods.

Mason nodded. "It's our best bet, but I don't think Moloch is going to make it easy for us. He said the information I got from him wouldn't do me any good. The data that I did manage to get ahold of, though, did have one of those companies listed."

"Good," Zahra said, looking at the city around her, drenched in night. "Why bring me here, though? You could have told me all of this in the car."

"I had to make sure that I didn't find Moloch in here instead of you."

"Ah, I get it. Well then, let's get out of here and take care of Moloch."

"Done," Mason said. The two of them opened their eyes to the sight of the car's cabin around them once more.

"Where to from here?" Zahra asked, pulling herself into a sitting position and squinting in the overhead light.

"That's why I said to go to the ESA. The company we're looking for is in Pennsylvania. By the way, can we stop at a take-out? You wouldn't believe how hungry I am after all of that Matrix-style punching and kicking!"

Zahra guffawed and began searching her vPhone for an off-ramp on the ESA side of the border while the electric car soundlessly accelerated into the night.

Chapter Five

"FBI!" Zahra exclaimed, holding her credentials a foot from a security guard's face. He was seated behind a large, white counter just inside the door of a small lobby blocking entry into the rest of the building.

"I can see that," the guard said, shifting in his cheap chair. "Did you need something?"

"We need to take a look at one of your computers," she said before checking the information on her phone. "The file we need is called Stardust-One."

"Right," the guard said, taking a look at his system before frowning at the screen. "That's on an auxiliary backup to the secondary backup."

"We just need five minutes," Zahra stated.

"Tirith Software is a secure facility," the guard lectured. "Do you have a warrant?"

"Don't need one," Zahra said. "This is our data, which your company carelessly left on one of its systems."

"Well—" the guard began before Zahra raised a hand.

"Look, we're not here to sue. As it turns out, we might have a need for that data after all and we were a little too hasty in deleting it.

Giving us access might help us and it will probably earn good credit towards future contracts with your company."

"If it's information that already belongs to you, then it should be okay. I am going to need to check with my superiors, though."

"Go ahead," Zahra said with a smile, while the guard tapped a number on his vPhone.

Zahra and Mason walked to a position ten feet away from the desk.

"What if they check in with head office?" Mason whispered.

"Then we're going to be in it pretty deep, but we'll know fast because the guard will make some excuse to hold us here while the FBI sends a team to arrest us or—"

"Or?" Mason asked, waiting on her words.

"Or it will take a few minutes for the FBI to get word of what we're doing, in which case they might come looking for us in about five to ten minutes."

"Do you think they'd do that?"

"We're off the grid. If our names came up in an inquiry, our superiors would want to detain us for questioning or Moloch might just be our superiors now. Just stay alert," Zahra whispered back.

"Alright," the security guard said, getting up. Zahra nearly went for her sidearm but managed to keep her right hand by her side. The guard walked around the heavy counter and stood within a few feet of them. An impressive semi-automatic rifle hung from a strap on his right shoulder. "My manager approved your entry. They said you can look at the Stardust-One backup, only."

"That's all we need," Zahra said, placing a confident grin on her face.

"Follow me."

Zahra and Mason fell into step behind the guard as he escorted them past several closed doors, many of which had thumbprint identification pads next to them. It was only once they had reached the back of the building that the guard stopped at a steel door next to an emergency exit.

"This is it," he said, using his thumbprint to open the door.

"We just need five minutes," Zahra said, taking a step into the room.

"My manager said you've got up to fifteen."

"That was very nice of them," Zahra said to his face before she closed the door and rolled her eyes. "The manager gave us fifteen minutes because he loves us so much."

"I heard," Mason said, chuckling. He sat down at the terminal and stretched. The monitor looked like an old 1950s television, but the screen projected a hologram into the air. "Okay, I'm into the main folder. What was the filename again?"

"Stardust-One," Zahra replied, just as Mason's stomach issued a disconcerting noise. "Must be that mountain of food you ate from that take-out," Zahra said, looking down at him.

"I told you I was hungry!"

"Yeah, well eating that many burritos can't be good for anybody. Let me see," Zahra said, watching over Mason's shoulder while he searched through the many directories and long-forgotten files that had accumulated on the drive. After a minute, she pointed at one file name floating in the air. "There it is!"

Zahra reached over his shoulder, tapped the file on the 3D screen and felt her face fall. "There's nothing in here! It's empty!"

"I was worried about that. Moloch's covering his tracks, again. I think it's time we got out of here," Mason said, logging out of the computer and standing up.

"Good idea."

They left the room and began retracing their steps towards the front of the building. They had only made it a short way when the same security guard who had escorted them earlier appeared in the hallway, rushing towards them.

"Hey! Stop!"

"Oh, shit!" Zahra exclaimed, looking at the empty corridor behind them. "Run!"

The pair spun around and rushed in the opposite direction.

"Stop, or I will shoot!" the guard bellowed as they raced away.

"He won't shoot," Zahra said between breaths.

"You certain of that?" Mason asked, fists pumping.

Zahra shook her head. "No."

"I was worried you'd say that. Where are we headed, anyway?"

Zahra nodded at a red emergency exit sign above a door at the end of the corridor. "There."

"Won't that set off the alarm?"

"Do we care at this point?"

Zahra was almost at the red door when it was flung open. She found her momentum carrying her out onto a wide concrete platform sparsely covered in picnic tables for lunching employees. Zahra nearly fell but managed to keep her balance and bring herself to a halt.

She heard the door slam behind her just a moment after Mason appeared in her peripheral vision. Zahra stopped, drew her gun and spun on her heel to confront whomever had opened the door. She was surprised to see Mason helping a long-haired woman in a lab coat move a picnic table against the exit.

"That's unsafe, you know," Zahra said, putting her gun back in its holster.

"But it keeps that security guard inside for a minute," the woman said, just as they heard a thump from the door, followed by bellowing and a series of four-letter words.

"Thanks for the help," Mason said, backing away from the door even as the picnic table was wrenched upwards a foot by a particularly strong shoulder.

"We should get to the car."

"I wouldn't if I were you," the woman said, shielding her dark eyes with a hand against the bright sunlight.

"Who are you?" Zahra asked.

"Ernestine Paul, but my friends call me Ern," she replied. "Your car's on camera now. They'll be able to track it by its plates. We should use my car."

"Why are you helping us?"

"Lotta reasons. I'll tell you once we get out of here. We'd better go, that table won't last long against Ron," she replied, raising an eyebrow at the door. "He works out."

"Can we trust her?" Mason asked.

"We don't have a lot of options here."

They both nodded at Ernestine. "Lead the way."

She led them across the platform and into a rear parking lot where a silver vehicle waited. Ernestine pressed a button on her fob and the doors opened upwards, allowing them to pile inside quickly.

"Garrett's. Hurry," Ernestine said to her car's computer the moment her body hit the chair. The car acknowledged the order and sped off, breaking the local speed limit.

"Who's Garrett?" Zahra asked once she had settled into the vehicle.

"A friend and I think you could use a few right now."

"You do know that we're the FBI, right?" Mason asked.

"Considering what the FBI has done to Natives over the last hundred and fifty years, you're lucky you're on my good side or I'd throw you both out of the car right now."

"It's moving," Mason observed.

"I know."

"Cherokee?" Zahra inquired.

"Mi'kmaq," Ernestine corrected, straightening her brown hair. "I know who you are and I know why you were at Tirith Software."

"You seem to know a lot about us," Zahra said, glancing out of the forward windshield as the car accelerated into the countryside. "Aren't you worried that we're going to get you in trouble?"

"The whole world's in trouble if that super-hacker, or whatever he is, takes over everybody's heads."

"Moloch," Mason supplied.

"Named after a demon, huh? Why am I not surprised?"

Mason grimaced. "It's appropriate, though. Trust me."

"You went up against him?" Ernestine asked, cocking her head sideways at him. A thin smile appeared on her rose-red lips.

"Twice, but it almost killed me both times," Mason replied. He shifted in his bucket seat at the back of the cabin.

"Wow," she said. Her reserved smile turned into a grin.

"Okay, Ern, how do you know about us and how do you know about bodyhackers?" Zahra asked, leaning forward in her chair.

"Bodyhackers? Yeah, that makes sense. I've been working at Tirith for over ten years. The last five were as a senior developer. Guess who worked on that code for mindhackers as a junior?"

"That was you?" Mason asked, eyes widening.

"Guilty as charged. It's Doctor to anyone who isn't my friend, by the way," she said, frowning at them. At the sight of their reactions to the statement, her contagious smile returned. "Don't worry, you guys can call me Ern. I worked on one part of the code, but the FBI assumed that I can't put two and two together, or they didn't care. But I knew someone would try to use it one day. Then, a few months ago, I noticed strange things happening in the news: too many people behaving weird, and too many people dying, if you know what I mean. When you two showed up, I knew you had to be checking into it. When I realized you were in trouble, I made my move."

"I have to tell you," Zahra said, licking her lips, "just helping us right now could get you in trouble. We're not exactly in direct contact with the rest of the FBI right now."

"There's a silver lining to the cloud after all," Ernestine said, chuckling. "Ron doesn't chase people around for no reason. Don't worry about it. I know what's going on and I want to help."

"This would be a good time," Mason said, glancing at the trees flying by his window. "We need to stop Moloch and we hoped to piece together the code he used to upgrade himself. We thought that might lead to him."

"But you found that he deleted everything," Ernestine said.

"Yeah. How did you know?" Mason asked.

"It fits in with everything else."

"You worked on the code," Zahra said. "Can't you tell us what we need to know?"

"I only worked on one piece of it. There was only one team that I know of that worked on the assembled code."

"Who?" Mason inquired, sitting up.

"It was Ed Blunt and five others," Ernestine said, digging a few bottles of water out of a cooler in the side compartment of her car. She handed one to each of the agents.

"Do you know their names?"

"I do, but it won't do you any good," she replied.

"Oh, no," Mason said, shaking his head at the familiar words. "What happened to them?"

"They're all dead," Ernestine stated, taking a long drink from her bottle of water.

"That can't be a coincidence," Zahra said, crossing her arms.

"I didn't think so either," Ernestine said. "Two of them died natural deaths over the years and you all know about Edward." They both nodded, and she continued. "The last three though," she said, pointing at them with a red, lacquered fingernail, "that's what got me suspicious."

"Why?"

"They all died in the last three months," she replied, setting her bottle of water on the floor.

"What?" Zahra said. "How?"

"Oh, it looked like a coincidence and the news never reported any of it because they didn't know they worked together. Top secret and all that. I did, though, and I paid attention. Three deaths in three months. All of them strokes, heart attacks, one of them committed suicide, but I knew there was something fishy there. So, I looked into it and it all started to make sense. It had to be someone who got ahold of the assembled code. He's making sure that no one can follow him. That's why I wasn't surprised when you told me he deleted it."

"Jesus," Zahra said, putting a hand to her brow. "How many people are under this guy's control?"

Ernestine sighed. "I already calculated that. By now, this Moloch has already taken about five percent of the population. Do you know how many people that is?"

"Millions," Mason replied.

"Three hundred and fifty million," Ernestine clarified. "And, that number's going up every minute, every second."

"He's covered his tracks pretty well," Zahra said. "I hope you can help us find someone to deal with this psychopath."

"You find Ed," Ernestine said, glancing at the floor. "We were pretty close for a while."

"Edward Blunt's dead," Mason said.

Ernestine slowly shook her head. "Only in the papers."

"They're usually right," Mason said. "I heard about it at the time. He left a will and instructions for his company and then vanished. That's got suicide marked all over it."

"You didn't know Ed. I did," Ernestine said, inflecting her words and pointing at her chest. "There's no way he'd ever kill himself. It's more like the complete opposite of that."

"Okay," Mason said, slowly. "Then how do we find an incredibly rich guy with endless resources who doesn't want to be found?"

"You sound like a smartass," Ernestine replied, smiling. "That's okay. I can work with that. You can find him through Freenet."

"Oh, God," Mason said, turning his chair towards the window.

"Freenet? Isn't that the online hippie group?" Zahra asked.

"It's a rebel underground created by a bunch of hippies who are all about 'free' vU, 'free' education, 'free' democracy, blah, blah, blah. It started up about twenty years ago. No one takes them seriously."

"You better," Ernestine said. "Ed started that hippie group."

"What?" Mason asked, squinting at her. "He did not!"

"Ah, yeah, he did," she said, raising her eyebrows. "Ed was misunderstood. He wanted the vU, vGames, vLibraries, all of it, to be free. If anybody knows how to find Ed, it's them."

"Time to go see the hippies," Zahra said, smiling at Mason.

"So, this Garrett guy is one of them?" Mason inquired, ignoring her.

"Not really, no," Ernestine replied, picking up her water bottle again and taking a sip.

"Then why are we going to see him?"

"He's my black market guy. Seeing that you don't have access to FBI resources, I figured you might need him."

Zahra looked at Mason and then back to their new host. "I don't like the Black Market, but we could use someone like that right now."

"Good," Ernestine said, turning her attention to the view through the windshield, "because we're almost there."

Zahra and Mason followed her gaze as the car slowed and took a left onto a dirt path nearly overgrown with vegetation. A thick stand of trees leaned over the disused road making it difficult to see what lay at the end of the overgrown path.

"Are you sure we're in the right place?"

Ernestine chuckled at the question. "He did all this on purpose. You could call it his secret lair. I think he got that from one of those vGames he plays."

"Garrett sounds kinda paranoid," Zahra commented.

"With who's after him, he's gotta right to be paranoid."

The car drove down the road at a much slower speed due to the uneven ground, which caused the vehicle to shift from side to side. After a few minutes on the old path, Mason and Zahra watched it open up onto a broad field of tall grass. From it sprung a one-and-a-half story house covered in peeling siding. It had once been white but now looked closer to a light grey. Dark shingles, worn smooth, covered the steep roof and dusty windows lined every wall.

"It looks dilapidated," Zahra said, raising her eyebrows.

"The important part's not," Ernestine said as the car pulled into a small clearing directly in front of the house. It stopped mere feet from a sun porch with torn screens and a faded front door at its center. The trio got out of the car and stepped into the tall grass.

"Is there a part of that house that's not ready to fall down?" Zahra asked while she and Mason followed Ernestine to the front door.

Ernestine laughed and opened the flimsy wooden door. "It's okay, trust me."

They entered a small living room with worn wooden boards covering the floor. A few pieces of dusty, ratty furniture were scattered across the room. The computer scientist walked past the living room and stopped just short of a greasy kitchen. Zahra briefly glimpsed overturned furnishings in front of an old iron stove covered in decades-old grease and grime.

Ernestine opened an old door to their left and walked into a postage-stamp sized bathroom. A yellow toilet with an unknown, murky liquid floating in it sat next to a basin that had collapsed to the floor.

"If you need the bathroom, we can wait outside," Zahra said, grimacing.

"It's the way in. You coming?"

Zahra looked at the toilet and did her best to position herself as far away from it as possible, while Mason refrained from touching anything in the room, especially the walls, which had long streaks of brown and yellow decorating faded wallpaper.

Ernestine reached out and knocked on the wall. "Garrett?"

A large, thick steel door replaced the sight of one wall.

"A hologram," Mason remarked, examining the edges of the door where a glowing strip of rainbow light framed it.

A voice came from all around them, sounding male but with carefully enunciated words. "What's the secret password?"

Ernestine snorted and shifted her weight to one foot. "Fuck off!"

There was a pause of a few seconds before the voice returned. "Good guess."

Ernestine giggled as the door opened. She took relaxed steps down the stairwell leading to a basement made of sandblasted concrete. The room was crowded with stacks of contraband ranging from weapons to prohibited foods. The only indication that a human inhabited the space was the presence of a few couches and chairs next to a small kitchen tucked away in one corner of the room. Every piece of furniture was pristine, the kitchen was gleaming, and the couch's leather still had the smell of the factory on it.

At the center of it all was a wide desk with steel legs and a wooden top upon which sat a ubiquitous 1950s-style monitor projecting a three-dimensional representation of the Milky Way galaxy. In front of it sat a man with distinctly Asian features and of average height, but Garrett looked as though he hadn't achieved his second full decade yet. A set of sunglasses with round rims reminiscent of the fifties sat on his nose.

"He's a child," Mason said, looking down at the seated man, dressed in black pants and a matching shiny dress shirt.

"I'm twenty-five," Garrett corrected with a scowl before regarding Ernestine with the same expression. "What did you bring them here for?"

"They're—"

"The FBI," Garrett said, interrupting Ernestine's reply.

Mason and Zahra looked at each other with a questioning glance before returning their attention to the youthful man sitting in front of them. "How did you know that?"

"Cameras at the edge of my property," he said, swinging his monitor around to face them. Garrett pressed a button on the small keypad in front of him, and the image of the galaxy turned into a close-up of Ernestine's car and its occupants as they turned onto the path. "That's all I needed to get your details. The FBI are looking for you, by the way."

"I figured they'd have to be by now," Zahra said. "You seem more mature than twenty-five."

"Thanks," Garrett said before pointing at his friend, "but she didn't answer my question. Why did you bring them here, Ern?"

"They need our help," she replied, stone-faced.

"Everybody needs help," he sneered before turning his disapproving stare at Mason. "So, mindhacker, huh?"

"That wouldn't be on the FBI vSite," Mason said.

"I did a little more digging."

"Are you going to ask to see my tubules now?" Mason asked, holding up his right hand.

"Hey, I never ask on the first date. Besides, you wouldn't be the first mindhacker who's been in here," Garrett said, tapping his temple with an index finger.

"So, you're not a virgin anymore?" Mason asked, smiling.

Garrett's frown turned into a wide grin. "I got my first mind-job when I was sixteen! Didn't know what she was doing," he replied and smiled. "Couldn't get anything outta me."

Mason chuckled, turning his attention to Zahra. "I think I'm starting to like him."

"Too bad the feeling's not mutual," Garrett interjected.

"Definitely starting to like him," Mason reiterated before returning his attention to Garrett. "Ern's right, we need help to rescue the world from certain destruction."

Garrett's grin turned into a sarcastic smile. "Unless I buy a timeshare, right?"

Ernestine sighed. "He's not kidding. Everybody, and I mean everybody, is in danger."

"From what? Mindhackers?"

"More like a super-mindhacker," Mason replied. "This one can take over your mind and body in less than an hour and hundreds of millions are already under his control."

"Sounds like some fucked up conspiracy theory bullshit to me," Garrett said, turning the monitor back to face him. The holographic galaxy was reflected in his fifties-style sunglasses.

"Garrett," Ernestine said.

"What?"

"They're my friends."

Garrett looked up at her words and relaxed his stony expression. "Well, the FBI is after you, which is a point in your favor and you are Ern's friend and she doesn't say that a lot. Who's going to pay?"

"I've got savings and a credit card," Zahra replied, showing him her vPhone.

Ernestine walked around Zahra and stood in front of Garrett. She raised her eyebrows and frowned down at him. "I'll pay."

Garrett looked at the floor for a moment as he replied. "Okay. Fine. What do you need?"

"We need to get into Freenet," Ernestine responded.

"Wow!" Garrett exclaimed. "I've got some strange requests for something on the vU before, but Freenet? Why don't you just ask me for my right nut while you're at it?"

"It's on the menu?" Mason asked.

"Funny. I can't just get you into Freenet, you know."

"Who can?" Zahra asked.

"Nobody, but you. They don't give out invitations. I can give you the key to Freenet's front door, but I don't think you're going to like it."

"But, isn't that all we need?" Ernestine asked.

"It's not that simple," he replied, crossing a leg over one knee. "It's up to you to solve two puzzles to get in."

"Puzzles?" Zahra repeated.

Garrett turned the monitor around to show them the projection again, which had a blank screen with just two lines of text on it. "The first is more like a riddle. Here," Garrett said, pointing at the holographic screen. On one line was the riddle, and the next was a nonsensical series of numbers and letters.

"Where does no child dare to go at night?" Mason read aloud.

"24GO32?" Zahra said, reading the second line.

"That's how you get into their online hideout," Garrett replied.

"But do you have any idea where it might be?" Mason asked.

"I don't know! I never wanted to find those hippies," he replied.

"This is the safest place I know to stay and look around the vU," Ernestine said to the investigative pair.

"I don't run a flophouse, you know," Garrett interjected.

"No, you run a bunker under an old flophouse. So let us stay. We need somewhere to hide out," Ernestine said.

"If it's money you need," Zahra began.

Garrett snorted and turned his chair to face the opposite wall.

"How about delivery?" Mason asked, looking at the spotless kitchen. "I get the idea that there's probably none out here and you probably don't even want delivery drivers to come here."

"Delivery from where?" The chair turned towards them with Garrett, now staring up at them through his round, black steel-rimmed sunglasses.

"Wherever you want. You seem like someone who doesn't want to be seen in public."

"I don't."

"Well, how about I get you whatever you want while we're here?"

"Even Italian?" Garrett asked, eyes narrowed at him.

"You got it."

Garrett looked around the room slowly, his face eventually facing Mason's again. "Alright, you can be my beer bitch, but I don't want any of that cheap, nutrient paste the Netholics eat."

"Wouldn't dream of it," Mason said, holding up both hands.

"Make yourself comfortable," Garrett said, nodding towards the couch and its two companion chairs. "vU's free here."

"Thanks, Garrett. Let's figure out that first line," Zahra said, motioning towards the living area. The three of them sat down and began their search for Freenet.

Chapter Six

"Why would it be in a movie?" Zahra asked, her chin resting on her fist.

"It sounds like a horror movie, that's all," Ernestine replied.

"Where does no child dare to go at night?" Mason quoted again from the text Garrett had given them. "It does sound like something out of a horror movie."

"There are interactive horror movies," Zahra said.

"And games, but which one? There are thousands of them!"

"Maybe it has something to do with where the line is online," Ernestine said before looking up at the youthful man sitting twenty feet away. "Where did this come from, Garrett?"

Without looking up from his work, he replied. "The Freenet site, where else?"

"Maybe we should all go online and start there," Mason suggested.

"Yeah, I was thinking the same thing."

"All of us?" Zahra asked, scrunching her nose.

"Come on," Mason said, reclining on the leather couch. "I know you don't like going online this way, but will you do it for the whole world?"

"Ugh," Zahra replied, reclining in her chair. "I guess I have to."

Everyone folded their hands on their laps, leaned back in their seats, and closed their eyes. When they opened them, the group stood in an empty room with white walls and a single exit. The room didn't have any windows, but a bulletin board was on each wall. The one opposite the door had 'Freenet' spelled out in white letters above it.

"Do you always use an avatar?" Ern asked, taking a closer look at Mason's beefy features. She smiled once she noticed the simple, worn jeans and black tee shirt his avatar wore. "And, do you have a clothes account?"

"Oh! Forgot," Mason said, opening a digital window in the air. After tapping a few buttons on the menu, his appearance reverted to his real-life one, but he still wore the same clothes. He noticed Ernestine gazing at his black tee shirt with a faded band's image across it and smiled back at her. "Virtual clothes cost money and I don't see the point, except for games. Besides, I'm on a budget and I can't buy swanky things like you!"

"It's still better," Ernestine said, unconsciously patting the sapphire dress she wore before looking around the room. "This is it?"

"This is it," Mason confirmed, walking to the bulletin board under the letters. At its top were the words 'Main Page'. The only other thing on its surface was the riddle Garrett had given them earlier:

Where does no child dare to go at night?
24GO32

"Not much to see."

Ernestine walked across a simple, green carpet to one of the other boards in the room. "This is the 'About' page. All it says is 'Freenet is for free, equal access to the most important informational medium in history.'"

"Well, all I'm interested in is what we're looking for," Mason said, looking at the last board in the room. "I think the links page might help."

"Why's that?" Zahra asked, joining him at the bulletin board. She straightened a black jacket she wore over a vibrant red blouse and grey slacks.

"Because, there's only one link here."

"vMaps," Ernestine read from the board. "Does that really narrow it down? I mean, that's a map of the entire world."

"It is, but you can go everywhere on it," Mason replied.

"You know, I heard that tourism across the world went down by something like fifty percent after vMaps came out?" Zahra said.

"Yeah, but I hate to admit that I never tried it," Ernestine said. "Is it true that you can go into people's homes?"

"You can't interact with anything other than to open doors, but yeah. You really never used it?" Mason asked, raising an eyebrow.

"Not my thing, but that's not the point: you can go anywhere that children would be, right?"

"Yeah, I suppose so. I never really thought about it," Mason replied, still staring at the link on the board.

"Then the way into Freenet has got to be somewhere in there."

"What if they're not being so literal? What if the place they're talking about is a child's mind, or something?" Zahra asked.

"It's still a good place to start," Ernestine said, glancing her way.

"I guess we should get to it then," Mason said, holding a finger over the piece of paper on the board. He tapped it twice and vanished from the room.

Zahra and Ernestine marched up to the bulletin board and followed suit. In the blink of an eye, the threesome stood on a street corner in downtown New York. This version of the metropolis was frozen in time, however. At the moment it was scanned into the vU, every person on the three-dimensional map was hurrying off to their destinations or just hanging around, but the cars on these streets never moved, and neither did any of its inhabitants. The grass here never bent in the wind and the clouds never made it to the other side of the sky.

Ernestine looked around the intersection they stood in. "I don't think we're in a place where there are lots of kids hanging around."

"So, where?" Zahra asked, looking up at the tall, gleaming skyscrapers around them.

"A playground, maybe?"

"vMaps: open interface," Mason said. Directly in front of him, a large globe of the Earth appeared. He zoomed in on a playground in a suburb on the outskirts of the massive city and tapped it twice. Their surroundings had a ripple of change flow across them before the trio stood on a grassy field with blue swings and slides at its center. The playground was empty, however, and sparkling droplets of rain were forever frozen in the air.

In every direction was street upon street with rows of bungalows in muted colors. Trees towered above perfectly mowed lawns. Zahra looked around the sleepy neighborhood and sighed. "I'm not sure we're getting anywhere. Kinda pleasant, though."

"But, the answer's here," Mason said. "Somewhere in this map. It's gotta be."

"But, it's like trying to find a needle in a haystack!" Zahra exclaimed, turning full circle.

"That's just it, though, isn't it? This riddle doesn't have specific coordinates. So, it would have to be a place anyone could access just about anywhere," Mason reasoned.

"That's the riddle!" Ernestine exclaimed, returning her gaze to the group. "It's something that applies to everyone, right?"

"Yes!" Mason said. "Yes! It doesn't ask where a specific child is afraid to go, but where *every* child is afraid to go. Then, where is every child afraid to go at night?"

"Well," Ernestine replied, trying to touch one of the drops of rain hanging in the air, "I was afraid of my closet at night when I was young. It was always so dark and my brother would tell me the boogeyman lived in there." Ernestine looked at the grassy ground and shivered.

"Yeah, me too," Zahra said. "I don't know if every child was afraid of that closet when they were sitting in bed at night, but I was."

"It's a child's closet!" Ernestine exclaimed. "That's the way in!"

"We're in the perfect place to give it a try," Mason said, looking at the many homes around them. "Let's take a look."

They walked in earnest towards a randomly chosen bungalow just as unremarkable as the many others around it. The small team was soon moving up a paved driveway to a house with beige siding and a plain concrete stairway to the front door.

"Looks like we're in the right place," Mason said, pointing at two small bikes that had been dropped at the bottom of the driveway. The lawn beyond was strewn with all manner of brightly colored toys. Mason stopped at the front door and placed a hand on the handle. "Here goes," he said, opening the screen door. Mason twisted the doorknob on the inner door and pushed it open. "Good, this is a home with the interior mapped."

They proceeded into a small living room with a simple, brown couch and chair complimented by a delicate coffee table. A boy and girl were frozen in the middle of playing a board game with small plastic players exploring various rooms of a holographic house, looking for clues.

Mason led the way across a faded brown carpet and into a kitchen where the mother of the family was chopping vegetables. The hand of the thirty-something mother was still in the air above a grey counter, forever holding a butcher knife that would take an eternity to slice another carrot. She had her back to them, so all they could see was auburn hair and a long, white dress covered in flowers.

Ernestine stopped to look at the back of the woman. "I always wonder about people in photos like this. Who are they? What are they like? What do they do?" she asked before noticing that her other two companions were already progressing down a hallway to her right. She turned from the sight of frozen food preparation and caught up with them. As her back receded from the kitchen, an unseen face of bright rouge and dark eye shadow blinked once and looked in the direction they had gone.

"So, none of those guys ever move?" Ernestine asked as they walked into the nearest bedroom in the hallway.

"They were scanned in the middle of doing chores on purpose."

"Why?" Ernestine asked as they walked around a small four-poster bed decorated for a little princess.

"Most families believe that it gives them a kind of fame by being in the maps. I'm not sure why," Mason replied. "Here it is."

They stopped in front of a white closet door on a wall painted peppermint green, but none of them attempted to open it.

"So, what's supposed to be in there?" Zahra asked.

"I don't know."

"Time to find out," Ernestine said, flinging the door open. Their eyes widened at the sight of a pile of clothing and dusty toys.

"I was hoping for more," Mason remarked.

"This is the way into Freenet?" Zahra asked.

"Maybe we were wrong," Ernestine said while trying to pick up a plastic doll from the closet floor.

"Maybe it's just a little more complicated than we thought," Zahra said.

"What do you mean?" Mason asked.

"The riddle asks where a child is afraid to go at night, right? Shouldn't we be looking in the closet at night, then?" Zahra asked. She closed the door and then asked for the vMap controls. A globe popped up in the air in front of her. Zahra selected the night setting by tapping a small icon in one corner of the representation, which switched from a small, yellow circle to a white crescent. The seemingly small change plunged the entire room into darkness.

"Try again?" Mason asked.

Zahra took in a deep breath and opened the door. This time, instead of a closet was a gleaming black door with glowing iron lamps on either side of it. "That's the entrance to Freenet?"

"It's gotta be," Ernestine said, shrugging her shoulders.

"But we've got a mixture of numbers and letters for the password," Zahra said, gesturing at a numeric keypad next to the door.

"Could it be that the numbers are associated with the letters, you know, like on some phones?" Mason asked. He brought up an old image of a phone on his personal display, which had the letters A, B, and C over the number one, D, E, and F over the number two, and so on.

"I'll give it a try," Zahra said, typed the number 244632 into the keypad and pulled on the steel handle to no avail. The three teammates looked at each other in bewilderment.

"But, what else could it be?" Mason inquired.

"I work with numbers and have to figure out how they relate to each other all the time," Ernestine said, bringing up the passcode on her wristphone's display. 24GO32 hovered in the air directly in front of her. She began tapping the numbers and separating them. "G is the eighth letter in the alphabet and O is the sixteenth." The G and O change to the numbers 8 and 16."

"So, that's the code?"

"That would make it a seven-digit code," Ernestine replied. "This is a number sequence and they want us to put more of it in. These numbers are the exponents of 2. 2 to the first power is 2. 2 to the second power is 4. 8 is 2 to the third power. You get the idea. The rest of the sequence is 64 and 128 for the first seven exponents."

"Why not just go with what's already there?" Mason asked.

"It wouldn't be that easy. It's exponents of two. That they want more numbers in the sequence is buried in the problem. They need two more because the base of the exponent is two."

"Good enough." She typed 248163264128 into the keypad, held her breath and pulled against the door handle. Everyone sighed as it opened to the sight of a long corridor, although this one was of the more unconventional kind. A coil of clouds stretched from the doorway to a sparkling white oval door on the opposite side of the ethereal corridor, but there was no bridge to connect them. Sections of the clouds turned clockwise while others went the opposite way, creating an effect akin to vertigo. Flashes of pink lightning from within the grey clouds lit the path in front of them every few seconds.

"Down the rabbit hole?" Mason asked, looking at the psychedelic corridor in front of them.

"Just another day in the FBI," Zahra remarked.

Zahra took a tentative step into the cloud corridor and was relieved to find her right foot resting on an invisible platform suspended above the clouds. Her two companions followed closely behind her as she worked her way to the bright white door, which on closer examination, was made of ivory with olive branches carved across its surface. When she reached the door, she closed her hand around a platinum handle and pulled to no effect.

"Do we knock now?" Mason asked.

A voice emanating from the door answered him. "We know who you are Agents Deane and Washington. Access denied."

Ernestine moved in front of them and stared at the door as though it was a camera monitoring her movements. "I'm Ernestine Paul."

"We know who you are."

"Then you know I was a close friend of Ed's. I've come here about him and what's going on in real life. Ed told me you're all smart people," she said, raising her voice with the last sentence. "You must've noticed the string of deaths. The rest of the team that worked on the Stardust Code are all dead."

"What of it?"

"Someone's taking over millions of people while you hide behind a door!" Ernestine yelled.

There was an audible sigh from the entrance. "Access granted." Ernestine tried the handle again, this time finding that the door opened easily.

They expected an office, but instead, the trio walked out onto an expanse of sand with Roman ruins at its center. The plateau was surrounded by mountains, with one side open to a beautiful vista and a precipitous drop. Ernestine took a step inside, feeling the dry air on her skin and looked up into the night sky.

"Can't be Earth," she said.

"Why not?" Mason asked.

Ernestine pointed at the sky. "Three moons."

The other two followed her gaze up to the three satellites of pale white, yellow, and blue. Zahra turned her attention beyond the ruins, looking out onto a vast expanse of rugged desert. "You're right. We're on a plateau high up in the mountains. I never read of any Roman ruins being somewhere like this."

"Come on," Ernestine said, taking a step down ancient, cracked steps. "We shouldn't keep this Freenet guy waiting."

"They look like Roman ruins to me," Mason remarked, following them into a large clearing where great walls once stood.

A strange, solid iron gate sat at the center of a crumbling exterior wall. The gate opened and a man of average height with a potbelly and bald pate walked through it. A thin mustache met an equal beard following the elusive line of his jaw. The man adjusted black-rimmed glasses on his face and opened his thin lips as he approached. "Ernestine Paul. Born in 2041, worked her way up from humble beginnings, got a doctorate in computer science, became one of the most eminent specialists in her field and was one of Edward Blunt's closest confidantes," he said and then held up his hands at the sight of Ernestine's open mouth. "Oh yes, 'Ed' to his friends."

"You must be Ray," she said before drawing him into a deep embrace.

"I am," Ray said, smiling as he put his arms around her.

"Ed said that you're a bit of a windbag."

Ray laughed and pulled away, straightening his simple, white dress shirt and grey trousers. "And, he said you have a sharp tongue."

"Maybe," she said, chuckling.

"He also said that you had a great laugh and he was right. What can we do for you and why are you hanging around federal agents?"

"They're the agents assigned to investigate one of the murders related to this bodyhacker."

"Bodyhacker? Good name. So," Ray said, turning his head from Ernestine to Mason and Zahra, "the FBI are finally looking into this."

"That's a little complicated," Mason said.

"Oh, yeah? Tell me," Ray said, crossing his arms.

For the next several minutes, both Mason and Zahra went over the events of the last couple of days. By the time they finished, Ray's impassive expression had changed to a frown and he held a finger to his lips. "Three hundred million taken over by this Moloch character, huh?"

"And fifty," Ernestine added.

"And fifty," Ray said with a nod. "Okay, Ed is alive and he wanted a nice, quiet retirement, but these are special circumstances. We'll help you."

Ray turned to lead them into the ruins, but Mason spoke up. "Did Ed Blunt really found Freenet?"

Ray regarded him and crossed his arms a second time. "People have this idea in their heads about Ed having been some kind of king of capitalism, the man who could sell anything to anyone at any time of day, but what no one seems to know was that what Ed really wanted was for people to be able to get a good education, have food in their bellies, and a roof over their heads."

Mason crossed his arms and shifted his weight from his left foot to the right. "Bullshit!"

Ray's eyebrows crossed and he opened his mouth to respond, but Ernestine spoke before he could. "We knew him, Mason. You didn't."

She walked past him and fell in line behind Ray as he led the way into a large collection of crumbling stone walls and pillars lying within the main gates. Mason and Zahra followed after she rolled her eyes at him. As they walked, they saw rooms without ceilings or furniture pass by one at a time. Some were large areas the size of ballrooms, some the size of an office, but all of them were empty, with only the gentle rays of three full moons to illuminate them.

"I thought that Freenet claimed it was a big organization," Mason said while they walked further into the standing ruins.

"It's even bigger than you think."

"So, what's all the empty space for?" Mason asked.

Ray chuckled at the question. "It's not empty. We've done our best to live off the grid in here, but if someone was determined to get in, they could. So, we have extra layers of protection. One of them is a 'Hide' command." He pointed at a large court and a crowd of people appeared like ghosts before becoming solid. They were at desks, huddled around tables, or busy at workstations. After mere seconds of visibility, they faded from sight.

"I see."

"Not anymore," Ernestine said.

"I've got to admit," Mason said, "I liked the entryway into here. That ivory door sparkled."

"Like it? I got it out of Far Fantasy XLV," Ray said, stopping at the entrance to a small room. He waved a hand across it and a stone table surrounded by Roman-style chairs appeared. The quartet sat down on thick, forest green cushions padding each seat.

"Tea? Coffee?" Ray asked.

Mason and Zahra shook a hand or a head in response.

Ernestine looked at the two agents in surprise and then back to their host. "I'll have something!"

"What did you need?"

"Ah," she said, looking up into the night sky for a moment. "Tea. Orange Pekoe. Just milk." He looked at the table's surface and a cup and saucer reminiscent of the Ming Dynasty grew out of it. Milky tea bubbled up from its bottom, eventually filling the cup. She picked it up and took a sip.

"Mmm. Ed mentioned once that you make good virtual food and drink."

"No need for a vRestaurant here. I make a terrific lasagna, too. Ed's own recipe. Best on the vU," Ray said.

"I went to a vRestaurant once that was supposed to have the best lasagna. Nice place. It was kinda like this, but the lasagna wasn't so good. Not for a hundred bucks, anyway."

"A lot of the vRestaurants have lower quality food. Here there isn't any extra code to downgrade the flavor. It's always the best."

"I believe it," Ernestine said, savoring her tea.

"Ah," Mason said, holding up an index finger, "on second thought, I think I will have something."

"What would you like?" Ray asked, forcing a smile onto his face.

"Tea. Earl Grey. Hot."

Ray guffawed at the statement and then glanced at a spot on the table where another cup and saucer grew from the stone. This one filled itself to the brim with a steaming, dark brown liquid.

Mason took a sip of his tea and found both eyebrows hitting his hairline. "Wow! Maybe I should try the lasagna!"

"Maybe another time," Zahra interjected.

"In response to your earlier assertion," Ray said, while Mason sipped his tea, "Ed Blunt co-founded this organization almost twenty years ago with a number of his other colleagues, most of whom were on the team that worked on the Stardust Code ten years ago."

"The ones who died recently?" Zahra asked.

Ray nodded and frowned. "Yes. He believed that what we're trying to accomplish here is important. Just before he retired, Ed gave us a considerable amount of money to support our efforts and to make sure that we stay protected and hidden. That can get expensive."

"Protected from who?" Zahra asked before looking at Ernestine and Mason's drinks. She held up her right index finger. "By the way, could I get a strawberry smoothie?"

"Done," Ray said, just before a tall glass rose from the table's surface. It was full of a thick, cold, pink liquid in seconds. "Ed knew that we would need protection from you."

Zahra's eyebrows rose as she sipped her strawberry smoothie with a satisfied smile. "Us? You mean the FBI?"

"All of you. The government, the FBI, the police, the judiciary, even the presidents. All of the state governments want our group disbanded and never spoken of again. The more extreme ones would love to see us in prison, or worse."

"I did hear rumors in the FBI that you were a problem, but not enough of one for us to get involved," Zahra said.

"You wouldn't unless they were actually coordinated, which they aren't and that's good for us," Ray said. "Now tell me, what does the FBI need from us to stop this 'bodyhacker' that's on the move?"

"We need Edward Blunt," Zahra replied.

"Yes, not an easy task, even for us."

"Ernestine said you were the only people who could get us in contact with him," Mason said.

"And she'd be right," Ray said, leaning back in his chair. "But you have to realize he didn't just leave his number with us."

"The word is that he died," Zahra said.

Ray sighed and leaned his elbows on the stone table. "And that's what he wants people to believe. It's easier to retire to a tropical island somewhere when you know no one's going to come looking for you. Ed wanted to spend his last years in peace."

"In the Bahamas?" Mason asked with a grin.

"Something like that. He didn't want to be bothered by a reporter or a fan, but he knew that something like this might happen, so Ed left a trail of breadcrumbs to follow."

"God!" Mason exclaimed. "More puzzles?"

"To tell you the truth: I don't know what lies down that path," Ray replied. "I never went looking for Ed because I never had to. What I can do for you, though, is to give you that first breadcrumb. From there, you're on your own."

"I hope it's not a long trail," Ernestine said.

"Ern," Zahra said, turning her attention to her, "you've kept up your end. You can go home at this point."

"To what, my job?" Ernestine asked. "That's gone by now and I didn't want it, anyway. I've got an empty house full of old memories and that's it. I might as well come with you. Besides, I want to see Ed again. I never realized how much I missed him until after he was gone."

"Are you sure?" Zahra inquired.

"Nothing else to do," Ernestine replied, shrugging.

"What's this first breadcrumb, anyway?" Mason asked.

"A set of coordinates," Ray replied, pulling a vTablet out of the air and handing it to Zahra, who tripled the tablet with two quick taps to the upper right-hand corner of its screen. She gave a copy to Ernestine and Mason.

"Ah, these coordinates are in Namibia," Mason said, already having brought up the information on his vMap.

"Makes sense for someone from here who wants to get lost," Zahra said. "It's got a coastline with lots of desert, people speak English as a second language and it's got a pretty sparse population. Good place to hide."

"Hide yes, but retire?" Mason asked. "If that's where he went then I think I'll stick with the Bahamas as my place to get old."

"That doesn't mean he retired there," Ernestine said, shaking her head. "We could go all the way there to find an empty warehouse with nothing but a note on the walls."

"I really hope not," Zahra said, "because it's a really faraway place to go for a note. Mason?"

"I've already sent the coordinates to my real phone."

"The question is: how do we get there?" Ernestine asked, putting the tablet in her pocket, which shrunk to the size of a fingernail before disappearing inside. "You don't have the resources of the FBI available to you now. We need planes, cars, maybe even a boat, depending on how you want to get there."

"I think we can help you there," Ray said. "We do have a plane and money."

"Thank you, Ray," Zahra said, standing up. "I guess we'll figure a way to get the rest of everything as we go."

"That's where Garrett comes in," Ernestine said, also standing. "Thanks for the help."

"You're welcome," Ray said, staying seated. "Just don't make this an everyday kind of thing."

"How do we leave?" Mason asked, glancing at the hallway.

"Just go back the way you came," he replied.

"Thanks," Zahra said. She nodded at Ray and then led the group into the ruined hallway. Zahra avoided talking until the glittering ivory entry door had closed behind them. "Just how good is Garrett?"

Ernestine smiled as they walked through the vertigo-inducing hallway. "I wasn't lying. He can get you just about anything you need, even though it's not always completely legal."

"That's good, I guess," Zahra said, approaching the door. "Namibia. We might as well be going to China. They're about the same distance away."

"Hey, it's a nice place, or so I heard," Mason remarked.

Zahra opened the closet door to the same child's bedroom at night and closed it behind them.

"I guess this makes us the boogeymen," Ernestine said as they walked out of the room.

"vMap: daylight," Zahra said once they were in the hallway to the kitchen. The place was abruptly lit again by the subdued light of a rainy day. "I think we should take a look at some travel apps before we leave."

"Good idea," Mason said as they entered the kitchen.

"We can meet in Chat Room 42. Hardly anyone goes there anymore. It's a nice, little cafe that looks out on an active volcano," Ernestine said.

Before they could round the corner, a butcher's knife flew past Zahra's head, missing it by less than an inch before burying itself in the electronic wall behind her.

The threesome stopped in their tracks and snapped their heads 'round to see the woman frozen in the middle of chopping vegetables had turned to face them with a ferocious grin. Her makeup was smeared across a distorted face.

"WHERE DID YOU GO, PIGS?" the woman screamed at them while taking menacing steps toward the small group. The irises of her eyes began to dart about the room at impossible speeds.

Mason stared at the hag in horror and yelled at his teammates. "Log off the Net now! NOW!" He waited the split second for Ernestine and Zahra to double-tap the back of their hands and then did the same just as the wretched hag's frightening face came to within a foot of his.

All three of them woke up in Garrett's compound, breathing heavily.

"What was that?" Ernestine asked, jumping up from her seat.

"What in the craziest of crazy hells was that?" Zahra demanded, sitting up straight in her chair.

Mason's eyes opened and he took a flying leap from his couch, only to fall onto the concrete floor. Zahra tried to help him back into his seat, but Mason resisted sitting in the same place, instead choosing one at the other end of the couch.

Zahra sat down beside him, panting for breath. "Who was that, Mason?"

Mason's hands shook as he responded. "That was Moloch."

"Wow," Garrett's voice said from the center of the room. "You guys look like you saw a ghost."

"You don't want to know," Ernestine said.

"How could that be Moloch?" Zahra asked, staring into Mason's eyes. "He's taking over minds, not the vU!"

"I knew he wasn't done yet. Moloch's doing more than just invading people's minds; I think he's starting to infiltrate the net, too."

"How?" Ernestine asked, leaning against a concrete wall.

"He can get his drones to go online whenever he wants. They must be forming some kind of stronger, bigger Moloch online."

"But he was in one of the images on the maps! They're not alive, Mason! They might as well be mannequins," Zahra said.

"I know. That's the one thing I can't explain. Moloch must have discovered new code along the way that lets him actually manipulate the vU itself."

"You aren't saying what I think you are," Ernestine said, slumping her shoulders.

"Even the vU is compromised now," Mason stated. "We're going to have to be really careful out there from now on."

"Well, where we're going is not online," Zahra said.

"Speaking of which," Ernestine said, directing her words at Garrett. "Wanna tag along?"

"Why on Earth would I want to do that?" Garrett asked, glancing up disinterestedly from his work.

Ernestine grinned in response. "To meet a dead man. Why else?"

Chapter Seven

"I'm starting to have second thoughts about this," Ernestine said. She watched as Garrett put a small knapsack in an overhead compartment of Freenet's small, private plane. "I know you don't like to be out in public."

"It's not a big deal, besides I get to meet my hero," Garrett said. He stood back and wiped the dust from his black golf shirt and khakis. The young hacker proceeded to busy himself with setting up a small command center on two grey seats at the back of the small, beige cabin. Zahra waited until Garrett was fully engrossed in his duties before standing next to Ernestine.

"His hero?" Zahra repeated, watching him take a seat at the back of the cabin.

"Ed Blunt," Ernestine replied.

"Oh. Creator of the vU. Well, he wouldn't be the first. What's with him spending all of his time in that bunker, anyway?"

Ernestine sighed and took a seat near the front of the cabin. Zahra sat down beside her, all the while trying to keep her pearl suit from getting wrinkled. "He's a little, what's the word, agoraphobic after doing this for so long, but that's not how it started."

"How did it start?"

"Garrett got into all of this years ago after he had to make a choice," Ernestine said, tugging down the seventies-style brown leather jacket she wore over a red blouse and tan bell-bottoms as she got comfortable.

"And he chose to build a bunker in the middle of nowhere?" Zahra inquired.

"Ever heard of helicopter parents?"

"Oh," Zahra said, glancing in Garrett's direction.

"Everything was decided for him, no matter how much he fought. Everything was scheduled. His adult life was already decided: he was going to be a doctor, have a wife and three kids. Two boys and one girl," Ernestine said, leaning back in her chair. "His parents even planned on buying the house next to them so he would have to live next door and they would watch over Garrett for the rest of his life."

"Did he have any choice in this?"

Ernestine shook her head. "Oh, no."

"So, he's in a bunker because of his parents?" Zahra asked, adjusting her seat.

"We're taking off," Mason interrupted as he walked down the aisle.

"Got it," Ernestine said, buckling her seatbelt.

Zahra looked up at the sight of Mason casually dressed in a pair of jeans and a blue tee shirt stretched over a lean body. She raised an eyebrow. "We're off-duty now?"

Mason adjusted the copper sunglasses on his face and smiled. "Come on, Zahra. We're not exactly on the payroll anymore. It's more like we're on the FBI's most-wanted list now. Time to blend in."

Zahra sighed. "Yeah, I guess so."

"We deserve a break for a few hours, so just relax!" Mason exclaimed before making his way down the aisle.

Zahra smiled, settled into her seat, and faced Ernestine. "So, he's hiding in a basement in the woods because of his parents?"

"He's not hiding from them, but he did plan for months to make his exit and, as soon as he graduated, Garrett was out of that door for good. Never looked back. He went to university, but he dropped out after a few years and had bills to pay. Garrett got into some shadier things and ended up working for some bad people. One of his so-called friends ended up owing them a lot of money and blamed it all on him.

So, he ran and happened to run into me. I lent him the money start over. He built that bunker and then he started up a business. That place really was a boarding house for a while, you know."

"So, who's after him? The mafia?" Zahra asked in a whisper.

Ernestine responded with a solemn nod of her head. "And we're talking about the kind of people who would do more than just beat you with a baseball bat. Garrett could end up at the bottom of a river if they're still mad at him and he doesn't want to take that chance."

"But he's still coming with us on a trip?" Zahra asked.

"Private plane and he arranged the automated car service so that no one would see his face. Besides that, the people we're talking about are powerful, but even they wouldn't have contacts in Namibia," Ernestine responded.

"And Ed Blunt's his hero?"

"Ed was always headstrong; Never let people tell him what to do. I think Garrett admired that and he was the world's first trillionaire."

"That's true," Zahra said, craning her head to take a quick look at Garrett engrossed in black market opportunities.

Their conversation continued, but eventually, they both fell into a black hole of sleep, only waking up a short distance from the St. Helena Airport, where Garrett had already procured a small yacht to travel the rest of the way to the Namibian coast.

He only emerged briefly in the fresh air next to his companions when it was time to get in and out of the automated cabs. Even then, Garrett rushed for the hover-yacht he had personally reserved and was happy only once he was out of sight on the lower deck of the surprisingly spacious vessel.

A large cargo ship hovered on the horizon, while the white and blue yacht glided out of a small harbor and around the island before making a beeline for the coast of Namibia. It effortlessly floated above the water for the next two hours until it arrived less than five kilometers off the desert coast. Zahra, Mason, Ernestine, and Garrett gathered on the top deck, looking out over the waves onto a sandy beach while the ship's autopilot brought them in at a reduced speed.

"Wait," Zahra said, as the sandy coast came into view, "doesn't Namibia have a coast guard?"

"I looked it up," Garrett replied. "The government's been cutting back on their defense force for decades. There's just one coast guard and it's forty years old. It uses, get this, propellers."

"I haven't seen one of those since I was a kid," Ernestine said.

Zahra watched the sand pass below the boat as it came to settle on the Namibian beach. A small gangway exited from the yacht's hull and came to rest on the sand at a gentle angle.

"Let's find out what's here."

Ernestine was the first on the ground and watched blue waves lapping at the beach while the rest of the group walked down the gangway. "How far away is it?"

Mason brought up a three-dimensional map on his vPhone. "About half-a-mile inland. It's almost straight back from here," he said, pointing at a small path leading from the beach and into a rocky desert.

"Hmm," Ernestine commented as they began their walk. "It's not as hot here as I thought it would be. There's even a breeze coming in off the ocean."

"It's winter here," Zahra said. Her eyes settled on the rusting hulk of a hundred-and-fifty-year-old cargo ship in the distance before she turned to face the desert beyond. "Where in Namibia are we, anyway?"

"Near the Skeleton Coast National Park," Mason said, glancing at the map on his phone.

"That helped." Zahra looked ahead, seeing only a dark, low ridge nearby and nothing else. "Are we sure that Edward Blunt didn't put us all on some wild goose chase?"

"Well, I don't know about you," Garrett said, sunlight glinting off his Fifties-inspired sunglasses, "but I'm going to those coordinates. Something's gotta be there."

"I hope you're right," Zahra said as she did her best to navigate over the ridge in sneakers.

"You really should have gotten some good boots," Mason remarked, raising his right foot to show off his.

"It's not far," Zahra said, rolling her eyes at his footwear. "I can manage."

It was just over a low ridge that a strange sight came into view. There, sitting in a depression overshadowed by a higher ridge behind it, was a concrete structure with battered solar panels on its roof and a row of wind turbines next to its thick walls. The building was just one story in height with curiously empty doorways and windowsills.

"It looks abandoned," Mason said.

"For a long time," Ernestine agreed, stopping beside him.

"Appearances can be deceiving," Garrett said, walking towards the open door.

The other three people in the team looked at each other, shrugged, and headed towards the entrance, as well. Once inside, they stood in a small living room with a layer of sand across the floor. The only furniture in it was a wooden chair with big, blocky green cushions.

Garrett glanced around the room with bright sunlight coming in from a window on each wall before heading into a rear room with a single window. A broad, steel table sat at the center of the chamber. A stack of dark monitors, kept company by a lone keyboard, covered it. All around the table was an extensive collection of burned-out dishes and antennae pointed at a single chair.

The chair was made of yellowed plastic and seated on it was a skeletal body, its head thrown back as though it was howling a deep laugh from an open mouth with a grey tongue. The body, itself, had been slowly disintegrating for some time, but not as badly as the few dirty tatters of clothing still hanging from it.

"Is this some kind of joke?" Garrett demanded, looking down at the corpse as though it should answer.

"I really hope so," Zahra said, moving to one side of the table to get a better look at the body. "Ernestine, is there any way you can confirm that it's him?"

Ernestine avoided looking at the deceased and, instead, dug around the sand piled under the chair. She uttered a gasp when her hand stopped, grabbed something, and emerged from the sand with a metal card in it. "I know what this is," Ernestine said, turning it over and over again in her palm. Her voice cracked slightly as she continued. "It's Ed's National Award for Programming. He took it with him everywhere. This was Ed. It had to be."

"He could have planted that!" Garrett exclaimed, pointing at the floor.

"You don't know how much that award meant to him," Ernestine said, carefully laying it back where she found it. "It was the only time that he got recognition from his peers."

"Maybe he really did die ten years ago. Maybe he planned to stay here," Mason said.

"Without any windows?" Garrett asked, pointing at the empty holes in the wall.

"Maybe the desert took out the windows during a sandstorm?"

"And left no trace behind? No, this looks a little too staged. Either that's not Ed, or something else is going on here," Garrett said.

"Is there something we can do to get the computer running and find out what he was up to?" Zahra asked.

"Nah," Ernestine replied. "The panels and wind turbines out there are in pretty bad shape. You wouldn't get more than a few watts out of them, if you're lucky. Not that it would make much of a difference. That computer's never going to work again."

"Well, I'd hate to admit that we've hit a dead-end—" Mason began.

"No!" Garrett exclaimed, slapping the top of the table. "Ed was a genius! He wouldn't be so stupid to set all of this up and then just croak! There's more here than meets the eye. Think about it: Ray said that this was the first in a trail of breadcrumbs. So, why would he give us his home address right from the start?"

"Maybe it took him by surprise before he could do whatever he was going to do," Zahra said, looking down at the man's remains.

"I don't buy it," Garrett said, looking at the ceiling. "I DON'T BUY IT!"

Ernestine stood in front of the body, a frown on her face. "He's right: Ed was a genius. He planned for every possible outcome, even this. Ed wouldn't let this happen without leaving a message or something."

"I'm going to look around," Mason said. "Even though I'm kinda just humoring you two, to be honest."

Ernestine and Garrett turned to the equipment behind them. Garrett picked around the desk, stopped, and squinted at one piece of blackened technology. He pointed at it with an exclamation on his lips. "This!"

"Yeah?" Zahra asked, her warm, brown features perking up.

"I don't know what this is!" Garrett exclaimed.

"That's a good thing?"

Ernestine leaned in, examining the burned-out piece of technology, and nodded. "Garrett knows just about every vU related tech on the Black Market and so do I. This is something I've never seen before. It looks like it was custom made."

They heard Mason shout from the other room. "Holy Shit! You guys have got to come and see this!"

"You go, I'll be there in a second," Ernestine said.

Garrett and Zahra ran toward Mason's voice, finding him in the only other room in the house they hadn't investigated. He stood in front of a giant, blue battery protected by a thick box of Plexiglas filling much of the room.

"Have you ever seen a battery this big before?"

"It's gotta weigh a ton," Garrett said, looking at its top. "I've seen smaller types of this make before. I got them for a few customers."

"What kind of voltage are we talking about here?" Zahra asked, taking in just how high and wide the battery was.

"Look, these are densely packed monsters. Even the smaller ones are in the high kilowatt range," Garrett said, looking at the battery. "Why would Ed Blunt need this much power?"

"I think I know," Ernestine replied from the doorway.

"You figured out what that equipment was for?" Garrett asked, his eyes wide behind the sunglasses perched at the top of his nose.

"Enough to know that he would need a lot of juice. I can't tell you exactly what each part of it does, but that room's full of different tech that can only have one purpose: digital conversion," Ernestine said.

"You're not saying—" Garrett interjected.

"I am. I think Ed uploaded himself onto the vU," Ernestine finished.

"No wonder he needed so much power," Garret said, crossing his arms.

Zahra regarded both of them. "So, he's not dead?"

Ernestine sucked in a breath and released it. "Depends on how you look at it. Ed's body is dead, that's for sure, but his mind isn't. It's in the Virtual Universe now."

"That's impossible, isn't it?" Mason asked.

"It's supposed to be," Garrett said, "but now I'm not so sure."

"Okay," Zahra said. She leaned against a wall and crossed her arms. "Why come out here just to do this?"

"If it was anywhere else, someone would eventually stumble across the body and figure it out like we did," Mason replied.

"Then how does coming all the way out here help us?" Zahra asked, waving an arm around the place. "If this is the first breadcrumb, then where's the second?"

"That is a good question," Garrett replied, looking around the room.

"Isn't this about putting together that Blunt isn't dead?" Mason asked. "If that's the solution to the problem, then the next breadcrumb has gotta be around here somewhere."

They spent several minutes looking around the hovel, only to find much of what they had before. The group returned to the sandy living room, with sweat beginning to form on their foreheads. It was Garrett who spotted something and smiled. "This guy came all the way out here just so he could fry his brains. So, why is there a chair?" Garrett said, walking over to it. "Don't you think that a cushion would get pretty eaten up out here?"

"It ate up Ed's clothes pretty bad," Zahra replied.

Garrett leaned over and felt the surface of the cushion. "This is plastic!"

"It doesn't look like plastic."

"This is really high-quality plastic. Probably made to order," Garrett said, trying to lift the plastic cushion. "It's part of the chair."

"Is there a way to get in there?" Zahra asked.

Garrett felt the top of the plastic cushion. "Not up here. Hold on a second." He got on his back and peeked under the chair. "Yup, there's a panel on the bottom. Anyone got a knife or something?"

Ernestine took a switchblade out of her boot, to everyone's surprise. She looked at them before handing the knife to Garrett. "A woman's gotta protect herself, you know."

"Amen," Zahra said, with a nod and a smile.

He pried off the panel to the compartment. Garrett reached inside and felt around until his fingers stumbled across something. He grabbed it and produced a piece of paper from the plastic cushion.

"Paper?" Ernestine said. "Who uses that anymore?"

"It's made of plastic, too. High grade; it even feels like paper," Garrett replied.

"Paper would degrade pretty fast out here," Zahra said. "It makes sense."

"What does it say?" Mason asked.

Garrett unfolded the poster, gawked at the paper and then read the words across the page: "For a good time see Rudi G."

"Very funny," Zahra said, crossing her arms.

Garrett turned the small, plastic poster around for everyone to see. The group got a view of a smiling, scantily clad male with blond hair and blue eyes suggestively splayed across the poster. Behind him were clouds of steam and the writing across it was in bright red.

"Oh, you weren't kidding," Zahra remarked, looking the poster up and down.

"Back to what I was asking before: Is this a joke?" Garrett asked, holding the poster up in his hand.

"Maybe not," Mason said. "Look at the bottom: it's got a vU address. '@ the Wide World of Porn, 13th Floor, Room 1313. I think our Ed had a sense of humor about superstition."

"And porn. What's your point?" Ernestine asked.

"This is our next breadcrumb. I think that Rudi's got something for us," Mason replied, taking the poster from Garrett.

"Oh," Zahra said, looking at the poster, "I'm sure he does."

"Not that," Mason stated. "I get what Garrett was saying now: This guy's the next link in the chain. We find Rudi, talk to him, and we get one step closer to Ed."

"And hopefully not the clap," Garrett added. He found himself staring at the plastic cushion again. "You know, I think there might be a pattern here, but I'm not sure yet."

"I know what you mean. I just can't shake the feeling that I've seen that Rudi guy somewhere," Mason said, taking a second look at the erotic poster.

"Ex of yours?" Garrett asked with a big grin on his face.

"No. I just feel like I know him from somewhere."

"Let me know if you come up with anything," Zahra said, looking through a doorway framing a dipping red sun, bringing a strong, warm wind across her face. "I think it's time we left. The coastguard might have only propellers to work with, but they still won't be happy to see us."

"What about this?" Mason asked, holding up the poster. "I can take a picture of it, but do we want to just leave it here?"

"This path isn't just for us," Zahra stated, receiving an appreciative nod from Ernestine. "Put it back so that someone else looking for Ed still has a way forward."

Mason took a photo of the poster with his wristwatch, which produced a perfect image of it in 3D a moment later. He gave it back to Garrett, who, in turn, put the poster back in the hollow chair, sealing the compartment shut.

"I wonder how long it will be before someone opens that up again?" Ernestine wondered aloud before a foreign voice screamed back at her in response.

"OPEN WHAT, PIGS?"

Everyone's attention was drawn to the entrance where a man with ebony skin and short, black hair stood. He was impossibly tall and his smile was far too broad for any human face. Bright, white teeth stood out on its visage, but they were long and pointed.

Mason drew in a deep breath. "Moloch."

"There's my pig. What are you doing here? Looking for Ed Blunt?" the man asked in a low distorted voice. The man's voice bore the heavy accent of the region, but it no longer belonged to him. He stooped to clear the doorway and entered the abandoned building in a menacing manner. "He's not really dead, is he?"

Zahra yanked her pistol from its holster and aimed it at the chair. Two bullets exploded against it, causing the chair to erupt in flames. Wood burned and plastic melted, quickly filling the room with acrid black smoke.

"NO!" Moloch screamed, leaping at Zahra. Mason jumped in front of her and the foes flew into a fast flurry of fisticuffs. The scuffle only lasted a second before the man bearing Moloch's consciousness jumped at the flames and began frantically patting them out.

"Go!" Zahra exclaimed to the group, who took no time to obey. The team raced from the building and over the ridge at full tilt for their yacht less than a mile away on the beach. Behind them, a trail of smoke billowed out of one window shrinking in size with every step. It was only after five minutes that Garrett stopped, panting heavily.

"I spend way too much time in a chair," he said, between puffs.

"Are you okay?" Ernestine asked, breathing heavily herself.

"Just give me a second."

Both Mason and Zahra drew their weapons and trained them on the ridge, watching for any sign of the tall man with black eyes while Garrett caught his breath.

"I don't know why I'm bothering," Zahra said, glancing at Mason. "You're the only one who could hit Moloch with how fast he moves."

"Still, I appreciate the backup," Mason said with a sideways smile at his partner.

"I just wish I didn't have to destroy that poster, but we can't risk it falling into Moloch's hands. How is he changing people into monsters like that?" Zahra asked.

"With what he knows, he can probably play with their DNA by now."

"God, it's starting to seem like nowhere is safe from him," Zahra said.

"And, it's only going to get worse."

"Okay," Garrett said, straightening up. "I'm ready to go."

The foursome broke into a run again, this time making it to the yacht, where Zahra rushed to get the ship onto the ocean. She was relieved once she saw the small vessel lurch away from the beach and only turned from the yacht's controls once it was a ways into the surf. The quartet assembled on the stern deck as the sun came out from behind a cloud to light up the viridian waves around the yacht.

"It'll take a few hours to get back to St. Helena. I think we should get on the vU soon... No!" Ernestine exclaimed, her stare glued on something behind the boat. Her companions turned to see a small stick figure of a man bounding across the sand towards them. Upon reaching the water, the ocean churned beneath him as he ran across the water's surface at a phenomenal speed, bound for the yacht.

"Christ!" Garrett exclaimed at the approaching demon.

"Shoot to kill, or at least, slow him down," Zahra said to Mason, who took out his weapon again and aimed it at the Moloch man while she turned and raced for the small bridge of the yacht.

Mason fired a round at the crazed entity managing to already catch up with the fleeing boat. He ensured his pistol was set high enough to fell most human beings, but the maniacal Moloch dodged the bullet as though it was flying no faster than a balloon on a light breeze.

Zahra reached the bridge in record time and pushed the lever controlling the boat's speed to maximum. The yacht began to pick up the pace, but the demonic force pursuing them was not disheartened. Mason looked at the churning water beneath the entity a second time and smiled. He lowered his aim and fired again. Moloch again dodged the shot, but this time the effort caused him to fly into the ocean like a comet.

"I've got it as fast as it will go," Zahra said, appearing beside him with her pistol drawn only to see that the man infested by Moloch was plowing head-first into the waves behind the yacht. "How did you do that?"

"After a bit, I realized that I could see something you guys can't: he wasn't actually running across the water."

"It sure as hell looked like it!" Ernestine interjected. "It looked like it was the anti-Christ walking on water!"

"Which scares the hell out of people, but it's what a good con-artist does, Ern," Mason said. "He wasn't walking on water. Did you see the water churning beneath him? He was moving his feet so fast that they were acting like propellers."

"No," Garrett said, looking back at the beach receding behind them. "It can't be."

"That's what I saw."

"Yeah, how did you do all of that, anyway?" Garrett inquired. "You were as fast as him. You see things others can't."

"I've got some of the same code that he does."

"You're not turning into him, are you?" Garrett asked, narrowing his eyes at Mason.

"No," Zahra replied for him, "he is not, but it's the only way we can fight him."

"We wouldn't have made it without him," Ernestine said to Garrett's doubting stare.

"I guess so, just don't try any of that on me."

"I thought we could use the boat trip back to the island to go look up this Rudi on the vU, but I'm guessing we could all use some rest, first," Ernestine said.

"I know I can," Garrett said, still breathing hard. He left to go below decks with Zahra in tow.

"I'm hungry," Mason said.

Ernestine looked at the receding coast of Namibia at dusk and then back to him. "You burn lotta calories doing that superman stuff?"

Mason smiled and patted his growling stomach. "How'd you know?"

"Makes sense. Come on, I could use a bite to eat, too."

Ernestine sat slack-jawed as she witnessed Mason's meal in a tiny gallery lined with faux wood. He started with a full three-egg breakfast, only to go on to have tuna-fish sandwiches for lunch. When he began to tear into a slice of pizza, Ernestine put down the croissant she had been nibbling on. "I've seen my whole family wolf down a buffet, and *all* of them didn't eat as much as you just did."

"I know. It's weird after doing something like that. It's like I suddenly need ten thousand calories because every part of my body is crying out for it."

"I can see that," Ernestine said.

Mason munched on a slice of pepperoni pizza, only opening his mouth to talk. "You didn't mention a family before, just a house full of memories."

"Yeah," Ernestine said, finishing the rest of her croissant. "I don't like to talk about it. I could use a drink. Want one?"

"Mmm!" Mason exclaimed, mouth full of pizza.

She grabbed two bottles of beer from a small fridge across from the booth they sat in. Ernestine placed them both on the table, having to stoop to return to her seat. Mason twisted the cap off his beer and downed half of it in one gulp.

"Don't add a drinking problem on top of your gluttony!" Ernestine exclaimed, laughing as she sat down and opened her bottle.

"I won't. By the way, if you don't want to talk about your family, that's okay with me."

Ernestine looked at her beer and a thin smile appeared on her face. "Did you know I haven't had a drink in twenty years?"

"Shit, is that because of me?" Mason asked, finishing his pizza. He leaned back from the table, a smile on his face and rested both hands on his stomach.

"Thank God you stopped eating! I thought you were gonna take a bite out of that fake wood on the wall!" Ernestine exclaimed, giggling, but her laughter trailed off and she shifted her eyes to the tabletop. "I didn't fall off the wagon, because of you, Mason. I fell off because of whatever that thing is that's chasing us around. That's the kind of thing that makes you pick up a bottle, again."

"Wow, though. Twenty years," Mason said, taking a much more restrained sip of beer from his bottle. "It's a shame that you have to start over again."

"Not a big deal. I only stopped because of my family."

"That bad, huh?"

"It's not what you think," Ernestine replied. "They didn't drive me to drink because they were bad. I started because they were dead."

"What?" Mason asked, creases furrowing his brow. "How?"

"Did you hear about the St. Mary's Protests that happened about twenty years ago?"

"Yeah. I think the whole world heard about it. You're not saying…"

Ernestine nodded her head deeply, but only once. "That's right. My parents were there and both my brothers."

"My God," Mason said. "I'm so sorry."

"Yes," Ernestine said, leaning back into the booth, "they ended up calling it the Aboriginal Day Massacre."

"I heard your prime minister went to prison for that after he resigned," Mason said, holding up his beer.

"PM Harry Harper. Yes, he did."

"So, your family was among the, what was it, seventy-eight people that were killed by the police that night?" Mason asked.

Ernestine put down her beer and then looked up at Mason with shining eyes. "But you want to know what everybody else wants to know: Why wasn't I there?" Ernestine asked, her voice shaking. Mason made a noise of protest, but Ernestine put her hand up. "It's okay. I was in university at the time on the other side of the country. I didn't even know they were there until it was too late. No one thought it would turn out the way it did."

"Still, I'm sorry, Ern," he said, holding her hand.

"I am, too," she said, squeezing it. "I inherited their house and everything in it. When I walked through that door the next day, it was like they had just walked out for a minute. Half of me expected them all to come in any second and all of me wanted it more than anything. They would be so loud when they came in. The whole house would be so quiet and then it was like having a circus in there. I think I miss that about them the most. That house has been way too quiet for way too long."

"So, that's why you said your house was full of memories."

"Those memories can drive you crazy and they almost did. I was scared if I picked up a bottle, I'd never put it down again so I stopped altogether. I got really mad and really weird for a bit. Ended up joining the Native Wolves," she said, putting her empty beer bottle on the table.

"You mean that extremist movement?"

"Well, not that extreme," Ernestine replied. "It was only for a year, though. It made me realize that there are people out there even crazier than me. Learned a lot about guns, though."

"I was worried about dragging you into a dangerous situation, but it sounds like you can handle yourself," Mason said.

"On just about anything," Ernestine said, inclining her head towards him. "They even taught me how to handle some of those heavier guns. Some of those things weighed a lot, let me tell you!"

"I bet."

"What about your family?" she asked.

"I don't like to talk about it," Mason began to Ernestine's open mouth, "but since you told me what happened to yours, it's only fair. My parents were never comfortable with me getting the mindhacker implants."

"But it was your dream, right?"

"No, it was a way to make money," Mason replied with a chuckle. "My family's very poor. My older brother joined the army, but with all the cutbacks that happened after the USA broke up, the government doesn't pay as much and their pensions have been cut back a lot."

"What about your parents?" Ernestine asked, putting her empty bottle to one side.

"My parents," Mason replied, smiling and putting down his bottle of beer, "are very accomplished artists."

"Well, that's great."

"The problem is that their paintings aren't worth very much. They live in a small condo and paint. A lot," he finished.

"They sound like nice people."

"They do, but they saw me getting the implants as selling out. I saw it as a way of making enough money to not have to eat dog food every day."

Ernestine leaned into the table. "It couldn't be that bad."

"I know, I know, but they barely get by. I wanted more than that," Mason said.

"You never know: they could end up having their paintings worth millions someday."

"Yeah," Mason said, guffawing. "With their luck, it will be the day after they die!"

Ernestine laughed, leaned a cheek against her hand, and smiled at Mason. "That's the way it happens with some artists, but it's not about the money for them. You should give them a call sometime."

Mason finished his beer and put it in the galley's small sink. "Yeah, I suppose I should. They don't really have anything against me. Maybe I have something against them."

"Yeah," Ernestine said, getting up with a chuckle, "they're poor! Get over it and be happy. In the end, all you ever really got is your family."

Mason turned to face her. "What about orphans?"

"They make their own, if that's what they've got to do."

"You're a very insightful person, Ern," Mason remarked.

"I know!" Ernestine exclaimed, slapping the table with a hand. She began to follow him out of the galley and up the stairs, but the computer scientist's brow creased and she slowed her steps. "But, why join the FBI? You'd make a lot more money doing other things, you know."

Mason stopped in his tracks and turned around to face her at the top of the narrow stairs. "I was a mindhacker for hire when I started."

"Really?" Ernestine said, increasing her pace up the stairs.

"It's some of the highest pay you'll ever see," he replied, leading the way into a large, open lounge forming the forward half of the yacht's main deck. "Information can bring down empires now, so it's more valuable than gold."

"So, why did you leave it?" she asked.

"Over a year ago I was hacking into someone's mind. Same as usual: dig out a secret from some corporate snob's head. It was high pay, too."

"How much?" Ernestine asked.

"Five million for a few minutes of my time. Well, for the actual job. I still had to gain access to the guy somehow. Lucky for me, he still took the subway. He got off at a station that not many people go to, so it was easy to catch him in a dark hallway. All I needed was a few minutes," Mason said, perching himself on the edge of a couch in one corner of the spacious lounge painted in soothing greens and blues.

Ernestine sat at the edge of the opposite, plush, green couch. "So, what happened?"

"There was an accident. I lobotomized him."

"You did?" Ernestine said, creases furrowing her brow.

"Something went wrong. I got the information I needed, but just seconds after I left his head, he went limp."

"I heard of that happening before, but I thought it was pretty rare."

"Very rare," Mason said, raising his eyebrows. "Funny thing is it was the FBI who hired me to do the job."

"But you weren't an FBI agent then."

"No, but I used to take up an FBI contract from time to time from an agent named Benny Carter. He was also the guy who arrested me after what happened," Mason replied, crossing his arms.

"He arrested you when they were the ones who gave you the contract?"

"The contract didn't include turning my mark into a vegetable," Mason replied. "I was given a choice: go to prison for three years for Virtual Assault in the First Degree or work for the FBI for six months catching people like me."

"But, didn't you say that was more than a year ago?" Ernestine asked.

"Yeah, I decided to stay with the FBI once my time was up."

"Why? Why not go back to what you were doing before? It pays better."

Mason glanced at the floor before looking up at her, sheepishly. "There's a man in a hospital out there, goes by the name of John Tate, who's hooked up to life support for the rest of his life. His family still hopes that he'll wake up one day, but that's never going to happen. I've got to live with that, and his name is always going to be burned into the back of my head."

"I get it, but you're going to have to learn to forgive yourself sometime," Ernestine said, getting to her feet.

"That's why I stayed with the FBI."

"Why didn't your contact become your partner?" she asked.

"After that, there was too many bad memories. I took their offer on condition that I was assigned to someone new."

"Which was Zahra," Ernestine interjected.

"Yeah, my handler seemed disappointed, but I'm sure he got over it."

"It looks like it worked out in the end," Ernestine said, getting up and tapping him on the shoulder. "Come on, I think it's time we got some rest, too."

Chapter Eight

The intrepid team napped for two hours 'til they reached St. Helena, where, upon waking and feeling refreshed, the motley crew got into an auto-cab and boarded their plane. It was only once it had taken off and the cadre felt safe that they readied themselves to enter the vU again.

"Is there any way to avoid Moloch when we're online?" Garrett asked.

"I've encrypted our stream with protocol obfuscations, multiple firewalls, and we're bouncing the signal off about fifty satellites. If he finds us again, it won't be for a while," Ernestine said, adjusting her seat to a more comfortable angle.

"Okay, we've got about five hours before we arrive back in the ESA," Zahra stated, straightening her pearl suit now that she was reclined. "Let's make good use of them."

"Will do," Mason said. He closed his eyes and logged onto the vU.

He opened his eyes to the sight of red steel doors. Small strips of paint were peeling from the doors set in a brick wall on a cracked concrete sidewalk. A red neon sign above the entrance read 'The Wide World of Porn'.

Ernestine looked up and down the street they stood on but found it was impossible to see anything beyond a short distance in any direction as an impenetrable darkness swallowed up all light beyond that point, although freshly fallen rain made the dark streets sparkle. "I thought this was a whole world."

"This is just the entrance," Mason replied.

"If you say so," Zahra said. "I've never been any place like this before."

"Me neither," Ernestine said.

"Ah, no," Mason stuttered, breaking eye contact with Zahra, "neither have I."

"Yeah," Garrett said, giggling. "Me neither. Wouldn't think of it on my worst day!"

He took the lead, red neon letters reflecting off his round sunglasses, and opened the crimson-colored doors. The rest of the group hesitated for a moment and then boldly walked through the entrance and into a small stand of red and violet bushes perched on the edge of a cliff.

Zahra took a deep breath and looked at the bushes on either side of her. "Roses and lilacs?"

"Something to do with diversity," Garrett said, inhaling their perfume. "Everyone is welcome here."

The group took a few steps and looked out on an impossible vista. The small ledge they stood on looked out onto a vast area without a discernible floor. A great distance away stood a great nude stone Atlas, but this version of the colossus had a female counterpart. The two titans faced each other, both struggling to hold up a sparkling red sphere the size of a planet.

"That's the Wide World of Porn?" Ernestine asked, slack-jawed.

"That's it," Mason replied.

"You seem pretty sure for someone who's never been here before," Zahra remarked, slapping him on the shoulder.

"But, where's all the floors? Where's the world? I thought I'd be in some bar with greasy, naked people everywhere," Ernestine said, crossing her arms.

"Disappointed? That's all over there," he said, pointing at the impossibly massive rose sphere in the distance.

"That's just a big crystal ball."

"Oh yeah?" Mason said. "Zoom in on it."

"I'm probably gonna regret this." Ernestine brought up a window reminiscent of the ones on old computer systems and pressed a plus sign in the window's top corner. Only once she zoomed in a few times could she make out more detail.

"Are those floors?" she asked, squinting at what looked like tiny lines across the large ball.

"Zoom in again."

Ernestine pressed the button three more times and the image became a mass of glowing red with countless floors stacked on each other. "My God! There must be hundreds of floors!"

"Thousands," Garrett corrected.

"And you would be the one to know," Zahra remarked.

"Naw."

"So, how do we get from here to floor thirteen?" Zahra asked.

"You just say: 'I want to go to floor thirteen," Garrett stated. The moment he finished the sentence, he vanished from sight.

All three of them repeated Garrett's words and found themselves looking at a large lounge with a translucent floor. Many subdued colors swirled across its surface, giving the room the illusion it was resting on exotic gasses. The ceiling was of the same material but slowly cycled through every color of the rainbow.

Across the groovy room were dozens of couches, chairs, and divans of blue, making the many naked bodies splayed across them stand out. Some furniture had two people engaged in various stages of sex and others had considerably more than two on it. A few had just one body occupying it, although even they were clearly enjoying themselves. The walls, the ones that were close enough to be clearly seen, that is, were full screens showing various themed sex films.

"I…" Zahra began, finding herself faltering. "I don't think I'm ever going to use my eyes again."

Ernestine looked around herself and began laughing so hard that some of the people on the couches stopped what they were doing to stare at her quizzically. Once she realized how much attention she was getting, Ernestine managed to reduce her laughter to an enormous grin, though she did have tears streaming down her cheeks. "I'm sorry, I'm sorry! I was just thinking of something someone told me! Really funny story!"

The still aroused people around her stared for another few seconds but soon forgot about the computer scientist once they got back on their respective wagons.

"What was all that about?" Zahra asked.

"Look!" Ernestine exclaimed. "Even online some people don't know what they're doing!"

Zahra looked around and started to giggle, which resulted in both of them dissolving into barely controlled laughter.

"Let's get them out of here before they start pissing themselves," Garrett said, taking Ernestine by the arm.

"Whole other floor," Mason remarked, doing the same with Zahra as they led them from the room through the nearest exit.

"That was embarrassing," Garrett remarked, hauling Ernestine into the hallway.

The moment the double doors closed behind them, Zahra and Ernestine were doubled over in laughter and holding each other for emotional support while Mason and Garrett, both visibly annoyed, waited for them to stop with crossed arms.

"Hey," Ernestine said, straightening up, "at least you know that it's the motion of the ocean that counts."

"Funny," Garrett said.

Mason smiled and shook his head. "You know how big this floor is."

"As wide as a planet," Ernestine said.

"Yeah, so we need to find Room 1313 sometime this year."

"Alright, alright," Ernestine said, her smile straightening out. "There must be a way to get around if each floor is this big."

"Room 13471118?" Zahra said, reading the sign on one of the doors. "Yeah, I think we've got a way to go."

"There should be an elevator around here somewhere," Garrett said, walking down the hallway.

"I thought we were staying on this floor?" Zahra asked as a door came into view but this doorway was different from the many others they had passed.

"This elevator takes us across the floor, not to another one," Garrett said as the wide door opened in front of him. They got into an elevator with transparent ice blue walls deliberately programmed to look like fields of light rather than glass. "Room 1313, please."

"Error: There is no Room 1313," a soothing female voice said.

"No Room 1313?" Garrett repeated.

"I thought you knew this place well," Zahra said.

"I didn't say that."

"You implied it," Zahra stated with raised eyebrows.

"Not the same thing."

"No Room 1313?" Mason asked. "Elevator: What's the nearest room number to 1313?"

"Room 1300001 is the nearest room number to 1313," the voice said.

Garrett sighed and looked at the others. "Any ideas?"

"Think of it this way: there must be a Room 1313. So, it is here somewhere. We just have to find it," Mason said.

"Maybe we should start at the first room, 1300001," Zahra said. "It's the first room, so maybe there's some clue or something there."

"Good enough. Elevator: Take us to Room 1300001."

The room winked out for a split second before the elevator's voice spoke again. "Corridor 1, Room 1300001 through 10."

The team got off the elevator at the end of a long hallway in an art gallery. Pearlescent walls glowed and large paintings hung from the walls. There were even low benches running down the center of the corridor set up for people to appreciate the broad canvases. Between the paintings were five doors on each side of the gallery, numbered appropriately, and soft classical violin music played in the background.

It was only once they began their walk down the corridor that Mason noticed the more lurid details of the paintings on the walls. He walked over to the plate mounted under one painting and read it aloud: "Snow White and the Seven Salacious Dwarves."

Zahra saw the fairy tale depiction on canvas was considerably less than loyal to its source material and let out a guffaw. "Look, Ern: horny dwarves!"

"If you're laughing about that, don't look over there," Ernestine said, pointing at a large painting on the opposite wall depicting a certain rogue having intercourse with a well-known princess.

"Sex Wars?" Zahra said, reading the plate below the painting.

"Can we just get to the first room, please?" Garrett pleaded as he walked ahead of them.

"Sure, sure," Zahra said, giving the painting one last look before following the group.

They walked past more paintings depicting different interpretations of classic stories before arriving at the end of the hall with one door on either side of them.

"That's it," Mason said, pointing at the door to their right.

Ernestine squinted at a picture of stuffed toys on the door. She opened the door and peered in before closing it again with a grimace. The rest of the group collectively raised an eyebrow at the sight of her bewildered expression. "Furries."

"Oh," the other three said, nodding.

"Where's 1313?" Mason asked.

"Would that have something to do with it?" Zahra asked, pointing at a large plaque between the two doors on the wall.

Garrett took a closer look at the plaque and read what was printed across its golden face. "This plaque was placed here on June 14th, 2074, in honor of the completion of Floor 13 of The Wonderful World of Porn."

"Why do they have to call it that?" Ernestine asked, shaking her head.

"You're missing the point," Garrett said. "Did you notice the date?"

Ernestine looked up at the date on the plaque, agape. "That's the exact date that Ed disappeared ten years ago."

"Yes!" Garrett exclaimed.

"And that's the symbol for his company, not the World of Porn's," Ernestine said, pointing at the Blunt Programming Logo.

"Yeah, why did he go with that anyway?" Garrett asked. "I always wondered why the red door with the green window in it."

"Ed said that red represented the blood and sweat he put into the company, but the door leads to greener pastures, which is why you can see green through the window. It meant that hard work paid off," Ernestine replied.

"There might be something here," Garrett said, checking through a list of information about that vWorld on a window he brought up. "This floor was finished six days before Ed disappeared. The plaque's date is wrong."

"The door leads to greener pastures. I wonder, Garrett, do all the hallways start off with an empty wall right here?" Zahra asked, patting the same wall where the plaque hung.

"No!" Garrett replied, smiling. "The first room should be right there, not across from door two."

"Let me take a look," Ernestine said, bringing up a window in front of her. She began examining the code in the program.

"Looking for an Easter Egg?" Garrett asked, bringing up a code window in front of himself, as well.

"Is it Easter now?" Zahra inquired from behind them, crossing her arms and shifting her weight to her right foot.

"In games, sometimes, the programmers will leave behind cool little things like unmarked quests, hidden messages, or even hidden doors for players to find. They're kinda like a gift, so gamers started calling them Easter Eggs after what a programmer once called them."

"So, there's one here?" Zahra asked.

"That's what they seem to think," Mason replied while Ernestine and Garrett dug further into the code.

"Ah!" Ernestine said, pointing at the plaque. "There it is. A simple 'show' command." The plaque became transparent, revealing a small, black door standing behind it. The number 1313 was clearly marked across it, bringing a smile to everyone's face.

"How do we get to it?" Zahra asked, noticing the wall, although transparent now, was still blocking their way.

"Ah, that's easy," Ernestine said, punching a few commands into her window. The wall vanished from sight a moment later. "An even simpler hide command." She marched to the wooden door to open it but was surprised when it wouldn't budge. A broad window popped into existence a moment later. Across its upper half was a screen with a single question and the bottom consisted of an electronic keyboard. Both were in the ubiquitous fifties style with a holographic interface and old-fashioned typewriter keys forming the board.

Garrett looked up at the words floating in the air above them. "Who was Edward Blunt's last wife?" he read out loud.

"He had three, didn't he?" Mason asked, even as Ernestine took a step away from the door, her wide eyes staring up at the large letters.

"Yeah, the third marriage was about forty years ago to Mariam Gates, right?" Garrett asked.

"Ah, Mariam wasn't his last wife," Ernestine interjected, avoiding their eyes, "I was."

"Are you serious?" Zahra asked in a raised voice.

"It was only for three months when I was thirty and we knew it was a bad idea real fast."

"How could things go wrong with the world's first trillionaire?" Garrett asked, his eyebrows raised.

"Well," Ernestine replied, keeping her eyes on the question floating in the air between them, "Ed was working all the time. He was a genius and it was hard not to fall for him, at first. Thing is, I'd go home at the end of the day to an empty house. He was great when he was there, though. It just wasn't often enough. He was married to his work."

"Get anything in the divorce?" Zahra asked with a broad grin.

"No," Ernestine said, with a shake of her head and a laugh. "It was only for a few months. I didn't want to make a big fuss, so we kept the marriage quiet and the divorce even quieter."

"Is that really true?" Mason asked.

"It's not a big deal," Ernestine replied.

"It kinda is. Look at the code on the door: You only get one try."

"Ern," Zahra said, indicating the keyboard.

Ernestine went up to the virtual board and typed in *Ernestine Paul*. The words replaced the floating question in the air, blinked twice, and then turned green. They could hear the distinctive click as the door unlocked.

"She's Ed's ex-wife!" Garrett exclaimed, putting his arm around her.

"Yeah, and most people don't know that," Mason said. "Ed only wants someone who knows him really well to find him."

Ernestine opened the door to Room 1313 and went in, followed by her companions. What they saw once they were on the other side of the entrance stopped them dead in their tracks: The quartet stood in a room with walls made of fog, making the area seem both small and infinitely large at the same time. At the center of the room was a king-size, four-poster bed made of simple iron, but highlighted with neon-red lights.

A nude man with blond hair and a generous mouth sat on the broad bed. His body was slender but defined and his features were angular, further accentuating sparkling pale blue eyes belying a deep sadness.

"What do you want me to do? I can do anything you want," he whimpered.

Ernestine couldn't resist taking off the black jacket she wore over her blue leather suit and then placed it over the man's exposed areas. He looked up in surprise.

"What are you here for?"

Zahra and Ernestine looked at each other in utter shock at what the room appeared to be, while Mason and Garrett tried to avoid looking at the simulated man altogether.

"We're not here to take advantage of you," Zahra said, her face seeming longer than it had been in years. "We're looking for Ed."

"Oh," Rudi said, looking away, "then I have what you need."

"Great!" Zahra exclaimed.

"But," Rudi said, his image flickering for a moment, "the only way you can get it is by killing me."

"What?" Zahra exclaimed, both eyebrows nearly hitting her hairline.

"That is why my creator made me. I know where he is. I'm the next breadcrumb. In order to get that location, you have to destroy me," Rudi said, looking up into her eyes.

"I can't," Zahra said, her dark eyes beginning to gleam in the soft light.

"Zahra," Garrett interjected, "he's just a pile of code. All Rudi is, is a program."

"I still say I recognize him from somewhere," Mason said, examining Rudi's face from afar.

"Time and a place," Garrett remarked.

"Not as a sex-toy. I saw him somewhere else," Mason said.

"He's much more than that," Ernestine said, looking at the pitiful creature in front of her. "I can see it. This A.I. is more advanced than others. We can't just decompile him for the code we need. It would kill him." She sat down on the bed next to him and held his cheek like she would a son's.

"Ern," Garrett interjected in a soft timbre, "if we don't extract the information we need, we're done. I mean, he's just a male prostitute and not even a real one!"

At Garrett's interjection, Rudi looked at the floor and all three of his companions glared at him.

"I don't care if he's just a complex program," Ernestine said, holding his face in her hands. "He's still self-aware and he deserves to live."

"Coming from someone who spent most of their life programming," Garrett stated, crossing his arms.

"Maybe that makes me the wrong person to be here," Ernestine said, looking up at him, "but maybe knowing Ed makes me the right person at the right time. I won't destroy an A.I. just to get what I want. I do want to find a way to free him, though."

"From what?"

"From this," Ernestine replied, looking around.

Garrett sighed, shook his head, and smirked. "He's just a sex program, Ern."

"He needs to be free of this cage. That's what Ed would want. I won't destroy you just to get the data I need, Rudi, but I will help to get you out of here and into a new world where you'll be happy."

"I'm not even sure that's possible," Mason said, looking around the strange room. "His code might not be able to function outside of here."

"We have to try."

"Are you sure?" Rudi asked, looking deep into her eyes. "You only get one chance."

"I vote we decompile the A.I. He's just a program. No offense," Garrett said, raising his hand at Rudi's dejected face.

"I'm with Ern," Zahra said. "Rudi's more than just code and I won't kill him just to get what I need and this isn't a vote. I'm in charge of this investigation."

"Your investigation went sideways," Garrett said, creases appearing across his face as his expression soured. "It went sideways the first day, Zahra and, if you didn't notice yet, me and Ern over here, we're not FBI agents. And, the FBI is looking for you, right now, so you're in charge of shit."

"I'll try not to take that personally," Mason interjected, grimacing.

"So, we vote. Period."

Zahra held up both hands, turned her back on him and walked away.

"Even if I voted for you," Mason said to Garrett, who was watching him closely, "all I would do is tie up the vote two-to-two. What good would that do?"

"Do I get a vote?" Rudi interrupted.

"No!" Garrett exclaimed.

"Yes," Zahra said, turning around and returning to the edge of the bed. "It's his life and he should get a vote. How would you vote, Rudi?"

"I'd vote not to die!"

"That's not fair," Garrett said, pointing at the artificial prostitute.

"It doesn't matter, anyway," Mason said, "because I'm not about to commit murder just to get what I want, even if it is simulated murder."

"Thank you," Rudi said.

Garrett turned away from the group and marched for the door. "Whatever. You just screwed up the only chance we have of saving the world for some fake floozy."

"That's your final decision?" Rudi asked, looking at the group around him.

"Yes," Zahra said, hearing the door slam behind her as Garrett left.

"Then," Rudi said, releasing a long exhale of breath, "you passed."

Mason looked up from his comfortable stare at the floor. "What?"

"You passed," Rudi said again, getting up from the bed. Zahra and Ernestine averted their eyes as he handed her coat back to her. "I don't need this now."

"I would think you did," Ernestine remarked, trying to keep her eyes on his.

"What would have happened if we tried to decompile you?" Mason asked, standing next to Zahra.

"Nothing," Rudi said with a shrug. "You would have found yourself outside of that door with no way to get back in."

"Just one chance," Mason said, nodding at Zahra and Ernestine in understanding. "Even if someone figured out what we did afterwards they wouldn't be able to get back in and change their answer."

"What about you?" Ernestine asked. "I can't just leave you here in a place like this buck-naked."

"Oh, yeah," Rudi said, looking down at his fit form. "I keep forgetting. Ed's a great guy, but he forgot to write a modesty subroutine into my program. The place only looks like this for anyone who comes through that door." He looked up into the air and the dungeon cell they stood in changed into a Roman villa of tall pillars and walls painted in soothing colors. A large, open courtyard appeared behind Rudi. The area was accented with wooden furniture covered with numerous deep cushions and pillows.

Tiny, glowing sparks of light rained from a cloudless sky, only to fade into the ground beneath them. The entire planet was at the point just before sunset, causing the horizon to glow in oranges, pinks and purples. The Aurora Borealis danced high in the sky above them.

Many people occupied that peaceful place. All of them wore modern dress of many different colors and fabrics, and the group wasn't limited to just two sexes. Rudi took in the sight of the many people having conversations or playing games and smiled. A pair of white khakis and a warm, white sweater appeared on Rudi's body. "I'm not in a dungeon and I'm not alone. This is my villa and the world I live in is the size of England, so there are plenty of people to spend my time with."

"I think it is England, say, about two thousand years ago?" Mason asked.

"Yes," Rudi said, grinning in appreciation of Mason's observant eye. "This is the height of the British end of the Roman Empire during the third century, A.D. This villa really did exist once in the real world, but Ed made a few improvements on the original."

"Like modern clothing and even Greatest Retros," Mason said, pointing out the people there who looked like they had just walked out of a 1950s film.

"I'm very glad to see that dungeon wasn't real," Zahra said, still looking around her ancient, yet magical, surroundings. "But, where's Edward Blunt?"

"I almost forgot!" Rudi exclaimed. "I was excited because you're the only people to make it this far."

"There were others?" Zahra inquired.

"About half-a-dozen, but all of them chose to destroy my program because they felt their needs outweighed mine. So, here's what you need to know: Ed's in a game."

"There are thousands of games out there," Mason scoffed. "Tens of thousands. That narrows it down a bit, but nowhere near enough."

"I know, but he did leave another clue: You need to look into a science fiction game with me in it," Rudi said.

"That's where I've seen him before!" Mason exclaimed, snapping his fingers. "You're in Star Lore!"

"Star what?" Zahra asked, curling one side of her lip.

"It's a whole franchise! I'm surprised you haven't heard of it."

"I'm very busy. Wait," Zahra said, holding up her hand, "how can he be here and in a game at the same time?"

"Because both he and his doppelganger's body, face, and voice were supplied by an actor. I think I've seen him in a few interactive movies, too, but his likeness is used for one of the lead characters in Star Lore."

"Star Lore is about what, exactly?" Zahra asked.

"It's about these Great Houses in another universe fighting for dominance and there are these futuristic magicians in it, too. He's in the first game," Mason replied.

"Okay, are we talking about science-fiction?"

Mason looked at Ernestine and then back to Zahra. "Science-Fantasy, but basically yeah, why?"

Zahra lowered her hand and exhaled a long, nasty breath. "I hate science-fiction!"

"Oh, maybe you should stay home next time," Mason said.

"No," Zahra said, looking up at the impossible sky above them. "This is my assignment and I'll get it done even if I have to fire a blaster or a photon torpedo."

"Different universes."

"Like I would know," Zahra said before returning her attention to Rudi. "So, he's in that game and that's where we need to go. How many bread crumbs are on this trail, anyway?"

Rudi smiled. "There isn't that much further to go. At least that's what Ed put into my question-and-answer matrix."

"Did Ed leave anything else?" Zahra asked.

"As a matter of fact, he did. When you log into the game, don't use your regular ID. Login as 'BluntlyEd' and the password is 'Scenerio0Wins'."

"Sounds a little ominous," Mason remarked.

"Now, if you'll excuse me, you guys came in right in the middle of a conversation I was having with someone. Stay as long as you like, but once that door closes behind you, it can never be opened again," Rudi said, turning away. He left them and joined a small group of people sitting on a collection of wicker couches with burgundy cushions.

"I almost want to hang around for a while," Ernestine said, taking in a deep breath of the cool air. "It's kind of pleasant here."

Zahra looked around and frowned. "Yeah, great. How long until Moloch finds us again?"

Ernestine exhaled. "Maybe it's time we got going."

The trio gave one last long look at the beauty around them and turned for the exit, which had transformed into a black door on the wall of the villa behind them. They opened it and walked out onto the museum floor with the same perverted paintings as before. Garrett had his arms crossed and was leaning against one wall. His round sunglasses reflected a very different Robin Hood from mythology mounting Maid Marian.

"So, what happened?" he asked.

"It was a test," Zahra quoted. "If we tried to decompile him, we would've walked away with nothing."

At her words, Garrett stood up straight and uncrossed his arms. "It was a test to see if we'd do the right thing?"

"I guess you could put it that way," Zahra replied.

Garrett looked at both of them in amazement. "That's it! They were are all tests!"

"Can you give me a little more than that?" Ernestine asked.

"Not here," Garrett replied, looking around the museum walls, suspiciously. "That Moloch dude can't be far away. We should log out of vU now."

"I just tried," Mason said. "I can't log off the vU."

Ernestine and Zahra tapped the back of their wrists twice and shook their heads. "Neither can we."

"That can't be good," Garrett said.

"There should be a main hub at the center of every floor. We can manually log off there," Ernestine said, staring at the elevator at the end of the hallway.

They marched towards the end of the corridor where the elevator had deposited them earlier. The quartet couldn't resist shivering as they felt a chill pass through them as they walked. They hurried their step but found the broad, tall corridor had begun to shrink. At first, the ceiling was as high as a church's, but now it was just half that and shrinking fast. The walls changed in color to burgundy and went from hanging with large canvases to holding paintings of landscapes one would find in a country home.

Garrett came to an abrupt stop in a moderately sized kitchen with white tiling and cupboards. A small five-piece dinette sat in one corner of the room and a back door stood against the opposite wall.

"It can't be," Garrett breathed, staring at his surroundings.

"Where are we?" Zahra asked, noticing darkness beyond the one window in the room. A gut-wrenching scream from somewhere behind them answered her question.

Garrett hurried past the group and down the hallway, where they glimpsed an ornate, wooden door with a stained glass window. The group followed him to the front of the home, where a dining area sat on one side of the hallway and a parlor on the other. The dining room hosted a simple, battered table with a few scratched chairs around it. Of the two other inhabitants, one was a skinny blonde wearing cut-off jeans and an incredibly tight tee shirt, while a lanky boy in bell-bottoms and a red tee stood across from her.

"They look like the neighbors!" the young woman exclaimed. "What are they?"

"What is she talking about?" Zahra asked.

The two characters continued their conversation as though they hadn't heard her. Garrett stared at the couple in horror. "I know where we are."

"Where?" Ernestine asked, looking between Garrett and the couple conversing about a demonic horde.

"This is a vNovel. It's called 'Ghost Town'."

"You read horror novels?" Ernestine asked.

"Guilty pleasure."

Zahra shrugged. "I'm more into trashy romances."

"Then this one isn't for you. It's one of the better ones I saw and better means scarier," Garrett said, taking his attention away from the panicked couple in the dining room.

"We need to get out of here," Ernestine said. "Fast."

"Moloch's gotta be behind this," Garrett said. "We need to get out of this book."

"How do we do that?"

"Whenever I'm in one of these online novels, I can usually just stop it wherever I want to," Ernestine said.

"Stop Ghost Town," Garrett said. "Pause Ghost Town." He shook his head. "I don't think that's going to work."

"The other way is for the book to reach the end, right?" Zahra inquired.

"Yeah, that would take some time," Garrett said, returning his attention to the scene unfolding in front of them. "We're only in the prologue. We've got about twelve hours to watch before we're done."

"Twelve hours?" Ernestine repeated. "Oh, Christ. We're dead, for sure."

"Let's get out of here," Garrett said, leading the way to the door. They were just closing it behind them when the young hippie in the dining room slammed a Gothic tome onto the old table and opened it.

The companions ran down a short walk to the edge of the road where cars from the 1970s littered the streets of a small village populated with Victorian-era homes. The community was full of people of all ages, dressed in bell-bottoms and suits with flared lapels, but they were running about a street in utter chaos. Dark, demonic creatures in the crowd around the quartet were dragging their human doppelgangers into homes with strange, glowing portals coming from within their many mirrors.

"What kinda book is this?" Ernestine demanded.

"You know this isn't actually in the book. The people at vNovel found that it was coming up two hours short so they expanded the prologue…" Garrett began. He trailed off once he realized the demonic creatures and the pedestrians around them had stopped and were now staring at them.

"That never happened in any book I ever watched," Ernestine remarked.

"That's because it's not supposed to. We're invisible bystanders. Something's wrong here."

Just as Garrett finished his sentence, a menacing howl came from everywhere at once. A dark entity rose from the shadows across a road made long and thin by the sodium streetlights. It was ten feet tall, had cracked grey skin leaking smoke and possessed the legs of a goat. Sharp black teeth and long horns protruded from its head. The demon's eyes were like spotlights projecting a cold, blue light. The entity looked directly at Garrett and screamed at him. In response, the people and demon doppelgangers began to walk towards them, slowly at first, but each step was quicker than the last.

"Run!" Garrett exclaimed. All four of them turned tail and flew down the street as fast as they could. Once they had made it a short distance, the foursome looked over their shoulders to see everyone had transformed into the very demons that had been assaulting them earlier. They were crawling down roads and over houses like an army of evil ants for Zahra and her cadre.

Just as they made it into the woods outside of the small village, Garrett stopped, breathing heavily.

"You know that you're not actually out of breath, don't you?" Mason asked, stopping next to him.

"Doesn't matter," Garrett replied, panting. "My heart's still pounding like a jackhammer. God, of all the things I ever wanted to see it wasn't one of those things chasing me down a road, much less an army of them. They freak me out!"

"I think that's exactly why Moloch brought you here," Ernestine said, out of breath. "He wants you to be scared."

"How are these characters interacting with us? I thought this was just a vNovel?" Mason inquired.

"Moloch must've changed the code," Ernestine replied, also taking the time to rest. "It's the only thing that makes sense. He brought in sub-routines from a game to make it interactive."

"Can't we just die, then?" Zahra asked, looking at them in the dim light of a full moon. "Won't we just wake up on the plane?"

"We already found that we can't leave the vU with the usual commands," Mason said. "Our avatars here won't die when attacked."

"And you don't want that," Garrett said. "Think about one of those things attacking you and you can't die. It could disembowel you, like, ten times and you still wouldn't die."

"So?" Zahra said. "We're not really here, right?"

"But, you can still feel pain and you'd feel the pain of one of those things torturing you over and over again for hours, even days," Mason replied.

"It would be a living hell," Ernestine said, fearfully looking towards the edge of the village, where the sounds of snarling and growling were starting to grow louder in the distance. "We'd all go insane after a while. What do we do?"

"We can't get captured by any of those things. We'd never get out of here. Ern, didn't you say that Moloch would've had to take code from a game to make this work?"

"Yes," Ernestine replied. "It's the only thing that I can think of."

"Then that code's compatible with cheats, right?" Garrett asked.

"Yes! That might buy us some time!" Ernestine brought up a window and tapped in several commands just as sounds of gurgling and grunting began to close in on them. "Okay, we've got cheats. So, just think of what you want and you'll have it."

"Yes!" Mason said, pulling an AK-47 out of the air. He aimed at dark bodies beginning to appear from behind trees and fired. The bullets slammed into the demons, but to everyone's dismay, they just kept coming.

"Great, now you've let them all know exactly where we are!" Zahra exclaimed, pulling a Glock out of the darkness.

"You have to shoot them in the head!" Garrett yelled.

"Why didn't you say so?" Mason said, correcting his aim. Three of the demons fell to the mossy ground seconds later.

"There's too many of them," Zahra said, firing at the creatures as they began to close in on them. "We really are just buying ourselves time."

"Running somewhere else would just bring us to the boundaries of this world and they're not far from here. If we go there, we're as good as dead," Garrett said, holding up his own automatic rifle and firing.

"So, what? We're at Custer's Last Stand?" Mason asked.

"I know how that one ends," Ernestine said. "It's not so good for Custer. I still have access to the code. Can't we use that to our advantage?"

"Don't these novels have bookmarks?" Mason inquired, taking down another five dark doppelgangers.

"So, you can pick up where you left off!" Garret exclaimed, slapping his forehead with his hand. "Ern, can we advance the bookmark?"

"Let me see," Ernestine said, examining the code. "Moloch tried to lock down that command, but he didn't do a very good job. Must've been in a hurry. Okay, where do we advance to?"

"The end!" Mason and Zahra exclaimed.

"Go to Bookmark: Epilogue," Garrett replied. "Minute five."

"Got it!" Ernestine exclaimed. Night turned to day and the small group found themselves standing in front of the same house they had started in, but there were now modern-day moving vans and cars in the driveway. A woman of average height and casual dress spoke to a woman standing on her front porch.

"He's not in there, Mel," the tall, dark woman said.

"Then where is he?" Mel asked.

"Okay, we're at the end," Garret said, watching the first woman walk away from the house while Mel returned inside. "It's just another minute or two."

The quiet of the neighborhood erupted with a demonic scream and the ground shook.

"Not again," Garrett said under his breath.

Just as the same dark demon began to rise out of the pavement for a second time, the entire street, village and sky above them winked out to be replaced by the sight of the museum of naughty paintings.

"Oh God, I never thought I'd be so happy to see smut on the walls," Zahra breathed.

Ernestine brought up a window in front of her and worked frantically for a moment before closing it. "Okay, I've put a freeze command on this floor. It'll stop Moloch from changing anything again, but it will only last for a few minutes. We've got to get to that hub now!"

Her friends didn't even bother to acknowledge what she said; they simply bounded down the corridor for the nearest elevator. As they ran through the gallery, the paintings quickly began to take on a more sinister feel. What was once consensual became nonconsensual and what was human became inhuman. The foursome piled into the elevator and Ernestine stopped at the control panel, breathing hard.

"Central hub, Level Thirteen," she said, still panting for breath.

"Right away, pigs," a sinister male voice replied.

"How the fuck is he doing that?" Garrett demanded.

"I'm not sure," Ernestine replied, staring at the glowing red walls around them. "He hasn't gotten past my freeze command yet, but Moloch's still getting in somehow."

The elevator moved without moving, pinging its arrival. Ernestine and her friends burst out onto a wide, circular, open area. It was a hundred feet across and had a large, round white tower at its center surrounded by a ring of consoles covered in panels glowing in blues and greens. The core, itself, was suspended over a great void and only accessible by four bridges located at each point of the compass.

Mason looked up to see that the transparent decks above them stretched on to the point that one couldn't see where they ended. "Wow."

"Yeah, don't look down," Ernestine said.

Mason, of course, couldn't resist and looked down to see the deck below him was also transparent and continued downwards twelve floors, ending with an infinite drop into nothingness. He forced his eyes to focus on the central tower and began moving in earnest towards it. Just as they reached the bridge, the group heard a thunderclap. The force of it shook the deck below them, stopping them in their tracks.

"What now? Is it going to rain inside?" Garrett asked.

Ernestine shook her head but kept her eyes on the vast expanse above them. "That wasn't thunder."

"What was it, then?" Zahra asked.

The sound issued again all around them, but this time the deck shook harder beneath them. Zahra followed Ernestine's gaze in time to see a ripple travel across the walls and floors above them.

"That was the sound of Moloch trying to get in. We've got seconds," Ernestine replied, looking at the consoles on the other side of the chasm in her sights. "Go!"

The quartet broke into a full sprint for the nearest bridge. They were only halfway across it when a third, terrible peal of thunder reverberated across every surface of the main hub. The decks below them jumped as a giant fist pounded against the entire world. The force was too much for the quartet to keep their balance, sending them to the floor.

"He's going to destroy this entire vWorld just to get to us!" Mason yelled with half of his face pressed to the deck.

"We're almost out of time! Hurry!" Ernestine exclaimed once she was on her feet again.

They rushed for the consoles, just reaching them when the world shook so violently that the transparent deck below them cracked and the pearl walls began to crumble.

"My God," Zahra breathed as she looked at the chaos around her.

"Touch the consoles now and think 'Emergency Exit'," Ernestine screamed at them as a cacophony of metal twisting and glass shattering came from above them. The other three members did as she said, feeling the glass floor beneath them shatter and give way before the blink of an eye had them in the plane's cabin again.

"It's like he's a god in there!" Mason exclaimed, sitting up in his seat.

"And it might end up like that out here, too," Ernestine said, opening her eyes. "He's getting stronger by the minute. I'm going to have to take some big steps to hide our identities online and construct some major firewalls. This is going to take some time."

"We can go to my place," Garrett said, rubbing his neck. "It's untraceable and it's got the best protection money can buy."

"Are you sure?" Ernestine asked.

"It's the best protected, heavily armed place I know, besides I've got personal stakes in this now. We'll go to my place."

"What were you saying, Garrett?" Zahra asked, sitting up and rubbing her temples. "Something about a pattern before that monster started coming after us?"

"Yeah," Garrett said, bouncing to his feet. He began pacing back and forth in the aisle. "I didn't want Moloch to hear this, but all of these tests are a test of character. Ed Blunt wants to see if we're worthy of meeting him."

"Ernestine?" Zahra asked, turning her attention from Garrett to her.

"He wouldn't want to waste his time with just anybody," she said, nodding her head.

"Figuring out that Ed's still alive was to gauge our analytical skills. The prostitute tested our sympathy and compassion," Garret said, stopping and glancing at the floor. "I failed, but you guys passed. Maybe I'm too much of a fan. I'd probably do a lot worse just to get a chance to talk to him once."

"You realize that now. That's what's important," Zahra said. "I think you're right about going to your bunker, Garrett. We'll wait until we get there before we go on the vU, again."

Chapter Nine

"Since it looks like you guys are going to be coming here a lot," Garrett said as he threw his black duffel bag onto a leather couch, "I should show you something."

"Do we have to?" Mason asked, collapsing onto a couch and rubbing his eyes.

"Yes, douchebag!" Garret said, sitting at his main computer located in the center of the room. "If any of you get into trouble, input: 'I've gotta a bad feeling about this.' into the main keyboard right here."

Mason guffawed and Ernestine grinned in response. Zahra eyed the others, frowning. "I don't get it."

"It's said in just about every one of those movies…" Mason said, trailing off.

"Which movies?"

Mason shook his head and Garrett smiled. "Never mind. Inside joke."

"Okay," Zahra said, elongating the word.

He input the code into his keyboard and a section of the concrete wall shifted and slid out of the way. Garrett leaned against the entrance, nodding at the dark hole behind him while his friends gathered around it. "It will stay open for a minute after you put the sentence into the computer."

"Is it a dungeon?" Zahra asked, grimacing at the darkness.

"You know," Mason said, "if there's an emergency I don't know if we'll have time to have an orgy in your secret S&M room."

"Prick!" Garrett exclaimed, pointing at him and smiling. "This is my escape tunnel if my weapons and booby traps fail. It goes on for a few hundred feet and comes out behind the property. The house goes back to Prohibition, so the tunnel came with the property. That's why I bought it. If there's an emergency, this will get us out fast, especially if we're outnumbered. There's a car at the exit with some supplies in the trunk. Really good supplies, like the one I have taped under my desk and all over the place."

"Garrett," Zahra asked, a forced smile on her face, "have you thought that maybe you're being just a little paranoid?"

"You think! I've got one of the biggest mafias in the world waiting for me to surface again just so I can wash up on a shore somewhere with my balls in my mouth! I'm not kidding, that's what they do to traitors!"

"The Ciccio Family?" Mason inquired, raising an eyebrow.

"Yeah, how'd you know?" Garrett asked.

"They're the only ones who still do that."

"Oh," Garret said, with a hard swallow. "So, suffice it to say I need a lot of guns and an emergency escape route because they really would come for me if they ever found out where I am and they wouldn't send just a couple people out here. They'd send, more like, twenty."

"Are there any lights in that tunnel?" Mason asked, looking past him and into the black maw.

"Don't worry, they come on the second you walk in."

"Like this?" Mason asked, taking a step into the tunnel, which activated recessed glowing blue lights in the ceiling. "Good color!" he exclaimed before the door began to close on him.

"Hey!" Garrett exclaimed.

Mason moved at lightning speed to the point that he blurred out of existence before appearing in the room next to Zahra.

"That was fast!" Garrett exclaimed.

"I'll go make a sandwich," Ernestine stated before walking off to the small kitchen against the opposite wall.

"Thanks," Mason said, rubbing his stomach. After a loud growl issued from it, he called after her. "Wait! I'll help you. I don't think one's going to be enough."

***

"Ugh," Zahra said, reclining in her seat across from Ernestine. After the feel of virtual silk online, she viciously tugged at the artificial fibers of her sapphire slacks and black blouse. "I don't know if I'm ready for this again. It's getting really late."

"What is it with this whole thing about not wanting to go on the vU?" Ernestine asked while Garrett made last-minute preparations on the fifties-style computer systems behind them. Mason was in the opposite corner of the room on a leather couch, staring at the news on a 3D display coming from his vPhone.

"It's—"

"And don't say it's because you don't have the time!" Ernestine exclaimed, pointing a long-nailed finger at her.

Zahra shook her head and laughed. "Okay, it's not just because of that. I was married once."

"Really?" Ernestine asked before smiling. "Well, you're not the only one."

"Yeah, but your husband was a tech guru. Mine wasn't rich and he wasn't smart, but he had a nice smile and he had kind eyes."

"Ah!" Ernestine said. She relaxed her head on the headrest but kept her eyes on Zahra.

"We met in university and we stayed together for years, but he had a problem," she said, glancing at one of the computer monitors nearby.

"What's that?"

"He ended up with an addiction to being online."

"He was a vAddict?" Ernestine repeated, craning her neck.

"It was," Zahra replied, hesitating on her choice of words, "bad."

"But, there's plenty of vAddicts who lead totally normal lives now."

"Not him," Zahra said, chasing away a tear from the corner of her eye with her forefinger. "He spent so much time on the vU that he lost his job, his home, and," she said, hesitating to finish her sentence, "his wife."

"You split up with him?" Ernestine asked, frowning.

"Kyle was so funny," she said, looking up at the basement ceiling. "He always made me breakfast on the weekends and then we would go to the opening night of a new movie. Kyle would buy the popcorn for both of us, extra butter. And then, he started spending more and more time online. I kept warning him about it and I kept throwing out cold suppers.

"One day, he went online and he stayed online. Two weeks later his work called to say he was fired. We tried that Netholics Program, but it didn't take. A month after that I found out that we didn't have the money for the mortgage. Three months later, I left him."

"I'm sorry, Zahra," Ernestine said, reaching out her hand.

Zahra held it tightly while she continued. "The divorce was finalized over a year ago, just before I started working with Mason. The next day the police came to my door asking me to identify the body."

Ernestine said nothing but watched as Zahra's eyes became glassy.

"He looked a lot like Rudi, so I guess my vote for him to live was an easy one. After Kyle's suicide, I didn't want anything to do with v-Whatever. So, I stopped going online. These last visits were the first time in a few years."

"I'm sorry we had to put you on there," Ernestine said.

"It's okay. I was worried at first, but now I know I can go back. It was time I moved on, like you did."

"Okay, we're ready to go," Garrett said, getting up from his seat and taking off a pair of headphones. "We're logged in as 'BluntlyEd' and I put in the unique password. Star Lore is loading right now."

"Time to get going," Ernestine said, letting her hand go.

Mason turned off his watch and got into a comfortable position on the deep, plush couch. Garrett sat down on the opposite end and the quartet closed their eyes.

They opened them to the sight of a round command center fitted with wood-paneled walls. The forward section of the bridge looked out on a five-story gap holding a large holographic screen across the forward wall. It displayed a vast starfield canvas of blue and green glowing gasses.

Zahra turned to see a command chair sitting between the gap and a round situation table. Iron and stained glass lights reminiscent of Tiffany lampshades were fastened over every station, which was part holographic and part liquid crystal display.

"What is this?" Zahra asked.

"A Bluestar command center," Mason replied.

"What's a Bluestar?" Ernestine inquired before pointing at two manned consoles perched at the edge of the gap with a broad view of space. "And, what are those things?"

"They're what's called a Great House and those stations are for the pilot and co-pilot," Mason replied.

"What about the green guy at one of them?"

Mason chuckled. "He's an orlock. There's seven different races in this game."

"Oh, little green men. I get it," Zahra said, before settling her eyes on a blond human seated at the co-pilot's station. "Isn't that Rudi?"

"His likeness, yeah," Mason replied.

"I thought this was sci-fi," Garrett said. He stood at a station that sensed his thoughts and created Steampunk controls for him out of the liquid crystal display as he approached. "Whoa!" Garrett moved a brass lever on the control panel with a glossy, black finish and went on to press one of a dozen colored glass buttons on the panel. "This looks like something from the nineteenth century, dude."

"That little dome-light that looks like it was made at Tiffany's sensed your thoughts and created that panel. The better question is: Why did you want nineteenth century controls?"

"Well, these clothes aren't from the nineteenth century," Zahra remarked, looking down at the green blouse and black slacks under a light leather jacket she wore. "These look like something from the future. At least they're simple."

"Simple?" Ernestine repeated, looking down at a long, flowing sapphire robe over the dark blouse and slacks she wore. She picked up a staff with two stacked crystals at its peak and looked at it. "This doesn't look simple to me."

"Oh," Mason said, with a smile, "you're a mystic, but I don't think you have to worry about it."

"Are you sure?" Ernestine said, turning the staff around in her grip. "I think I'm a wizard."

"Mystic," Mason corrected. "You can cast spells, but I don't have you have to worry about the staff."

"Good," Ernestine said, leaning the staff against a nearby bulkhead. She pointed at the bubble, "But, what's that?"

The quartet stared at the multi-story holo-screen with a view of an expanse of space where several warships glided past their flagship. The Bluestar vessels were of different sizes but shared a design lineage and were painted a deep, vibrant blue with grey trim. The ships' bows were spherical and connected to a cruciform-shaped main hull with thick wings extending to each point of the compass. At the end of each wing was a long, rectangular hangar, with a green permaglass hangar door covering the back and front of it. All four hangars were, in turn, connected by a thick outer ring. Four round engine ports glowed from the flared stern of the vessel.

"Those are the good guys," Mason said.

"There's a lot of them out there," Garrett remarked. "That's good. Any idea of what it is we're supposed to be doing?"

"I don't recognize this specific command center from the game," Mason said, looking around him. "I think we're on a star carrier, though."

"Is that good?" Ernestine asked.

"It's one of the heavier ships in the game, so yeah, it's good."

"Oh, I see," Zahra said. "Those smaller ships with the globes have guns instead of those big hangars. The bigger ones have the hangars and extra guns."

"Those guns are called 'pulsers'. The bad guys have 'shredders'," Mason supplied.

"Sounds bad," Ernestine remarked.

"It ain't good."

"Is that what we're here for?" Garrett asked, pointing at something that had just appeared at the center of the large screen in front of them.

"What the hell?" Mason said, squinting at a tiny red blob, growing in size by the second. "No, it can't be. Anything but that!"

"What is it?" Ernestine asked.

"I think, but I'm not sure," Mason replied before looking down at his clothing, noticing the bands around the cuffs of his black leather jacket for the first time. "I'm a general! Ah, helm?"

The extraterrestrial with olive skin seated at the helm station in front of them replied, "Yes, Mason?"

"Zoom in on that ship."

The orlock pilot nodded and the ship jumped in size from a small dot to a gargantuan burgundy vessel with six points.

Mason sighed and slouched. "I was worried that's what we were looking at."

"It looks like a big, red starfish," Zahra said.

"It's miles long."

"Please," Garrett said, his eyebrows rising over his shades, "tell me those guys are our friends and why did he call you by name instead of general?"

"The military doesn't work the same way here," Mason said, shaking his head. "It's more of an informal militia. And, those are the bad guys, like *the* biggest baddest guys in the game. It's a Blackstar mobile fortress. They can destroy entire fleets by themselves and have hundreds of fighters in their bays."

"So," Ernestine said, straightening her black top. "How do you take them down?"

"I don't know!" Mason exclaimed. "You never have to deal with them in the game. I heard they're going to be the bad guys in Part Two!"

"That doesn't help us much," Ernestine said.

"Mason," a tall alien with blue skin said from his round station on one side of the round center, "the Blackstar fortress is going weapons hot."

A great, fiery orange eye on the upper main hull of the enemy ship began to pulsate, slowly at first, but it increased in rapidity with every flash.

"Oh," Mason said. "Charge barriers and batteries."

"Barriers and batteries?" Zahra repeated.

"It's how they say to raise shields and arm weapons here."

"Oh," Zahra said, leaning against a heavy chair with a high back. "Is this a throne?"

Mason sat down on the chair and looked up at her. "Close, it's the captain's seat."

"Oh," she said, eyeing the throne before an amused smile appeared on her face.

"They're launching fighters," a broad-shouldered, dwarfish woman said from behind them. Two of the fortresses' arms disgorged swarms of small, red six-winged fighters that dove for the Bluestar ships.

"Jesus Christ!" Garrett exclaimed, getting most of the bridge staff's attention. His cheeks turned red and he pretended to cough. "Oh, ah… carry on."

"Mason, they're firing!" the orlock officer exclaimed.

The team looked up in time to see the fiery eye's flashing become solid. It fired a bright, orange beam that sounded like a dragon breathing fire as it bisected the night sky and hit one of the blue and amber ships nearest it. The ship exploded within seconds of the beam tearing across its hull.

"Jesus Christ!" Garrett said again, eliciting the same reaction from the bridge crew. "Sorry!"

"This doesn't look like it's going to be easy," Ernestine remarked as the disintegration beam destroyed two more frigates before vanishing.

"I think that's the point," Mason stated. He returned his attention to his simulated crew. "Launch all fighters. Have the Hornets and the Griffins go after their fighters. Spartans and Thunderbolts take on the mother ship."

"They can't go up against that, can they?" Ernestine asked, pointing at the mobile fortress.

"We might as well go all in," Mason replied, shrugging.

Mason brightened as the fleet launched a hundred or more of their own fighters, but grimaced once they saw how quickly they were mowed down. Several ships blossomed into fireballs and the Blackstar mothership's main gun began flashing again.

"Get us out of here!" Mason exclaimed to his subordinate.

"I can't! Their fighters have surrounded us!" the helmsman exclaimed.

The ship disgorged another destructive orange beam, which burst through the holographic screen. The entire control center vanished in an explosion of shrapnel and wood before the program reset and the center returned to its previous state.

"Great," Garrett said, "you got us all killed in less than five minutes."

"I know what to expect now. I'll give it another try," Mason said, still seated in his chair.

"Mason, Mobile Fortress Twelve is almost here!" the same orlock pilot said again.

"Okay, this time launch all fighters now, charge barriers, and lay down a full barrage from our pulsers," he said to the command crew. He was about to turn his head to speak to an android crewmember when he noticed something in the corner of his vision flicker for a moment. His eyes darted about the many consoles and stations nearby, but he couldn't figure out exactly where it was coming from.

Mason returned his attention to the battle and watched as their ships disgorged all of their fighters in less than a minute. The moment the great, red starship came into weapons range, the blue and gold ships fired everything they had. Pulses of bright amber starlight and torpedoes flew into the mothership as it glided into the fleet like a duck across a pond. The mobile fortress came to a stop at the same place it had before and disgorged a legion of fighters. Once they were away, it fired bright torpedoes and shredder beams into Mason's fleet.

Less than five minutes later, the foursome watched as the enemy juggernaut belched a great stream of flame from its cyclops eye and hit the hangar attached to their main hull. It exploded as the beam traversed across the center of the vessel, hit the buried spherical command center and split it in two. Mason looked up in time to see the ceiling of the command deck collapse into splinters of wood and shrapnel. They were just an inch from his face when the game reset for a second time, leaving it again untouched.

"I think I know what I did wrong," Mason said, looking at the giant red ship with black trim as it began to loom large on the screen, again. "This time we'll pull back. This is the command ship and it shouldn't be right in the middle of the fight."

Ten minutes later, he hit his armrest with a fist as three glowing torpedoes made the entire front bulkhead of the C&C vanish. Things were back to normal a split second later.

After another two hours, Zahra tapped him on the shoulder. "I think you've tried just about everything."

"I don't get it. I've always found a way to win," Mason said.

"Maybe it's time for someone else to try," Ernestine said before raising her hand at the change of expression on his face. "Even if it's just to give you a break, so you can give it a fresh eye later."

"Alright," Mason said, getting up from the command seat. "Who's next?"

"Zahra," Ernestine said, "you're the senior partner and you always take the lead. Why don't you give it a try?"

"I'd say no, except that I've been watching Mason play—"

"You mean watching Mason lose," Garrett interjected.

"For two hours now," Zahra finished. "I guess I could take a shot at it."

"Be my guest," Mason said before looking up at the ceiling to speak to the computer. "Make Zahra Player One." He patted the reduced number of bands on the sleeves of his jacket. "After losing that many times, I guess I deserve a demotion."

"He said it," Garrett interjected, "I didn't!"

"Okay, let's try going all out this time," Zahra said, taking the command seat as the sleeves of her jacket grew an increased number of bands. "Helm?"

"Yes, Zahra?"

"Turn on those barriers, get those pulsers ready and take us in at full speed. Let's go right for them. Tell all of our ships to do the same. Forget the fighters. We'll take them out by getting up close and personal," Zahra said.

Ernestine and Garrett looked on as the great red, six-pointed starfish seemed about to swallow the main viewport. Mason again noticed something in the periphery of his vision. No longer having to keep his attention on the battle unfolding in virtual space, he caught a holostation flicker for a split second.

"Huh," Mason said, keeping his attention on the station.

"Something important?" Ernestine asked, following his eyes.

"Don't know. It's probably nothing."

"Shit!" Zahra exclaimed.

The four-letter word caught the attention of the two, who looked back at the large screen just as a flurry of torpedoes and shredder beams lashed out from the enemy ship and hit the command ship with their full force.

"Barriers are overloaded!" an officer on one side of the command center exclaimed.

"Retreat!" Zahra yelled, but it was too late. The bridge dissolved into chaos as stations exploded, bulkheads burst and long wooden splinters flew across the room. Command and Control reverted to its formerly pristine condition moments later. "Well, that went nowhere fast."

"I think you beat Mason's record!" Garrett said, laughing.

"I don't do this often," she said. "We'll try something different."

"I hope so," Garrett remarked.

"Garrett," Ernestine remarked, "sometimes less is more."

"Fine, fine," he said, taking a step towards the back of the center.

"Okay, Tactical, tell all of our ships to form lines. Scout carriers in front, light carriers in the middle, us at the back," Zahra said, concentrating on the expanse of space in front of her, occasionally lit by flashes of color from nearby nebulae. "Send those fighters in right away to intercept theirs."

Mason's line of sight was attracted to a nearby station that winked in and out of existence again for a moment. "Huh."

"Zahra," the man at tactical reported, "their fighters are already overwhelming ours."

"Damn," Zahra breathed. "Tell the frigate wing to go in right away to support them."

Within fifteen minutes, the fortress had breached all of their lines. With most of her ships destroyed, Zahra sighed and planted her face in her palm as the center exploded from a direct hit. She looked up to see the command decks back in one piece a moment later. Zahra continued through several more scenarios over the following hour before shaking her head.

"Pause Game," Zahra said. "I've tried everything I can think of that Mason didn't already try."

"My turn!" Garrett exclaimed, rushing forward to the main chair.

"Be my guest," Zahra said, getting up from the command seat. "Make Garrett Player One."

Garrett, dressed in black with four golden bands decorating his sleeves, settled into the big chair with a broad smile.

"The enemy is closing on us, Garrett," the orlock pilot said as the great, red starfish expanded across the screen for the hundredth time.

"Sometimes the best defense is a good offense," he said. "Put all power into the barriers and take us in at full speed."

"Now, that is something we haven't tried," Zahra said from his left.

"I know. We're going to ram the fleet into them!"

"What?" Mason said.

"Wait, wait," Zahra said, placing a hand on her partner's shoulder. "You never know: it might work."

The gargantuan red mothership dominated the screen to the point that they could see the fortress' curiously shaped hexagonal Art-Deco domes in detail. The protective bubble in front of them shattered as the mobile fortress' hull smashed through the carrier's decks and bulkheads. A moment later, the game reset.

"I think you just beat the record for shortest attempt," Mason said.

Garrett released a long sigh, got out of the command chair, and dragged his feet to the back of the command center.

"Pause game," Ernestine said. "Do you have any other ideas, Garrett?"

"Naw, that was my only one," he said, nodding to Zahra and Mason, whose images were reflected in his sunglasses. "Everything else I can think of, they tried already."

"Yeah, me too," Ernestine said, gazing at the distant image of the red leviathan on the five-deck screen above the cavernous gap in front of them. "I can't help but feel like we're missing something."

"We have to win, what else could it be?" Garrett inquired, looking over his shoulder at her.

"No," Zahra said, taking a step towards the holoscreen, "she's right. This whole scenario is an unwinnable battle. The question is: How do you win a no-win scenario?"

Garret snorted. "You don't!"

"So, this is a test of character, like in that old movie from the twentieth century," Mason said.

Ernestine gazed at the starboard side of the command deck. "Mason, what did you see over there?"

"Oh, that?" Mason said, looking in the same direction. "It's just a glitch."

"What do you mean?"

"A station over there would flicker for a second," Mason replied, taking a step towards it.

"A flicker, like it was being updated, maybe?" she asked.

"Yeah," Mason said, taking another step towards the LCD console, "now that you mention it, and it keeps happening around the same time."

"Does it happen at around the same time, or at exactly the same time?" Ernestine asked, moving to that side of the center.

"I'm not sure, why?"

"Which one is it?" Ernestine asked, standing in front of a row of holostations sporting a seat and a crescent-shaped console. The manned stations had panels covered in controls customized for each person, while unmanned stations possessed featureless black panels. The chair for each station sat on top of an amber glass disc, making it look like each station was floating on a golden pool of water. A large screen was mounted on the wall in front of them.

Mason stood beside her and pointed at one station in particular. "That one."

"This is just a dummy console," Ernestine said, closely examining it. "It's just for show. Garrett, stay in command for now. Resume Game."

"Here we go again," Garrett said, settling back into the command chair.

The moment the enemy ship opened fire, the console flickered for a moment as Ernestine and Mason watched. Ernestine sat in the station's seat and the console immediately created controls according to her thoughts. She watched as the flat, black crystal panel became liquid and formed black dials, switches, and buttons embedded in a silver panel. "Look at that! It's not a dummy anymore. It works!"

"Do you think this is what we're supposed to be looking for?" Zahra asked, joining them at the station.

Ernestine pressed a plastic switch on the console and a three-dimensional holographic model of their flagship popped into view. The computer scientist began to manipulate the dials and levers on the panel and watched as the model rotated on its X-axis and then its Y. A sudden jolt through the deck caused some parts of the model to turn red. "This station is for repair management. Look: it's color coded. Green team is headed for that damaged section because it's green now. See, that Blue Team is headed to that area," she said, pointing at a blue part of the ship.

"How does this help us?" Mason asked.

"That part of the ship," she replied, pointing at a small, red dot on the model, "was damaged before we were hit."

An explosion from behind them sent the command decks into a conflagration before they reset to their previous appearance. Ernestine, Zahra and Mason looked at the console, now a featureless dummy again, and regarded Garrett.

"I promise I'll do better next time!"

"Just try to keep us together long enough to figure out what's going on," Ernestine said. "We just have to wait until the battle starts again."

"That's the exact time the console changes?"

"It was last time," Ernestine replied, pressing her lips together.

Sure enough, the moment weapons fire began, the console flickered for a moment as though it was blinking out of existence before becoming solid again.

"There, right at the same time!" she exclaimed before accessing the working console again. A holographic model of the ship popped into view and Ernestine zoomed in on one part of the star carrier colored in red. "See, this one section says that it's damaged, but we haven't taken any damage yet."

A jolt went through the ship and a few sections of the model turned different colors. Mason sighed and glanced at Garrett before returning his attention to the model. "We have now."

"That's a good thing," Ernestine said, pointing at different sections of the ship that had turned various colors with small, moving dots representing repair teams on their way. "See! There it goes again. Those repair teams are going to their assigned places to handle damage, but no one's assigned to that red one."

"So," Zahra said, looking at Ernestine, "shouldn't we go and take care of it?"

"No one else is gonna do it," she replied with a smile.

"Well," Zahra began before the console exploded in her face. Within a second, the console was whole again, but no longer functional. "That's starting to get annoying."

"Zahra," Mason said, "maybe you should take command. You managed to last the longest of all of us and we could really use the extra time."

The comment brought an audible sigh from behind them as Garrett shrunk in his seat.

"Sorry, Garrett," Ernestine said, smirking.

Garrett got up, still frowning, and let Zahra take his place on the command chair. "Make Zahra Player One," he mumbled.

Zahra sat down and began issuing orders. Ernestine waited until the console became functional again before zooming in on the same place on the 3D model. "Okay, I identified it: Deck Twelve, Room Fourteen."

"Okay," Garrett said. "Let's go.'

He headed to the back of the command center with everyone else in tow but was stopped by security personnel dressed in green fatigues. The guards stood on either side of the exit, which was comprised of a set of double doors placed at the back of the center.

Garrett smiled and strode towards them. "Stand aside. We're leaving the bridge."

"No, Sir," was the reply from both of the guards in a monotone.

"Garrett," the pilot said, suddenly standing behind him. "We are in the middle of a battle and the senior staff can't simply leave during a crisis."

"Well," Garrett said, turning around, "we're doing it, anyway. So, get out of the way."

"No, Sir!" the guards repeated, louder than before.

"Is this normal?" Garrett asked, looking at Mason.

Mason's mouth was open and he slowly shook his head from side to side.

"We're going anyway," Garrett said, after a pause before turning back to the exit. He tried to move past the men, but they aimed their pulse rifles at him in response.

"Arrest them!" the pilot exclaimed.

"Sir," the soldier said. "Please, put your hands behind your back."

"Great!" Garrett exclaimed, complying with their orders. "Get us out of here."

"Take them to the brig," the pilot said.

The rest of the team was also put in handcuffs and removed from the command decks. Mason leaned towards Garrett as they were escorted down a corridor with walnut wainscoting and burgundy wall panels. "Is this also part of your plan?"

"We'll break out of the brig," Garrett replied, just before they heard the loud roar of a heavy shredder and the corridor dissolved into a firestorm. They blinked and found themselves in the command center again just before the battle.

"I guess it was worth a try," Ernestine remarked. "So, how do we get out of here and get to that room?"

Mason sat down, stared at the opposite paneled wall, and sighed. "Pause Game."

Garrett ran a hand through his hair. "So, we can't leave and we can't win. Was Ed always this big of an asshole, Ern?"

"He could drive you crazy," Ernestine replied, "but he was always worth it. There's gotta be a solution. Ed wasn't a practical joker."

"We can't leave the bridge," Mason said, glancing at the exit.

"No!" Zahra exclaimed, getting up from the bench. "You just said it: *We* can't leave the bridge, but maybe one of us can! The solution is not to go as a group but just send one person. It's deceptively simple!"

"Jesus," Ernestine said, standing next to Zahra, "could it be?"

"Let's find out," Zahra said, seating herself on the command chair again. "Resume Game."

"Who should go?" Mason asked.

"Ern, you're the expert in code and you knew Ed personally. You should go," Garrett replied.

"Makes sense to me," Zahra said, getting a grin from Ernestine. "Get ready."

"How do I talk to you when I leave?" she asked.

"Oh," Mason said, getting up from his seat. "Just use your vPhone."

Ernestine tapped the virtual watch on her wrist. "Got it."

"They're going weapons hot!" the pilot exclaimed for the umpteenth time.

"Bring us to the back of the line, Captain. Launch all fighters. They're all to concentrate on taking out the enemy fighters. The rest of the fleet will support them."

"Yes, Zahra."

"There it is," Ernestine said, pointing at the flickering console. Mason and Garrett manned the station, bringing up the same holographic representation of the ship.

"Here goes," Zahra said, looking at Ernestine. "Ern, take care of the damage on Deck Twelve, Room Fourteen."

"Ah," she replied, "yes, Ma'am?" Ernestine turned for the exit and walked to the set of double doors, feeling a pit in her stomach as she reached the security guards. She breathed a sigh of relief when the pair didn't stand in her way, but remained at their traditional places on either side of the door.

Ernestine walked out of the Command Sphere and into a corridor, turned her vPhone on and held it a few inches from her mouth. "Can you hear me?"

"Yup," she heard Mason's voice reply. "You are now a red dot on the model. It looks like you're assigned to take care of that damaged section. Walk to the end of the corridor and take the elevator to deck twelve."

"Got it," Ernestine said, moving at an earnest pace for the only set of doors she saw in front of her. She got onto an elevator with wooden wainscoting and liquid crystal displays depicting a quiet glen, making it appear as though the elevator was surrounded by grass and trees. Ernestine requested deck twelve and arrived in under a minute. The deck moved beneath her as soon as she stepped off the elevator.

"How is everything going up there?"

"Bit of a run-in with a torpedo, but we're actually doing pretty well this time," Mason replied from the other end of the line.

"Good," Ernestine said, "because I really don't want to do this again."

"Same here."

She walked down a broad hallway with Tiffany dome lights lining the ceiling. One wall had a long row of tall, narrow viewports running alongside it. Ernestine found her eyes held for a moment by the sight of the major battle unfolding in space outside before shaking her head and resuming a hasty pace. She came to a T-intersection and stopped.

"Where to now?"

"To your right. You're doing great. It's not much further."

"Good," Ernestine said after another shake of the deck below her.

"Oh, things are going a little worse now. Might want to hurry."

"Great."

Ernestine followed their instructions until she was standing in front of a door that looked like the entrance to a first-class stateroom, judging by the richness and quality of the entryway. Ernestine turned the brass doorknob, hearing a click as she did. She pulled the door open and a bright, white light hit her, making her squint.

"What's going on?" Mason's voice asked.

"It's a white light," she replied. "I'm going in."

"Really?" Garrett asked over the intercom. "I think I heard something about what happens when someone walks into a bright, white light."

"I'll be okay. Ed set this up," she replied.

"Good luck."

Ernestine took a deep breath and walked into the room. Once she was standing on the other side of the threshold, the light vanished and was replaced by a long corridor where the walls, ceiling, and floor were made of stars. The last person she expected to meet again was standing right in front of her…

***

"Ern?" Garrett said, staring at the silent red room on the holographic ship. "Ern, come on! Don't do this to me, man!"

"Where is she?" Mason demanded, hastily turning the model of the ship around with his hand. "This doesn't make any sense! She was right there!"

The console shut down, as did the hologram. Mason and Garrett watched as the command crew vanished from their positions, followed by the ships battling beyond the glass dome.

Zahra stood up and looked from the view of nothing to the duo. "What's going on now?"

The command decks transformed into a white gazebo covered in ivy with a small, round five-piece dinette at its center. Beyond it were trees and cobblestone paths.

"Whoa," Garrett said, placing his hand on the round table. "It's made of glass! Pure glass!"

"I like the cushions," Zahra said, looking at the plush, royal blue cushions perfectly placed on every chair and then at herself. "Where are we and what are we wearing?"

"We look like something out of the Victorian Era," Garrett said, looking down at the immaculate blue jacket he wore with black trousers. His hair shined with oils. "I look like a rube."

"You look great," Mason said before looking down at the chocolate trousers and jacket he wore over a purple waistcoat. He tapped a brown top hat he wore. "I look like friggin' Willy Wonka!"

"Hey," Zahra said, pulling a multi-layered emerald dress up a few inches off the ground. "Consider yourself lucky. Oh, I swore I'd never wear high heels!"

The trio turned and walked down one of four short stairways onto a cobblestone path. Garret looked at the sky. "Wow!"

A hundred feet above them was a glass dome, and beyond that was a golden ribbon of light undulating across the night sky.

"It must always be autumn here," Mason said, his attention drawn to the birch trees around them decorated with leaves of red, orange, yellow, and purple. The grass was a perfectly manicured pale green. "I wonder where this path goes?"

They walked a way down the cobblestone walk only to come to the edge of a thick glass dome supported by a thick, riveted wrought iron frame. Mason walked up to the glass enclosure and put his hand on it before looking out on the barren landscape beyond. "Hmm, the glass is cold. I bet there's no air out there."

"Even if there was," Zahra said, frowning at the dark landscape beyond, "I still wouldn't want to go out there. Looks like a moon of Jupiter."

"That doesn't look like Jupiter to me," Garrett said, pointing at a great, red gas giant in the sky, with a thick golden ring sitting just above the horizon. A green sun glowed in the distance beyond it. "I don't think this place exists anywhere in reality."

"Is this some kinda prison?" Zahra asked.

"I don't think so," Mason said, turning around to start the short journey back to the gazebo. "Losing meant doing that battle simulation over and over again."

"And over again," Zahra said, looking up at the night sky above them.

"So, what is it, then?" Garret asked.

"I think it's a waiting room," Mason replied.

"It's not like any waiting room I've ever been in," Zahra said, settling her eyes on the gazebo as it came into view.

"Ed must've made it," Garret said as the stairs approached.

"It would make sense."

"If this is a waiting room, then what are we waiting for?" Zahra asked, placing a high-heeled leather boot onto the first step.

"Ernestine must've gotten into that room. I guess we wait here until she's done whatever it is she's doing," he said before his mouth dropped open at the sight of the glass dinette. "When did that get here?"

The other two followed his gaze to a silver platter with triangular cut sandwiches and delicate cups of tea. Zahra put a hand covered in white lace on the back of one chair and considered the cup of Earl Grey. "I'm really not a tea fan." The moment the words were out of her mouth, the cup transformed into a crystal glass filled with a light, white Riesling. Zahra settled into the seat and picked it up with a smile. "Now, that's more like it."

The others sat down and began their light meal while making small talk, but all the while, their eyes would occasionally glance up into the night sky above them with images of Ernestine flashing across its pin-pricked canvas.

Chapter Ten

"Hello," said a white-haired man with a Londoner accent. Around him, the corridor of space vanished and was replaced by a desert expanse soaked in the deep blue light just before sunrise. A village a short distance away slept with the half-constructed pyramids of Giza and the Sphinx beyond it.

"You always did like that fifties 'Greatest Retro' look," Ernestine remarked, smiling at his tan trousers and cardigan worn over a white dress shirt. His company's logo, a red door with a round, green window, stood behind him.

"You probably know that I'm Ed Blunt. I know you've come a long way to find me, but don't stop now, you're almost there."

"My Ed," Ernestine said, taking in the elderly man and recommitting his face to memory.

"Now, if you're one of my ex-wives, you shouldn't have bothered."

Ernestine frowned and crossed her arms.

"Unless it's you, Ern," he said, at which point a smile slowly started to spread across her face. "I'd be glad to see you again. My biggest regret was not being there for you when you needed me. All I could see was my work and I should've seen you."

"Ed," Ernestine said, shaking her head, slowly.

"And now onto the boring part. Where am I? You've gathered so far that I must be in a game and you're right. The question you must have is: Which one?" he asked with an enigmatic smile. "Look for me in Sword & Sorcery. It's my favorite RPG and the one place I wanted to spend my extended retirement."

Ernestine's eyes widened at the statement. "You never told me that!"

"Well, now you know where to find me and you've passed all of my tests to get here. Good luck."

The recording vanished, as did the view. Ernestine was now looking at a gazebo where her friends were enjoying high tea. She looked down at her garments and gasped. "Oh God! Victorian dress!"

"Ern!" Zahra exclaimed, jumping up from her chair. "What happened?"

Ernestine raised her dress high enough to see her footwear. "Anything but high heels!"

"Amen," Zahra said with a laugh.

All three of her friends gathered around her. Ernestine lowered her layered dress and smiled a wistful smile. "It was Ed. Well, it was a recording of him. I got his location."

"And?" Garrett asked, looking over his sunglasses at her.

"He's in a game called Sword & Sorcery," Ernestine replied.

Mason's ears perked up. "Seriously?"

"What?"

"That's my favorite game! I was just there a couple of days ago," Mason replied before a small smile appeared on his face. "I can't believe that was just a few days ago. It feels like months."

"Well, it turns out it was Ed's favorite game, too," Ernestine said.

"I should've known," Mason said. "It's one of the oldest games on the vU."

"How big is Sword & Sorcery?" Garrett asked.

"About the size of the UK, why?"

"I was worried you'd say something like that," Garrett replied, beginning a slow walk towards the dome's edge.

"Why is that a problem?" Zahra asked, falling into step next to him.

"How are we gonna find him?" Garrett asked. "He's in a game the size of a country!"

"He's gotta a good point," Ernestine said, trying to keep up with the other three. "That's it, these friggin' things are coming off." She spotted a bench just a short ways away and sat down. Ernestine subsequently began wrenching off her shoes.

"I feel that," Zahra said, sitting beside her and doing the same. Soon, they both stood up again with two pairs of high-heeled boots lying on the ground.

"So," Garrett said, eyeing their painful footwear, "how do we find this particular needle in a haystack?"

"Ed wouldn't be walking around for everybody to see," Mason replied.

"So, what? He's hiding in a dark corner or something?" Garrett asked.

"Ed would make sure to leave anyone looking for him some kind of symbol or something to locate him," Ernestine replied, sighing with each step.

"What would he use?" Garrett asked.

Earnestine laughed and snapped her fingers. "That's why he had his logo behind him!"

"What?"

"Ed's recording! He had his company's logo behind him, and I was wondering why until now. He put it there as a hint of where to find him in that game!" Earnestine said, though she was speaking so quickly that she started to stammer.

"His logo?" Mason said, his eyes lighting up. "Yes! I saw his logo in the game! I talked to an older guy who pointed out that cottage to me. I know where to go!"

"Then it's time we got out of here. Sword & Sorcery?" Zahra asked, looking at everyone around her. They all nodded in approval and Zahra looked up into the night sky and said: "I want to go to Sword & Sorcery."

The rest of the group did the same and winced as the bright light of the noon sun hit their eyes, except for Garret, who smiled at their discomfort and shifted the sunglasses on his nose.

Zahra immediately looked down at her clothes and smirked. "From Victorian era dress to medieval. I don't know which one's worse," she said, taking in a pale blue and white cotton dress with a ring of dirt around the hem. "Why am I automatically a poor wench?"

"Don't knock it," Ernestine remarked, taking in a shiny, tight leather hunter's outfit she wore, complete with bow. "This doesn't work for me."

"Hey, you look good in leather," Zahra said. "I look like I should be bringing a jug of beer to a bunch of greasy, old fat guys."

"It's not that bad."

"I can tell by the smile on your face that it is," Zahra said, turning her attention to the two men in the group. "Now, look at these two: Robin Hood and the Magician! Of course they would get the fun stuff to wear."

Garrett turned away from his view of the river and looked at Zahra from behind his ever-present shades, giving a modern take to the green tights and vest he wore. "You can change what you wear, your faces, everything, you know. Just bring up your menu."

"I'm okay being me, but these clothes have got to go."

Both Zahra and Ernestine thought a screen into existence and accessed the game menu. In less than a minute, Zahra changed her mode of dress to a shiny brown leather suit with a frilled white dress shirt, while Ernestine opted for a conservatively tailored medieval green dress and leather boots.

"That's better. Now we can go," Zahra said, looking around. "Where do we go?"

"Over there," Mason said, pointing at a tall elm tree near an incredibly wide river. "That's where that old guy was the last time I was here."

"Did he look like Ed?" Ernestine asked as they walked towards the river.

"If he did," Mason said, "I would have noticed."

"That would be a little too obvious, wouldn't it?" Zahra said, taking in a deep breath. "Wow, the air here is really fresh."

"Simulated air," Garrett corrected before pointing at a fallen tree with a man sitting on it. "Is that him?"

The former agent followed his eyes and grinned. "Yes! That's the guy! Come on!"

Mason led them to a small, white-haired man in a grey robe, only stopping once he was five feet away. Just as before, the man took a moment to notice them, causing him to jump and then laugh at his reaction.

"I'm sorry," he said, slapping the log in amusement. "I was deep in thought."

"That's what he said last time," Mason said over his shoulder. "You're OverForty506, right?"

"Yes, but people around her call me De," the man said, narrowing his eyes at them. "How did you know that? Wait, aren't you the one who was here a few days ago? Your avatar was different."

"AntiFed386 or Mason, whichever you want," he replied.

"De?" Ernestine repeated, noticing the man's expression radically change at the sight of her. "That's Ed backwards and 506 is his old street number."

"It is," he said, nodding his head, but still staring at Ernestine.

"And you're even older than your avatar in real life?" Mason asked.

"Yes," he said, in a distant voice, his eyes locked with hers.

"Say, around a hundred years old by now?"

"Right as rain," De replied from a million miles away.

"So," Ernestine said, taking a step towards the stunned man, "what's so special about the house across the river?"

"That red door with the green window is identical to the logo for vNetworks," Mason interjected.

"Ern, I…" De said, faltering.

"You don't look anything like you used to," she said.

De looked up into the sky. "Emergency Update Situation Zero Four." He flickered for a moment and then looked back at the group and smiled. "Ern! I was hoping you'd show up some day. I'm glad it wasn't too long."

"Did you see that? That was a software update," Ernestine said, "meaning limited memory allocation. You're not Ed, are you? You're a program."

"Guilty on all counts," De said, clapping his hands together. "I am programmed with much of Ed's personality, but this character's memory is eaten up by operating in this environment. Once you're gone, I will have to revert to how I was."

"I didn't think you'd spend all of your days sitting by a river on the off-chance that the world might be in danger."

"Not my first choice, no," De said. "I am the gateway to Ed. It's through me that you can get his exact location."

"He's in that cottage across the river, isn't he?" Mason asked.

"The one place in this game you can't get to. It's the perfect place for him to retire," De said. "You're smarter than most people who've stopped to talk to me."

"Thanks."

"Now, the big question," Ernestine said. "How do we get to him, De?"

"My program is actually the start of a broken quest," he replied. "I can only give it to you by choice."

"A broken quest?" Zahra repeated.

"It's kinda like those Easter Eggs I mentioned to you before," Mason replied. "Sometimes games are hurried into publication and some quests can't be finished in time and others weren't working and there wasn't time to fix them. Gamers call them broken or unfinished quests."

"But," De interjected, "my quest was intentionally broken and no one can fix it unless I ask them a specific question to get it started. You wouldn't believe how many people have come along trying to 'fix' my code or find a way to get me to ask them the correct question to start the quest. They all eventually got bored and moved on."

"So, do we pass?" Zahra asked.

"Yes. It's not just because of you, Ern, although you're reason enough just by yourself," De said, at which point Earnestine grinned. "It's also because of you, Mason. You took the time to stop and talk to me, you asked what I was doing here, and no one else ever cared. Well," he said, straightening his back and standing up, "here goes. The Quest: I'm just an old man in need of some help. Will you aid me in my time of need? Wow, I can't tell you how great it was to finally say that!"

The quartet laughed out loud and regarded the simple smile on the ancient man in a grey robe.

"Yes," Mason replied, "We would be honored to help you."

"Good man!" De exclaimed, rolling back on his heels. "Now, what I need is something simple but difficult, easy but hard—"

"Oh God!" Ernestine exclaimed. "Ed was never much for writing or riddles. I'm sorry."

"He always thought he was pretty good at it," De remarked.

"I know."

"It does kinda fit in with this place," Mason said, glancing at the medieval village in the distance.

"Can I continue?" De asked.

Ernestine sighed. "Go ahead."

"What I need is something simple but difficult, easy but hard, if you ever find one, it will be on a bard."

"Three stars," Ernestine said, looking down her nose at him.

"I would've given it four," Mason said. "It is an Ed Blunt original."

"So," Garrett said, shaking his head and rolling his eyes, "what does it mean?"

"I'm afraid that's all the help I can give you," De said.

The group turned away from the elderly man and walked back to the road running through Lothering, less than half a mile away. A breeze brought cloud cover, cooling the day and shading their eyes.

"Something difficult and hard that you'd find on a bard," Mason paraphrased. "What do you find on a bard that you don't find on anyone else?"

"In this game?" Garrett asked. "Everyone has weapons and tools. Do bards in this game have musical instruments?"

"Well, yeah," Mason replied. "In this part of the country the bards carry a lute."

"A lute," Zahra said, looking at the approaching village, "aren't they simple, stringed instruments from medieval times?"

"Simple to make, but hard to play!" Mason replied. "That's it! Wow, Zahra, you're getting good at this!"

"Thanks. Where's the nearest bar?" Zahra asked.

"It's just ahead in Lothering," Mason said before blowing a raspberry. "You're not going to believe this: It's called The Bard's Quest."

"I should've known," Ernestine said, slapping a hand to her brow. "There's Ed's sense of humor again."

"How do we get the lute? Can't we just buy it?" Garrett asked.

"I have built up a lot of coin in this game. We could try to bribe him into giving it to us," Mason suggested as the bar came into view.

"That sounds too easy," Ernestine said, pulling her dress off the ground, which now had a thick layer of dust around its hem. "Jeez, Zahra, maybe I should've gone for pants as well! Aren't these quests or whatever supposed to be long and difficult?"

"Yeah, but this is just a side quest."

"It's a what?" Zahra asked.

Mason had his mouth open to reply, but Garrett was already responding for him. "Main quests are long and involved, but side quests are usually simple kill/reward or 'fetch me this' kinda quests. They're not supposed to take a lot of time," Garrett replied. Mason raised an eyebrow at him. Garret smiled and placed a booted foot onto a cobblestone walkway just outside of the stone pub. "You're not the only one who plays games, you know."

"What he said," Mason said, pointing a thumb at Garrett. He stood in front of the door to the two-story building, which had an oriel window on either side of it. Above the entry was a round, wooden sign with blue and green detailing around the words 'The Bard's Quest'. "This is the place," he said, pulling the door open.

Zahra and Ernestine's noses scrunched up the moment the warm air from the bar hit their faces. "I didn't realize they went for such realism in this game."

"Yeah," Ernestine said, pinching her nose. "It smells like a brewery in there."

"You get used to it," Mason said, looking around the tavern. He pointed across the wooden floor at a woman dressed in lively colors and holding a simple, stringed instrument from which came a lilting tune. The bard was backlit by a roaring fireplace as she sang and danced. "There she is."

"Should we try to blend in?" Ernestine asked, looking around at the growing number of people staring at them.

"Yeah, let's go to the bar," Mason replied, leading the way to a simple, rectangular counter made from wooden planks at the center of the pub. Mason stopped at the counter in front of a gruff, bearded man with arms the width of tree trunks. "Four mugs of ale."

"Yeah, yeah," the man growled.

"You know, I'd rather have a glass of," Zahra began before the bartender's stare killed the words on her lips. "A mug of ale would be great."

"Damn right it would be," he said, slamming four iron mugs onto the countertop, causing beer to spill out onto its rough surface. A slow, moist palm with thick fingers moved over the drinks. "Four gold pieces."

"Sure," Mason said, taking four gold coins from a purse at his belt. The money glowed in the firelight as it fell into the bartender's wet palm. A fifth and final piece tinkled as it dropped onto the small pile. "For your trouble."

A small, wet-lipped smile appeared on the bartender's face before he turned to help another patron. Each person grabbed a mug and commandeered a simple, square table with four chairs close to where the bard played.

"Take a drink," Mason said to everyone's disheartened faces. "Trust me."

The other three took a careful sip from their mugs. Garrett looked at the mug for a startled second and then took another one. "This is really good! Judging by that bartender, I thought—"

"It would taste like piss?" Mason asked, noticing that the other two members of his group were also much more liberal now with their imbibing. "It's an old game and that means great food and great beer."

"Shh!" a voice hissed from the table next to them.

Mason coughed and nodded. "We should listen to the bard."

They listened as the entertainer sang of far-off places where wild wars were won. The eventual arrival of peace brought a satisfying ending to the story as the bard finished. She took her applause with a smile, and bowed before taking a break.

"Here I go," Mason said, finished his pint and stood up. "Wish me luck."

"He isn't going to hit on her, is he?" Garrett asked, leaning in towards Ernestine.

She laughed and leaned back in her chair. "I've got to say that I'm a little surprised to be in here trying to get a lute away from a bard. I never knew that Ed was so big into gaming."

"I read something about it years ago, but I never really gave it any thought," Garrett said, taking a long draught of his beer.

"I thought I knew him better."

"There's always something you don't know about a person," Garrett said. "You're not in this just to get out of the house, are you?"

"No," Ernestine admitted, putting her drink down. "I wanted to see Ed again for a long time. I never felt like we really wrapped things up between us, and I guess I saw my chance by joining up. Now I'm starting to think there was more to it than that. I guess I realize just how much I really missed him all these years."

"We are in big trouble!" Mason exclaimed. He slapped both hands on the table and leaned into the center of it.

"What?" Zahra asked.

"She won't give up her lute for anything. I even offered her ten thousand gold pieces for it!"

"Do you have more?" Garrett asked.

"Yeah," he said, glancing at the bard over his shoulder, "but she gave me the impression that no amount of money would be enough. She wants something else."

"Like what?" Ernestine asked, pushing her drink away.

"I don't friggin' know!" Mason exclaimed, sending a bewildered glare at the woman behind him. "She wouldn't say! She just smiled when I asked if there was anything else she'd take in exchange for the lute."

"She wants something," Zahra said, leaning back in her comfortable wooden chair. She kept one hand on her mug of beer.

"Is this place like other RPGs where the bartender has a shop for buying things?" Garrett asked, looking up at him.

"Sure."

"Did you ever browse his inventory before?" Garrett asked.

"Yeah, there wasn't much there, except this unbelievably expensive lute on…" Mason began before smacking the side of his face with his hand. "Oh no! Do you know how much that lute is?"

"No, how much?" Zahra asked.

Mason frowned at the question. "It costs a million coin. That's why nobody ever buys it! It's just a really expensive lute with no special enhancements or powers or anything! I always thought it was some kind of programming error with the cost."

Ernestine smiled at the rest of her friends. "That's why it's there. Nobody wants it because it's the only way to solve this side quest. I bet its code allows it to respawn in less than an hour."

"It's a *million* gold pieces," Mason restated, dropping his shoulders towards the top of the table.

"Do you have that much?" Zahra asked, smiling up at him.

"Barely!"

"Then do it," Zahra said, watching his face fall. "Look, it's just virtual coin. We'll find some way for you to get it back."

Mason looked around at them, but didn't find a single face sympathetic to his cause. He sighed and straightened up. "Fine." He went to the bartender, who attended to him within moments. "Hey, barkeep," he said, quietly. "Can I see your wares?"

The bartender smiled, nodded, and a menu popped up in front of him with several foods and tools to buy like, axes, rope, and even Shepherd's Pie. Mason scrolled to the bottom of the list, seeing a glowing lute at the bottom of it on sale for one million coins, exactly. He selected it, bit back a cry, and pressed the purchase button.

The menu disappeared and the bartender held a glowing wooden lute in his hands, which he gave to Mason, who did his best to put a smile on his face as he accepted it. He turned around and looked at his friends still seated at the table. Upon seeing the lute, they gave him the thumbs up, causing him to slump even further.

Upon presenting it to the bard, she jumped up and down, hugged him and accepted the gift. His teammates watched as she pulled the strap of her own lute over her head and handed the instrument to him. Mason turned to face them, his painted-on smile vanishing from his face.

"Here's your fuckin' lute," he said, plopping into his seat and tossing it onto the table.

"Well," Garrett said, gulping down the last of his beer and standing up, "no point in sitting around here. Let's go and get Ed."

Zahra and Ernestine also got up from their chairs, but Mason remained seated. "Just give me a minute!"

Zahra put a hand on the back of his chair. "It's just money, Mason, and it's not even real money!"

"I know, just give me a minute!"

Zahra looked around at the rest of her comrades, gulped down the rest of her beer and picked up the lute from the table. "Minute's over! Come on, time's a wastin'!" She pulled him up off his seat and the quartet walked out of the bar. The cool breeze coming in off the water hit them as they walked out onto the street, bringing a smile to everyone's faces except for Mason, who dragged his feet to the river.

This time, De was already standing and facing them as they approached. Zahra gave Mason the lute and stood back. Mason managed a more sincere smile to reflect De's, stopped before him, and presented him with the musical instrument. "Here is the lute you requested."

"Lute?" De repeated. "The quest wasn't for a lute!"

"What?" Mason demanded, eyes bulging from his sockets.

A broad smile broke across De's face and he held his sides as phlegmy howls escaped his mouth, now all teeth. "You should have seen your face!"

"Friggin' Ed and your sense of humor!" Ernestine exclaimed from behind Mason.

"Come on, Ern, that was funny!"

"We've always had different opinions on what's funny," Ernestine said, placing a hand on her hip.

"Alright, alright," the robed man said. "Yes, you were right. The quest was for a lute. You just need to give it to me."

Mason huffed and held up the lute as though it weighed a hundred pounds. "Here. Take it, before I change my mind."

"Brilliant!" De said, snatching the lute from his hands. De regarded it for a moment, a smile on his face as he brought his eyes to within an inch of the instrument, examining its surface in detail. "Yes, yes, this is it. I know exactly what to look for." He let the lute fall to the ground and grinned at Mason. "This is exactly what I need!"

Mason drew in a deep breath once De lifted his right leg and crushed the instrument beneath his foot. The mindhacker put both hands over his mouth, making his next question difficult to hear. "Why did you do that?"

De glanced at the smashed lute. "Don't worry, those things respawn every hour."

"Told you so," Ernestine said under her breath.

"You stepped on a million-coin lute!" Mason exclaimed, clenching his fists and feeling his mouth turn into a frown.

"Oh that," he said, glancing again at the broken lute. "It's the key to this particular gate; One that has to be destroyed to open the lock. Look!"

De stepped aside and the small group of friends looked out on the broad river.

"Is something supposed to be happening?" Ernestine asked, watching the serene scene.

De pointed at the ground next to him, where individual strands of ice rose from the grass and came together like a puzzle to form a step and then another. As the staircase formed, rays of midday sunshine hit it, causing mist to rise from its steps.

"It's made of solid ice!" Zahra exclaimed as the steps continued to appear in front of them. The ground shook and the river in front of them began to move strangely, as though it was being pushed aside by something below the surface. Then, a great, glittering bridge of ice broke from the water, rising to meet the steps that had formed in front of it.

"You better get going," De said, pointing at the bridge. "It really is made of ice and it's timed to become too unstable to cross in less than an hour."

"Thank you!" Zahra said, feeling a cold breeze coming off the ice structure spanning the river as she placed her foot on the first step.

"Thank you for letting me do that for the first time," he said.

The rest of the group thanked him as well and stepped onto the bridge.

"It's got fog coming off it!" Ernestine exclaimed as they walked across the pale blue surface enclosed by thick railings of ice.

They walked in awe with every step as the other side of the river gradually approached. It was sometime later that they placed their feet on solid ground again. Zahra looked behind her and saw part of the railing collapse under the heat of the afternoon sun. "Wow, you really do have just enough time to get across."

"There it is," Mason said, standing at the bottom of a path leading up to a small, stone cottage with two windows. Between them sat a red door with a round, emerald window in it.

"It took so much to get here and now I'm not sure I can get my feet to move," Garrett said, looking up at the house on the hill.

"He's supposed to be dead and he's my ex-husband. I've got a lotta questions for him to answer," Ernestine said, placing one foot in front of the other, while picking the hem of her dress off the path.

"Yeah, me too," Mason said, walking beside her.

"I think they're trying to say: 'Don't be scared'," Zahra whispered to Garrett before grabbing his hand and pulling him up the path.

"The one place you can never get to," Mason repeated, looking at the green lawn adorned with tall oak trees.

"The one place we had to go," Ernestine said. They stopped at the front door and looked at each other.

Mason indicated it with his hand. "You were his ex-wife."

"You're the one who needs him the most."

"I'm the one who's going to have a nervous breakdown if someone doesn't open the fuckin' door," Garrett said from behind them.

Ernestine straightened her green dress, looked at the red door, and sighed. "Here goes." She held up her right hand and knocked on it.

"It's about time!" a voice exclaimed from inside. "Come in, come in! It's unlocked."

Ernestine tried the round doorknob, finding that it turned easily. She opened the door to the sight of a medium-sized room with broad, thick floorboards. Yellowed walls reflected the light from beams of sunshine streaming in through the windows. The dust in the air made them into spotlights, but they didn't illuminate an individual but sections of the floor. The entire room was covered in books and papers, but underneath all of it was a desk, couch, table and a few chairs.

At the center of the mess was a man just standing up from a high-backed, plush leather chair. "My God! Ern! I hoped it might be you!"

Ernestine looked at the man from head to foot. "You can't be a day over thirty. You got the Retro Fifties look right, though."

"What?" the man asked, squinting his eyes at the middle-aged woman standing in a sparkling sunbeam. Edward looked down at his hands, fresh with the flush of youth. "Oh, yes! Ern, you knew me better this way:" he said and then transformed into a man of eighty. "Better?"

"Now, that's the Ed I knew," Ernestine said. "Still a short, little squirt."

"You haven't changed," Ed said before a wide grin lit his face. "I missed you. I'm glad it's you who came and not someone else."

"Well," Ernestine said, moving to the side.

Edward's eyebrows rose at the sight of the trio standing behind her. "Brought some friends, I see. Well, come in, come in. I haven't had company here in, well, ever!"

"Same sense of humor," Ernestine said, taking in the untidy atmosphere around her. "Same mess."

"You got so sick of the house being a sty even when there was a daily cleaning service!" Edward exclaimed as he drew her into a deep hug. "I should've been kinder to you."

"It doesn't matter anymore," Ernestine said, pulling back from the embrace to take in his seamed face. "I just wanted to see you again."

"And I wanted to apologize. I should never have left you alone in that house with nothing but the memories of your family."

"Thanks, but there was plenty of blame to go around."

Mason took advantage of the pause in the conversation to clear his throat. Ernestine and Edward jumped at the noise. They separated and straightened their clothes.

"Ah, yes," Edward said, clearing his throat. "You brought guests, Ern. Care to introduce them?"

"Yeah, this is Garrett Cho, my go-to for just about everything since you died, or seemed to have died."

"Garrett," he said, pumping his hand. "I'm glad someone could be there for her."

"It's an honor to meet you. I'm a big fan," Garrett said, grinning from ear to ear. He took off his sunglasses and squinted sparkling brown eyes at Edward. "You've been a big inspiration to me."

"Took off the shades, huh? Judging by your friends' reactions, that's a big deal. Now I'm the one who's honored," Edward said.

Garrett quickly put his sunglasses back on. "I've got a million questions."

"We'll have plenty of time for that later," he said with a warm smile, before turning his attention to his next guest.

"This is Zahra Washington," Ernestine said as Ed shook her hand. "She and her partner are FBI agents."

"FBI?" Edward repeated, looking at Ernestine. "*You're* working with the FBI?"

"We're working under the radar right now," Zahra replied.

"The circumstances here are unique," Mason said, stepping forward. "We need your help."

"That's Mason Deane," Ernestine whispered in Edward's ear.

"Yes. A mindhacker, correct?" he asked. Ed took a step towards him and looked into his eyes. "No, not anymore. You've got code you shouldn't have."

"How did he know that?" Mason asked, looking at Ernestine.

"Because he's Ed Blunt."

"I designed the code," Edward said, spritely jumping back from Mason a full foot and clapping his hands together once. "It's code that was never meant to get out to the public, which means that someone's trying to become a bodyhacker, also correct?"

Garrett grinned and looked at Zahra. "He's good!"

"It's the prime probability," Edward said. "I bet it took Ern, here, even less time to figure it out."

"I had to start from scratch," she stated and sighed, "but I noticed the deaths."

"Yes, the deaths," Edward said, looking at the wooden floorboards for a moment. "Keith, Joanne, Rodney, Jamie: I knew them for a long time. They deserved better."

"They did," Ernestine said with a nod.

"What I don't understand is how this guy became a bodyhacker. I thought that was impossible," Mason asked. "The FBI destroyed the code a decade ago."

"It's not possible to destroy all of the code because it's in all mindhackers, everywhere. You see, the original concept was to create bodyhackers, not mindhackers. If you have the code, you have the capacity," Edward replied, carefully watching the expressions on their faces change.

"Why did they change their minds?" Zahra asked.

"Because of what it could turn your average person into. Think of all the times that you wished you could reach into someone's heads and change their minds. Then imagine you could in a very literal manner. The temptation to abuse such a gift was far too great. Ultimately, mindhackers were the better option to go with," Edward said, crossing his arms.

"But, why not just destroy all of that restricted code, then?" Garrett asked.

"Because the FBI wanted to keep the code in case another nation came up with what we did. It was taken from us, classified top secret, and locked away on a closed server deep in their headquarters. Somehow this person stumbled across that information."

"Was his access that high?" Zahra asked, looking at Mason.

"I don't know," he replied, with a shrug.

"I know you said to wait," Garrett said, fidgeting, "but, I gotta ask: What was with all of the tests? I figured out what a few of them were for, but I didn't get the big picture."

"Ah," Edward said, turning away from them before taking a step towards his chair. "Why did I put you through all of that? Good question. Excuse me, while I change into someone a little more comfortable." Before their eyes, Ed grew an inch, his white hair became a light brown, and his eyes changed from a cloudy pale blue to a bright sapphire. He was now a young man in his twenties, but still wearing tan trousers and a white dress shirt.

"Ed, I gotta ask: What's with the face?" Ernestine asked.

"You remember me as being eighty," Edward said, taking quick steps to his chair in the middle of the room. "This is what I looked like when I was in my twenties."

"Oh," Ernestine said as he sat down in his chair and looked up at her. "You were handsome back then."

"Thank you," Ed said, raising an eyebrow before returning his attention to Garrett. "You seem like a smart man, Garrett. You already know getting into Freenet was a test and what it was for."

Garrett blushed. "I could be wrong, but I thought it was to find out just how smart we are."

"Exactly," Ed said, pointing at him, "and my former abode in Namibia was where I permanently entered this world and left behind my mortal coil, but not everyone could figure that out and where to go next without good analytical skills, which you demonstrated."

"And, the prostitute measured our compassion for others, even one made of ones and zeros."

"Which you also passed," Edward said.

"Uh," Garrett said, scratching the back of his head, "not all of us. I wanted to destroy him to get the information. Everyone else didn't."

"Oh," Ed said, narrowing his eyes at Garrett, causing him to shrink where he stood. "Didn't pass, huh?"

"I know what you're going to say," Garret said, lowering his head. "I don't belong here."

"What I was going to say," Ed said, his features softening, "was that you learned a lesson and you had three friends to help you realize which choice was the right one, in the end."

"He did," Ernestine said, looking down at him with a bright smile.

"Then there was the conundrum in the Star Lore battle simulator," Ed stated. "That was to test if you could think outside of the box."

"What about that expensive lute?" Mason interjected.

"That was to see how serious a gamer you are."

"Edward," Ernestine said, rolling her eyes.

"Well, all of those first tests were to make sure that some moron with an Ed fixation didn't come through that door, but I also wanted someone I liked. So, I made sure that whoever got here appreciates games as much as I do," he said, shrugging.

"He did end up paying a lot of money in that game to prove it to you."

"Oh yes," Edward said, looking at Mason with a smile. "Want your money back, do you?"

"Well," Mason said, "it is just virtual money."

"No, it isn't," Edward said, scoffing. "I know it means something to you because it would mean something to me, too. It represents countless hours scouring dungeons for treasure and fighting dragons! Don't worry, by the end of the hour, you'll have your million back plus a little more for your trouble."

Mason chuckled. "Just like if I completed a regular quest."

"It's the least I can do."

"Ed," Ernestine said, taking his smooth hand into hers, "why do all of this? You could have lived a few more years in the real world."

"A few more?" Edward repeated, bringing her hand to his cheek and closing his eyes. "A few more years might have been worth it if it was spent with you, but I was ninety, Ern, and by then every day could be your last and you become acutely aware of it. I could have lived a few more years, but I would have died and there is always more to do. You know me—"

"You won't be finished until the world ends," Ernestine interjected, shaking thoughts of tears from her head.

"If you're lucky," Edward said. He opened his eyes and looked up into hers. "There's always more to do and I needed more time. Here, days pass by like hours in the real world. Here, I will never age and I knew someone might come looking for my help. There are things I've done that I regret—"

"Everybody has regrets," Ernestine assured him as he let go of her hand and stood up.

"My regrets can destroy entire worlds," Edward whispered, looking deeply into her eyes. "So, I did this."

"I'm glad you did," Mason said, speaking up. "Someone did stumble on that FBI database and now they're taking over people's bodies and minds."

"And he's starting to take over the vU, as well," Edward said, keeping his gaze fixed on Ernestine.

"How did you know?" Zahra asked, taking a few books off a nearby couch to sit down.

"It's buried there in the code, if you know where to look. The deaths of my colleagues were a start, but then I noticed some strange behavior on the net by far too many people. It was if they all were of the same mind."

"That's exactly what it was," Garrett said, still standing near the exit.

"I thought so. Come in and sit down," Edward said, looking at the mess around him. "Just dump whatever on the floor or wherever. I know where it all is and it can't get wrinkled or go missing like in the real world."

"How did you notice things were wrong in the vU?" Zahra asked.

"Mindhackers aren't aware of this little fact, but we intentionally embedded a kind of identification mark in the code. I can't track where one of them is, but I can see their 'fingerprints' if they've been somewhere."

"And you saw them somewhere?" Ernestine asked.

"I started to see them everywhere. That person must have been doing this for months now."

"He has," Mason confirmed.

"And he'll be beyond anyone's reach, soon. Tell me, has he already figured out how to manipulate DNA?"

Ernestine thought of the man-turned-monster running across the ocean's surface off the coast of Namibia and grimaced. "Yeah."

"Hmm," Edward said, taking up a position near the center of the room. "You, Agent Washington, have a psychopath on your hands who's going to eventually take over the majority of the population and have complete control of the vU."

"Can't he take over everyone in the population now?" Garrett asked, leaning against one wall of the room.

"You would think so," Edward replied, inclining his head towards him. "It's theoretically possible, but the greater population would inevitably become aware of him and fight back."

"What happens then?" Zahra asked.

"A war unparalleled to anything anyone's ever seen in all of history. We're talking about more than soldiers and tanks and missiles, do you understand? No, children will be fighting parents inside their own homes? Someone like this—"

"Moloch," Mason interjected. "His name's Moloch."

"The Canaanite God who demands a great sacrifice? And usually children, at that. How appropriate," Edward said, nodding. "Well, this Moloch will escalate matters very quickly. Whole cities will fall under missile barrages and hundreds of warships will hit the bottom of the ocean. Eventually, countries controlled by Moloch would launch nuclear attacks on others still largely independent of his influence. It will be a war of billions against a single person."

"I hoped we could make you understand how big our problem is," Mason said, taking a seat on a paper-covered chair. "Now I see it's way worse than I ever thought it could be."

"Well, it wasn't my intention to demoralize you or my ex-wife," Edward said, returning to his seat. "Quite the opposite. I wanted you to know just how much is at stake."

"Mission accomplished," Garrett interjected. "I think I just left a puddle on your floor."

Ed chuckled and placed two fingers at his temple. "Yes, I can see why Ern likes you. As to this Moloch: I became aware of his existence a while ago but didn't know who he was or what his intentions were until recently, but even then I had to wait for someone to come along with information from the real world, something I couldn't get on my own."

"What do you need?" Ernestine asked.

"What I need is to access the mind of one of his victims so that I can begin work on a virus to take Moloch down."

"I'm not sure how we're going to do that," Ernestine said.

"I was almost a victim of his, but I guess that doesn't count," Mason remarked.

Edward's eyes sparkled and he jumped to his feet, taking slow, cautious steps towards Mason, but with an intrigued smile on his face. "Almost a victim?"

"Yes," Mason replied, watching his feet as they slowly advanced towards him.

"He did invade your mind?"

"Yeah," Mason replied, with Edward now just a few feet away.

"Perfect!" Edward exclaimed, clapping his hands a single time. "You have just what I need!"

"But," Mason said, taking a step back, "he's not in my head anymore. I did manage to get him out of there."

"And I bet it wasn't easy," Edward said, "but I don't need him to be in someone's head, you see. I just need someone who still has the remnants of the code he used to get in there."

"Will it hurt?" Mason asked.

"No," Edward replied, standing in front of him. He raised a hand and motioned it towards Mason. "May I?"

"Okay, I guess."

Edward moved his hand through Mason's head. He shivered but didn't move for the second it took for Edward's hand to complete its journey.

"Now, that wasn't so bad, was it?" Ed asked, turning away.

"It was a little uncomfortable."

"And it's over now," Edward said, moving to a large table with a holographic workshop on it. Transparent cubes with numbers floating across them hovered in the space above the worktable. "Now I can get started." He placed his hand in the holo-workshop and touched one of the cubes. The cube turned from blue to red and a matrix of numbers floated inside it. "It will take some time, but I believe that I can make a virus to keep him out of everyone's heads in a day or two."

"What about the vU?" Mason asked.

"Ah," Edward replied, clapping his hands again, "that's not as easy to fix, but first thing's first." A screen on his display flashed and turned red, causing a frown to appear on the centenarian's face. "Oh, that's not good."

"What?" Ernestine asked.

"This Moloch of yours is moving faster than I anticipated. I planted several alarms around Freenet that would only get tripped if they were in danger."

"One of them got tripped?" Garrett asked. He left his place at the wall and moved closer to the display.

"All of them did. An attack on Freenet is imminent. I need someone to warn them. I can't without revealing myself to far too many people."

"We'll help, but I'm not sure what we can do," Mason said. "We've been trying to fend off Moloch online and haven't had much luck."

"It usually involves a lot of running," Garrett said.

"I can help you with that," Edward said, a smile reappearing on his face. "I may not have a physical body anymore, but I've got a lot of cheats."

"So do I," Garrett said, sighing. "Everybody does."

"Do yours work everywhere on the vU?"

Garrett straightened. "Everywhere?"

"No matter where you go, these will work," Edward replied. He took a transparent, blue ball the size of a baseball from the top of his desk. The orb had tiny lines of three-dimensional code glittering within it. He tapped the ball thrice and three identical copies of the ball popped out of it. Edward threw one at each of the other people in the room. The moment it hit their chests, the digital ball vanished. "Good, now all you have to do is think of what cheat you want to use and it will happen."

"Really?" Garrett asked, arching an eyebrow at him.

"Why not give it a try?"

Garrett pulled a Tommy Gun out of thin air and smiled while he cocked it. "Nice!"

Mason waved his hand across the air in front of him and an entire cabinet full of heavy weapons popped into existence. "Not bad."

Ernestine looked at the wall and a door appeared in it. "This could be useful."

"Ern!" Edward exclaimed. "That's my wall!" He walked over to the door, touched it with an index finger and the exit vanished back to where it had come from. "I just had that painted."

"No you didn't," Ernestine said, taking him by the hand.

"You're just as much of a matriarch as you ever were."

"That's news to you?"

"And just as beautiful and intelligent," Edward said, placing a hand on her cheek.

"You're so full of shit," Ernestine said, blushing.

"At any rate," Edward stated, withdrawing his hand. "It's best to have you on your way. Freenet could be invaded in as little as an hour. You need to evacuate them before that happens."

"Ed," Ernestine said, "even if they are invaded, they're not really here. They're not in any real danger, are they?"

"No, but you should know by now that Moloch could block their exit from Freenet."

Zahra looked at Mason, an image of the glass floor in the Wide World of Porn giving way beneath them in her mind. "He did that to us already."

"And he'll do it again. There are hundreds of them and Moloch could put them through hours, even days of the worst pain imaginable before they found their way out. That could be enough to leave them permanently traumatized in the real world, or worse."

"Then we should go right now," Mason said.

"Good luck," Edward said. "Come back and see me once you're done and say hi to Ray for me."

"How do we get back?" Mason asked.

"Just say 'Dead Ed' to my avatar out there and you'll get back."

"I want to go to vMaps," Mason said, vanishing from sight a moment later.

Ernestine and Zahra gave the same command and disappeared as well. Garrett watched them vanish and regarded Edward. "I've got so many questions."

"I know," Edward said, a faint smile on his lips. "I promise we'll get to every last one of them in time."

Garrett nodded. "I want to go to vMaps."

Edward waited for him to leave his world and then rushed back to his table and its virtual workshop, where he began a new program that would take days to complete.

Chapter Eleven

"Where's the nearest child's closet?" Zahra asked, looking at the skyscrapers of New York surrounding them like the bars of a jail cell.

"You think I know?" Mason replied.

Ernestine's eyes jumped from one tower to another. "That one! It's a high-rise."

"Go!" Zahra exclaimed. The group of four rushed past a woman frozen in time, flinching as a wave of water created by a taxi took forever to hit her. Long raindrops were suspended in the air and a thin fog surrounded everything. They ran through the entrance of a tall, blue skyscraper in the frozen landscape, past the lobby, and up the stairs to the second floor.

"Here," Garrett said, spotting a toy that had been accidentally left outside one of the condominiums. His three companions gathered around a mustard door with a steel letter and number spelling out '2B'. Zahra took the lead and opened the door, which led into a white corridor with a small, silver chandelier casting cold light across a reflective hardwood floor.

The corridor opened out onto an expansive, open-concept kitchen and living area. Zahra looked to her right and left, spotting the main bedroom with the second bedroom opposite it. "Here," she said, taking a quick left into a room with a pale blue carpet, a bed covered in cartoon characters, and a closet door to their right.

"vMaps switch to night view," Garrett said.

The misty light outdoors changed to star-studded night and Zahra opened the door to the child's closet where the Freenet entrance waited for them. Zahra punched in the code, pulled the door open, and ran across the vertigo walkway with the rest of her cadre in close pursuit. Once Zahra arrived at the ivory entrance, she mercilessly banged on it with a clenched fist.

"Ray!" she screamed at the glowing impediment. "Ray!"

"Well, well!" a familiar, disembodied voice exclaimed. "Look who's back!"

"Ray," Ernestine interjected, placing herself in front of the door alongside Zahra. "This is an emergency! Let us in!"

"Okay, okay."

The door clicked open and the four friends rushed through it into the ancient ruins lit by three moons. Ray was just unlocking the iron gate when the intrepid team stopped mere feet from him.

"You guys look winded," he said, pushing open one side of the gate.

"Is everything okay here?" Ernestine inquired, panting for breath.

"Yes," Ray replied, leaning against one of the gate's posts. "Why wouldn't it be?"

"Ed sent us," she said.

"Ed?" Ray repeated, straightening up.

"Ray," Mason said, his eyes flitting about the ruins, "Moloch's on his way right now."

"Shit!" Ray exclaimed, gritting his teeth. He looked around the moonlit sandy field and jumped at the sight of a shadow slowly extending across it. The rest of the group noticed that his eyes had settled on something behind them, turning in time to see the shadow expand to fill the entire area in front of the gates like a pool of black water. Ray turned to the gates and yelled into the ruins: "Pearl Harbor! Pearl Harbor! Damn, my Hide command is down; No one has any protection!"

From the darkness of the great shadow lying in front of them rose scores of dark heads, followed by shoulders, torsos, and eventually feet.

In the pale moonlight, Mason made out eyeless sockets and gnashing teeth. Grey, torn skin glistened in the night.

"Fuck!" he exclaimed. "I hate zombies!"

"What's your contingency plan?" Zahra asked, facing Ray.

He turned back from the gate with a revolver in his hand. "Everyone's armed and ready to fight, but we're not soldiers, Zahra."

"Then you need to evacuate. We'll buy you time, but you're going to have to hurry."

"We've already started," Ray said before eyeing the four people around him. "What exactly are you going to do to slow them down?"

Garrett pulled a Tommy Gun out of thin air and aimed it at the zombies who were now lumbering towards the gate and shrieking like a crush of banshees. "This!" he exclaimed and began to empty the clip on the approaching horde. Limbs were blown off the undead army, but they kept coming.

"You're supposed to aim for their heads," Mason said.

"I'm trying! Do you know how hard it is to aim these things?" Garrett said before three of the horde dropped from multiple bullets impacting their craniums. "Now, that's more like it."

"Cheats," Zahra explained to Ray's questioning eyes.

"Oh."

"You can leave this to us," Zahra said, pulling a contemporary pistol from her pocket. She aimed at one of the zombies and squeezed the trigger. The explosive round blew the zombie's head apart.

"I'll stay and help," Ray said, firing at one of the undead. "I have a few tricks up my sleeve."

"If you want," Mason said, taking a futuristic weapon reminiscent of a double-barreled percussion pistol from his breast pocket. He aimed at one of their enemies and fired a bright energy pulse at them, causing their heads to vaporize. The headless zombie stopped advancing and fell to the sandy ground.

"That's not fair," Garrett said, looking over his shoulder at Mason.

"Hey," Mason said, smiling, "we can use whatever we want with these cheats, so why not use a few weapons from Star Lore?"

"Yeah," Ernestine said, taking a step towards the horde now within a short distance of the gate. "Like something from a fantasy game, right?" she asked and then threw a fireball into the center of the crowd of undead. It started as a small firework but exploded into a firestorm the moment it hit the ground. The zombies were now all aflame, but still moving forward.

"You gotta—" Mason began.

"Hit them in the head," Ernestine finished, nodding. "I know, I know." She stretched out her hand in front of her and lighting flowed from her fingertips at eye-level with the zombie horde. The lightning chains electrocuted several of their skulls and they fell to the ground, fried.

"Nice," Mason said.

"I always wanted to try that spell," Ernestine said. "I designed the code for Wizards and Warlocks III and never got to play it."

"You did pretty well for a first-timer," Mason commented before shifting his body to take down another member of the undead getting too close to the group.

"They just keep coming," Zahra said as another dozen undead rose from the shadows.

A small, pulsing spark flew into the center of the new additions and flashed a bright light. Where the shamblers had been standing was now empty space. The quartet looked back to where the light had come from to see Ray beaming.

"What was that?" Zahra asked.

"I call it a delete grenade."

Garrett shrugged and turned his attention back to the attacking bodies. "Hey, it delivers what it promises."

As if taking notice of their numbers, Moloch's zombies stopped for a moment, looked into the shadows below them and a hundred more zombies rose into existence.

"We're fucked," Garrett said while attempting to mow down as many attackers as possible with his Tommy Gun.

"We only need to buy another five minutes or so," Mason said before vaporizing the heads of two more of their attackers.

"You got any more of those delete grenades?" Zahra asked.

In response, Ray tossed two more pulsating lights into the fray, making a few dozen more of Moloch's undead vanish from sight. "That's all I've got."

"That helped. We can make do, now," Zahra said.

Ray fired his revolver at another member of the undead before something caught his eye. He looked down to see a shadow cast by the outer wall in the corridor behind him creep across the ground. "Oh, no."

"What?" Zahra asked, keeping her attention on the attackers in front of her.

"I think Garrett's right," Ray replied, watching a handful of eyeless heads rise from the floor behind them. "We're surrounded!"

Zahra looked past Ray, her eyes bulging from their sockets at the sight of the moaning minions. "Everyone, retreat into the ruins! Ray, close and lock that gate. We'll cover you."

Ray fired a virtual bullet into one of the shambler's heads in the hallway and swung on one thick heel. He rushed for the entrance, keys in hand. Zahra and her friends opened up with a storm of fire, both literal and figurative, before retreating from the gates while Ray pulled them shut. The four defenders fired through the gaps while Ray shoved the key into the hole and locked the gate. They turned to confront the few undead behind them as countless more threw themselves at the gates in a frenzy. The motley team turned to watch the army of undead clamoring to get in.

"How tough are those?" Garrett asked with a nod at the wrought iron gates.

"The gates are only as good as the programming behind them. Luckily, I designed it and it's pretty complex. They'll hold for a few more minutes, but those eyeless things are showing up in here now."

"We'll do our best to get them away from your friends," Zahra said, marching into the ruins.

"I don't know if that's enough. Those things are probably popping up everywhere and if they get to any of my people—"

"Then those Moloch monsters could tear them apart for hours or even days."

"And I'm not going to allow any of them to be subjected to that kind of trauma," Ray said, walking towards the first open area in the ruins.

Zahra's audible gasp increased his step. Ray stopped at the edge of the area where pandemonium was unfolding. A hundred of his people were visible and under attack. Zombies lay in the area, bullet holes in their heads, but many more were pulling and ripping at the human beings. Screams filled the air as arms and legs were torn from their sockets, only to be tossed onto the bloodied sand.

"We can't stop all of them and, even if we do, more will rise to take their place," Ray said, his voice breaking, even as Zahra picked off a few more of their attackers with precise shots from her pistol.

"Is there a hub nearby where they can manually exit?" Ernestine asked, staring at the horror in front of her.

"Yes, but they can't use what they can't reach. This is the worst case scenario any of us ever considered," Ray said, looking at the carnage surrounding them. "We can't salvage this. I'm going to have to destroy it all."

"Are you sure?" Zahra asked, turning to face him.

"The only way to force everyone here out of Freenet and back into their homes, their real homes, is to make sure it doesn't exist anymore."

"Leave by a hub in the vWorld or destroy the vWorld to manually eject everyone," Ernestine said, nodding. "You'd have to have the delete command for it. A command console, right?"

"Right," Ray said, tears slipping down his cheek as he looked around at his screaming comrades. "It's just down the hallway, but I won't make it on my own."

"If it ends all of this," Mason said, hitting a few more of the undead around him with his pulse pistol, "then we're right behind you."

Ray motioned with his head to the hallway behind them and the entire group began taking quick, cautious steps towards the exit. The shadow in the partially enclosed hallway moaned and released several more members of the undead, who immediately headed for them.

"You're mine," the dozen undead in front of him said in haunting unison.

"Moloch!" Ray exclaimed before pointing his revolver at one of them and firing a bullet directly into its face. The zombie dropped to the ground, giggling and gurgling.

"What the fuck is with the laughing?" Garrett demanded just before a dozen more of Moloch's shamblers rose from the shadows before them.

All five friends ferociously fired into the fray, causing the shamblers to fall like dominoes. Zahra and her team rushed through the exit and down the shadowy hallway made mad by the midnight moonlight streaming through the open ceiling.

"How much further?" Zahra asked as more of the zombies ascended from the shadows. They stopped and fired before Mason realized that more were coming from behind them. He and Garrett focused their fire on the shambling undead massing at their rear while Zahra and Ernestine fired on the ones in front of them.

Ray fired a few more shots and then clenched his teeth. "It's not more than another twenty feet, but I don't see how we're going to make it."

"You can't!" Moloch's minions hissed through broken teeth. "We will feast on your fearful flesh!"

"God!" Zahra said, rolling her eyes before she blew one of their heads off.

"The cheats," Ernestine whispered through clenched teeth at her.

"We're already using them!" Zahra exclaimed, firing more shots at their adversaries.

"We're using them to make weapons," Ernestine said. "Ray, where's the control room?"

"Just over there," he replied, pointing at a doorway a short ways down the hallway.

"Thanks," Ernestine said, blinking at the empty space in front of her. A red door appeared out of thin air. Mason peeked around it, seeing a second one appear just inside the open doorway they were trying to reach.

"I wish I thought of that," Zahra said, looking from one door to the next.

Ernestine opened it and stepped through. "Come on!"

"You two go first," Garrett said, emptying his Tommy Gun into the growing crowd of undead behind them. Mason and Zahra withdrew from the fight and followed Ernestine through the doorway. Garrett stopped firing and turned towards the door when one of the zombies lunged at him, grabbing him by the shoulder.

"No!" it screamed at him.

Garrett turned around and aimed the gun at his attacker. "Yes!" He unloaded several rounds into the zombie, wrenching himself free of its grip. Garrett came out on the other side in a small room surrounded by stone walls but with an open ceiling, like much of the rest of the structure. He closed the door behind him and it disappeared immediately.

The group heard numerous moans and roars coming from the corridor. Zahra looked at the doorway and then back to Ernestine. "They're going to be here in seconds."

"But they won't be able to get in," she replied. Ernestine blinked at the open doorway and wrought iron bars appeared in it. The zombies flew into the thick bars, empty sockets aghast at the unexpected encumbrance. Arms were shoved through the gaps in the bars in a futile attempt to grab at them.

"You've got a knack for this," Ray remarked.

"Where's the control console?" Ernestine asked.

"Right here," he replied, walking to the opposite wall. He waved a hand across the center of the wall and a large, grey box with a single red button appeared in it.

"You know what they say about red buttons," Ray said, hand hovering over it. He looked at the four people huddled around him and then at the zombies hissing at him from behind the metal bars. "I'm sorry to say this will mean we won't see each other again for a while."

"But we will see each other again," Zahra said. "That's what's important." She placed a hand on his shoulder and nodded.

"Well, at least this will give me a chance to redecorate once all this is over," Ray said. He slapped the button and the entire world around them vanished in a bright flash of white light. They found themselves standing outside the same closet a moment later.

Ernestine opened the door and looked inside. "Just what I thought: nothing. Freenet's gone."

"We shouldn't stay here," Garrett said.

"No," Zahra said, reaching out and closing the closet door. "We should get back to Ed and tell him what happened."

"I want to go to Sword & Sorcery," they said, vanishing from the small bedroom.

They reappeared in the same place as before, just a ways down from the small village of Lothering, with *The Bard's Quest* tavern at its spiritual center. Their style of dress returned to the same as the last time they were there.

The group of friends rushed for the fallen tree near the river. Legs only stopped pumping once a small man in a grey robe jumped at the intrusion.

"Oh!" he said, jumping to his feet, laughter on his lips.

"Yeah, yeah, you didn't see us," Mason said.

"Well, no I didn't."

"Dead Ed."

"I see," De said. His face went blank and the river nearby began to move in both directions.

"Do you see that?" Zahra asked, putting her hand out in front of her to block the sight of the setting sun.

The quartet looked at the river in time to witness a long depression form in the water. Within moments, that section of the river was dry, with a wall of water on either side of it held back by invisible forces.

"Seriously?" Garrett asked. "Ed went ahead and parted the sea?"

"Ed and his friggin' sense of humor," Ernestine replied, taking a long stride towards the corridor. "Let's get going. Something tells me that Moloch is right behind us."

After crossing a hundred feet in silence, Mason looked at the riverbed and then behind him. "Whoa!" he exclaimed at the sight of a wall of water keeping a distance of just ten feet behind the group. The moving wall met the other side of the river just after the foursome marched out of it and onto the green grass. Each step seemed faster than before as they hurried to the front door. Ernestine arrived at the top of the stairs first and knocked on the door.

It opened to the sight of the younger Ed's smiling face. "How'd it all go?"

"Freenet's gone," Ernestine said.

Ed's shoulders sagged and he opened the door wide. "You'd better come in."

They piled past him and Edward slammed the door shut behind them. "Tell me what happened."

"Moloch happened," Mason replied. "He got there right after us. What you thought would happen, did. Ray had to destroy Freenet just to get everyone out."

"Was he torturing them?"

"Yes," Mason replied in a whisper.

Ed walked away from the door and began to pace in front of the large table near the center of the room. "Then Ray did what he had to. Freenet will take a while to get itself back together, but those people got out, hopefully, without too much damage being done."

"I just wish we could've gotten there sooner," Ernestine said.

Ed stopped pacing and regarded her. "I know. Thank you for trying. I want you to know that I've been looking deeper into Moloch and I know who he is now and I have his exact location."

"Then, all we have to do is find the fucker and blow his head off," Garrett said.

"Not so fast," Ed said. "In my online travels I located what I needed to stop Moloch and that requires two things: one, his virtual code, which you provided, Mason."

"And?" Zahra asked.

"I need some of the code from his real-life implant so that I can shut down all of his hosts."

"What do you mean: Shut them down?" Zahra repeated. "They'll go back to normal?"

Edward avoided her brown eyes as he replied, "They'll go into a coma."

"Are you telling me that you want to put… what was it?" Zahra asked, gesturing to Ernestine.

"Three hundred and fifty million," Ernestine said, eyes cast to the floor.

"Three hundred and fifty million people into a coma? Do you have any idea of the kind of chaos that's going to cause?" Zahra demanded, flashing her eyes at Ed.

"I know, but the alternative is to see that number keep going up."

"It's probably closer to four hundred million by now," Ernestine interjected, looking up for a moment.

"Which only makes my point all the clearer," Edward stated, pointing a finger at the floor. "We have to stop him in real life, too, or all of this will start again."

"You want us to kill him?" Zahra inquired.

"No," Ed said, returning to the holographic projection playing above his large worktable. He pointed at long lines of code running down one of the red screens. "I need you to get a copy of the hardcode in his implant."

"Oh, shit!" Mason exclaimed, putting a hand on a nearby windowsill to steady himself. "Do you have any idea how hard that's going to be?"

"What does he mean, Mason?"

"I need it," Ed reiterated, glancing at each of them.

Mason looked at Zahra with a sullen face. "Most of the information you'd want from anyone is somewhere on the vU, but there's one thing that you can only get from them in person and that's the hardcode wired directly into their implant. It's not published anywhere."

"So?"

"So," Mason replied, looking her in the eye, "the hardcode that Ed needs is in Moloch's implant, as in the one in his actual, real-life head."

Zahra stared at Ed. "Is that true?"

"I'm afraid so," he replied, turning his back to her to look at the screens above his table. "It's the only way to stop him, Zahra. I appreciate your concern for the hundreds of millions of people that will suddenly need medical help not to mention entire countries that will have all of their resources strained far past their limits, but it will still save lives in the end."

Zahra held the bridge of her nose between two fingers and squeezed her eyes shut. The room was silent while Zahra considered their options. She shook her head and opened her eyes. "I guess we don't have much of a choice."

"We could let them die," Garrett interjected. "Nothing survives of the host, right?" There was an immediate din following his words which Ed refrained from. Instead, he looked between the four arguing friends with an intrigued expression. Garrett took in a deep breath and shouted everyone down. "Hey! I didn't say that I liked it, but it is an option. If what Moloch says is true, they'll just be empty husks for the rest of their lives."

"I'm not going to take the chance that Moloch is actually telling the truth," Zahra said, crossing her arms. "What I am going to do is go with Mason and stop Moloch in person."

"His real name is actually Theodore Manson. He supposedly vanished about a year ago. According to the FBI, he's still technically missing," Ed said, gazing again at the holographic readouts above his worktable.

"The FBI has a file on him?" Zahra asked.

"Oh, yes," Ed said, turning from the desk. He took a manila folder from its surface and handed it to Zahra. She perused the virtual papers within it while he continued. "Ted Manson, aged thirty-one at the time of his disappearance. The FBI suspected him in the death of one Benny Carter, his handler."

Mason's head snapped up. "Benny Carter?"

"Yes," Ed asked, looking at him with bright eyes, "you knew him?"

"He was my handler before I joined the FBI," Mason said, turning his attention to Zahra. "It was right before I started working with you."

Ed walked over to his chair and sat down. He placed a finger on his temple and looked up at Mason. "Can that be a coincidence?"

"I don't know," Mason replied, hesitantly.

"Did you change to Zahra as a partner because your handler had other duties?"

"No. He wanted me to be his partner," Mason said, looking at the floor. "I wasn't comfortable working with him and asked for my partner to be someone new."

Ed followed his gaze to the floor and then back to his eyes. He leaned forward and cocked his head towards Mason's lowered face. "May I ask why you weren't comfortable working with him anymore?"

"He's the guy who gave me the mind-job where I ended up lobotomizing John Tate," Mason replied.

"Does Moloch know that you share a common thread?" Ed asked.

"Sort of. He saw John in my head. I guess you could say that there's a kind of shrine to him in my innermind."

"A shrine?" Garrett asked. "You knew him that well?"

"Hardly knew him at all, but what happened to him was my fault and that shrine is to remind me to stay human for the rest of my life."

"I didn't think you weren't human," Ed said, straightening his lean figure. "But it does prove that you are, just like the rest of us."

"Is there any connection between the two?" Zahra asked.

Ed searched Mason's eyes before he responded. "Some people think there are no such things as coincidences. I believe that the word came into being for a reason. In this case, however, it seems too convenient to be one. No, you two are connected somehow."

Mason looked up and met Ed's searching stare. "That's what I'm afraid of."

Ed's smile thinned. "Me, too."

"What else was in his FBI file?" Zahra inquired, taking a spot next to Mason and holding up the thick manila folder.

Ed glanced at him and then looked carefully at Zahra and Mason's faces while he responded. "The FBI investigated him thoroughly when they considered recruiting him. As a toddler he burned another child with a lighter multiple times. That got my attention."

"Some toddlers don't understand that they're hurting others sometimes," Garrett said. The dark lenses of his sunglasses reflected the soft lights of a rustic, five-armed chandelier hanging from the ceiling.

"Yes. An easy explanation and one bought at the time except for one case worker who claimed he was 'sociopathic'."

"What happened then?" Zahra asked, narrowing her eyes at him.

"Ted didn't improve in elementary school, not at all. He was in numerous fights that resulted in the police being called because of just how far he would take those little quarrels of his. Ted was then sent from school to school and things only got worse from there."

"There's the sound of the other shoe dropping," Garrett said with a wry smile.

"In high school, he was arrested for assault three times, one of them serious enough for stronger charges to be pressed, but the school went easy on him. Influential parents, you understand. Then, he tried to burn the school down. Again, his parents stopped anything serious from happening to our dear Ted.

"After that, he was disinherited and estranged from his wealthy, reputable family. I'm not sure of the specifics but it had something to do with an assault and a restraining order taken out by his parents. The first thing he did was to sign up as a mindhacker," Ed said, shifting his eyes between their faces. "You know, that old story."

Zahra listened to the tale while flipping through the pages in the folder one by one, her eyes searching every sentence for answers. Now, she looked up at Ed with raised eyebrows. "Was a psychological assessment ever done?"

"Ah," Ed replied, leaning back in his chair with a smile, "good question! You'd be surprised how many people wouldn't think to ask that. Yes, the FBI did a psychological analysis of him the moment he stepped foot on the premises."

"And?"

"He passed with flying colors," Ed responded, getting up and grabbing a piece of paper from the desk. "Did quite well. A little too well. The psych staff decided to observe him secretly on the job because they had suspicions that their subject had a high I.Q., but was possibly psychopathic. Amazingly, he managed to pass that test, too and there was never another question." He handed the sheet to Zahra, who snatched it from his grasp and began to read it as soon as she could get it oriented correctly. "It's quite the read. Bestseller, if you ask me, because it's all fiction."

"What do you mean?" Ernestine asked, having taken a seat near his.

"None of the conclusions you see on that sheet are the truth," Ed said, pointing at it. He grabbed a mug from the table, drank the last sip from it, and then returned it to the tabletop. "No, he was too clever, that one. Our dear Ted managed to fool a formal investigation and, when they tried something a little more subtle, he recognized what was going on and showed them exactly what they wanted to see."

"So, what's your assessment?" Ernestine asked.

Edward turned a serious eye to her. "I think you're dealing with a psychopath with a genius level I.Q. One who has a penchant for murder and cruelty because those are the only two emotions that make him feel anything at all. I don't envy you having to meet him in person."

"But," Ernestine said, getting up from her chair, "we're going to have to."

"Yes, and the sooner you deal with him the better."

"Even with my enhanced abilities," Mason said, "I was barely able to hold him off last time."

"Which is why you need to enhance them a bit more," Ed said, taking a translucent ball from his pocket. "This will bring you up to the same level of physical manipulation as Moloch and then some."

He tossed the ball at Mason, which disappeared the moment it hit his body. "I can defeat him with this?" Mason asked, looking down at the spot where the ball had vanished into his chest.

"Let's hope so. This is a full manipulation of your DNA this time and not a minor bit of tinkering. So, it will take about an hour to reach its full effect. Better not to put the Superman outfit on 'till then.

"Oh, I also just gave you the retrieval program that will access Moloch's implant and obtain the code I need. There's one more thing:

A bit of a bonus that comes automatically with the completion of your task."

"What bonus?" Zahra asked.

"I need to make sure that our dear Moloch returns to his former self. Even without his hosts and the vU, he could still be a danger on his own. The retrieval program will have a piggyback virus on it that will start the regeneration of his original DNA. Within an hour at most, he will be plain, old simple Ted again."

"How long, exactly?" Mason asked. "He could be a real problem if he's still got all that strength and speed."

"Don't worry," Edward said, a smile on his face. "You'll see a drop of about half his speed and strength within minutes, but he'll still be unusually strong and fast. Be careful."

"That makes things a little easier."

"How far away is he?" Zahra asked, raising an eyebrow. "If it's in another country we might have a hard time getting a plane this time."

"You're in luck," Ed said, snatching another piece of paper from his desk and handing it to Zahra, who copied it and sent it to her vPhone in real life. "He's less than fifty miles away from your current whereabouts. Here's the address."

"Another coincidence," Mason said, looking at Ed, who smiled in response.

"Which is very convenient given what you two already share," Ed said, straightening up. "No, he's less than fifty miles away from you because he's looking for you."

"That's impossible!" Garrett exclaimed. "My place is untraceable!"

"For the average person, yes, but this is no average man. I don't think he's compromised your cloak of invisibility just yet, but he's getting closer. You'd better get going before he narrows your location down even further."

"It can't be," Garrett said, shaking his head.

"We're going to need to come up with a plan on how to get in there, not to mention getting all the details on the place," Mason said.

"The plan is up to you," Ed said, opening the door. "The details I can help with. A phone number is on the back of the address I gave you. Call me when you want to talk shop."

"We'd better be going," Ernestine said. "Exit vU."

Chapter Twelve

The quartet's eyes snapped open and they were on their feet a split second later.

"Shit!" Garrett exclaimed, rushing to his chair. He plunged into its leather comfort, sitting ramrod straight.

"Is anything wrong?" Ernestine asked while she and the others crowded around his desk.

"Nothing's been set off, yet," Garrett replied. "I'm bringing up all of my live feeds on here," he said, reaching into the monitor's holographic projection. The black market guru brought up a dozen camera feeds across it.

Mason looked at the images and sighed. "Nothing."

"Yeah, yet," Garrett said. "I don't think we should wait for them to get here, though."

"I'll get the car ready," Mason said.

"No, we'll use the tunnel," Garrett replied, looking across the room at the hidden door in the wall. "It's probably going to be the only time I get to."

Garrett went to type the necessary commands into the computer when the holographic screen in front of him began to flash and flicker.

His hands fluttered across the typewriter-style keyboard before he hit the top of the table with both fists. "I've got no control over anything!"

"What the…?" Mason asked when a new sound came from the monitors.

"Mason?" a distorted voice asked.

"Who's this?"

"It's not supposed to be anyone," Garrett replied, shaking his head. "This place is untraceable!"

"Mind Mutilator Mason Deane? And that must be Garrett Cho, Mob Meat and Mason Masturbator," the voice said.

"What?" both of them demanded, frowning at the blank monitor.

"It's a male voice," Ernestine said, leaning closer to the monitor, "and it sounds cruel. I think Moloch just found us."

"And the wagon-burner! Her Indian Name must be: 'Likes her men old and dead'! Dig 'lotta gold today, Chief?" the voice sneered. "The only one missing is that trans-trash-used-to-be-a-man-and-is-now-a-woman trailer trick."

"You son of a bitch!" Ernestine bit out while Zahra took a step back from the table. The monitor returned to its standard green, but a three-dimensional face came from it, still sneering at Zahra.

The visage, itself, was one that anyone might have walked past on a crowded street and never noticed. Dark hair framed brown eyes, an average nose, lips and chin. He was a completely nondescript man until he smiled cruelty.

"Does everyone know that you used to have a prick, you pussy?" demanded Moloch through a curled lip.

"Fuck you, T—" Zahra began before Mason shook his head and put an index finger over his closed lips.

"What was that, Moron Mason? Thinking of banging fake pussy?"

Mason sighed and crossed his arms. "How do you know so much about us?"

"That thing called the vU, moron. Tell me: what was lobotomizing a man like for you? Is that why you have a prison in that innermind of yours? Thinking, maybe, that jail is what you deserve? I've done millions now and I can tell you there's something really satisfying about it. It's almost as good as killing someone in real life, but far more gratifying to personally snuff out their minds. Did you know that there are pain centers in the brain you can't find with a scalpel or a sledgehammer?" he replied, looking at the four faces around him.

"Are you trying to scare us?" Ernestine asked, putting her hands on her hips. "Does that bit work with anybody?"

"Aww," the face said, pouting its lips, "did I hurt the little squaw's feelings?"

"Squaw!" Ernestine roared.

"He's just trying to get under your skin, Ern," Mason said, taking a step toward the monitor. "Don't let him. Moloch doesn't just try to get into your head with nanobots."

"Oh," Moloch said, turning his face to him, "thought you were being insightful, eh mind-job, or should I say hack-job?"

"You really hurt my feelings," Mason replied in a monotone. Ernestine slipped away from the computer and sat at one of the other terminals in the spacious room.

"And you're not even half as smart as you like to think you are."

"Takes one to know one," Garrett said out of the corner of his mouth.

"Hey," Moloch's face said, as it turned in Garrett's direction, "I hear you're going to wake up one day with your balls in your mouth! How about I let your old castration comrades know where you are, huh? Maybe they want to do a little bit of free surgery tonight? I'd hate to be the one to break this to you, but you're chances of making it through this one are not so good."

Garrett took a few steps back from the computer monitor and swallowed, which didn't stop Moloch's verbal attack on the man.

"That shut you up, huh? Do you think your little bonk-the-bros basement is invisible? I bet your mafia buddies will have a whole list of things to do to you when I give them a little more on your background."

"I've had just about enough of you," Zahra said, taking a step toward the monitor.

"And I don't want any of you!" Moloch exclaimed, scrunching his nose. "You're not a man or a woman, anymore. You're just an it."

"You're just a distraction, Moloch," Zahra said, a smug smile spreading across her face. "I know you get off on these little games you like to play, but there's something else there isn't there?" Zahra asked while Garrett joined Ernestine at their terminal in the corner of the room. "You're just buying time, aren't you?"

Moloch didn't reply, but a slow grin spread across his face.

Zahra nodded and crossed her arms. "Yeah, I thought so."

"Got him!" Ernestine exclaimed from her desk. The image of Moloch winked out and was replaced by the feeds from the remote cameras. "He was just buying time to find us, which means that he had to have put a tracer on one of us. Did the zombies touch any of you?"

Garrett raised a hand and grimaced. "One of the zombies grabbed me just before I went through that door in Freenet. He must've tagged me then."

"Guys," Zahra said, leaning in to peer at the live camera feeds, "we've got company."

The other members of her team gathered around her and spotted a car turning into the driveway of Garrett's bunker. It stopped at the entrance, positioning itself to block the exit. Several men dressed in dark suits with silk shirts got out and took slow steps down the path, pistols in hand.

"The Ciccios?" Zahra asked, looking up at Garrett.

"I'd bet my life on it."

"You kinda are," Mason remarked, raising his eyebrows at him.

"Time to turn on the defenses," Garrett said, rushing to another computer.

"Can't Moloch just turn them off?" Zahra asked, taking a pistol from her holster.

"No," Garrett replied, tapping commands into an older computer standing against the back wall. "This computer is on a closed system. No vU. The only thing it does is control the area around here."

They heard a bang in the background and one of the camera feeds emitted a bright light and went dark.

"Was that an explosion?" Zahra asked.

"A little C-4," Garrett responded. "No big deal."

"How did you get your hands on C-4?" Mason asked with an incredulous expression on his face.

"I deal with the Black Market!" Garrett replied, keeping his eyes on the computer. "That took out two of them, but there's six more. They must've taken two cars to get here and they probably have a lookout in both."

"Can you take care of it, or should we make a break for it?" Mason asked.

"I think I got it," Garrett replied, watching as another pair of assassins shot a camera, making its feed disappear from the screen. "That one was about a hundred feet away." He brought up a map of the house and the surrounding area. Garrett tapped one section of it, which turned red and flashed. "Wait for it." A second later, there was another bang and the sound of yelling. "Got them," Garrett said, shaking a fist.

"Wait," Zahra said, pointing at one live image showing four people walking past it. "Isn't that right outside of the house?"

"Crap!" Garrett said, tapping the house and turning it red. "I don't believe it! They let four of their own men die just to distract me. That's not the Ciccios' style."

"Maybe it's not the Ciccios who are giving the orders," Zahra suggested.

"Do you think that Moloch's controlling them?"

"At this point, he could have people everywhere," Ernestine said, taking a Taser from her purse.

"Yeah," Mason said, taking out his pistol.

Everyone watched as the four henchmen moved through the house, shooting the cameras. When one pair reached the kitchen, a loud bang came from above and the floorboards shook, sending dust and dirt onto the concrete floor nearby.

"That's the first two," Garrett said. He pointed at a camera feed of the filthy bathroom the last pair of henchmen had just walked into. He pressed a button on the keyboard, the camera flashed and the feed was lost. Another bang shook the ceiling above them. "That's the last two." A distant alarm in the house went off moments later. "I think those last two started a fire."

"Then we better get out of here."

"I'll open the emergency exit into the tunnel," Garret said, returning to his primary terminal.

"What about the lookouts in the cars?" Zahra asked.

"Those lookouts are sitting in a couple of cars alone," Garrett said, taking a gun from where he had taped it to the bottom of his desk. "The car I've hidden isn't anywhere near them."

"Sounds good," Zahra said before a new, impossible sound came from above them.

Thump… thump… thump…

"Footsteps?" Ernestine asked, lowering her voice.

"One of the lookouts?" Zahra whispered, looking up at the ceiling. They could hear a crackling sound and the faint smell of burning paper.

"I don't think so," Garrett replied. "They wouldn't be so stupid as to follow the guys who disappeared."

"Whoever they are, they're almost at the bathroom."

They listened as the footsteps got louder and then abruptly stopped. Thin coils of smoke began to appear between the narrow cracks in the floorboards above and the smell of burning insulation and plaster began to find its way to their nostrils.

Zahra, along with the others, aimed their weapons at the staircase. The heavy sound of the metal door opening came from the top of the stairs and the footsteps began again, but this time, they were accompanied by the sight of army boots and fatigues coming into view. Three pistols followed the boots until a soldier arrived at the bottom of the staircase and turned its head.

"My God!" Zahra exclaimed at the sight of a face with empty eye sockets and grey skin. It looked at them and smiled broken teeth.

"DNA manipulation," Mason breathed.

"Mason!" the zombie exclaimed in a long, gurgling drawl.

Their moment of shock was interrupted by the sounds of dozens more boots pounding across the floor above. Mason shot the guard twice through the chest, but the ghoulish man didn't even appear to take notice.

"Can you take them?" Zahra asked him.

Mason shook his head. "It takes an hour, remember? The enhancements I have right now aren't enough against one of these guys, let alone a whole platoon."

The drooling zombie cackled at Mason's response and turned his head to stare with eyeless sockets at Garrett, who was nearest him and still standing at his terminal. Garrett fired his pistol, hitting nothing but air as the strange, shambling man moved faster than any human being could. In a fraction of a second, he had already smacked the pistol from Garret's grip. More boots marched down the steps. Garrett typed the last word into his keyboard while Mason and Zahra fired more shots into the soldier's head, finally bringing him down.

The wall behind them opened and the secret tunnel was exposed, albeit only briefly. Garrett managed only a few steps towards them before more Moloch monsters mobbed him.

He stared at them for a moment, hope lost in his eyes. "Go!" Garrett exclaimed, and when they didn't move, his expression hardened. "NOW!"

Zahra and Mason took a few steps into the exit, but Ernestine stayed where she was. "Garrett!"

He opened his mouth again to speak, but one of the soldiers surrounding him grabbed him by the head with an iron grip and placed his knuckles near his face. Three tiny tubules appeared from between them and punctured the soft tissue at his temple. Garrett whimpered and went limp seconds later. Orange flames from above lit the room in an eerie glow and smoke began to choke their throats.

"The host never survives," the platoon of undead hissed at him as his eyes closed.

"Garrett, NO!" Ernestine screamed at the growing military body in the room.

"We've got to go," Zahra said, grabbing her.

Ernestine yanked her arm away and watched helplessly as one of the soldiers picked Garrett up and threw him over his shoulder. The Moloch host ignored trails of flame as he marched up the stairs with their unconscious friend. The movement caused Garrett's sunglasses to fall from his face, its lenses smashing across the floor. The last sight of him was his bobbing shoes just before they disappeared.

"Garrett! GARRETT!"

Mason grabbed Ernestine by both arms and yanked her back just as the entrance to the tunnel started to close. Now that Garrett had been removed from the room, the soldiers turned their attention to the trio vanishing behind a closing door.

Zahra was still firing at them when a single arm flew from the closing crack in the door and began using its brute strength to force it open. Mason let Ernestine go and took out his pistol, firing two shots into the shoulder of the super-strong soldier, taking his arm off with the explosive bullets. There was an angry scream and the door closed with the appendage lying on the floor in front of them.

"Garrett!" Ernestine screamed at the door.

The only response was the sound of fists banging on metal.

"Ern," Mason said, putting his pistol back in its holster. "We've got to go."

"We need to get Garrett!" she exclaimed over her shoulder. Ernestine placed a hand on the door and sobbed.

Mason slowly shook his head at Zahra. His partner walked up behind her and gently placed a hand on Ernestine's shoulder. She put her other hand on the door and withdrew it a fraction of a second later. "The door's already hot. Mason's right. We can't help Garrett right now. Those soldiers banging on the door right now are probably on fire. We need to go."

"We need to get Garrett before Moloch takes him as a host," Ernestine said, taking her eyes off the door for a moment.

"They already have," Zahra said, her voice breaking.

"No, not Garrett!"

"Come on," Zahra said, taking her by the hand and leading her into the corridor.

The trio jogged down the narrow tunnel with only small LED lights to guide them. They moved at a quick pace, but they did so in silence for their fallen comrade. It was only once they found the car Garrett had intentionally left near the exit and were on their way toward parts unknown that Zahra spoke up.

"Did you see their uniforms?" she asked, keeping her eyes on the road, despite it being a self-driving electric car.

"What?" Mason asked, coming out of a daze to look her way.

"Those Moloch soldiers or whatever you want to call them. The uniforms they were wearing were from the same division that helped us in Alabama," Zahra replied, still looking through the windshield. "Those things were the soldiers that helped us just a few days ago. Now what are they?"

Mason paused and found himself looking out of the windshield, as well. "I don't know."

"I remember thinking at the time that some of those boys looked so young. Enlisted, you know? Couldn't have been more than eighteen or nineteen."

"Half of them, at least."

"Now they're gone," Zahra said, finding her voice break, "and so is Garrett."

"How can you say that?" Ernestine demanded in a hoarse voice. Her eyes were pink and her makeup was running down her cheeks. "He was your friend!"

"I say it because he was my friend," Zahra said, putting her face in the palms of her hands, "and I just got him killed."

"That's not your fault," Mason stated.

"Yeah? Whose fault is it?"

Mason put an arm around her shoulder. "Moloch's. He's trying to manipulate us all. He'd want you to believe that. Garrett wouldn't."

"Tell me we're going to get him," Ernestine said.

"You know we are," Zahra stated, taking her hands away from her wet face.

"No," Ernestine said, moving into the space between the two forward bucket seats. The shadows in the car left only her face visible and she stared, unblinking into Zahra's eyes. "That's not good enough. I need to know that we're going to get him. I need to see it in your eyes."

"We are going to get him," Zahra said, staring back into Ernestine's face. "For Garrett and for Tommy."

"There are a lot more people involved here than just them now. He's got millions of lives to pay for. Millions."

"You're right," Zahra said. "We will bring him to justice."

"Justice?" Ernestine repeated. "Justice? I've seen what justice means: There are six cops out there who were suspended with pay for six months for murdering my entire family! That's justice!" she exclaimed, tears finding their way down her cheeks. "Moloch's going to pay. Say you're going to make him pay!"

Zahra nodded and took both of Ernestine's hands in hers. "He's a war criminal now and he is going to pay dearly for what's he's done."

Ernestine gripped Zahra's hands tightly, nodded and then vacated the position between them. She collapsed into her bucket seat at the back of the car and stared out into the darkness lurking on the other side of the window.

"How did he know so much about us?" Zahra asked. "And, don't tell me he got all of that online."

"That's what he told us, but it can't be true. Moloch's found his way into databases he shouldn't be able to access."

"Jesus!" Zahra said, slapping her forehead with the palm of her hand. "Of course! By now, he probably has access to the FBI and CIA databases and God knows what else."

Mason took out his pistol and checked the magazine. "How much ammo do you have left?"

"Not enough."

"Same here," Mason said, checking the number of explosive bullets he had left in the pistol's magazine. "I wish I didn't have to say this, but Moloch can take over someone's mind in as little as forty-five minutes."

"Not with Garrett," Ernestine said, her voice box raw. "He'll give him one hell of a fight."

"I'm counting on it," Mason said, slapping the magazine back into his gun. "Because, once Moloch's taken over his mind, he'll know we're coming for him. We've got an hour, at most, before Moloch sounds the alarms."

"He liked you, you know," Ernestine said, looking at him with a wistful smile.

"I liked him, too."

"No," Ernestine said, shaking her head. "I mean he *really* liked you."

"Oh," Mason said, looking at her from the corner of his eye. "Why did he insult me all of the time, then?"

"It's his way."

"Wow," Mason said, smiling and looking out of the windshield. "I should've known that was all just banter."

"Don't think you missed something. He wasn't great at making new friends."

"You know if it wasn't for," Mason began before the rest of his sentence died on his lips. He glanced at Zahra. "I just wish I had gotten to know him better."

"Where are we going?" Zahra asked.

"The coordinates Ed gave us. They're about a half-an-hour away. Man," Mason said, putting his pistol back into its holster, "I just wish we had more guns."

"Check the trunk once we've stopped," Ernestine said, slowly. "Garrett was always prepared."

"Yeah, he did mention something about that," Mason said, "but we've got to come up with a plan before we get there."

"We don't have time," Zahra said, checking the time on her vPhone.

"We do online," Mason said. "Hours in there are just minutes in the real world."

"Won't Moloch come for us again?" Ernestine asked.

"We could go to Ed's, I guess," Zahra replied. "We might be safe there."

"I don't want to bring Moloch to Ed's front door before he's ready for it," Mason said. "I just don't know where we could go where Moloch won't find us in less than five minutes online."

"That's the way he wants it," Ernestine said, staring out of the window. Her voice came from a distance even though she was just five feet away from them. "He takes away our safe places online and then he takes away the one safe place we had in real life so that he can isolate us; make us feel alone."

"Well, it didn't work," Zahra said. "What we need is to find somewhere online where Moloch won't think to look."

Ernestine looked away from the window. "There might be a way, but it wouldn't last for very long."

Zahra and Mason turned their chairs towards her.

"I could take control of a deactivated site for a few minutes."

"You can do that?" Zahra asked.

"It's actually not that hard to do. It's just that the webmasters will pick up on it in about five minutes of real time and shut us down."

"That still gives us about an hour on the vU," Mason said.

"Whenever you're ready, Ern," Zahra said, reclining in her seat.

Ernestine took a few moments to access the vPhone on her wrist, during which she tapped numerous commands into it with a holographic keyboard. She nodded at her two companions. "We're as ready as we can be."

The three of them closed their eyes and opened them to the sight of darkness.

"Kinda dark in here," Mason said, putting his arms out in front of him.

"Hang on. I'll turn the power on," Ernestine said. An interactive window appeared and the shadows of hands moved across it. An orange sun switched on like a light bulb and illuminated a vast desert with an abandoned city of tall concrete structures in the distance. "We'll need something to sit on," Ernestine said. A moment later, a dark, stone table surrounded by wooden chairs winked into existence just a few feet from them. A much larger window appeared and hovered in the air above the table.

"It's warm but not hot," Zahra said, taking in a deep breath and releasing it. "The air's kinda dry, though."

"What was this place?" Mason asked, looking at the distant, abandoned city.

"It's a stored piece of a much bigger game," Ernestine replied. She pointed at the cement city some distance away. "That was a city in a sci-fi game, but there wasn't enough people coming here to keep it going, so it was archived."

"Was it called 'Space Colony'?" Mason asked after a pause.

"Yeah," Ernestine replied. "How'd you know?"

"I used to play it. I think I came here once. You're right, there wasn't many people here, so I never came back. There weren't many Orange Giants in that game, though. It's as beautiful as I remember it."

"I'd love to hear about it sometime, but we're in a hurry. Ern, see if you can get Ed on the line," Zahra said, taking a seat at the head of the table.

Ernestine looked at the phone on her wrist. "Call Ed," she said to it. They heard the sound of a ring tone and then a familiar face appeared on the large screen.

Ed looked down at the small group with a warm smile that disappeared once he saw their expressions. "Where's Garrett?"

Ernestine stayed silent.

"Garrett didn't make it," Mason said after a moment.

"Oh," Edward said, taking a deep breath and then exhaling it. "And I told him that we'd have plenty of time for questions later. I was wrong and I don't like being wrong."

"We're all still reeling from it," Zahra said. "I wish we had time to mourn, but we arrive at Moloch's estate in less than hour and we don't have a whole lot to go on right now."

"Yes, and incidentally," Edward said, "thanks for not coming in person, this time. Now that Garrett's being absorbed into Moloch, I have even less time than I did before. I'm going to shut down the quest that allows people to access my home and change the password. If you need to visit me in person in the future, the password will be Apollo."

"Got it," Zahra said. "Now, we're going to Moloch's front door and we don't know what we're up against."

"And that's where I come in," Edward said, clapping his hands once, "and I've got something good: the schematics of the house you're going to."

"Residential or commercial?" Zahra asked as a holographic representation of an unusual looking home appeared in the air above the table.

"Residential, but it's not what you're expecting," Edward replied. "It's the primary residence of one Robert Alexander Coombs, a billionaire with a penchant for designer homes."

"Oh," Zahra said, looking at a dozen large concrete columns holding up a house two stories off the ground, "is that a Vadé?"

"A what?" Mason asked.

"You've never heard of her?"

Mason and Ernestine looked at each other and shook their heads.

"She's designed some of the most unique homes for celebrities and billionaires. Look at all of that glass and the wraparound deck on the first floor! That home has to be worth something in the range of fifty or sixty million dollars."

Edward scratched his nose and grinned. "You are full of surprises, Zahra. Yes, this architecture is by Vadé and has the unusual and somewhat unique quality of being constructed some seven meters off the ground. It has all of the latest in security: cameras, sensors, alarms, you name it."

"And this is the house we need to break into?" Mason asked.

"I'm afraid so. What do you have at your disposal?"

"If we were still in contact with the FBI," Zahra said, putting both elbows on the table, "just about everything. As is, there's just the three of us."

"Luckily," Edward said, leaning back from the camera feed, "you've got me, too."

"I thought you're stuck in the vU, cut off from reality?"

"Oh, there's a lot you can do online," Ed replied, rubbing his hands together. "For instance, all of that security is done by a remote company who manages all of their clients online. It's heavily encrypted, of course. Virtually unbreakable."

"But," Ernestine said, smiling, "you can get into it, right?"

"Well, I did build it," Edward replied, reflecting her smile. "I can take care of the alarms, the sensors, and I've taken the liberty of recording footage from their cameras, which I can put on a loop the moment you arrive. There are security patrols, which I can help you to avoid, but you may not be able to avoid all of them."

"Is there any way you can get video of the patrols?" Zahra asked.

"Unfortunately, I already have," Edward replied, his arms moving just off-camera. The hologram of the estate vanished and was replaced by live feeds of one of the patrols. Edward froze the image and zoomed in on the faces of two security guards dressed in black.

"That man needs a shrink," Mason said at the sight of one of the guard's faces transformed into that of a demented clown's complete with white skin, but this one perpetually smiled sharp, bloody teeth. The second's was somehow burned to the point of having part of his face raw and bubbling while other parts had shredded flesh barely clinging to it.

"It's all about scare tactics, but you already know that," Ed said.

"I'm glad that you've taken care of security, Ed," Zahra said, "but how do we get into the building with it being two floors off the ground?"

"Yes, back to the blueprints," Edward said, changing the camera footage to a 3D representation of the house. "You see, this house may be built in the air, have marvelous views of the Atlantic and the surrounding countryside, but like all other homes, it needs sewer, water, power, etcetera, etcetera. For that, you need a basement where you can put a heater, hot water tank, perhaps even a washer and a dryer—"

"Ed," Ernestine interrupted, sighing, "get to the point."

"Ah, yes," Edward said, while the three-dimensional view of the house changed to that of a basement located beneath the heavy, concrete columns. "Some of the heat, water, and whatnot are provided via the many columns you see, but the way up to the house is by way of the main support column at the center. It has an elevator and a staircase."

"We can't just walk up to an entrance that exposed. The minute we do, we're dead," Zahra said, looking up at the blueprints.

"Wait," Ed said, with a knowing smile, "there's another way in." He changed the image to one of real-time at night, where two wide garage doors were visible from the rear end of the building. "Don't you just love it when there's room for a four-car garage?"

For the first time since they left Garrett's bunker, the trio smiled.

"One that would give us easy access?" Zahra asked.

"The very same," Ed replied. "With the cameras on a loop, the alarms and sensors disabled, you'll only have to deal with the patrols. The elevator and staircase are both accessible from the basement, but I suggest you take the stairs as they are the least traveled. From there, you can go up to the second floor, where the bedrooms are located."

Mason watched as the image of the backyard switched back to the hologram tracing a path up through the building and to the second floor. "What's wrong with the first floor?"

"Nothing, that's where the living areas are, but you're looking for Moloch, correct?" Edward asked.

"Yes, but doesn't he still eat and crap like the rest of us?" Mason inquired.

"I'm sure he does, but it is four o'clock in the morning and even his body requires sleep. I do suspect, though, that he is using that time to spend on the vU so that he can continue communication with all of his legions of hosts."

"So, he'd be sleeping in a bedroom," Mason concluded.

"The master bedroom, I believe," Edward said, making a large room at the front of the house flash in green. "Considering that Bob the Billionaire now belongs to him, he would feel completely entitled to the best room in the place."

"That does give us a direct, simple objective," Zahra said, looking at Mason. "No wandering around."

"So, once I'm there, how do I get into his head? Do I have to confront him in his innermind, because I didn't do so well against him last time," Mason asked.

"Ah!" Edward exclaimed, changing the hologram to an image of a hand with tiny tubules extended from between its knuckles. They were close to the left side of a computer-generated face. "No, you don't have to fight him inside his head. I'm sure that would be destructive to both of you."

"Good," Mason said, sighing.

"You will have to get very close to him, though," Edward said, while the hologram showed the mindhacker tubules getting closer to the artificial person's temple. "One inch and you'll have to inject him with my virus right here," Edward stated, pointing to the soft tissue at his left temple.

"That's not going to be easy."

"Luckily he'll be asleep so you can catch him unawares," Edward said. "It's your best shot."

"What if he wakes up?" Zahra inquired, shifting her attention from the hologram to the screen with Edward's face on it.

"Then you'll need to think of something."

"How long do I need to be in contact with him?" Mason asked.

"That's the bad news," Edward replied, avoiding eye contact. "Three seconds."

Mason sighed and looked away. "That's a long time."

"And it won't be easy. Best of luck. I'll be around to give you more help, if I can," Edward said.

"Sounds like a plan," Ernestine said, pushing herself away from the table. "We should get back."

"Same here. Call me through your vPhones under the new phone number you'll have on them once you start your operation. Bye for now," Edward said, his image fading from the screen.

"There's just one thing," Zahra said, putting a hand up. Ernestine had gotten up but turned back to face the table. "I've gotta ask: Ern, when Moloch, Ted, talked about me being trans, you got mad at him. How did you know?"

"I didn't," Ernestine said, a slow smile spreading across her face.

"Then how did—"

"I don't care if you're trans. I care that someone was picking on my friend."

"Oh," Zahra said. "Thanks."

"Any time."

"What about you?" Ernestine asked, turning her attention to her partner.

"Ah," Mason said, keeping his eyes on Zahra. "I—"

"Oh," Ernestine said, tapping the back of her hand twice, "time for me to go. Turn the lights off when you're done."

"Well, that just leaves the two of us on this whole planet," Mason said once she had vanished from sight. "You can't say that every day."

Zahra glanced at the ground, having trouble keeping eye contact with Mason. "I know I never told you I was trans, but—"

"It doesn't matter," Mason interjected. "I kinda got the idea that you were over the last few months."

"But I never brought it up," Zahra said.

"Zahra," Mason said, taking the seat nearest to her, "sometimes what you don't say it just as important as what you do say."

"When did you start to get all old and wise?" Zahra asked, pushing a strand of hair away from his forehead.

"Well, seeing inside of your head helped," Mason said, a grin breaking across his features. "Me in there all ready for a date. I looked better in a cardigan than I thought I would."

Zahra blushed and looked at the desert floor. "You should wear one sometime."

"There's a version of you in my mind, too," Mason said, winking.

"Oh, and what do I look like in your mind?" Zahra inquired, crossing her arms.

"Whips and chains?" Mason said, laughing. "Ow! No, you're not ready for a date in my mind. You're sitting in my version of a food court, kind of like yours."

"Great minds think alike," Zahra remarked before squinting at his remark. "Hold on: why am I sitting in a food court?"

"Because you're one of a few of my favorite things?" Mason said before Zahra pinched his arm. "Ow! That's what Moloch said when he saw you there."

"That's why it's not funny."

"You know why you're there," Mason said.

"Thanks for letting me into your mind. You saw my dark side and most people don't and you didn't get all weird around me afterwards. Thanks."

"I saw that bungalow in the dark side of your mind. Is that what was making you so depressed back then?" Mason asked.

Zahra got up from her seat and sat on the desk in front of him. "That's the old house I shared with my ex-husband. It's also where he committed suicide."

"Oh, Jesus! I'm sorry, Zahra!"

"No one as much as me, but I had my time to mourn. My grandmother was there to support me," Zahra said, glancing at him.

"Grandma's Mouse Cake," Mason said, smiling.

"It's *Mousse* Cake, and yeah. She always made it for me when I felt bad. So, she made it a lot, especially when I was a kid being bullied for being trans. It cheered me up every time."

"Sounds good."

"You know it was. You had two slices!" Zahra exclaimed before she glanced at the ground. "If all of this makes you feel uncomfortable, I can get you transferred the second everything's back to normal."

"You don't have to do that," Mason said, taking her right hand into his.

"You're really okay with this?" she asked, her voice breaking. She glanced at their entangled hands and fought back tears.

"I was since the day I met you," Mason said.

Zahra laughed and squeezed his hand. "Weren't you wearing a torn pair of jeans and an old sweater the day we met?"

"Yeah," Mason said, smiling his boyish grin. "It wasn't my best day when it started, but it became that because it was the day I met you."

Zahra's smile broadened. She leaned over and caressed his cheek. Mason put his arms around her waist, pulled her towards him and the couple kissed in the heat of the desert. The only sound they heard was the distant howl of the wind through the lonely cliffs in the distance, which tussled their hair a moment later.

"That was perfect timing," Mason said, once she leaned back on the desk.

"The kiss or the breeze?"

"Both," Mason replied, smiling.

"Come on," she said. "It's time to get back to reality."

Chapter Thirteen

"Everything okay?" Ernestine asked once the couple's eyes popped open.

"Everything's fine," Zahra replied as Mason held her hand.

"I'd say that's new," Ernestine said, crossing one leg over the other, "but I'd be lying."

"I always say you're an insightful person, Ern," Mason said.

"I know! It's a good thing you guys woke up. We're getting close to the house. I got the autopilot to increase our speed a little past its limits."

"Alright," Zahra said, letting Mason's hand go. "Time to get started."

The car stopped five minutes later a safe distance from the concrete residence. The group exited the vehicle into the autumn evening. Zahra looked up at the dark blue of the sky and took a pistol from her holster. "It's going to be sun up in less than an hour. We need to hurry."

"Kinda cold," Mason said, exhaling a visible breath.

"Now, we have guns, but I'm a little worried about you, Ern," Zahra said.

"Garrett always planned ahead," Ernestine said. She walked to the rear of the navy electric car and opened the trunk. She pulled out a long-barreled submachine gun a second later. "He was ready for the mafia if they came."

"Wow!" Zahra exclaimed. "Anything in there for me?"

"Take a look," Ernestine replied.

Zahra joined her at the back and smiled at Mason. "You have got to see this."

"What?" Mason said, making a beeline for the trunk of the car. He walked around the corner of the vehicle, where a small armory awaited him.

"I don't think heavy arms would be much good in this situation. Especially not that one, unless you're planning on blowing something up," Zahra said, following his eyes to a heavy gun some four feet long.

"Hey, I can admire it, can't I?"

Zahra chose a second pistol as a backup, which she attached to an ankle holster. Mason put his pistol away, took a submachine gun out of the back of the car and patted it. Ernestine chose to fit herself with two copies of the same submachine gun, which had straps to carry over her shoulders when needed. They all took silencers and extra magazines before closing the trunk.

"Well, we're as ready as we're ever going to be," Zahra said.

Ernestine told her watch to call Ed and waited until she heard the sound of the other end being picked up. "Are you there, Ed?" she whispered.

"I'm here," the voice responded in a louder tone.

"Shh!" Ernestine exclaimed in response.

"I created those watches, remember?" Ed said at the same volume. "You're on private mode and only you can hear my voice. Tell the others to go live with me, too."

Ernestine relayed his instructions, and soon, all three team members heard his articulate timbre.

"Are you at the house, yet?"

"We just got here," Ernestine replied. "It's just on the other side of a stand of trees."

"And you're facing the back?"

"Yes," Ernestine replied, still whispering.

"Good."

"I wish we had time to change," Zahra said, zipping up a black jacket over her bright, red blouse.

"Hey, most of what you're wearing is black," Ernestine stated. "Why did I decide to wear beige today of all days?"

"You might blend in with something," Mason said.

"Like what?" Ernestine asked, raising both eyebrows.

"Maybe they have some rock gardens you can vanish right into," Mason replied, smiling.

Ernestine stifled a giggle and pulled at his brown tee shirt and worn jeans. "Well, even jeans are a better choice than this."

"I'm sure that the finer parts of fashion are very important, but you might want to concentrate on breaking into the rich man's house right now," Ed's voice said through their watches.

"We're on our way," Zahra whispered, removing her pistol from the holster at her side.

She motioned for Mason and Ernestine to follow her. The trio carefully walked into a dark hedge. On the opposite side was a strip of firs stretching out long branches over thick underbrush. They crouched and moved forward at a restrained pace, although their eyes rarely moved from the dark shadow of a home looming over the large yard before the trio.

The moon came out, illuminating the entire area. Zahra exhaled a long trail of visible breath at the sight of the house. A great structure twice as wide as it was long stretched out across a green lawn, dimpled by the occasional birch tree. Thick supports held up a high-perched blocky building with a wrap-around deck and floor-to-ceiling opaque windows. The concrete foundation and basement were hidden by a manicured green lawn stretching out from beneath the main house like a green floor beneath a concrete bed.

"Was he afraid there'd be a tidal wave?" Mason asked, looking at the strong concrete pillars holding up the home.

"I think it's more about the view," Ernestine whispered back.

"Isn't the glass a mirror during the day and transparent at night?"

"Not this one," Zahra replied, looking at the distorted reflections of the forest in the windows. "That makes this a little harder."

"Do you see the garage doors?" Ed asked through her watch.

"Wait," Ernestine replied, lifting her head through the underbrush. She spied a dip in the landscape where a fifteen-foot depression held two steel doors on a concrete wall. "I bet there are lights right above those garage doors that will go on the second you get close."

"Not anymore," Ed's voice said.

"Thanks," Ernestine whispered back. She turned her attention to the others huddled around her. "Let's go."

"Wait!" Ed's voice exclaimed, freezing them in their tracks. "There's a patrol moving into your area. Get down and wait for them to pass."

The team hunkered down and peered through the bushes. The cold began to pierce their clothing, but it was easily forgotten once they heard the sounds of approaching boots crunching across the frosty grass. Within a few seconds, the sounds were joined by the sight of two men dressed in black, both with lengthened canines and wearing grotesque expressions on their faces. They stopped walking not far from Mason's place in the underbrush and looked around. The team held their breath while seconds passed like hours. After a moment of eternity, the guards resumed their patrol. It was only once they disappeared around the corner of the house that Edward spoke again. "Now! Go!"

The trio sucked in a deep breath and moved as quickly as they could across the dark, green lawn caked in frost and gleaming in the fading moonlight. Ernestine breathed a sigh of relief once she saw that the floodlights above the garage doors stayed off as they approached.

"What about the keypad?" Mason mouthed to Zahra once he huddled next to them.

Ernestine pointed at herself and carefully removed the cover of the keypad. She deftly manipulated the wires within and soon, the keypad turned from red to green and they heard a click from within the locking device. Ernestine pulled it up and her two companions sprinted past her and into the basement of the building.

They held their breath until the door closed behind them.

"Huh," Ernestine said, looking around. "No cars."

"I thought you were a computer scientist," Zahra said, leaning against a concrete wall.

"I am. I never said that's all I ever did. There is a reason why I know Garrett as well as I do."

"She was part of the Native Wolves," Mason said.

"Really?" Zahra asked, facing her.

"It kept me busy," Ernestine replied, shrugging.

"We're in," Zahra said to her watch.

"Excellent, I—" Ed began before the trio noticed two security officers were standing within mere feet of them.

Ernestine drew in a breath at the sight of one of the officers wearing a white goalie mask made of living skin. The other was wearing a strange Halloween mask and it, too, was somehow part of its face.

The Halloween guard raised his vPhone to his mouth but was interrupted when Mason's foot hit him in the face with a blow that snapped his chin up in the air. The second was hit with the mindhacker's fist a moment later. Feet and fists flew across Ernestine and Zahra's field of vision in a blur of frantic movement.

"Hangman!" Zahra exclaimed at Mason.

Zahra pointed her weapon at the air above the fighting individuals but didn't have to wait for long. Within seconds, the Halloween man's head was above everyone else's. Zahra aimed, fired with pinpoint accuracy and watched as the monster's cranium came apart.

The fight of fists and feet continued until Mason called out from the blur of movement in front of them. "Passed out!"

"Got it," Zahra said, aiming at the floor. "Aim at the floor. The target will only be vulnerable for a split second." Ernestine followed suit. A moment later, the hockey-masked monster was forced to the floor, but struggling hard.

"Got him!" Zahra exclaimed and fired her gun. The monster's head had a sizeable hole in it a moment later. Ernestine's shots ended up buried in the floor.

She harrumphed. "My aim's off."

"It's been years since you fired a gun. You'll get better at it."

"Yeah, hopefully in the next five minutes," Mason interjected.

"Don't listen to him," Zahra said, rolling her eyes.

"It looks like those enhancements Ed gave you worked," Ernestine remarked.

"Yeah, I just wish they were working an hour ago."

"That's not your fault," Ernestine said, "What was that you were saying, anyway? They sounded like code words."

"A code that Mason and I developed if one of us can't get away from someone and the other needs a clear shot. 'Hangman' means that one of us will get the individual above our shoulders, 'passed out' means get him on the floor, and 'wide target' means there is more than one."

"I'll try to remember that," Ernestine said, raising her vPhone. "Ed, where do we go from here?"

"Straight ahead. There are a few different corridors in the basement but the elevator is at the center of the building. All roads lead to Rome, in this case," Ed replied through the phone on Ernestine's wrist.

"When in Rome," Mason said, turning from the bodies and taking a step towards the center of the basement.

"Could any of them be lying in wait in one of these rooms?" Zahra asked. The FBI agent kept her weapon pointed at the door, but she couldn't resist glancing at the unmarked steel doors as they passed.

Mason kept his eyes on the metal door at the end of the hallway. "I don't see why they would if they don't know we're coming, but keep your eyes peeled."

The two cautiously moved forward until they reached a thick concrete wall, at which point Mason placed a careful hand on the door handle and opened it a crack. He took a peek around and then nodded at his two companions behind him. Mason took a tentative step into an empty room with a concrete box and two sets of doors at its center.

"Empty," he said.

"Are you sure?" Ernestine whispered from the doorway.

Mason pointed at his ears. "Enhanced hearing as well. Nobody's here. There's the staircase," he said, pointing at one of two doors with the appropriate symbol on them.

"Go," Zahra said, moving into the small room with Ernestine following closely behind her. Mason opened the door to the stairway as quietly as he could and listened for a moment.

"It's clear," Mason said.

Zahra motioned with her gun for him to continue and the threesome took slow steps up the staircase. Mason only stopped on the first floor for a few seconds to listen at the door before continuing to the second story in the dim stairwell.

"Where's the master bedroom?" Mason asked his watch.

"Out the door and to your right. Keep walking 'til the end. It's the last door on your left."

"Got it," Mason said before taking a deep breath and noiselessly opening the heavy door. He and his cadre crept down the long hallway and past another door before arriving at the end of the corridor with a single wooden door on their left. The end of the hall featured a floor-to-ceiling glass window looking out on a vast expanse of countryside with a sliver of coastline. Already the deep blue of early morning was turning a pale sapphire.

Mason turned to the door on his left and felt the resistance of a lock. He looked up at the two faces beside him, both of whom had the same reaction as him.

"We've got a problem," Ernestine said.

"What's that?" Ed's voice whispered back.

"This door is locked!" Ernestine exclaimed. "I thought you took care of all the security."

"I thought I did. There shouldn't be a locked door in the whole place. Let me see," he said. Ernestine and her friends watched the hallway, sweat trickling down their faces while only the occasional sound issued from their vPhones. "Ah!" Ed exclaimed, making all three of them jump. "The lock to the master bedroom is accessible only by an access code on a manual keypad next to the door."

Mason looked up to see a black, unadorned keypad without a single light on it. "Do you know the code?"

"That I don't."

"Can you get in there, like you did at the front?" Zahra asked, shifting her attention to Ernestine.

"Maybe," she replied. Ernestine carefully began to remove the keypad's faceplate, paused, and put it back in place. "No good. The faceplate's wired. If I try to remove it, an alarm will go off right away."

"Can we guess it?" Zahra asked.

"The information I have says that this lock has a four-digit combination. Perhaps it's his birthdate?" Edward suggested.

"Too obvious," Mason replied. "It'd have to be something that he would remember but wouldn't be information just anyone could get ahold of online."

"Doing a deep search on John Alexander Coombs," Edward said through the wireless connection. "Cross referencing with anything four digits long... Ah! Poor guy, he had a daughter who died when she was just a baby. He kept it out of the news. She was born on May 28th."

"It's the best we got," Mason said.

"Assuming that Moloch didn't change the code to one of his own," Edward interjected.

Mason tapped in 0528 and was relieved when he heard the bedroom door click. Mason mouthed the words *Wait here,"* at Ernestine and Zahra before creeping into the bedroom running the length of the house.

Ernestine and Zahra watched as he made his way past a few leather couches and chairs arranged to face each other. In the dim light of the room, they watched Mason bend over the bed, hover there for a few seconds and then return to them, closing the door behind him as quietly as he could manage.

"Boy, was that ever close!"

"You did it?" Ernestine asked.

"No, it wasn't Ted! It was that Bob the Billionaire dude," Mason replied.

"God!" Zahra exclaimed, white teeth glowing in the dark.

"Then where is he?" Ernestine asked.

"The most likely place he would be was the master bedroom," Edward's voice intruded.

"We've got maybe one more shot before Moloch knows we're here," Mason said.

"Then we have to narrow his location down."

"Wait," Mason said, looking at the vPhone on his wristwatch. "Ed, you said that the master bedroom was the place he was most likely to be, why?"

"It's what the computer projected."

"Of course it would be," Mason said. "That's why Moloch wouldn't be anywhere near it!"

"Excuse me?" his vPhone asked.

Ernestine regarded Mason, wide-eyed. "Ed, he's right. Moloch would know that most people would look in the master bedroom first, so he knew he couldn't stay there."

"So, he's in another bedroom?" Zahra asked, looking at the doors on the opposite side of the hallway.

"If he's not in that one, then I don't think he's in one of the others," Ernestine replied.

"In the living room downstairs, then?" Zahra asked.

"That might be a little more likely," Edward replied.

"No," Mason said, "that's not the way he thinks. Moloch wouldn't be in a kitchen or a living room. He'd be off where no one would ever expect to find him, like a closet. Ed, are there any closets that would be big enough to fit a cot in?"

"Maybe," Edward replied. After a moment, his voice came from the vPhone again. "Yes! There's a general-purpose janitorial closet in the basement that could be easily converted into a small bedroom."

"It would be back the way we came," Mason said, taking quick, careful steps to the stairwell.

At the door to the stairway, Mason again opened it a crack and listened for a moment before returning his attention to his companions. "I don't hear anything."

He led them down the dim stairway and back into the basement, where Edward directed them to a corridor on their right. They crept down a short hallway, stopping at the first door they encountered.

"I think he's here," Mason said.

"How do you know?" Ernestine asked.

"It's the mindhacker implants," Mason replied, tapping his temple. "You can feel a kind of buzzing in your head whenever you're near another one."

He nodded to each of his teammates. Ernestine brought up her submachine guns and Zahra took out her backup pistol, using both to cover the door. Mason twisted the doorknob and pulled it open.

Inside was a small space surrounded by concrete with only one dim lamp on a narrow shelf to light it. All of the cleaning products and equipment had been removed, leaving only a single cot, a narrow desk and a simple, wooden chair. A feeble ray of light illuminated the face of the man lying in bed. He looked like any other white male of average build, height, and weight, except this man had a cruel curl to his lips, sharp cheekbones and peaked eyebrows.

Mason looked at the man's face and then back to his companions, giving them a curt nod before ever so slowly creeping into the room.

He kept his eyes on those of his target the entire time, taking one careful step after another. Mason felt sweat starting to find its way down his forehead and into his eyes. His heart nearly tore itself from his chest with every beat, forcing him to take a deep breath of the musty, stale air in the room. Mason stood next to the top of the bed and began to reach out with his right hand to the man's left temple. The agent extended the tiny tubules from between his knuckles. They were just an inch from Moloch's head when he opened his eyes and smiled up at Mason.

"I heard you were coming."

Mason froze at the sight of the man's murderous brown eyes staring into his own. Before he could react, Moloch was on his feet and racing for his companions. Mason wrenched himself from his paralysis and lunged for Moloch, catching him by the back of his shirt and hauling him backwards. Zahra ran into the room, dragging Ernestine behind her and slammed the door shut behind them.

"Ed," she said, panting into her vPhone, "lock the door to this room."

"Got it," he replied while Mason and Moloch squared off.

"Wait," Ernestine said into her wristwatch, "lock all of the doors in the building and then cut the power."

"How are you going to get out if I do that?" Edward asked while Zahra kept her pistol trained on Moloch.

"Don't worry about that right now. Locking the doors will slow down Moloch's people."

"Who gave you superhuman strength and speed?" Moloch asked Mason with a wicked smile.

"Wouldn't you like to know?" Mason replied, blocking a punch Moloch threw at him.

His foot flew out at Moloch's face, but the bodyhacker moved his head out of the way with impossible speed. "I really would. Not just anyone could give you those abilities. It would have to come from someone who knows the system even better than that squaw over there."

Ernestine tightened her grip on her gun and frowned, but said nothing.

"You'll just have to keep guessing."

"No, I don't," Moloch said, flying at him as though he was launched from a catapult. Mason was in front of him one moment and then beside him the next. He grabbed Moloch and used his momentum to throw him into the desk, causing it to crack and collapse under his weight. Moloch looked up at him, wiping a trickle of blood from his mouth.

"Garrett's memories are in here now. I know that Edward Blunt is in the vU and I know that's who the squaw was just talking to. I also know where he is and how to get to him thanks to your old pal. I think it's time I visited him. He's got something I need."

"Like a conscience?" Mason asked.

"Humor to cover up your myriad insecurities. Ed's got what I want, doesn't he? He can make me live forever."

"Like hell," Ernestine said, pointing the muzzle of her gun at Moloch's head.

"What's the matter, wagon burner? Trying to protect your sugar daddy?"

Mason took advantage of his distraction and landed a blow to his nose, which issued the sound of a nasty crunch followed by two streams of blood flowing from his nostrils. Moloch was on his feet in a fraction of a second and flew at Mason, who caught the full force of his bear hug. Both of them landed on the bed, which buckled under their combined weight and inertia. Moloch was lying on top of the FBI agent and holding him so tightly that Mason realized the bodyhacker was aroused.

"I feel like we should catch up," Moloch said, purposely releasing hot, rank breath across his face. "I'm going to humiliate you in so many different ways, you know. Some of them even after you're dead."

"You call that catching up?" Mason asked while Moloch kept grinding his erection into him.

"How about talking about old friends, like Benny Carter?"

"What that you killed him? I already knew that."

"No," Moloch said, deliberately thrusting against Mason. "You didn't lobotomize anybody! Benny did and what's even better than that is the FBI covered it up and used it against you!"

Mason's jaw dropped open at his words and Moloch thrust both of his hands around his throat. He clawed at Moloch's hands, helpless to release the iron grip around his neck. Ernestine and Zahra fired shots at Moloch's head, but he flew into the air, the bullets whizzing by him. Moloch let gravity slam his body back into his rival, but this time,

Mason was ready for him. The agent wrapped one hand around his waist and the other was at the bodyhacker's temple.

"We could talk about you, *Ted*: Is your innermind always some shitty office in an Art Deco nightmare?" Mason asked, at which point Moloch's face froze. He took advantage of his moment of hesitation and pierced the man's temple with his tubules. Moloch's eyes closed while Ed's virus did its trick. Mason withdrew from his mind, pushed the man off him and stood up.

"Keep your eyes on him," Mason said. He carefully extended a foot, poked Moloch in the side and shook his head. "I didn't think the virus would knock him out."

"It should only take seconds to start working," Ernestine said, looking down at his inanimate form.

Zahra took a few steps towards the body and poked the bottom of his shoe with her toe. All three teammates started and turned towards the door when a loud bang made it jump and tear itself partway off its hinges.

In that split second, Moloch leaped to his feet and drew a knife from a hidden scabbard at his calf. He lunged at Ernestine's turned back, but his hard features dropped and his trajectory towards her wavered as he felt some of his strength and speed leave him.

Mason spotted the rush of movement from the corner of his eye and reacted. Even surprised, he had his submachine gun off his shoulder and traced a bead across Moloch's flying body in less than the time it took him to traverse the room. Moloch's knife was just a few inches from Ernestine's back when Mason fired. A spray of red flew from Moloch's right temple and his sagging body flew away from Ernestine once Mason followed up with a powerful kick. His lifeless body hit the wall and collapsed into a pile on the floor.

Ernestine turned back in time to catch the sight of Moloch's corpse hitting the wall, but the smile and nod from the computer scientist let Mason know everything he needed to know. The door came off its hinges and slammed to the floor, bringing everyone's attention back to the exit.

"Wide target!" Zahra exclaimed. The team swung their pistols up to the door and fired at the first of two burly security guards with creepily clownish faces. Bullets flew at different spots in the doorway. The clown-monster tried to evade them but discovered that there was still one headed for it regardless of where the nightmare clown moved his head. The guard fell to his knees and then to the ground, face down.

"Again!" Zahra said when the second came through the door. The next ghastly guard was also unable to evade all the slugs fired at him and soon joined his host-comrade. Zahra lowered her weapon and then regarded her two friends. "Thanks. I'm glad you realized what I was trying to say with the multiple target code."

"No problem," Ernestine said. "The question is: how many guards are there between us and the car?"

"By now everyone knows what Garrett knew. Every host within a hundred miles is probably converging on this place," Mason replied, taking a step into the corridor. "We've gotta get out of here."

"Unless we can get them all to stand in that doorway, we need to come up with some other way to stop them," Zahra said, motioning with her head to where both expired security guards lay.

"It's okay," Mason said, "I'll be able to aim my SMG and fire shots at multiple targets."

"Should the rest of us just sit around and have tea?" Zahra asked, putting a hand on her hip.

"You two are very important. Remember that they might be fast, but those SMGs can fire a thousand rounds a minute and even Moloch's hosts can't evade them," Mason replied.

"Best way out?" Ernestine asked her watch.

"The same way you came in," Edward replied. "Good luck."

"Mason, you take point. We'll cover you back to the main lobby and then to the back exit."

Mason nodded, took the lead and the group moved as one body down the hallway towards the center of the basement. Once in the corridor, they heard distant sounds of metal crumpling.

"It's coming from all around us," Zahra observed, briefly looking at the ceiling.

"They're breaking down the doors to get to us," Ernestine said, keeping her eyes on the approaching door to the lobby. "We're going to have a lot of them here soon."

Mason disappeared through the door, returning seconds later. "We're clear. Come on."

The trio continued into the main room and were just walking past the elevator when the door to the main stairway began to cave in under repeated blows. Mason looked back at Ernestine and Zahra. "Hurry!"

"Ed," Ernestine said into her wristwatch, "turn the power back on and unlock the door to the last hallway."

"Already done," his voice replied as the lights came on and the emergency lights turned off. "I'll also lock it again the moment you're through. Will do the same with the back door once you reach it."

"You're a lifesaver," Ernestine panted into her vPhone.

Mason pulled the door open and the team broke into the hallway just as the door to the stairway flew off its hinges on a trajectory for the trio. Mason closed and locked the door a fraction of a second later. Everyone heard the door click shut just before a loud boom shifted it.

"Run!" Zahra exclaimed. The three team members flew for the exit, hearing the door banging behind them. They reached the garage door in seconds, which clicked open as they reached it. Mason pulled up the broad door and flew out into the fresh air. Their flushed faces were bathed in the cool blue light just before dawn as the garage door lowered behind them and locked with a click.

"How long will it take for them to get through those doors?" Ernestine asked.

"I don't think that really matters right now," Mason replied.

Ernestine turned from the door to see the agent staring at the field where a hundred people stood in the glistening grass of the backyard. Some looked like nightmarish zombies, some like creepy clowns, but most of them looked like normal people until one saw the ghoulish grins on their faces.

"I bet you guys wish I had taken the big gun now," Mason said, wide-eyed.

"Can we get through them?" Ernestine asked.

"We're going to have to," Zahra replied.

All at once, dozens of people were running at the trio standing in front of the back door. Zahra took a step back, aiming both pistols at one of the attackers. "Now!" she fired a few shots, which the host nimbly avoided, but not the other that Mason had fired at its skull. That bullet exploded on impact, killing the host, whose body thumped to the ground.

Ernestine and Zahra began firing at the closest enemy while Mason peppered the host army with explosive bullets from his submachine gun, taking out a score of targets in seconds.

"Advance!" Zahra exclaimed, taking a few steps into the backyard. Mason dropped the empty magazine out of his SMGs, slapping in two fresh ones in less than a second.

Mason and Ernestine did the same and everyone fired again, taking out several more attackers. Thanks to Mason's enhanced physical and mental abilities, both of his hands became blurs of flesh while his submachine guns fired each round in a new direction. It only took another ten seconds before dozens more of their attackers died on the defrosting grass.

The remaining zombie-hosts looked around at the bodies surrounding them and launched themselves through the air on trajectories that would take them headfirst into the three intruders.

Mason managed to bring down several more in the moments it took to cross that distance, but four of them landed on him and his friends. Mason was already making headway with his attackers, but he heard strained grunts from Ernestine and Zahra as they attempted to fight off the zombie-people trying to overpower them.

Those sounds gave Mason a boost of adrenaline and he kicked off one of his clown-faced attackers, who flew through the air when the superhuman's foot hit him in the stomach. While the crazed clown soared across the glowing blue sky, Mason grabbed his gun with one hand and wrapped his arm around the other man's neck. He pressed the weapon against its head and fired a single round into it, causing the Moloch-host to go slack a second later.

Mason stood up and saw that the clown he had sent reeling a moment before was already returning. He stood and fired fifty bullets in less than a fraction of a second at the ghoul-clown, who tried to evade them, but soon fell to the ground, face down.

He turned his attention to the two attackers assaulting his friends. A young woman was trying to hold Ernestine down and inject her with nanobots while the other was fighting Zahra for her pistol.

"Hey!" Mason exclaimed at the young woman wearing a waitress' outfit. The woman's head turned at the exclamation and Mason took her down before she had time to realize who had fired the shot.

He pulled the second attacker off Zahra. He was a thin, older man with enhanced strength and a face that had been twisted into something demonic. The elderly man flew through the air, his bones breaking upon hitting the ground. He tried to get up and, when that failed, Moloch's emaciated host began crawling towards Zahra, cackling as he did. Mason narrowed his eyes at the Moloch monster and fired a single round into his head. He collapsed to the ground, finally finished.

Ernestine pushed the waitress off herself and got up, wiping away bits of grass and dew clinging to her beige slacks and blazer. "Oh, I hope the dry cleaners can save this suit."

"More will be on their way in minutes," Zahra said, also getting to her feet. "A lot more."

Mason nodded and the trio broke into a jog for the car, only slowing down to jump over a body. Once they arrived at their vehicle, they piled in and Zahra spoke quickly to the autopilot. "Los Angeles. No highways."

"We're going to L.A.?" Ernestine asked as she collapsed into the front bucket seat.

"It's a random choice that will take weeks to get to by the back roads. Moloch won't be able to trace us easily," Zahra explained. The car accelerated to its top allowable speed and sped off into the countryside while the red light of dawn appeared on the horizon.

"Good enough," Ernestine said, leaning back in her seat. "What was all of that going on between you and Moloch?"

"The fighting?" Mason asked, wincing as he put on his seatbelt.

"No, the talking. What was that about Benny and some Art Deco office?"

Mason rubbed his jaw while Zahra dug around the car in search of a First Aid kit. "I've spent the last year believing that I lobotomized John Tate. He just told me I didn't."

"But, can you be sure he was telling the truth?" Zahra asked, opening up a panel at the front of the car. "Ah!" she exclaimed, pulling out a small, white metal box with a red cross on it.

"No, but it gave him the distraction he needed. It would be nice if he was telling the truth, for once," Mason said as Zahra began to dab at his cut lip with iodine.

"Good timing with the name to catch him off-guard," Zahra said, administering to his lacerations.

"I knew that wouldn't be enough, though. That's why I brought up what his innermind looks like."

"But," Ernestine interjected, holding up an index finger, "how would you know what it looks like? I thought you told me that Moloch was in your mind the first time and you were in Reg's the second."

"At first I thought the same thing," Mason replied, accepting a cold compress from Zahra and holding it against his jaw. "Then I realized what Rose said when she went into Reg's head: Someone had already been there and she described it as an Art Deco office. That's what I saw, too. Then, I remembered Ted said something about remaking my mind and it all fit: What I saw had to be Moloch's innermind."

"So, the Art Deco office she described wasn't Reg's," Zahra said, with an appreciative smile, "it was Moloch's. You're getting good at this, Mason."

Mason kissed her quickly before leaning back in his chair. "Thanks."

"I'd hate to get between you two," Ernestine said, "but we should call Ed and tell him what's going on."

"What's going on?" a voice from their watch asked, making them all jump.

"Ed, you're still there?" Ernestine said.

"Of course! Why would I miss any of this?"

"Sorry," Ernestine said, planting her face in her palm and smiling. "With everything that happened in the last few minutes, I guess we forgot about you."

"I heard a lot of shouting and gunfire. I take it you're safe?"

"For now," Ernestine replied, "but Moloch is on his way to you."

"Well then, he needs a welcoming party. I'm going to need all of you back here. There's no point in contacting me from somewhere else now that he knows where I am. We're going to need to prepare."

"For what?" Mason asked.

"For his end. Maybe ours. Maybe the end of everything. We'll see," Edward said and hung up.

"Is he always like that?" Mason asked, looking at Ernestine.

"You'll get used to it. Time to go back online."

Chapter Fourteen

"If Moloch finds us here when we're online, we're dead," Mason said, reclining in his seat.

"I'll stay behind and keep an eye on things," Ernestine said.

"No," Zahra said, closing the top of the First Aid Kit. "I've got more experience with weapons. I'll stop the car for a minute and get more guns out of the back. If there's any problems, I'll text you."

"Okay," Mason said, closing his eyes. "Here we go."

He and Ernestine found themselves back in Sword & Sorcery, not far from where Edward's robed avatar stood. They hurried for De and didn't wait for him to get up from his tree trunk before giving him the new password of Apollo. De smiled and a door appeared from nowhere, which they quickly entered and walked into Edward's formerly unreachable cottage. The billionaire turned away from a table with several screens and transparent boxes hovering above it.

"We need a plan."

"Yeah," Mason said, crossing his arms, "against a man who seems to know more about me than I do."

"What did he tell you?" Edward asked, narrowing his eyes and cocking his head at him.

"Moloch told me I didn't lobotomize John Tate. My handler did and the FBI covered it up."

"Oh," Edward said. He grabbed a floating cube from above his desk and offered it to Mason. "That's why this information came in recently."

"What is it?" the agent asked, taking it from him and examining the numbers as they changed into words.

"It was sent to my email box less than a minute ago in real time. I've had it for less than ten in here. There wasn't time to finish analyzing it yet."

"How do you have an email?" Ernestine inquired.

"It's an alias. Few people have it. That's why its arrival perplexed me. You see, this is a classified file from the FBI that was buried by the department some time ago. What it covers appears to support what Moloch told you: You didn't lobotomize John and they deliberately kept it from you."

"What? Why?" Mason demanded, his eyes jaunting back and forth across page after page of information.

"They wanted you to work for them and no one else," Edward replied, looking between the digital report and his face. "They not only got you to join the FBI as a full-time agent, but they had projections that specifically said there was a high chance you'd stay on for many more years if you believed that you had made John into a vegetable."

"Are you saying they had John lobotomized just to get me?" Mason demanded, looking up from the cube with a frown on his red face.

"No, but they did take advantage of the situation and covered it up to keep the truth from you."

"Does Zahra know about this?" Mason asked, returning his attention to the large cube in his hands.

"I sincerely doubt it," Edward replied. "This information is so highly classified that, up until now, only a handful of people would have access to it. No, our scrupulous Zahra is far too low level to have ever seen it."

"Who sent it then?" Ernestine asked.

"Supposedly the sender was anonymous, but—"

"It was Moloch," Mason interjected.

"It seems the most likely answer," Ed said after a reluctant pause.

"Why would he just send this information to you? He actually did me a favor by telling me this," Mason asked, holding the glowing green cube in his hand.

"He created massive emotional turmoil in you at a critical moment, catching you off-guard. Luckily, you turned the tables on him, but I suspect he was willing to heal an old wound just to open a much larger one by revealing the FBI's involvement in your career choices."

"He's trying to wear me down?" Mason asked.

"Precisely, but in his own way, Moloch is giving you a compliment," Ed replied with a thin smile.

"If that's how he compliments people then I hope he never takes me out to dinner," Ernestine interjected.

"That would last all of about five seconds. Do you still remember our first date and what I said after the wine came to the table?" Ed asked, facing her with a wide grin.

"Flatterer."

"No, Mason," Ed said, returning his attention to the young agent, "Moloch is afraid of you and he put this speed bump in your way to slow you down. He wants to win this particular race more than anything and tired old Ted is afraid that he could lose. The information that I just received does more than that, though: It might just better prepare you for whatever else Moloch has to throw at you."

"What else is in it?" Mason asked, glancing at the cube.

"It appears that the FBI did their homework and then some. You see, Benny Carter hired you to do a mind-job on someone after he already did it."

"Why would he do that?" Mason inquired, shaking his head.

"To set a trap for you and cover up his crimes at the same time," Edward said, stone-faced. "Tell me, Mason: you never lobotomized a person before so how would you know if you had?"

"I don't know," Mason responded, sputtering out his words. "I only saw him collapse a few seconds after I was done."

"It happens so rarely that few people would know what to look for. Tell me, what did you see in his mind?" Edward asked, taking a slow step towards him.

"It was on the second floor of an old house in the main room. You know the one that's part of the stairs but there's some room for furniture up there?"

Edward blinked. "The hall?"

"Sure, but it was set up like an office. It had antique furniture and it looked like it was Victorian, but it felt, I don't know, later than that."

Edward sniffed. "Edwardian. Yes, that makes sense. Ordered, clean, and of a style just a decade or so earlier than Art Deco. You weren't seeing the brain of a man who was about to have a stroke. No, you were seeing inside the head of a man who was much like his successor. You might remember that his innermind was that of an office decorated in the Art Deco style."

"Moloch?" Mason asked, narrowing his eyes.

"And he was more like Benny than you might think. You saw *his* innermind, not John's, sixteen months ago."

"But, how could that be, unless…" Mason began.

"Unless Benny was already in there and in complete control, waiting for you to show up and get some unimportant information. Sure enough, there you were, he allowed you to access that information, off you went, and he gave his host a stroke seconds later. It worked so well that Moloch would use the same trick to try to frame Rose over a year later, with the added casualty of poor Tommy, that is. Rose never identified who hired her to do the contract?"

"We asked," Mason replied, "but she said they didn't have anything to do with what happened and to leave them out of it."

"I wonder if that's true."

Mason's eye widened and both he and Ernestine looked at each other. "Moloch? Moloch hired Rose?"

"Of course he did," Ed replied. "He needed a scapegoat and there she was. All Ted required was for her to show up and then everything would fall into place."

"Reg a vegetable. Tommy dead. Rose in prison," Ernestine said, counting them off with her fingers.

"Right," Ed said, pointing an index finger at her, "but this time the plan did not go off without a hitch because you and Zahra became involved."

"But my old handler couldn't take over someone else's head! Benny was just a regular mindhacker," Mason said.

Edward sat down, placed a finger at his temple and looked into Mason's eyes. "Was he?"

"Benny," Mason said, "Benny was a bodyhacker?"

"The first I suspect," Edward replied, returning to the large table at the center of the room. "Benny was on his way to becoming what Moloch is now, but Moloch realized what he was doing and wanted the same. He killed Benny for that information and then disappeared. He's spent months combing through classified reports, getting information from people's minds and now he's ready to fly. If you hadn't stumbled onto Moloch's plans, we would have likely found out far too late to do anything about them."

"Benny was using me for a patsy and then Moloch killed him. In a way, I should almost thank him."

"Don't thank him just yet," Edward said, turning around to face the table and its many holograms. "He is about to try to kill you."

"He can't kill me here; Just my avatar," Mason said to Edward's back.

"And you killed the original Ted in real life, but he still has millions of hosts across the entire continent looking for you. It's a good thing Zahra's out there. Hopefully, everything in here will be long finished before one of them finds you," Edward stated while he manipulated the many numbers floating in front of him.

"I'll text Zahra and warn her," Ernestine said, bringing up a screen in front of her.

"How are we going to keep Moloch out of here?" Mason asked, gazing at the yellowed walls and ceiling.

"Simple," Edward said, standing in front of the duo. "We invite him in."

"He's already on his way here," Ernestine stated, closing her screen.

"And he knows he can't make his way to this side of the river without the correct code. I've frozen the quest that allows people to get here and I've also taken De offline for a while. Moloch knows that I would do all of this and he'd be only too happy to destroy this game to get to me. After that, we would be playing hide and seek across the vU, and even as big as it is, he'd eventually find me," Edward said, leaning into the others and lowering his voice. "We need to invite him in right away; challenge him to a fight between you, Mason, and him. With that psychopathic attitude he has, he won't be able to say no without looking weak."

"You want the two of us to duke it out just to prove whose got the bigger dick?"

Edward smiled. "You'll find this will be more about who has the bigger brains, than uh, brawn. He must win in order to get the grand prize, which I won't have to give to Ted because you will win, Mason. By the time it's over I will have finished the virus that will end this, once and for all."

"Thanks for the confidence, but what is it that you're going to promise Moloch to get him to agree to all your terms?" Mason asked.

"What he's always wanted," Edward said, sighing at the ceiling. "Immortality."

"Doesn't he already have it?" Mason asked.

"He can take over people's heads but it's not the same thing. What he truly wants is what I have: the ability to stay alive in virtual reality forever."

Ernestine nodded and glanced at Mason. "Whenever you go into the digital world, your brain stays in the real world."

"When a mind becomes completely digital like mine," Edward said, pointing at his head, "you've sent all that information into a digital medium and as you stay around your information can get corrupted over time."

"More like will," Ernestine corrected. "It was something I was going to ask you about: How do you keep this digital you from degrading?"

"It was a creative solution, and one I can't tell you I'm afraid. Moloch must know that I've overcome that particular difficulty and he wants to be able to do the same. He knows that with him forever in here, he can forever be out there. I'm the only one who can give him that."

The room shook from a great blow from somewhere above and some of the plaster in the ceiling fell to the shiny, wooden floor, kicking up papers and dust. The trio looked at the ceiling as the tremor died away.

"I believe that our guest has arrived," Edward said, clapping his hands once. "It's time we had a talk with him."

"We'll keep off camera," Ernestine said, taking a few steps away.

"Good idea," Edward said, bringing up a wide digital screen in front of him. He tapped a few buttons at its bottom and the image of a strange, ethereal being appeared on the screen. It had a pale face, a small mouth smiling a scurrilous smile, and strangely gleaming all-black eyes. The man's haunting face was framed by closely cropped, obsidian hair. "I take this to be Ted calling?"

The thin lips and small mouth expanded into a nasty smile. "It's Moloch and you're Edward Blunt. Ed to his friends."

"Yes, but you already knew that. You need me for that last bit of code that will make you immortal."

"Yes," Moloch said, with a slippery grin, "and you will give me that information one way or another."

"I've got a better solution: a challenge. You fight Mason in a fair game of skill and the winner gets it from me voluntarily," Edward said, with each outstretched hand indicating the two rivals.

"That easy?" Moloch said, scowling. "I don't buy it."

"We both know that I could hold out long enough here to escape and lead you on a very long chase across this very big virtual universe. It might even be fun for a while, but we'd both tire of it eventually and we both know you'd probably win in the end. I say, let's get it done and over with now."

"Fine. Where?"

"Here," Edward said, tapping the floor with a heel.

"When?"

"Five minutes," Edward responded.

"Make it one," Moloch said, pursing his lips.

"As you wish." Edward tapped the screen twice, making it disappear and turned to his chief co-conspirator. "Remember that he can only kill your avatar in here, but he can still make you suffer. He has a long list of cheats to make himself almost invincible, but you have your own set, as well. Use them and outmatch him. Keep in mind that Moloch can, and likely will, communicate with you to keep throwing you off. Now, off you go and good luck."

Before Mason could say another word, the cottage room around him faded away and was replaced by the small village of Lothering.

"Is he going to communicate with us here?" Mason asked, holding his hands, palms up, to the sky.

"I don't know," Ernestine replied, looking around at the row of stone buildings near the river before locking eyes with Mason. "Are we supposed to have this big challenge here? Is it a joust or something?"

"I hope not. I'm really bad at jousting," Mason replied.

Ernestine had her mouth open to reply when the ground began to shake. Other players stopped what they were doing and regarded each other in surprise once it continued past a few seconds. Ernestine looked at the expressions on their faces and then back to Mason. "Is this part of the game?"

"Once in a while there might be a tremor if it's part of a quest," Mason said, watching a few stones at the top of one of the buildings come loose from their place and fall to the ground, pulling a plume of dirt and dust behind it. "But nothing like this."

The ground jumped, forcing many people to their knees. Characters and players alike streamed out of the many buildings in a rush. A cacophony of screams and ignorant shouts of joy filled the air.

"It sounds to me like some of these players think it's still just part of the game," Ernestine said, kneeling on the ground, hands clutching the earth.

Mason's legs trembled like the ground beneath him as he fought to stay standing. "There's no reason for them to think it isn't."

A second jump from the floor brought a strange gurgling sound to their ears.

"Ern, the river is draining!" Mason exclaimed.

Ernestine looked in the direction he was pointing in time to see the entire river emptied as though some great titan had pulled the plug out of a gargantuan tub of water. She clenched her teeth and looked up at Mason, her face twisted. "What's happening?"

"I don't know," Mason said, shaking his head.

Another great shake from below caused a few of the buildings' facades to collapse, taking some of the medieval characters along with it. The screams of panic returned but in greater numbers.

"Do you hear that?" Ernestine asked, pressing her ear to the shaking soil.

"I can't hear much of anything!" Mason shouted. His ears pricked up and his gaze went to the earth beneath him. "Wait, I can hear it now. It's some kind of rumble."

Ernestine pulled her ear from the ground with some difficulty. "It's getting closer."

A large steel and glass spire broke from the ground nearby, followed by floor after floor of a skyscraper rushing to meet the sky. The players looked around, stunned, to see the non-player characters around them vanish from sight. The spire rose a hundred feet into the air, followed by hundreds more breaking through the ground in random places across the countryside. Lothering crumbled to the ground when the broad, tapering top of a tall tower complex burst from the town center, erasing it from virtual existence.

Mason and Ernestine did a double-take as they found themselves rising into the air while the loose topsoil danced its way off the sides of the rising skyscraper around them. They found the departed earth had left behind consoles and a raised, padded chair at the center of an open area. Once they were high in the sky, walls rose around them and, from their tops, sprouted ceilings that reached out to the center of the area, enclosing a room filled with stations covered in cogs, switches, brass buttons and black dials. A thick, glass window in front of them gave a panoramic view of a much different vista than what had been there mere minutes before.

The duo got up and stood at the wide window in front of them.

"What is this?" Ernestine asked, gazing out on a glassy, silver city stretching for miles in every direction except where a purple sea crashed onto a pink coast to the east. She turned towards Mason, her eyes taking in his clothing. "And what are you wearing?"

"You mean what are *we* wearing?" Mason said, smiling. Ernestine looked at herself, realizing they both wore shiny, black armor emblazoned with gold vines. "It looks like it was made in the nineteenth century. This is a kind of powered armor, I think. Come to think of it: This reminds me of something I saw before."

"Reminds me of something out of a steampunk movie. This whole C&C does," Ernestine said, pointing at the impossible skyline. "Do those buildings kinda look like daggers and swords to you?"

"They are shaped like weapons, now that you mention it," he said. Mason's eyebrows went up and he snapped his fingers. "Now I know this place! This is War of the Worlds III! It's a strategy game."

"Some strategy game," Ernestine remarked, putting both of her hands on the railing and looking out on the sprawling metropolis in front of them. "What's it about?"

"Well," Mason replied, furrowing his brow, "you're not going to like it."

"Does it have anything to do with that book *The War of the Worlds*? The one by that guy, Wells?" Ernestine said, hearing loud rhythmic stomping in the distance.

"The same. It's based on the idea that there was more than one 'War of the Worlds'," Mason replied.

"It sounds like a giant is going for a walk. So, the book is supposed to be the first war?" Ernestine asked as the stomping got closer.

"And the second happened in the early twenty first century with the third being in the future on a human colony. Here they reverse engineered the tripods they salvaged from the last war and built their own," Mason said, pausing and looking out on the horizon.

Ernestine followed his gaze, feeling a small tremble in the earth with each rhythmic bang. "Wait, are you saying we're about to be attacked by those fighting-machines from *War of the Worlds*?"

From behind a row of skyscrapers came a tall tripod standing several stories high and made of shining metal. From the flattened oblong main body atop the legs were two articulated arms holding a device resembling a large camera. Many tentacles hung from the monstrosity like steel chains. Green smoke leaked from its many joints.

Mason looked from the fighting-machine to Ernestine and nodded. "I'm afraid so. We're playing the defense force for Elysium."

"Elysium?" Ernestine repeated, tilting her head up.

"That's the name of the colony we're defending."

Ernestine rolled her eyes. "The Ancient Greek afterlife? I should've known." The tripod aimed its giant camera at the face of one of the dagger-shaped skyscrapers in front of it. A lens at its center began pulsing with bright light, while an increasing crackle of energy came from inside of it. The camera box fired a bright beam of starlight into the side of the scraper and a dozen stories of the building exploded into a cloud of fire and shrapnel. "Holy shit! Didn't you say we have our own fighting machines?"

"Yeah," Mason said, looking down into the street from their perch some hundred floors off the ground, "but I used to play this game and you don't win by sending out your own forces, right away. That's suicide. You wait because there are booby traps and mines everywhere for those things to run into." The street beneath the tripod rippled with explosions, causing a transparent shield around the machine to briefly appear. "See? And there are automated gun emplacements to help you out, too. It's after you wear them down a bit that you can take them out."

"Oh. Sounds like we have nothing to worry about, then," Ernestine said, crossing her arms.

"You might think so, but those aliens' shields are really strong and then there's that," Mason said, pointing at the streets hundreds of feet below them.

Ernestine squinted at the small figures on the streets and then looked at the glass bay window in front of them. "Is this just glass, or does it have a zoom feature?"

"Of course," Mason replied. He touched one place on the window above him and then moved his finger diagonally across their view. The window zoomed in on the populace below. People were walking back and forth in confusion on the futuristic street. They wore the clothing of mages, bards, rogues, and soldiers.

"Are those the same people who were playing S&S?" Ernestine asked.

"Yup and now they're in a game where their abilities may or may not work, but it's certainly interesting that Ed allowed them to be a part of it."

"I think people should witness this," Ed's voice interjected. Mason and Ernestine's eyes darted around the room for the origin of his voice but couldn't find one. "Besides, I thought you could use the help. They do, indeed, have the same abilities from the other game."

"Where are you?" Ernestine asked.

"Same place as before. Don't worry about me. I'll get the code done and try to keep an eye on the game. Mason, know that Moloch's going to cheat from the beginning, but you can do everything he can. Moloch's intelligent, but he never set foot in a single game in his entire life. I checked. That's his biggest weakness."

"Thanks," Mason said, looking out on a city where a single tower burned brightly in the morning light provided by a red giant looming on the horizon. He turned from the sight of the gleaming city and sat down in the command seat at the center of the room.

"Anything I can do?" Ernestine asked.

"Over there," Mason said, pointing at a pearl console to his left and closer to the broad, fortified window. "A second player can control the defense towers. Don't worry about using up a lot of ammunition. The enemy's going to take them out fast."

"Got it," Ernestine said, walking to the console. As she approached it, a holographic display popped up showing the city with several green turrets mounted on towers dotting it. Ernestine manipulated the controls for a moment before she nodded. "Ah. Point and tap. Easy."

"Good," Mason said. "Target each one with everything you've got."

"On it."

Just as Ernestine acknowledged Mason, two sword-shaped skyscrapers exploded in a hurricane of fire. From out of the blazing tempest came three more tripods, wreathed in flame. Ernestine expertly assigned targets and priorities. Three turrets nearby hummed to life and turned their dual cannons on the attacking forces. Half-a-dozen explosions hit the lead tripod, causing its shield to glow.

"Wow," Ernestine said.

"That was pretty good for a first try," Mason said, still looking out on the vast city by the coast.

"No, I mean it hardly did any damage."

"They are tough," Mason said, shifting his gaze to the back of her head. "I should've told you: this is the hardest strategy game to play. You're trying to defend an entire city with inferior weapons."

"How many times did you play it?"

"Probably dozens," Mason replied while Ernestine hammered the tripods with cannon fire.

"How many times did you win?"

Mason smirked. "Once."

"Well," Ernestine said, examining the information on her screen, "I know you can do it again."

A face on a screen interrupted the vast view of the city under siege. It had familiar features of oily, black hair and eyes with a pale, white face. Thin lips were turned upwards into a cruel smile.

"Ted!" Mason exclaimed. "I'd recognize that evil emo look anywhere."

"My name is Moloch."

"Sure it is, but can you drop the disguise? It's not scaring anyone anymore," he said, sporting a more mocking smile.

Moloch sneered at the suggestion, but his face did become more like his real one. The black hair and white makeup, however, stayed in place. "I thought you'd like to talk while this intergalactic chess game plays out."

"Or, you're trying to distract me," Mason said, shifting his attention to the battle.

"But we have so much to talk about! Like you blaming yourself for something the FBI covered up and wasn't your fault! All that wasted time," Moloch said.

"We already got your 'anonymous' package. Bad move."

Moloch scowled at him but said nothing.

"I know that the man you killed was actually going to kill me."

"He still planned to, you know. I hacked into his mind to get the code I needed. Benny couldn't get to you right away, but he was going to, eventually. Do you know what he really was?" Moloch asked, leaning forward in his seat.

"I know that Benny was a bodyhacker and you killed him for his secrets," Mason replied, maintaining his attention on the battle unfolding before them.

"Very good," Moloch said. "But Benny was going to kill me, too, after you bailed on him."

"He needed a new scapegoat?" Mason asked, looking up at him.

"Yes, but I got there first."

"And you killed him which meant the FBI started hunting you! A smarter man would've taken care of Benny, quietly, and then used FBI resources to get to their goal faster," Mason said, returning his attention to the fighting outside. "Bad move."

"I've got a surprise for you," Moloch said, grinning broadly.

"I can't wait."

"I lost six turrets, but I did take down three of his tripods," Ernestine reported.

"Good work," Mason said.

"It won't make any difference," Moloch said, shaking his head. His image disappeared from the screen a moment later.

"Mason," Ernestine said, turning a frowning face towards him, "the players from S&S are starting to fight, but they're attacking us."

"What?" Mason demanded, tearing his attention from the sight of turrets lobbing shells at the fighting-machines.

"A bunch of them are trying to get into this building right now."

"Moloch! That's his surprise."

"I'll find out what's going on," Ernestine said, conjuring an interactive window from empty space.

Two more towers collapsed from bright rays coming from the tripods' little boxes. Bolts of fire and lightning from the chaotic crowd converged on several of their defense towers. Mason looked at the scene and frowned.

"Hurry."

***

Zahra was keeping an eye on Mason and Ernestine, both reclined in their chairs and unconscious, when she heard her vPhone beep. She read Ernestine's incoming text and then heard a surprising sound. She looked up in time to see another car, black and sleek, revving its engine and accelerating towards them at over a hundred miles per hour.

"Car! Emergency stop!" Zahra shouted at the dashboard, keeping her eyes on the vehicle careening towards them. The car's computer put the brakes on and the tires screeched. The other vehicle smashed into the front of her car at high speeds with a cacophonous crunch. Zahra's eyes widened as she saw the world spinning around her before everything went dark.

***

"Son of a bitch!" Ernestine exclaimed at the digital window hanging in front of her.

"Bad news?" Mason asked.

"Moloch just put a billion pound bounty on each of our heads. We're not talking about crypto here, either. This is a billion pounds in UK currency and he's told everyone exactly where we are," Ernestine said.

"I can help with that," Ed's disembodied voice said. "Just give me a few minutes."

The doors at the back of the room shifted from an explosion and began to give way. Ernestine looked at the doors, which were starting to glow red. "I don't think we have a few minutes."

"You've got cheats. I suggest you use them," Edward said.

"He's right," Mason said, getting up. "Let the computer handle the turrets. We need to stop the other players from taking us out."

"Aren't we supposed to have a huge number of those hit-points to keep us from getting killed?" Ernestine asked before pulling an assault rifle out of thin air.

"That doesn't mean we're invincible and the more they wear us down the easier it will be for Moloch to take us out."

The door was now incandescent and melted in front of them. The moment the floor was covered in slag, a small host of players flew in wielding swords, staves, and bows. Ernestine and Mason, now armed with a futuristic automatic rifle, opened up on the intruders.

Ernestine fired countless rounds per minute into the people surging through the doorway, but was still hit by some bolts of lighting and magical arrows, which she shook off. Mason turned his rifle on one rogue, who leaped into the room and attempted to stab him with a dagger.

"Hey, no fair!" the leather-bound rogue exclaimed once his dagger bounced off Mason's thick armor.

"Neither is this," Mason said, firing a beam of bright energy at the rogue, vaporizing the player instantly.

"I'm almost there," Ed's voice said. "Give me a few more seconds. Try to bribe everyone, huh, Ted? We'll see about that."

"Make it quick!" Mason exclaimed and pressed a button on the side of the rifle. He squeezed the trigger and a hail of bright energy pulses flew at the attacking players, mowing them down. As each avatar hit the floor, they vanished from sight, leaving behind a pile of clothing and equipment.

The back wall spanning the entire room exploded and a small army of players' avatars came marching through the smoke and debris. They aimed their weapons at Ernestine and Mason.

"Hey!" one exclaimed from behind a helmet made of enchanted glass. "Everybody see the new bounty?"

The army stopped and brought up windows in front of them or looked at digital vPhones on their armored wrists. All of the soldiers examined the new notice, some longer than others, before turning around and leaving.

"Ed," Ernestine said, lowering her machine gun, "how did you do that?"

"Easy," his voice replied from nowhere. "He put a billion pounds on each of your heads so I put four billion on his."

Mason stared at Ernestine for a second and then laughed out loud. "You just outbid him?"

"Exactly. Now focus on the battle. I'll have the maid clean up later."

"Let's get back to it," Mason said, returning to his seat.

***

Zahra opened her eyes to the sight of Mason and Ernestine, unconscious and still belted into their seats. They widened at the memory of the other car rushing for them, her head snapped around, and Zahra looked through the fractured windshield. Much of the front of the vehicle was a tangled mess of metal, but it was upright.

She heard car doors slamming shut. Zahra's eyes searched for where the sounds had come from. Through a cracked, dirty window she spied a man and a woman, both professionally dressed, walking towards the car. Each of them had a pistol in their hands and a cruel grin on their faces.

"Car," Zahra whispered, unlatching Ernestine's seatbelt and dragging her sleeping body to the floor, "car?"

There was no answer, but the crunching of gravel and sand got closer. Zahra released Mason from his seatbelt and pulled him to the floor as well. She took the pistol from her holster, aimed at the nearer of the couple and pulled the trigger. The woman collapsed to her knees, light brown hair now askew from the force of the explosive bullet that had hit her between the eyes and fell on her face.

The second dodged to his left, lowered one knee and aimed at the car. Two shots smashed the window on that side of the vehicle. Zahra jumped up into sight and fired at her attacker, neatly hitting him three times in the chest. She put her pistol back in its holster and gazed at the vacant vehicle parked a short distance away.

"Time for new wheels," Zahra said, opening the door.

***

Ernestine watched as a dozen medieval soldiers were mowed down by one fighting machine while another's shield gave out under an entire platoon of mages casting all manner of spells from their staves. The tripod, its shields down, had its legs collapse under it and the entire machine came crashing to the ground, bringing up a great roar from the attacking crowd.

"Those other players are helping us now, but they're also taking heavy losses. When are you going to get our machines out there?" she asked.

"How many turrets do you have left?" Mason asked.

"Just twelve across the whole city," she replied.

"Then it's time," Mason said, pressing a button.

"Why not wait until there's none left?" Ernestine asked, briefly glancing at him from over her shoulder.

"Because, they don't have the firepower to take a fighting machine down now. They can help our machines with supporting fire, though. Take a look at this:"

The sound of great cogs and pulleys whirring to life came from everywhere. Ernestine spied many crescent-shaped, large hangars across the city rumbling. Bay doors more than twenty stories high opened and dozens of large, silver fighting machines appeared throughout the city. Ernestine spotted one and sighed. "Four legs now. Four."

"It's because they're supposed to be built by humans."

"Okay. Just as long as they can fight those tripods," Ernestine said, keeping her eyes on managing the last few working turrets she had left.

"They're armed, but not quite the same way."

"Missile racks," Ernestine said. "That's what's on their shoulders and I think those are rail guns on the sides. It's not the same as that annihilation ray the others have." Half-a-dozen tetrapods fired a cloud of missiles at one of the enemy tripods and, while explosions enveloped it, they followed up with shells from long-barreled guns. By the time the smoke had cleared, the fighting machine belched smoke from several large cracks across its egg-shaped body. The tripod shattered and fell to the ground. Ernestine smiled. "It'll do."

"I think we might be turning the tide," Mason said, glancing up at the burning city in front of him.

A screen popped into view again with Moloch's face scowling from it. "You cheated."

"*We* cheated?" Mason repeated, looking up at his image. "You put a bounty on our heads!"

"And Ed punished you for going too far," Ernestine said.

"This is between me and the cheater."

"Fine with me," Ernestine said, frowning as she returned to her work.

"I understand why you feel stressed," Mason remarked.

"I don't feel stressed," Moloch said, gritting his teeth.

"Sure you don't, but this match probably means more to you than me. After all, your body out there in the real world is dead."

Moloch's frown turned into a thin smile bearing sharp, white teeth. "Bad move. I'm well aware of how advanced modern cloning technology is and I can just have a new me grown in a tank. I've already preserved my body tissue so that I can create as many as I want for as long as I want. I will have dominion over everything on Earth and in here."

"That could take some time," Mason said, glancing down at the battle statistics rolling across a small screen on the armrest of his chair.

"I never liked you, Mason," Moloch said, his lips in a thin line.

"Gee, why not?" he asked, keeping an eye on his readouts.

"You were supposed to be Bernie's mark, but you got out ahead of schedule. He chose me to be his next patsy and then he tried to kill me. That was supposed to be you and I ended up on the run," Moloch replied, keeping his narrow gaze firmly on Mason's face.

Three tripods beyond the window came apart at the seams, raining debris on a ravaged city populated by a dwindling number of medieval warriors.

Mason's face lit up as he regarded Moloch's image, looking down on him from the screen. "Bad move! I didn't put a gun in your hand and I sure as hell didn't tell you to kill Benny. You could've exposed him for what he was when I didn't even know what was going on. I got lucky and you decided to make yourself into a demigod. Oh, and by the way: you don't have many tripods left, Moloch."

Moloch tutted. "You're going to pay for that." His image vanished from sight.

Three tripods appeared from their hiding places behind large buildings and stood shoulder to shoulder in front of the command tower. The annihilation boxes held by articulated, mechanical arms began to pulse with sound and light.

Mason's eyes widened at the sight of the three fighting machines and his ears twitched at the increasing hum of their main weapons. "They're building up to fire a breaching shot right into the command center."

"Can it withstand that?"

"No!" Mason exclaimed. "He's not even supposed to be able to do that. Moloch's cheating again."

"We've both got lotta hit points though, right?"

"It will eat up all of them," Mason replied, standing up from his command chair. "I've got every machine in the area targeting them but there's not enough time."

"Run!"

Mason shook his head. "No time!"

The camera boxes glowed with bright, yellow starlight and all three weapons spewed bright beams of destruction directly at the bay window mounted some ten stories below the tower's peak. Ernestine screamed in protest and flung herself in front of Mason just as the beams hit the command center, shredding it to bits.

***

Ernestine opened her eyes to the sight of the clear, azure sky. She noticed a dirty hand gripping the tan fabric over her shoulder and felt her heels dragging through the dirt. "What's going on?"

The hand at her shoulder let her go and Zahra's face interrupted the sky above her. "Ernestine? You're out?"

"Not by choice," Ernestine replied, putting a hand up, which Zahra grabbed and helped her to her feet. She looked at the condition of their car and then at Zahra. "Got my text?"

"Yeah, just in time," Zahra replied.

"Looks bad," Ernestine said of the crumpled front of the car. "They rammed us?"

"They were aiming to hit us right in the middle of the cabin where we were all sitting. Ern, they were going so fast that they would have killed us all but, thanks to your warning, I stopped the car in time. Well, almost in time."

"Still, we're alive. That's all that matters," Ernestine said, looking at the two hosts' bodies and then at Mason's immobile one. "Moloch almost won out here and in there."

"Did you stop him? Here, help me get Mason into that other car over there," Zahra said, bending over to grab Mason's left shoulder while Ernestine grabbed his right.

"That's why I'm here. One of us had to take a pretty big hit."

"Can we revive him?" Zahra asked, her eyes lingering on Mason's sleeping face for a moment.

"Not yet. He'd lose the game."

"Okay, once we get him in the other car, we'll be on our way again," Zahra said.

"They found us out here?" Ernestine asked, glancing at the dry woods around them.

Before Zahra could reply, the sound of two cars coming in at high speeds filled their ears on the quiet back road.

"They're coming from both directions," Ernestine said, cocking one ear up.

"Great. Help me drag Mason back to our car. We're not driving anywhere right now and there's still weapons in that trunk."

"You drag Mason back between the cars and I'll look in the trunk," Ernestine said,

"Good idea. We can use both cars as cover that way."

Zahra dragged Mason into the space between the two vehicles facing opposite directions while Ernestine opened the trunk and grabbed everything she could in the limited time they had.

The former agent fired a shot at both vehicles' rear tires before sitting next to Mason. Ernestine leaned against the other car and waited as the clamor grew nearer.

Two black cars flew towards them from opposite directions, raising a long cloud of dry dirt behind them. Their tires screeched to a halt once they neared the sight of the collision and four people got out of each vehicle. A hail of bullets flew from both directions the moment Zahra heard the sound of many car doors slamming shut at once.

"They move in unison," Ernestine yelled from her place ten feet away.

"They're all thinking with the same mind," Zahra said, beginning to unload her magazine into the car in front of them.

"Hurry back, Mason," Zahra said before turning to fight the attackers behind them.

***

Mason groaned and sat up in a pile of debris, finding that the command seat formerly under him was now leaning against his side. He pushed it away and noticed a pile of empty power armor laying on the floor in front of him.

"Ernestine," Mason said and sighed, "you didn't have to do that."

He looked around the center, now smashed beyond repair. The forward observation dome had shattered, leaving a gaping hole in one side of the building. He got up and limped to the shattered window. Mason saw only a few players still running back and forth in streets littered with debris and lost equipment, but his tetrapods had turned the tide against Moloch's tripods, which were losing numbers and ground with every passing minute. Mason smiled at the sight of several more of Moloch's fighting machines exploding under concentrated fire. "You lose, Moloch," he whispered into the breeze.

Mason's head snapped up at the sound of a distant scream. A great, black cloud had formed near the city limits, lit only by the occasional discharge of red lightning from within. The cloud rested just above the tops of distant dagger and sword-shaped skyscrapers, but was moving towards him at a frightening rate. Mason squinted at the twisting tempest and brought up a zoom window in front of him. He magnified the cloud, seeing a small mote of a man at its center.

"Moloch." Mason's uttering of his name sent the distant body flying for him and the scream grew louder by the second. Mason braced himself as the storm sped towards the battered building.

"Remember that you can use every cheat he can," Ed's voice said from nowhere.

Mason stretched out both arms in front of him and released a series of fireballs from his fists, all of which hit Moloch with full force, but he continued to accelerate towards him. Mason pulled an enchanted long sword from the air and pointed it at Moloch as the baleful bodyhacker flew for him. Moloch hit the point of the sword with his full force, causing the weapon to shatter the moment it hit his chest.

He smashed into Mason, propelling the agent backwards. Skyscrapers flipped by his vison as Moloch slammed his body through a dozen buildings. Mason felt his strength declining, but wrapped Moloch in a bear hug and used his own abilities to force them into a downwards trajectory, slamming Moloch's body into the pavement with the force of a shooting comet.

Moloch, unfazed, jumped up from the concrete, shook it off, and smiled. "I'm going to kill you in here and out there. I've already got my people surrounding you in the real world."

Mason snorted and spat out a bit of blood. "I've got people to protect me."

"Not for long," Moloch said, his cruel smile returning. He launched himself at Mason with the wrath and strength of a deadly dragon. Mason thought a mage's staff into his hand, which he used to launch devastating elemental attacks on Moloch, who winced as a fireball engulfed him. Once the firestorm faded, Moloch fought back with his own devastating magical onslaught. Beyond them, the remainder of Mason's forces defeated the last tripod, bringing an eerie quiet to the battlefield beyond their immediate sphere of combat.

Mason placed a defensive bubble around himself while Moloch rained fire down upon him before reacting with his own counterattacks. As he launched attack after attack on Moloch, he felt blood begin to trickle from his mouth and nose…

***

"No, no, no!" Ernestine said, noticing more cars come to a stop both behind and in front of their wrecked vehicles. More shiny shoed feet hit the dirt and the sound of additional guns firing echoed across the wilderness.

"They've got us pinned down," Zahra said before popping up from her refuge to pepper her adversaries with fire, dropping two of them. She sat back on the ground as bullets hit the car and flew through the air above her.

"They had us pinned down the second they got out of their cars!" Ernestine yelled back.

"Keep them at bay!" Zahra replied before getting up to expertly take down another one of the people attacking them.

Ernestine froze when she heard the sound of a magazine clicking into place. She peeked out from cover and saw a tall man wearing sunglasses slap a magazine into a machine gun.

"Shit!" Ernestine exclaimed and dived for Zahra's position while the car behind her was riddled with bullets in a matter of seconds. She collapsed next to Mason and looked up at Zahra. "What do we do?"

***

Mason felt his body fly into the side of a tower shaped like a spike. The sudden crush of concrete, steel and glass winded him, causing a coughing fit of blood. The fit left him unable to find the strength to keep himself from falling into the great hole his body had created. A pair of vice-like hands gripped his shoulders, crushing them. Mason felt himself lifted into the air and then thrown from the building with such force that he could see the city flying by him at a ruinous pace. He felt himself smash through another skyscraper and then Mason's body hit the pavement before rolling for over a mile.

He started to push himself up off a hot street, basking in the red giant's sun, but became paralyzed once great pain coursed through his body. The same firm grip was at his shoulder again, picking him up and dangling him in front of an inhuman face.

Moloch had reverted to his previous features. All black eyes stared into Mason's soul. "I can do this all day, you know. I have the strength of millions of my hosts' avatars running through me."

"Geez," Mason said, spitting a glob of blood onto the ground, "why didn't you tell me?"

"Funny, pathetic Mason," Moloch said, tossing him at a concrete wall. Mason hit it and collapsed into a pile on the sidewalk. "Since it's your time to die, I'm going to tell you something," he said, his lip curling up at one side. "A little more salt in the wound."

"Can't you just kill me now?" Mason asked, looking up at him with a bloody smile.

Moloch snorted and squatted in front of him. "Did you know I was never even looking for you when this all started? At that point, I was only interested in killing you before you leaked out what I was doing." He laughed, discomfortingly, and stared down at Mason's pulped figure. "But then you made me aware that Edward Blunt was still alive and I could taste immortality on a level I never could have dreamed of before. Then you ruined the one chance I had by destroying that chair in Namibia."

"Sorry about that," Mason said, coughing up blood.

Moloch corrected his behavior by wrenching his arms from their sockets, causing them to hang limply from Mason's body. He screamed and Moloch let his vocalized agony abate before continuing, which took some time. "That's better. There's no need to apologize. You see, all I had to do was follow you, give you the occasional kick in your complacency and then take the prize from you, which I'm about to do. You're the loser here, Mason, not me. I'll tell you a secret, though: I'm going to assimilate Ed just like everybody else and then I'm going to delete him from the vU, just like everybody else. Now, we just need to take care of those powers," Moloch said, inserting his tubules into Mason's head. After mere seconds, he retracted them back into his hand. "That's better. No more enhanced speed or strength."

"That's it?" Mason asked, a bitter frown on his face. "No consolation prize?"

"You were supposed to be me; You were supposed to be Carter's murder victim, but he ruined my life, instead. It was you who made me, not Benny," Moloch said, leaning towards him and reaching for his feet. "Now, off come those legs."

"That's enough!" a voice boomed from around them. The vast otherworldly city and its few remaining occupants faded to black. Edward's cottage materialized around them a moment later. Mason was heaped in one corner of it with Moloch standing over him. Edward turned away from his holographic table to confront his nemesis. "You've won, Moloch. Leave him alone."

Moloch jumped up from his place in front of Mason and turned to see the young Edward Blunt in casual fifties dress. "It's an honor to meet you. I'm a big fan!"

"Thanks, I suppose."

"No," Moloch said, grinning. "That was what Garrett said when he met you: 'It's an honor to meet you. I'm a big fan.' He also had a million questions he never got to ask. Want to go over them now?"

"You are a bastard," Edward replied, slowly nodding his head.

"And you're dead. Now give me my prize," Moloch said, clenching his jaw. He seemed to expand while the entire room shrunk and darkened around him as though all the light in the world had dimmed. Once the lighting returned to normal, Moloch had transformed into a hulking grey minotaur with red eyes.

"Very well," Edward said, avoiding Moloch's eyes. "I'll keep my end of the bargain."

"Good," Moloch said, taking broad steps towards him.

***

"They're getting closer!" Ernestine exclaimed. She sighed and her shoulders slumped upon hearing the sound of more tires skidding to a halt on gravel. "Another car just got here!"

"We're going to get overrun," Zahra said. She glanced up at the trunk door hanging open and riddled with bullet holes to the point of looking like a blue slice of Swiss cheese. "Is there anything else in there that could help?"

"Wait," Ernestine said, putting a hand on Zahra's soiled shoulder, "could you give me cover in both directions for a second?"

Zahra picked up a second submachine gun and nodded at her. "I can try. Now!"

Zahra popped up from cover with each SMG pointed in opposite directions and let loose a barrage of fire across the area sending their rivals diving for cover. Ernestine jumped up beside her, pulled out a heavy weapon four feet long, aimed it at one of the cars and fired a large projectile into it. The car exploded the moment the explosive shell hit it, causing their enemies to react in a panic.

Ernestine swung the weapon around and fired two more shots, causing a pair of vehicles to jump in the air and land on the ground, wreathed in flame. She continued to swing the rifle from target to target until half-a-dozen cars burned in the afternoon sun. Ernestine dropped the heavy weapon and collapsed into a heap next to Zahra, who also laid on the ground, her back against the holed vehicle.

"I think we got them all," Ernestine said, massaging the aching muscles of her arm.

"You know," Zahra said, taking some effort to turn her head to look at her, "Mason wanted to try that gun out."

"I know!" Ernestine exclaimed, laughing.

"I hate to admit it, but I didn't think you could lift that thing."

"The people on my reservation have a saying," Ernestine said, leaving the sentence hanging in the air.

"What's that?"

"Never piss off Ern," she replied, her dirty face stone-serious for a moment before she chuckled, "on a good day or a bad one!"

Zahra joined in her contagious laugh and looked down at the still form of Mason. "I can't stop wondering when he's going to get up."

Ernestine stared down the long road glimpsed through the flame and smoke rising from the nearby cars. "I hope it's soon, because Moloch's going to send more people here sooner or later."

***

"I have a scrupulous conscience," Edward said as Moloch took menacing steps towards him.

"How awful for you," Moloch said, a gruesome grin on his feral face.

"Yes," Edward said, looking him in the eye. "I feel like I should be fair to you and give you a choice."

"A choice?" Moloch repeated, scowling at him. His cloven feet were now at a standstill.

"I can make you immortal or you can turn away now and take the right path. It would be simple with your cooperation to remove your awareness from all of the hosts you occupy. I can create a clone of you and you can spend the next eighteen years lounging around the vU until it's ready. It would have to be under restrictions, of course, so you don't try this again."

Moloch sneered at him. "You want me to give up everything I've gained and return to the small man I was? Is that it?"

"Don't knock it," Edward replied, a look of pity on his face. "Immortality can be a curse. Trust me, I know that better than most."

"I'll take my chances."

"Are you sure?" Edward asked, looking up into his eyes.

"Enough talk!" Moloch roared, increasing in size to the point that his horned head and grey wings fell just short of hitting the ceiling. He pointed at Edward's face with long, sharp talons hovering just inches from his eyes. "Now give me what I want or I will feast on your fearful flesh."

"Alright," Edward said. "This code is unique and I need to transfer it directly from my matrix to yours. That requires physical contact."

"What kind of physical contact?" Moloch demanded, eyeing the small man in front of him.

"It will only take a second. I need you to get on your knees," Edward said, noticing his furry chest puff out at the request. "Well, one knee, unless you want to transform back into Ted."

His chest deflated and Moloch took to one knee, the floor groaning as he did. Edward stood just a foot from his grotesque body. As he leaned in to place his hands near Moloch's temples, the bodyhacker grabbed Edward's in a terrifying grip. "Don't try anything."

Ed smiled and looked back at him with sparkling eyes. "There's nothing left to try."

The words brought a slight relaxation in the monster's musculature and Edward's hands exuded thick, glowing tubes from between the knuckles on both hands, now on either side of Moloch's head.

"This won't hurt a bit."

"Spare your bedside manner for the weak, old man," Moloch bit out, staring at him.

"As you wish," Edward said. His tubes entered Moloch's temples for a few seconds and then retracted back into his hands. "Done."

Ed stepped back from Moloch's large frame. The minotaur stood up to his full height and looked down at him. The bodyhacker flexed his muscles as his body pulsed with a new, golden light. The entire room winked out for a moment around him.

Moloch looked at his hands which were casting long, golden rays. He turned around to face his adversary and roared in triumph. Mason looked up from his misery to see a bright light coming from every piece of exposed skin on his body. Moloch marveled at his changing flesh and laughed while Edward looked at his back with a mourner's expression. "I can feel it! I can feel myself changing… becoming more! MORE!"

Mason glanced at Edward with sorrowful eyes, but Ed placed a finger over his lips and vanished from sight. The spectacle continued, growing in intensity until Moloch was too bright to look at. The blinding light reached its climax and faded from view, leaving a very different being behind. This one was not a minotaur, but Moloch returned to his original, nude form.

Ted looked at his human hands and felt his human face as his mouth hung open. "What happened? I felt something at first. Not anymore. Blunt!" he exclaimed with a roar. That roar turned to a whimper and he collapsed to the floor. "What did you do to me?"

Edward appeared from nowhere and looked down on Ted's weakened form. "You are not immortal, at least not yet."

"I felt myself changing!" Moloch protested, looking up into Ed's eyes.

"You did. The virus I gave you took away your abilities. You are now just, plain simple Ted, again. It also provided me with an important distraction."

"Distraction?"

"Yes," Edward said, standing over him. "You see, I needed time to find your control panel."

"His control panel's in his head," Mason said, looking up from his pain. "How can you get to it from here?"

"Ah," Edward said and stomped a foot on the wooden floor. Mason and Moloch looked up at the sound of all four walls falling like those on a stage. Around them stood an office in a 1920s office building, complete with Art Deco decorations. Ragtime music came from a nearby player and a nineties-style computer sat on a heavy, wooden desk.

Edward jumped back and clapped his hands together. "It's the old simulated world within a world trick! How many times have we seen that one?"

"That's impossible," Mason said, looking up from his heap.

"Yes, in real life it is, but Moloch's mind is completely digital now. I just had to enter yours, Ted, and then use the vU to simulate my cottage within it. While you were transforming back into yourself, I just sat down and helped myself to that old computer of yours. Now I have complete control of your mind and you. You know, I have a feeling I would have made a pretty good bodyhacker, myself!"

"You lied to me," Moloch said, looking from his control computer to Edward. "You promised me immortality! You betrayed me just like Carter!"

Edward took a knee next to his crouched form, a mournful expression returning to his face. "Oh, I didn't lie, Ted. I will give you the immortality you asked for."

He leaned over and touched Ted in the middle of the forehead with an index finger. Once he withdrew it, a red spot appeared and began to grow, at which point the diminished man flinched and gritted his teeth. "What are you doing to me?"

"Immortality comes at a price," Edward said, eyes glassy as he looked down on him. "Your nickname says what you should know better than anyone else: gods demand sacrifices."

Ted's entire head was now covered in streaming red code. His features started to fade as the code slowly expanded across his body.

Edward's voice broke, but he continued. "You're turning into a program, Ted. It will delete your presence from everyone out there, but more importantly, your program will act as a first-line defense against anyone who ever tries to do this again. You will be everywhere and eternal, but you will have no consciousness. No self-awareness. It is immortality."

"No! Not like this!" Moloch rasped as his body was consumed by ones and zeros glowing like rubies. Edward looked away while the code absorbed Ted as he whimpered, leaving nothing behind. Around them, the Art Deco office faded from view and was replaced by Edward's cottage.

"Nothing remains of the host," Edward whispered, got up, and stood in front of Mason's crumpled body. "Congratulations, you bought me the time I needed. Oh, a little gift," Edward said more cheerfully. He returned to his desk, grabbed a small, transparent green cube and tossed it at Mason, watching it vanish into his battered chest.

Mason's blinked and got up on his own two feet. He stretched his arms and legs before regarding Edward. "I'm back in one piece! Thanks!" he exclaimed, smiling with bright eyes as he looked at his limbs, now returned to their former glory.

"You're welcome. You gave me the time I needed to draw Moloch into a trap and disarm him. Thank you."

"Why did you lie to me about the code killing him?" Mason asked, looking at where Moloch had kneeled moments before.

"Because I knew he might have taken that information from you by force. If that had happened, he would have known what would really become of him and Ted would have never agreed to it. I had hoped that he might be out there somewhere in human form, with only his virtual self gone, but he prevented that from happening. I hope you understand why I did what I did."

"No, I get it," Mason said, stretching again. "Just don't do it again."

"Agreed," Edward said with a smile and turned towards his table, but stopped abruptly. His grin vanished, Edward turned back to Mason and pointed a finger at the ceiling. "While we're at it, I have one more deception that should come to light."

Mason looked at him from the corner of his eye. "Go ahead."

"The classified FBI file about you, Benny Carter and that whole mess: It wasn't mailed to me. I sent it to myself."

"But, why?" Mason asked. "Why did you want to undermine me like that?"

"Oh!" Edward said, shaking his finger at him. "But it wasn't me who was trying to hurt you, it was Moloch. When I heard what he said to you in that basement I immediately began a search to confirm that information."

"But you only had, maybe an hour, to find it," Mason objected.

"And an hour is a day in here," Edward said, holding up a hand to encompass his cottage. "It was plenty of time, once I knew what to look for."

"But why do it?" Mason asked.

"You needed the whole picture; not just what he wanted you to see. That kept you focused and gave me the time I needed."

Mason thought on what he said, smiled, and motioned with his head at the empty spot on the floor where Ted had met his maker. "So, you stopped him and anyone else from ever trying to do this again?"

"I've made it harder," Edward replied, sitting in his chair. "But there are no guarantees, my friend. Anyone can try this if they're sufficiently determined."

"Then how do you stop it if it happens again?"

"By being immortal," Edward replied, resting a chin on his hand. "I knew someone would eventually try this and that there would likely be more than one. Someone will always have to be here to stop them. I am the soldier at the gate who can never sleep, never desert, and must always be vigilant. Immortality can be a curse, sometimes, rather than a blessing."

"I have to admit that I kinda feel sorry for Ted," Mason said, straightening up in his seat, "and you."

"Well, it's not all bad. You brought Ernestine back to me and I plan to have you all over for dinner tonight. I make the best virtual food you've ever had, not like those vRestaurants. It's much better here. Now," Edward exclaimed, clapping his hands once, "it's time we did something for you for everything you did for me!"

"Give me back my abilities?" Mason asked, eyes lighting up.

Ed chuckled and leaned against his table. "No, can't do that. Too tempting, you understand. I will let you keep those cheats I gave you, though."

"All of them?"

"All of them," Edward confirmed before shaking a finger at him. "Just try to be subtle with it. I wanted to give you something you'd enjoy and it seemed appropriate."

"I was kinda hoping for more," Mason said.

Edward frowned, looked at the empty spot on the floor where Moloch had vanished, and then back to him. "Well, I suppose I could give you the same immortality as Ted."

"No," Mason said, holding up both hands. "I'm okay. Cheats. Good gift."

"I'm glad you think so," Edward said. He waited for a moment to pass before he couldn't keep his lips together any longer and let out an exasperated sigh. "Oh alright, alright, I do have something better! You know all those millions of people in comas right now, thanks to Ted?"

"Yeah," Mason replied. "People like Garrett. How many families out there have lost someone?"

Edward lowered his head conspiratorially towards him. "How about none?"

"But Moloch said nothing survives of the host!"

Edward's lips expanded into a tight smile. "He lied. I thought so, but when Ted was being converted, I saw the truth in his mind: the host lives on. They end up locked away in the equivalent of a prison cell in their own heads, but they are still there."

Mason straightened up at the news. "How do we get them out?"

Edward leaned back and laughed. "Why, you of course!"

"I'm not following," Mason said with an uncertain smile and a shake of his head.

"I'm delivering a new program into your implant. Well, it's going to be in every mindhacker's implant. With it, you will be able to enter the comatose victim's mind and manually restore them to their old selves. I also included a kind of 'tape worm' that will eat the memories of their time with Moloch. Thought it was best, all considered."

"I can wake up Garrett and everyone else?"

"Yes, even a man named John Tate. Ever heard of him?" Edward asked, an enigmatic smile on his face.

Mason's knees started shaking as he leaned against Edward's desk. He looked up hopefully into Edward's smiling face. "I can bring him back? I can bring back the man that I… I mean Benny, put into a coma?"

"Benny Carter was the first bodyhacker and this program will take care of him, too. His family will finally get him back."

"Good as new?" Mason asked in a whisper.

"Absolutely," Edward replied, returning to his work. "It's a whole new profession. Personally, I think you and the others should be called 'mind-helpers' now. I'll even give you a few dollars for your trouble!"

"Just like a quest," Mason said with a wistful smile.

"Now, you'd better wake up and check on things in the real world. From what I understand, you were under attack from a small army of Moloch's soldiers."

"Zahra! Ern!" Mason exclaimed, checking his vPhone for messages. "I've gotta get outta here!"

"You might be surprised at just how well they're doing. Tell Ern that everyone's invited to dinner tonight. We're having spaghetti!" Edward exclaimed, clapping his hands together once. "You can tell a lot about a person by how they eat that stuff!"

Mason watched his back for a moment with a smile before tapping the back of his wrist and vanishing from the unreachable cottage.

Chapter Fifteen

Mason found himself staring at a blue sky framed by fir trees. He sat up and looked around. "Did I miss something, again?"

Ernestine and Zahra had their backs resting against what was left of their car and laughed. "Yeah, we handled it."

Mason gave them a quizzical look and stared at their totaled vehicle. "What happened?"

"We'll tell you later. Is Moloch gone?" Ernestine asked.

"He's gone, but Ed deserves most of the credit. We've got a lot of work ahead of us. Well, I do anyways."

Zahra and Ernestine raised an eyebrow at Mason while the trio groaned to their feet. Ernestine rubbed her shoulder and winced. "You're all getting too old for this!"

Mason snorted. "By the way, thanks for throwing yourself in the path of certain death for me."

"I'd do it for anyone, I guess," Ernestine said cheerfully, wiping dirt off her beige khakis before looking at the smoldering wrecks around her. "How are we getting home?"

"Where's home?" Zahra asked, leaning against her and lifting the wrist with her vPhone on it. The movement made her cringe and forced her to hold the arm with her other hand. "I'll call a cab. Where are we going?"

"To the hospital," Mason replied. "The one where Garrett's most likely to be now that Moloch's gone."

"Ted, now that Ted's gone," Ernestine said. "What are you going to do?"

"Garrett's still in there," Mason said. Ernestine and Zahra regarded him, slack-jawed. Mason shook his head and smiled. "I'll tell you on the way."

***

Mason withdrew his tubules from Garrett's left temple and watched as he slowly opened his eyes. Garrett looked around a sterile hospital room, groaned, and put a hand over his eyes. "Why do I feel like I'm hungover?"

"Hey, Garrett," Mason said, hovering over him.

"Mason? What happened? Last thing I remember is being in my bunker and it was on fire," Garrett said, wrenching his hand back and staring up at him.

"You were in a coma, but we can explain all of that, later. We won, Garrett, in no small part thanks to you," he said. Garret grinned. Mason stood up straight and smiled back. "So, I hear you like me!"

"Oh, God!" Garrett exclaimed, covering his face with both hands. "Just put me back in a coma!"

Mason chuckled and crossed his arms. Zahra and Ernestine got up from a pair of chairs on the other side of the hospital room and sat down on his bed. Ern drew Garrett into an embrace that would last for some time.

About the Author

Kris Powers wrote an MMORPG, an interactive novel and hundreds of articles. He's a science fiction and fantasy fan, an avid cook and is learning Latin in his spare time. Kris is currently working on the first novel in his new science-fantasy universe, Star Lore. He lives in New Brunswick with the stray cats who keep showing up at his door.

To see more about this author, please visit him at:
www.krispowers.com.

Manufactured by Amazon.ca
Bolton, ON

37782732R00152